Close Cover

Also from Lexi Blake

Masters And Mercenaries
The Dom Who Loved Me
The Men With The Golden Cuffs
A Dom Is Forever
On Her Master's Secret Service
Sanctum: A Masters and Mercenaries Novella
Love and Let Die
Unconditional: A Masters and Mercenaries Novella
Dungeon Royale
Dungeon Games: A Masters and Mercenaries Novella
A View to a Thrill
Cherished: A Masters and Mercenaries Novella
You Only Love Twice
Luscious: Masters and Mercenaries~Topped
Adored: A Masters and Mercenaries Novella
Master No
Just One Taste: Masters and Mercenaries~Topped 2
From Sanctum with Love
Devoted: A Masters and Mercenaries Novella
Dominance Never Dies
Submission is Not Enough
Master Bits and Mercenary Bites~The Secret Recipes of Topped
Perfectly Paired: Masters and Mercenaries~Topped 3
For His Eyes Only
Arranged: A Masters and Mercenaries Novella
Love Another Day
At Your Service: Masters and Mercenaries~Topped 4
Master Bits and Mercenary Bites~Girls Night
Nobody Does It Better
Close Cover
Protected, Coming July 31, 2018

Masters and Mercenaries: The Forgotten
Momento Mori, Coming August 28, 2018

Lawless
Ruthless
Satisfaction
Revenge

Courting Justice
Order of Protection, Coming June 5, 2018

Masters Of Ménage (by Shayla Black and Lexi Blake)
Their Virgin Captive
Their Virgin's Secret
Their Virgin Concubine
Their Virgin Princess
Their Virgin Hostage
Their Virgin Secretary
Their Virgin Mistress

The Perfect Gentlemen (by Shayla Black and Lexi Blake
Scandal Never Sleeps
Seduction in Session
Big Easy Temptation
Smoke and Sin
At the Pleasure of the President, Coming Fall 2018

URBAN FANTASY

Thieves
Steal the Light
Steal the Day
Steal the Moon
Steal the Sun
Steal the Night
Ripper
Addict
Sleeper
Outcast, Coming 2018

LEXI BLAKE WRITING AS SOPHIE OAK

Small Town Siren
Siren in the City
Away From Me
Three to Ride
Siren Enslaved, Coming April 24, 2018
Two to Love, Coming Spring 2018

Close Cover
By Lexi Blake

A Masters and Mercenaries Novel

Foreword by Rebecca Zanetti

EVIL EYE
CONCEPTS

Close Cover
A Masters and Mercenaries Novel
Copyright 2018 Lexi Blake
ISBN: 978-1-945920-86-8

Published by Evil Eye Concepts, Incorporated

Sign up for the 1001 Dark Nights Newsletter
and be entered to win a Tiffany Lock necklace.

There's a contest every quarter!

Go to www.1001DarkNights.com to subscribe.

As a bonus, all subscribers will receive a free copy of
Discovery Bundle Three
Featuring stories by
Sidney Bristol, Darcy Burke, T. Gephart
Stacey Kennedy, Adriana Locke
JB Salsbury, and Erika Wilde

Foreword from Rebecca Zanetti

Dear Reader,

I think one of the nicest things Lexi Blake has ever said to me was, "I think you could be Charlotte Taggart. Your cardigans are just a prop." Since this happened after I'd chased Lexi around a book signing wearing a clown outfit (I was in the wig, not Lexi), I had to take this as genuine and incredibly kind. Charlotte, like the heroines in the Masters and Mercenaries series, is tough, authentic, and smart. I mean, who else would use a nail gun against terrorists and win? Plus, and this is a huge-assed plus in a world of plusses, Charlotte has Ian. I mean Ian Taggart! He's one of those sexy, snarky, brilliant characters who becomes the glue in a series and the guy you can't ever forget—nor would you want to.

As it turns out, I'm not the only reader obsessed with this series. Or the only author. Lexi has created a crossover opportunity for several awesome authors (you're probably already fans of them and I know I am), and how fun is that? Crossing these mercenaries into the Demonica Underworld is just fascinating and creates an amazing escape from reality for a while. All of the crossover authors have such terrific worlds set up to combine. Adding two worlds together and letting authors go wild with their imaginations is terrific fun for us. I'm sure it'll be a wonderful adventure for readers as well.

I'm excited to read all of the crossover books, and I know that you will enjoy your adventures in those worlds as well.

Happy Reading!
Rebecca Zanetti

Available now!
Close Cover by Lexi Blake
Her Guardian Angel by Larissa Ione
Justify Me by J. Kenner
Say You Won't Let Go by Corinne Michaels
His to Protect by Carly Phillips
Rescuing Sadie by Susan Stoker

Acknowledgments from the Author

This is a project I've had in my head for years. You see I started out in comic books and fantasy and science fiction. At heart I'm a true geek, and one of the things a geek loves is when worlds collide. They do it in comics all the time. Batman vs. Superman. The Avengers is the perfect crossover.

There are several ways to do this in the book world. I could have written in another author's world, but I wanted something more interactive. Something we as romance authors haven't done before. I wanted to get five or six of the best in the business together, form a plan, and roll out the characters before the audience even knew what we were doing. This was a crazy idea that would play out over the course of a year and a half and required a lot of work and a huge leap of faith.

I still have trouble believing these amazing authors said yes to me. Carly Phillips is a legend. Corinne Michaels is the brilliant new star. Susan Stoker can't write a book that doesn't succeed wildly. J. Kenner has the kind of career we all aspire to. And Larissa Ione writes the best paranormal around. I don't know why you said yes to me, ladies, but I'm so glad you did.

There was only one publishing house for this project and that was Evil Eye. I can't thank Liz Berry and MJ Rose enough for building a house where artists can bring their big ideas and know we're safe in your hands. Thanks to the entire crew at Evil Eye—Kim, Fedora, Kasi, Jessica, Asha, and Dylan. (I gave birth to the last one. Proud of you, baby boy!)

But this one is for the fans. I hope you enjoy this crazy crossover and maybe find some new writers to love!

Lexi

Prologue

The light in his face blocked out the view of the man interrogating him. Remy blinked in the glare and sighed. He should have known this wouldn't go the way he'd hoped it would. He'd come back to Dallas as a courtesy and now he had to worry that maybe he wouldn't make it out of this office again.

He should have filed his report and run the other way, but the truth was this had been his team and it was in ruins now. Well, what some would call ruins. They had been a fully cohesive unit and then the last few weeks had played out the way they had and their ranks had been decimated.

One by one they'd fallen…

The team he'd known so well these last few years was gone and it wouldn't be the same again.

"I want to know what happened," a deep voice said.

Remy sat back. He wasn't about to let that bastard know for a second that he was mildly intimidated. Besides, after everything that had happened in the past few weeks, the asshole probably had a right to take a chunk out of his hide. "It's all in my report."

There was the sound of shuffling and then his report slid across the desk and bounced into his lap.

"You mean this? This tells me nothing."

"It tells you everything you need to know about what happened in Papillon. I've documented everything thoroughly, including all the bloody parts and where I buried the bodies in case you need them for anything. Of course, given where I was at the time, those bodies might not last long. The bayou tends to take everything it can from a man if he's not moving. Sometimes even when he is."

As his brother had learned. God, he hoped his brother forgave him one day. Of everything that had happened in Louisiana, his brother's pain was the one thing he truly regretted.

Remy picked up the report he'd submitted only last week when he'd done all his exit paperwork. He thought he'd been extremely thorough in his mission report. His final report.

"Tell me what else you need from me, Tag."

It was his last report because he wouldn't be back here again. Not to work. After what had happened that wasn't possible. He was needed somewhere else.

Of course, given the fact that this dramatic interrogation scene was how Ian Taggart handled his exit interviews, maybe it wasn't such a bad idea to change careers.

He suspected the real problem was so damn many of them were doing the exact same thing. If it had only been him, Taggart would have crowned a new head of the personal security division, tried like hell to not give the sucker a raise, and gone about his business.

But that wasn't what had happened. Over the course of a few brief weeks, each man on the team had taken a case that had changed his life. And it couldn't help that Ian's own niece, Sadie, had left the company, too.

"I need answers. This was your team. How did they fall like a line of dominoes? Was it something in the water? Do you think the Agency did something to the team? We're still not on good terms. This would be a good way to fuck with me." The light winked out and Taggart stood up after pressing the button that opened the curtains. "Damn it, Guidry. I want to know what happened."

"It's complex and the truth is I can only tell you my side of it. We've all been through some crazy stuff in the last couple of weeks. You'll have to get the rest of the stories from Declan, Riley, Shane, Wade, and Sadie." It had been a busy few weeks. The truth was he was still reeling from all the changes, too. He thought about the last time the whole team had been together. It had been the night it all started for him. He'd thought he would be the only one leaving, but fate had different ideas. He was happy for that last night together. The next day was when their roads had split, taking them each in separate directions. He hoped it wasn't forever because he would miss those bastards.

Taggart turned on him. This afternoon the big boss was wearing slacks and a button-down shirt. Remy had rarely seen him in a suit. Taggart was far more comfortable in fatigues, even all these years after he'd left the military. Of course sometimes Remy wondered if Big Tag had really left the Army or merely started his own. "Do you understand the chaos I have to deal with?"

"You've known I was going to leave for a long time," he replied softly, because he did understand the last month had been hard on Taggart. The man hated change and he'd had a ton of it. "I let you know I was buying my family business back last year."

"I didn't realize you were going to spark a revolution," Tag shot back. "Look at what's happened. Declan gone. He's run off after some chick who can cook, and I think she put some crazy ideas in his head. Sadie's traded us in for some group of misfits at Fort Hood. Just good-bye, Uncle Ian. Gotta go break up some criminals, run from a crazy stalker, and find true love. Riley quit via text because he can't leave his lady love in LA. I built this division from scratch over years, finding the absolute best and brightest."

"You call us the full douche when we're all together," Remy pointed out.

Taggart waved that off. "An affectionate term. I built this all up and it fell apart over the course of a month. Of course I want to know what happened. I'm left with Shane, who smiles too much now. Does he honestly think smiling is going to stop a bullet? I get it. He's getting laid regularly by his very own smarty pants, but the happy thing is getting to me. And on the other end of the spectrum there's Wade. He got left out of the grand exit. He spent too much time with that country-western singer. He acts like he's in one of those songs. You know the ones I'm talking about. Someone cheats and drinks and someone's dog dies. What I'm saying is, Wade mopes. A lot. Now, personally I think moping will play way better on the bullet front, but it's annoying. This was a great team. I fed you all. I watered you. What did I do wrong?"

Oh, he was going to miss that jerk. He found himself smiling because apparently the team's happiness and joy was cause for Big Tag's fit. "You want to know the true story, Tag? At least my story. Like I said, you'll have to ask the others."

"At least let me understand one of you."

He leaned forward. "I'm going to warn you, it's got some parts you might not like. There's kissing in this story. And I do a small amount of groveling."

"You can skip those parts. Get to the bloody parts. Did anyone get eaten by a gator? That happened to Alex once. Not him, but to some bad people chasing him. I always miss the gator attacks." He frowned. "And I don't like any of this. I hate hiring people. It means I have to talk to them and I fucking hate talking to new people. Everything is changing and I don't like that either. I want to know who to blame. How the hell did this nightmare start?"

Remy sat back, ready to begin his tale. "Well, boss, like almost all really good stories, it started with a woman…"

Chapter One

Dallas, TX
One month earlier

Remy Guidry sat back in the comfortable chair he'd claimed only moments ago in the main conference room of McKay-Taggart. He wasn't sure why they were having this very normal weekly briefing in the main office instead of their man cave, but when the big guy called, he moved his team into place—whether that meant moving them into sniper positions or hauling them up a floor and making sure they weren't in work-out clothes.

His team. It was weird to think of them that way and to think about a potential future where they weren't around. He would miss them. He hadn't expected that when he'd taken the job a few years ago. He'd merely planned to use this time to his betterment. McKay-Taggart paid well and he didn't spend much. He'd figured a few years of putting his body on the line and he could buy his cousin's bar back in Papillon. It was a piece-of-shit nothing hole-in-the-wall, but once it had been Remy's whole damn world, that bar. He'd grown up watching his pop-pop mix drinks and sell bait out the back. He would sit on that dock and watch the boats go by and wonder when it would be him on that boat, heading out.

Now all he wanted to do was go home.

Except he'd been surprised to find a group of friends here. He hadn't meant to make them. They'd been like barnacles, slow growing and when not cut off, somehow becoming a part of him.

"Any idea why we're here?" Declan asked, sitting his massive frame in one of the chairs. "New assignments?"

Declan was one of those barnacles. Remy was pretty sure the ex-Air Force pararescue hadn't meant to find a bunch of brothers either. Of all Remy's men, Dec was the most secretive, the one he worried about. There was something…almost unworldly about the man. Like the stories his mom-mom would tell about the old ones still walking the earth. He came from a pretty crazy bunch of people, but Declan sometimes made him wonder if his mom-mom hadn't been right. "Big Tag sent me a nice note stating the whole group needed to be here at ten and ready for a meeting."

Riley Blade and Shane Landon strode in, both looking tan and fit from their time in LA. Dec had been on assignment with them, but somehow he'd managed to come back without a tan. Apparently when he hadn't been watching over superstar Joshua Hunt and getting his ass shot at, he'd stayed in his room, avoiding the beauty of Malibu.

"Nice note? Then it wasn't Tag, this is a trap, and we're all about to be brutally murdered," Riley said.

"What did it actually say?" Shane asked with a sort of detached curiosity.

"It said get the full douche down to the real world because I can't take clients into that sweat-soaked man cave you call an office. And dress like men." That was the boss.

Wade strode in, his boots ringing along the hardwood floors. "How exactly do we not dress like men, and I take offense to the group of us being described as a douche. What the hell does he mean by that?"

"It's like a gaggle of geese," Shane offered. "Or a pack of wolves."

"Or a murder of crows," Declan continued, his eyes dark. "Which is what I think about doing to Tag every time he calls us the full douche. I'm not a douche. Blade's a douche, but I'm not."

Riley sent Dec his happy middle finger. "Fuck you and your sad-sack jeans. Did anyone tell you the nineties are over?"

Sometimes they were a bit like bickering siblings, their camaraderie manifesting itself in manly insults and the rare but always fun blowup that resulted in wagering, someone getting his ass kicked, and then beers all around. Big Tag was an asshole, but he understood his employees. When he'd given the bodyguards their own office, he'd installed both a gym and a fridge that he'd filled with beer.

It wasn't the worst way to live, though sometimes it felt like he'd never actually left the military.

A vision of himself behind the bar, mixing drinks and shooting the shit the way his pop-pop used to came over him. It was a dream he'd started having years before when he'd spent his days killing and surviving. In his dreams he would see that bar and know it was his place in the world. Lately, the dream had changed slightly, merging with one he'd had since he was a teen first interested in the ladies. He was still behind the bar, but the door to the patio would open, the late evening sun illuminating the woman walking through it.

His woman. He knew that because his dream self damn near salivated at the sight of her, but she was a shadowy figure, her face always too backlit to make out her features.

How his friends and coworkers would laugh to find out Romeo Remy dreamed about his future wife. Which was precisely why he wasn't telling anyone about it. He'd learned long ago to keep those weird dreams he sometimes had to himself.

Shane was chuckling. "You have to admit you're a little on the Hollywood side, my man. You fit right in with that crowd in LA. I think that's why Joshua Hunt didn't like you. You're almost as pretty as he is."

"I admit to nothing but having a small amount of taste, and Hunt didn't like me because I was more popular at his club than he was," Riley replied. "And Tag would call us douches even if we were dressed like hoboes. He's wired that way. From him, it's almost affection."

Declan shrugged one big shoulder. "Better than a hug."

Wade took the seat closest to Remy and leaned over. "Hey, what was all that yelling about this morning? Sounded like a problem from home, man."

Remy frowned. He'd shut the door the minute he'd realized it had been his cousin calling. Apparently the solid wood door hadn't been thick enough to contain his rage. "Why do you think it was personal?"

"You started yelling in French," Wade pointed out. "You don't speak French unless someone calls you from home or Charlotte needs help ordering from the Paris Chanel store. Since Big Tag isn't screaming about how broke he's going to be, I assumed it was the former. Is it about the bar? Did he up the damn price again?"

The others had stopped their argument over whether or not Riley's designer clothes made him less manly and all heads turned to him.

"He upped the price again?" Shane asked. "Because you're already paying too much for that market."

"Way too much." Riley and Shane had done some investigating and concluded that his cousin Jean-Claude was an asshole of the highest order.

Remy could have told him that. "He didn't up the price." It was much worse. "He wants it all in cash in six weeks or he's going to sell out to a land developer who's been looking at our town. If the wharf goes, the town goes. No more shrimpers. No more small businesses. If he sells our land, the rest will have to sell, too. The whole town depends on having access to the water. If Jean-Claude sells the land, they'll immediately oust everyone who rents a slip in our marina. They'll evict the mechanic shop connected to the wharf and our entire way of making a living goes away. Unless we want to work in the big resort he's planning, we'll have to move. Most of those families have lived on that bayou for a hundred years, some more."

"How much?" Dec asked, his voice tight.

Remy shook his head because it didn't matter.

Dec gave him one of those looks that told Remy he could tell him or Dec would find out himself. "How much?"

Remy sighed and sat back. "I'm seventy thousand short. And that's seventy thousand short of merely qualifying for the loan. I thought I would have another two years, but my time's run out."

Wade held up a hand.

Remy knew exactly what he would say. "And no. Killing Jean-Claude wouldn't help anything. The wharf would go to a distant cousin, who's even greedier than he is. And no. Killing Jean-Claude and his cousin won't fix it because he's got a large family and they would keep coming."

"I'm only saying that between the five of us, we can kill a lot of people," Shane said.

"I can make a chart," Riley offered. "I'm a very organized killer."

"I appreciate it, but no." He was done killing, tired of all the blood on his hands. "I'm going to talk to the bank again. The last time I talked to them, the real estate boom hadn't started. Maybe they'll up the property value of my house." His rundown two-bedroom in a bad part of town. "No matter what, I'm going to find a way."

Whatever arguments might have come out of his teammates' mouths were silenced by the door opening and Big Tag walking in, his gorgeous wife, Charlotte, right behind him. Oddly enough, of the two, Charlotte scared him more than the former CIA assassin. Charlotte was utterly ruthless and did not mind leaving a man with two hand grenades waiting to go off while she sashayed away to have fun.

The hand grenades had been her twin daughters and yes, the "fun" might have been giving birth to baby number three. He prayed those two were done gifting the world with their spawn because he wasn't sure he could handle those two baby girls again. Not without a wife.

But they had gotten him thinking. They were stinky but awfully sweet. After he'd calmed down and accepted that he had to take care of two little girls and a dog who looked like he could kill but peed whenever new people showed up, he'd settled in. He'd found some cartoons and the girls had finally climbed up onto his lap and watched. After a while they'd fallen asleep and he'd studied them. They were cute and sweet and cuddled up like kittens looking for warmth. They were trusting in a way no adult could be. He kind of wondered what it would be like to have one of his own.

Big Tag had a future right there in those tiny things.

"Welcome to the civilized world," Taggart said, taking his place at the head of the table. "Riley, Dec, and Shane, welcome back from La-La Land. Nice job. The client didn't die and you managed to blow up a whole Mexican drug cartel and out a dirty CIA agent in the process."

"Not that it made him lose his job," Dec pointed out.

"But we know he's bad," Tag replied.

A whole lot had gone down in LA and it had a major effect on the London office, which suddenly found itself down a bunch of memory-blank soldiers it had been hiding and one operative who was now marrying a Hollywood star.

Charlotte sat down across from her husband, her strawberry blonde hair upswept in a professional bun. It made him wonder briefly how she'd worn her hair when she'd been a Russian mob assassin. She seemed to relish taking care of the day-to-day business of running McKay-Taggart. She pushed three envelopes out to each of the men who'd worked the LA job. "I think you'll find that Josh and Kayla were happy with your services and with helping train a new set of bodyguards for when they travel. They wanted to give you all something to show their appreciation."

From the way Shane's eyes widened, that must be a mighty big check. Sometimes the bonuses on certain jobs could be outstanding.

Damn, but he needed one of those jobs. He'd sent the others on the LA job because he'd wanted to stay close to home. Now he might be losing home altogether. But he wasn't about to show that fear here in the office. They had plenty of other things to worry about. "Do we have an update on the situation with Sadie?"

Sadie Jennings was Grace Taggart's niece, and for the last couple of years she'd taken her aunt's place as the office receptionist. She was a ball of sunshine in everyone's day, always willing to help out even in the dangerous stuff.

He was worried that level of loyalty was going to get the young woman hurt or even killed because a few weeks before, she'd been kidnapped. She was rescued, but one of the kidnappers got away and according to all the information they had, he was still after Sadie.

"Chase is keeping her hidden," Ian said, his voice grim. "But Jonathan Jones was recently sighted in the San Antonio area. Sean's driving down to Fort Hood for an update and to check in on her. Apparently she's got a bunch of friends down there, and some of them are military. He trusts them, but she's not safe until Jonathan is dealt with."

"Sadie is quite smart and capable," Charlotte said in a tone that made it obvious this wasn't the first time they'd talked about this issue. "She'll stay put until we are able to find the asshole."

Ian raised a hand as if to stave off the inevitable argument. "We'll find him. On to other things… Riley, you wanted some time off and I'm giving it to you. Go and have fun, but keep your phone on. If there's an emergency, I might have to call you back."

Remy got the meaning behind those words. After the LA mission, they didn't know what would happen with the Lost Boys. If the Agency came after them, it would be all hands on deck, and they might be going up against the CIA.

Riley nodded. "You need me, call, boss. I'll be there. But until then, I'm going to…rest for a while."

Yeah. Remy got those words, too. Riley would crawl into bed with a woman or two and not get out for a good long time. Exactly what he himself would do if he could. Find a good-time girl. One who didn't want anything more than a couple of orgasms because that was exactly all he had to give any woman at this point.

"Shane, your request to stay in Dallas for a while has been

approved," Charlotte said with a smile. "We've got a couple of short-term jobs around town so you can settle into the new place. Is it true you've got an outdoor shower?"

Shane smiled, the satisfaction clear on his face. "Country living with all the joys of the city. Best of both worlds. I can't wait to have my first barbecue."

"That leaves us with an assignment in South America. It's on the dangerous side and I don't know if we should take this one at all," Ian said, opening the folder in front of him. "It's a bodyguard assignment to a diplomat going to speak in Argentina, but I'm not sure about him."

"I'll take it," Declan said.

"I think we should talk about it, but if we decide to move forward, Wade should take this one," Charlotte said, starting to push the folder Wade's way.

A big hand came out, slamming over the folder and pulling it toward him like it was prey being dragged back into some predator's cave. Declan's. "I'll take this one."

A brow rose over Tag's eyes. "Damn it, Dec, you just got back from a long-term assignment and quite frankly you look like shit. Have you been sleeping at all?"

"I sleep fine and this one is mine." Declan didn't look up, merely opened the folder and started reading.

"I can't take it because I have a case of my own." Wade rode into the rescue like the cowboy he was. "I have a friend in town and he's asked me to watch after a lady from his hometown. Emily Young."

"The country singer?" Tag asked. "The one who played Top a while back?"

Wade nodded. "She's doing a full tour this time and she's attracted some crazies. She needs a full-time bodyguard. I head out to Houston tomorrow to join the tour. I hope it's all right. Remy approved it."

"We've all had some personal stuff we have to do," Remy replied. "I'll stay here and back up Shane and run the office."

"No, you won't," Charlotte said with a wry smile. "We have a job and it looks like you're the only one who can do it. This is why we called the meeting up here. We need you to meet with a client who's also a bit like family. I thought we could let them interview you and Declan to see who would work for them, but it looks like you get the job by default." She waved to someone outside the conference room.

"Excellent. Here they are."

He glanced up but couldn't see who she was waving at. Something raced along his spine, some small tendril of instinct that told him this was important. He didn't have the pure sight the way his great grandmother had, but he knew when change was coming and it was about to walk right through that door. Whatever this job was, it would be meaningful. To him? To the company? He couldn't be sure, but change was coming.

"The rest of the douche is dismissed," Tag said, getting up to open the door.

His coworkers all grumbled as they left, showing Big Tag how they felt, but in semi-polite ways as there were three women and two men waiting there in the lobby.

Remy frowned because he knew that group. They played at Sanctum, the BDSM club started by the founding members of McKay-Taggart. Well, four of them did. Will and Bridget Daley walked through first, Bridget looking pretty in her jeans and cotton top that couldn't hide her second pregnancy. Mitch Bradford was wearing his customary suit and his sweet wife, Laurel, looked like she'd come straight from her office. Mitch was McKay-Taggart's go-to lawyer and Daley's best friend.

The third woman was one he hadn't seen at the club before, but he could bet who she was. Lila Daley. He knew that because she looked a lot like her sisters—Laurel and Lisa.

Lisa. Freaking Lisa Daley, with the doe eyes and the slender feminine curves that made his mouth water every time she walked into a room. Lisa Daley, the good girl he couldn't have because he didn't do good girls.

At least she wasn't here. He got antsy when she was in the room. Sometimes he actually walked out of a room when she walked in because he knew if he didn't he would do something incredibly stupid like ask her to play or worse, ask her out on a real date.

He didn't date. He didn't take a sweet lady out to the movies and hold her hand and share popcorn with her and drop her at her door with nothing more than a kiss. Nope. He went to bars and picked up women who wanted a hot night of fucking. Or negotiated with submissives who knew the score.

But not with her. Never with her. The one time she'd asked, he'd practically run the other way.

I'm not interested.

He'd seen the hurt on that pretty face before he'd turned and walked away. The fact that she *could* be hurt made it plain she wasn't for him.

"Thanks for meeting with us on such short notice," Will Daley said as he settled his wife into a chair. The neurosurgeon looked worried, his eyes a bit bloodshot, as though he hadn't been sleeping. "We were all shocked at what happened. We thought this damn nightmare was over."

Remy sat up. What had happened? He liked the Daley family, his unwanted attraction to Lisa aside. Actually, her family was one of the reasons he stayed far away from the young woman. Lisa came from a family of high-powered doctors and nurses. Her brother-in-law was a top-tier lawyer and her sister-in-law a best-selling author. Lisa herself had a master's degree and would likely marry someone important.

What she wouldn't do was ever give up her comfortable life in the city to marry an ex-soldier who wanted nothing more than to tend bar and keep his hole-in-the-wall small town together. She would be horrified by where he came from, likely disdainful of the town's residents. Lisa was a big-city lady who wouldn't be able to handle his low-class baggage.

It didn't stop him from thinking of her.

"I knew it could happen," Bridget said. "I told you that judge is on the take. I can see it in his eyes. They're all in on it."

"Pregnancy makes you paranoid, baby," Will said, pulling her hand to his mouth for a kiss. "Remember when we had Brendon and you were absolutely sure the woman who had moved in across from us was working for Russian intelligence?"

"She worked for the IRS," Bridget shot back. "That's even worse. I bet she went through our trash looking for receipts."

Lila sighed as though this was a long-fought argument. "We don't know that the judge is on the take. We do know that jerk has a good lawyer."

Mitch shook his head. "Nah, that asshole got lucky. He should have found that problem in the beginning. He stumbled on it during cross."

"What's going on?" If Remy let them go on, they would start arguing among themselves and it would take forever to get to the point. "Who's in jail?"

"The problem is who got out of jail," Laurel replied, a frown on her face. "Have you been following the Jimmy Vallon case?"

"No," Remy admitted. It wasn't too surprising. Unless it was a sports score, he didn't follow the news. "What's it about?"

"Jimmy Vallon owns the largest valet service in the DFW area. He supplies restaurants and entertainment venues all over the Metroplex. About a year ago, he hired a new accountant who quickly figured out he was using some shady practices with his cash flow. She was smart enough to ask an expert and then went straight to the police to turn her boss in. Turns out Vallon was laundering money for a local drug distributor," Mitch explained. "So the police arrested him and up until yesterday he was absolutely going to be convicted and looking forward to doing some serious time. Then at the last moment, his attorney got lucky. He got one of the cops on the scene to admit to breaking chain of custody. Vallon kept a second set of books all by hand that the accountant discovered. Turns out there's about six hours missing between when they took the books from Vallon's office and when they were finally logged in at the police station. At some point in time two pages were pulled out and went missing. The main evidence was thrown out and a mistrial was called."

Remy wasn't sure where he fit into this, or the Daleys for that matter. "You're looking for an investigator? You want me to figure out what happened to the books? I'm not sure that's going to help anything at this point. Once evidence is thrown out, it's out."

Even he knew that much.

"We can't get the police to put her in protective custody because they don't have the resources. The truth is the prosecutor isn't even sure if he wants to retry the case," Will admitted.

"Because he's involved," Bridget insisted. "Because he's the one who set this whole thing up so Vallon doesn't do any time. Politicians. They're all on the take."

Her? Will had mentioned a "her." Remy put up a hand, trying to stop the argument. "Who is this mysterious accountant? I assume we're talking about the accountant because that's the only person who might be able to testify against Vallon."

He had a bad feeling about this. Lisa Daley had some kind of business degree. Surely she hadn't fallen into a job that put her firmly in some goddamn mobster's sights.

"Lisa," Laurel said, her face flushing with obvious emotion. "My sister was Vallon's accountant. It was her first job straight out of grad school. None of us can believe it. It's such a mess. She's the one who turned him in and now she's the only witness to his crimes."

He shook his head, his brain racing to try to find some way out of the trap he'd been placed in. None of the others could take on a job like this. It wouldn't be fair to put them on something this time-consuming after they'd just gotten back. But he sure as hell couldn't do it. Watching Lisa Daley every single day might drive him crazy. "Why would they come after her? She's not a serious danger to Vallon. They would need the accounting books. Juries want to see the actual evidence, not some hearsay."

"It wouldn't be hearsay. She has actual knowledge of the crime. I assure you she can testify." Mitch leaned forward. "And she might be much more effective than a bunch of books. Juries are funny things. They would absolutely rather listen to someone interesting speak about a crime than study boring numbers. Lisa is now considered a person of knowledge in the case. She's the only one who can testify as to what she saw in those books. The jury will either believe her or they won't. The trouble honestly isn't Vallon himself. Vallon's not violent."

Remy knew exactly what the problem was. "Nonviolent men don't do well in prison, and that means he's got plenty of incentive to talk about who he was laundering that money for. And Lisa is the only one who can send him there."

"My sister has an incredible memory for numbers," Lila explained. "She always has. I'm worried that somewhere in that big brain of hers is an account number that could potentially lead to a very bad man, but she won't listen to any of us. She won't go into hiding."

"Won't?" He was surprised at the bolt of pure panic that went through him. She was walking around out in the world in her designer shoes, her expensive handbag a target that said "please murder me" to all the happy mobsters. "Because you know *you* can lock her up. There's not a damn thing she can do about it if you do it right."

Will's jaw tightened. "She would never forgive me."

Laurel put a hand on her brother's arm, lending him her support. "Lisa can't stand to be locked in. She can lock her doors all right, but she has to know she'll be able to get out. It's a phobia from childhood. We asked about police custody, but she fought that the first time and this time around they won't consider it because of budget constraints."

"If she's in danger, lock her away," Remy insisted. Phobia or not,

Lisa was being reckless with her life. "If she's not smart enough to know it's for her own good, then take her safety into your own hands. It's as simple as that."

"Remy, as much as I tend to agree with you, these are our clients and we need to listen to what they want," Big Tag said quietly.

"Not when what they want will get Lisa killed," he shot back.

Will stood up, his face flushed. "Do you think I like this? I don't. I hate this. I'm worried about her every minute of every day, but I can't and won't betray her like that. You can't know what she's gone through and I'm damn sure not going to tell you because it's obvious you're smarter than the rest of us and nothing is going to change your mind."

Oh, that man was on the edge. Remy kept his voice as calm and even as possible. He didn't need to inject more emotion into the situation, but he did want to point out some logic. "Not at all. I'm not trying to be arrogant. You came here to ask me to do a job. Well, I'm giving you sound advice from someone who knows how to protect other people. There's a time you have to step up and be the head of your family, and that means making the hard choices."

Sometimes those hard choices put family members on opposite sides, but they had to be made. Remy was sure the hardest one Will Daley had ever made was to choose which expensive college he would go to. Oh, in the back of his head, he remembered some conversation he'd once had with Laurel about a trailer they'd lived in when they were kids, but it was clear that family's fortunes had turned and probably quickly since they all had impeccable manners and dressed like they only shopped at designer stores.

Bridget Daley's eyes narrowed. "Really? You think my husband has never had to make hard choices? You know what, Guidry? Fuck you. I love my sister-in-law so much I was willing to offer your ass a hundred grand to protect her while giving her the freedom she needs. Somehow I think I can find someone better than you." She turned to Taggart. "I want someone else. Someone who's not an asshole."

He'd forgotten that sweet-looking woman had some serious claws on her.

She also had serious cash. The Daleys all did.

A hundred thousand. One hundred fucking thousand dollars.

And that money was about to walk out the door.

Not to mention the fact that he didn't like the idea of some other man watching over Lisa Daley.

Taggart grimaced. "Assholes are all I have. It's kind of how they end up falling into the job."

"Then get me another asshole," Bridget insisted. "A smarter asshole."

"Look, Mrs. Daley, I'm sorry I offended." He had to fix this and fast. He'd been rude. He was almost never rude, but the idea of Daley letting his sister run around on her own because he was afraid she'd be mad at him got his back up. Someone needed to take that woman in hand.

She was already standing, but Laurel stood up beside her.

"Bridget, we talked about this. I want Remy to protect Lisa. He's good. I should know," Laurel said. "He watched over me. He's excellent at his job. I wouldn't have known he was watching me at all if Mitch hadn't been an overly possessive asshole."

"Hey," Mitch started and then kind of sighed and sat back down. "Fine. I can't help it. And I vote we keep Remy. He did do a good job. He protected Laurel even from me, but this is going to be a different kind of job. He can't watch her from afar twenty-four seven. He needs to be close."

"I would agree that this needs to be a close-cover assignment," Big Tag replied. "Hence the rather large amount the Daleys are willing to pay."

"But if she thinks you're there to protect her, she'll balk at the idea." Lila pulled her sweater around her like a shield, and Remy wondered what Lisa's stubbornness was costing her family. Not a one of them looked like they'd had a decent sleep recently.

He added selfishness to his long list of reasons to avoid Lisa.

Except it looked like he wouldn't be able to avoid her for much longer. Not if he wanted to save his hometown and solidify his future.

Besides, the fact that she was selfish enough to cause this much turmoil meant maybe he'd been wrong about her. Maybe she wasn't as sweet as she seemed and maybe that hurt he'd seen on her face that day had been shock at not getting her way. If she was some spoiled princess, then as long as he played it right, she would be fair game.

Close cover. Yeah, he might be able to handle that just fine. The woman had plagued his dreams at times. It might be good to get her out of his system before he walked off into the sunset.

"Can we find a female operative? One who could move into her apartment building and become her friend? What about that Kayla person?" Bridget asked. "She's cool and she's not an asshole. Didn't she watch over Mia Taggart while Case was being a massive ass? I don't know that I want to give this guy my hard-earned cash."

"You earned that cash by writing about triple penetration," Tag shot back.

"Do you know how hard it is to make that shit romantic?" Bridget turned on the boss. "Do you have any idea how difficult it is to make the act of lubricating various body parts sexy? I am a motherfucking genius."

"Yes, you do it so well," Charlotte soothed. "Bridget, Remy is our best bet and I happen to know that the apartment across from Lisa's opened up last week. I've already rented it. It will keep him close to her and her building has security cameras. He can cut into the feed and follow her when she goes out. We also installed her security system, so he would have easy access to that. It's a perfect setup. He can track her twenty-four seven."

He might have to be with her for weeks. Months, perhaps. That could be a problem. "I need the money upfront."

This kind of assignment would be split between McKay-Taggart and the bodyguard. It wouldn't give him everything he needed, but he could sell his house and that should put him over the top. He would give his cousin the money and his mom and siblings could take over running the place until after the job was done. Well, his sister could. Zep would just as likely drink the bar dry and try to sleep with every woman who walked in.

Now it was Will who looked at him suspiciously. "Why?"

"He's not trying to screw you," Big Tag assured him. "He needs the money upfront. He's trying to save his family business. Did your asshole cousin change the deadline?"

Remy frowned. "How did you know?"

Big Tag shrugged negligently. "I know everything. Also, I was downstairs earlier and speak some French." He turned to Will. "He's good for the job. He'll do it doggedly and he won't let anyone get close to her. And if it comes down to it, he'll be the bad guy. You know as well as I do she might need to be protected in a way she won't like. If Remy makes the call to put her in protective custody, he'll be the one who hurt her, not you. Your hands will be perfectly clean and you can throw in a couple of punches when you ride in to save her after she's safe. It's the perfect solution to your problem."

"She won't lose her family if things get rough," Charlotte promised. "She'll still trust you. She won't trust *him*, but that's all right because they don't have a relationship."

He would be the bad guy if it came down to it. It wasn't like he hadn't played that role before. He nodded Charlotte's way. "We're not even friends. I've seen her at the club, but we've never played. We've said maybe twenty words to each other."

Hello, Sir. I was hoping we could sit and talk and maybe discuss a scene between us.

So sweet and polite that his dick had hurt as he'd turned away. But he'd done it. And he would do it again. He would walk away from her at the end of this and he wouldn't look back.

"All right," Will said. "We understand this could be a long-term assignment. This is a twenty-four seven thing. I expect you to eat, breathe, and sleep this job for the next eight weeks. That's how long we think they'll take to make the decision whether or not they're going to retry Vallon. If it goes past that, we'll renegotiate. I'll have Moneybags here write a check and Taggart can pay you upfront if he wants to."

"And if she dies, I'll kill you myself," Bridget promised, her hand resting on her swollen belly as if the child she carried agreed with her.

"I'll do my best and I'll get started right away," Remy promised. "If she asks, I'll explain to her I'm putting my house up for sale and I need a place to stay."

It wasn't a lie. His house would be on the market, so it would be perfect to have a place to hang while the real estate ladies did their thing.

"So you'll do it?" Laurel asked, her eyes wide and pleading. Pleading for him to save her sister. He remembered how kind she'd been to him when she'd been his client. She never complained, included him in meals when she could, was always the perfect lady. Lovely manners, well-educated.

Very much like her sister, though he doubted Laurel would ever put her family through what Lisa was. Laurel Daley Bradford would have locked herself away in a heartbeat if it saved her family a moment's despair.

"Yeah, I'll do it. I promise I'll make sure no one gets close to her." No one but him. He wouldn't go into this planning to jump into her bed, but if it came up, well, he would be open and honest with her and if she still let him in, it wasn't like the wolf to leave the henhouse untouched.

As Charlotte started talking about the basic contract, Remy sat back and hoped his new client had better sense than he did.

Chapter Two

Lisa stared at the bank statement as though the numbers would change. Maybe if she willed it so, the decimal would move to the right and add some zeroes while it was at it. A lot of zeroes. She needed them since she'd been out of a job for over six months now. Stupid Jimmy and his stupid criminal activities.

She was supposed to be self-sufficient. She was twenty-nine years old and borrowing money from her siblings to pay for her apartment. They didn't know it, but she'd already turned in her car. The apartment was a deal breaker though. Moving wasn't an option. The notion of downgrading had been met with the idea of moving her in with Lila. It wasn't that she didn't love her sister, but Lila had a boyfriend who creeped her out, a boyfriend who looked at her like he wouldn't mind playing around on the side.

She'd mentioned it to her sister, who told her she was as paranoid as Bridget.

What the hell was she going to do?

You know there's a job waiting two stops over just for you. You can take the train. There's a nightly buffet so you don't have to pay for dinner and you'll get at least one meal every day you work. The solution is there. You're too proud to take it.

You're too ashamed to take it.

This was not where she thought she'd be after working her ass off to put herself through college. She was supposed to be the girl who picked herself up by her bootstraps, who got through everything with a smile on her face, who didn't need any help.

She thought she'd be married by now, happy in her career, maybe a baby on the way. She was supposed to have found her dream Dom at Sanctum and settled into pure bliss.

Life hadn't worked out the way she'd thought it would.

Sometimes she wondered if her mother had ever stood in this place and decided *what the fuck. Life sucks. Let's do some drugs.*

Wondered? Hell, she knew that was what her mother had done. Her mother had made that choice on a daily basis.

Would she? Would she finally find that place where there was nowhere left to go?

Or she could stop feeling sorry for herself, tell the world to fuck off, and go take the job where she would make a bunch of cash.

It wasn't like *she* would be stripping. She would simply be making drinks for men who were watching other women strip. That was all. Well, it would likely go hand in hand with fending the boss off on a nightly basis.

Jai, too cool to have a last name, had offered her the job two weeks ago. He lived in the building and they'd gotten to talking one day in the laundry room. Well, she'd been doing laundry. He'd been smoking outside.

Maybe he hadn't even been serious. Maybe she would walk into the subtly-named Cherry Pies and Jai would laugh and say she obviously didn't belong. He would tell her she was far too smart to end up in a strip club and hey, go find yourself another accounting job.

Nope. She had to think positive. This was going to work. She would bartend at night and look for a company that didn't mind hiring a known whistle-blower during the day. She would get back on her feet.

Lisa straightened the pretty Chanel blouse Bridget had given to her after she'd declared she would never fit into it again. The truth was Bridget was wildly successful and enjoyed changing out her wardrobe on a regular basis. Luckily she was just the tiniest bit smaller than her sister-in-law when it came to clothes, and they were a perfect fit on shoes, so Lisa had a steady diet of gorgeous designer clothes she could never, ever afford.

Okay. She could do this. Professional makeup. Check. Résumé in Kate Spade bag. Check. Shoes that were supposed to make her feel strong and powerful. Check. Pepper spray within reach and at full strength. Check and check.

I am a strong, independent woman. Nothing can bring me down except me.

And maybe an asswipe criminal who liked to clean other people's money. She nodded to the woman in the mirror and turned to her door. She was doing this. No more being afraid. No more pretending something better was coming around tomorrow. She made her destiny. She asked for what she wanted.

Her bag securely on her shoulder, she stepped outside. Maybe she should change her shoes. The five-inch Louboutins looked sexy as hell, but she had to walk quite a distance. Maybe she could feel powerful and invincible in sneakers. She was just about to change her mind when she walked right into a hard-muscled back.

She practically jumped away as she collided with the man carrying one half of a leather sofa. Somehow she managed to stay on her feet. "I'm so sorry."

It looked like 4C was getting filled quickly. Dayna and Jim Ball had only moved out two days before, but here was another neighbor to welcome to the building. Or not welcome, since it wasn't like it was a friendly place. She'd lived across the hall from the Balls for two years and had barely known the couple beyond their names and the fact that the wife didn't mind leaving her delicates hanging all over the laundry room waiting for any pervert to come and steal.

Or maybe this was a worker. A mover, perhaps, since he was made of muscles. Lots of sexy, masculine muscles.

"You all right?" a deep voice asked.

A deep voice with a ridiculously sexy Cajun accent that went straight from her ear down to her traitorous pussy. She heard lots of the Doms at Sanctum joke about how dumb their dicks were, but she was fairly certain her pussy could beat them all.

And that man was going to turn around and *not* be Master Remy. Nope. They were in Dallas and that was close enough to Louisiana that there could be another bayou boy here. It was some other gorgeous Cajun god of a man standing in her hallway, one she hadn't hit on and gotten rejected by, one she hadn't made a complete fool of herself over. It was another beautiful man. She would make a joke about the collision with him and then never, ever speak with again.

She'd learned her lesson and didn't want to take Being Humiliated by Remy Guidry 101 again. Her *A* had been well earned.

"I'm fine. Didn't even fall. Welcome to the building." It was best to retreat now. Whoever it was—not Master Remy, not Master

Remy—he was obviously busy, and she had things to do, too. It was way too late to change her shoes. They were good shoes. Bridget swore by them. She had to go get her strip-club job before some other sad-sack, couldn't-get-another-job woman took it from her.

She started to turn and then heard a heavy thud.

"Lisa? Lisa Daley?"

Run, Lisa, run. That was the smart part of her screaming in her head. *Dump the shoes right here and now because they will hold you back. Dump them and run like a gazelle evading a hungry lion.* The polite part of her stopped.

She slowly turned, forcing a smile on her face. "Mr. Guidry? What a surprise to see you here."

Yep, that was Remy Guidry. He was six-foot-five-inches of pure muscle. His hair was dark and she remembered when it used to flow around his face, brushing his shoulders when he would take it down before a hot scene. She'd been like a groupie, following all of his scenes, waiting for that moment when his hair would come down and she would pretend like she was the submissive he was about to put in bondage and suspend. A few months before he'd cut it, like seriously cut it. He'd been out of town for a few weeks and when he'd come back he'd had that military look. The new buzz cut had grown out a bit, but she'd been surprised to see how cutting his hair had made him even more masculine, the stark, gorgeous lines of his face no longer softened by the hair. Now he wore a muscle shirt, jeans, and boots, and there was zero chance of missing the way those shoulders moved, how strong his arms were.

His sensual lips curled up as though he could read her mind, and every thought she sent his way made him the tiniest bit more arrogant. And he was arrogant enough before. "Yes, this certainly is a surprise. You visiting someone here?"

She should say yes and then move out tonight. Pack everything up and run. Unfortunately, that would mean moving in with her married brother or sister and disrupting their lives, or with Lila and murdering her boyfriend. If only she had a car… Homelessness had never been more appealing. "No, I live here. 4B. Home sweet home. I suppose you're helping to move a friend in."

Someone had to have been holding the other half of that couch. Maybe she was going to get lucky and this was just one bro helping another. No big deal. They weren't even particularly good friends, so he wouldn't be around much. Maybe he'd lost a bet and he didn't even like the person who was moving here. She could live with that.

"Not at all. This is home sweet home. Temporarily," he replied, his hands on his lean hips. "My house is being extensively renovated so I can put it on the market. It could be a few months before I can move, so here I am. It's nice to see a friendly face."

Wow. He had two houses. That must be nice. And it was good to know her face was friendly. She'd been afraid it was twelve kinds of horrified. She still had it, the ability to not show her emotions on her sleeve. It boded well that she would be able to get through her interview without crying. "Yeah, well, welcome to the…hi."

Another man was standing behind him, his partner in getting that comfy leather sofa into the apartment. He was a lovely man wearing a T-shirt and jeans and sneakers, his hair neatly kept. Fit and handsome, she couldn't help but smile his way. He was a hottie. Too bad he had horrible taste in friends.

That was a terrible thing to think. Just because Remy Guidry hadn't been interested in her didn't make him a bad man.

The man who would have been considered very big had he not been standing next to Remy moved around the sofa, holding out his hand. "Hi, we haven't met. I'm Shane. I work with Remy at McKay-Taggart. I drew the short straw and had to help him move."

He worked with Remy, but he wasn't a regular at Sanctum. She'd remember seeing him there. He looked friendly and normal. Handsome, but her heart didn't threaten to explode from looking at him. She reached out and took his hand, shaking it with a smile. "Hi, Shane. I'm Lisa."

He gave her a smile that lit up the hallway. "It's nice to meet you, Lisa. And might I say, you are looking lovely today."

And he was polite. "Thank you."

Remy stood between them, frowning down like he'd never seen two people shake hands before. "Shane, I think I heard your phone ringing. You left it in the apartment."

Shane held her hand a moment longer before he shook his head. "Yeah, definitely. Gotta go see who that is. Catch you later, Ms. Lisa. I'm a friend of the big guy so I'm sure to be around."

He let go of her hand and stepped back into the apartment, where absolutely no phone had gone off unless its ringer was tuned to dog hearing or something.

"He's not a good friend, so don't expect much. He lost a bet and had to help me move. You know how it is with guys," Remy quipped, leaning back against the couch as though it was perfectly normal to have a conversation in the middle of the hall, a couch blocking most of the way. "I'm glad to see you here."

"Why?" Oh, god. She'd said that out loud.

His face softened. "Because you're a nice person to see. Look, I think we got off on the wrong foot."

No. They'd gotten off on a foot that had been promptly shoved into Lisa's mouth and way too far down her throat. It was a foot she'd been forced to chew on for months while she tried to get her confidence back.

She'd had a crush on the sexy Cajun ever since he'd been Laurel's bodyguard during that time between Mitch getting her preggo and properly marrying her. For a week or so, Remy had been Laurel's shadow, and Lisa had started dreaming about him. Then she'd gone through her training class at Sanctum and found out her dream man was also a Dom there. It had taken her months, but she'd worked up the courage to converse with him.

I'm not interested.

It was then she'd realized why human beings made shit up. *I have a girlfriend. Oh, I'm so sorry, I have a cold tonight and can't play. Aliens are coming and I need to go and find my laser gun. Hope you have fun tonight.*

The truth hurt. The truth gutted and left one feeling empty and hollow for months. That tiny lie, even when blatant, was so much kinder than the brutality of truth.

"Not at all," she assured him. "We simply don't have friends in the same circles."

And you weren't interested in me.

"You haven't been at the club much lately," he pointed out.

She didn't have a car anymore and there wasn't a nice neat train station close by. She'd agreed that she wouldn't play on nights Will and Bridget were playing or Mitch and Laurel, so she didn't have a ride in. Will and Bridget had taken Fridays. Mitch and Laurel Saturdays, and that left Lisa with Thursdays and Sundays. One day she would work the nursery in exchange for her club access, and the other she would be allowed to play. Until she'd turned in her car. She certainly wasn't going to force someone to pick her up and drop her off, and she'd looked at her budget and decided she didn't have enough to Uber in and out twice a week. She'd canceled all her nursery workdays and was fairly certain that meant her membership was gone, too. She missed the club and all her friends there. One more thing Vallon had cost her. "Yes, I stopped going a while back. Guess it wasn't for me after all. You know I tried it a time or two, but turns out I'm not as submissive as I thought."

Oh, she was in bed. She loved it for sex, but he didn't need to know that. He wasn't interested in that.

His eyes searched hers and she could practically hear his "bullshit." Not that it mattered. He could think what he liked. "I find that surprising. Wade Rycroft is a friend of mine, too, and he said you were the best trainee in your class."

Wade Rycroft was the Dom in Residence at Sanctum, when he wasn't off working as a bodyguard for McKay-Taggart. He'd led her training class and she'd found him to be a genuinely kind man. She'd always wished there had been something past friendship between them, but again, her pussy was a dumb creature.

"I'm an excellent student, Mr. Guidry. I like to do well, and sometimes that means compromising on what I want to get that *A*. It's something about me."

"It's Remy, Lisa." His words were low and deep, honey dripping from that sensual as sin mouth of his. "We're not in the club. You don't have to show me respect."

"But isn't it nice to simply respect everyone?" she replied. "Even people we don't particularly have much in common with. It makes life much more pleasant."

"Respect is something that should be earned," Remy said, but kind of waved the point away. "And you went to the club far more than a few times. You were a regular for over a year. You played every Thursday night. Was that because your brother didn't want you playing at the same time as him and his wife? Because Thursday isn't as fun as Saturday. I like to call it suspension Saturday. Now, I will suspend a sub on another night, but doesn't Saturday feel like the right time to get trussed up and suspended in a pretty cage of rope?"

Yep. It sounded awesome. But again, he wasn't interested. "I was never into suspension."

"That's funny, because I remember distinctly that you used to be in the crowd whenever Kai suspended Kori," Remy remarked.

She felt herself flush and hoped he didn't notice. It hadn't only been Kai and Kori's scenes she'd watched, but luckily he didn't seem to have noticed her watching all of his scenes. "I was curious at the time."

"But you aren't now?"

"No. I am not. You know, that's why we call it exploring. We try new things and realize they're not for us." Abruptly she remembered his reputation as a ladies' man. More like unrepentant manwhore. "Now, if you'll excuse me, I have an appointment. Like I said before, welcome to the building. Please remember we have a policy of quiet time after eleven at night. You might remind all your...dates. See you around."

She could have sworn his eyes had been narrowing as she'd turned, but she didn't look back. Nope. No way. No how. She walked on, her shoulders squared.

You have to be better than this trailer park if you're ever going to get anywhere.

From out of nowhere, the memory rose. She was eight and sitting on her bed, Lila brushing out her hair for school because their momma was in jail again and Will was left holding everything together.

But why? Standing up straight hurts after a while. Young Lisa hadn't understood.

It had been Lila's job to train her. *Proper posture is ladylike and proves you've been raised well. Then the social workers don't look at us so much. Then they buy the story that Aunt Elaine is here and just went off to the grocery store. If the trailer is neat and clean and we're all polite and proper, no one believes we're on our own. We have to be perfect or they'll come and take us apart, Lis. So be still and let me brush your hair.*

She'd washed it even after the water heater had gone out. For months they'd all taken cold showers and saved coins to use at the laundromat, all so no one would suspect they were four kids on their own.

She'd learned to pretend to be something she wasn't a long time before. And god, she'd learned not to ever fuck up. A smile on the face. That was how to get through life. The one time she'd failed... Well, she preferred not to think about that at all. Stupid Vallon had made her think about it and she wasn't going to let it ruin her again.

She never let life see her down because life had no problem showing her exactly how much further she had to fall.

She strode out into the late afternoon light and walked toward the train station, trying not to think about the gorgeous man she'd left behind. And wishing she'd changed her shoes.

* * * *

"You want to tell me what the hell that was about?" Remy felt weird as he picked up the end of the couch and barely managed to fit it through the door to his new home. Temporary home. He wasn't staying here for long.

It was awfully nice though. Probably the nicest place he'd ever lived, but then that wasn't so surprising since this was where the Daleys stashed their youngest sibling. Lisa was the only one of the Daleys who wasn't attached, and apparently she was very independent. The building had good security, a whole round of amenities like a dog park and jogging trails. Hell, anywhere he'd lived before Dallas, if he wanted to jog, he did it while trying not to be eaten by gators.

He couldn't stay for long because the paperwork was already in the works. He had done all the paperwork for the loan and in a few short weeks the marina and everything in it would be back where it belonged. In his hands.

Lisa Daley was nothing more than one last job. It didn't matter that he wanted her. It didn't matter that she was the most tempting thing he'd seen in forever. He wasn't getting involved with another woman who would need more than he could give her. He'd married one and that had led straight to the situation he'd been in for years. He wasn't about to lose his family and his inheritance over a spoiled rich girl again.

So why the hell was he feeling like a bear riled out of hibernation way too early? She'd looked utterly horrified at seeing him. Oh, he'd told her something different and he could see she'd been trying to appear normal and happy, but pure terror had been behind that smile. He had the feeling she'd wanted nothing more than to run as fast as she could.

And then she'd turned on that high-wattage smile when she'd caught sight of Shane. She looked at Shane like he was a cupcake and she'd been on a sugar-free diet for way too long. It bugged him.

"She's pretty," Shane replied, turning to head into the kitchen. He opened the fridge and pulled out two beers. "She reminds me of the lawyer's wife. You know, Mitch's wife. What's her name?"

"Laurel. There's a reason they look alike. She's Laurel's sister." Apparently he should be glad Shane didn't play at Sanctum or Lisa might not have needed a bodyguard. "And could you try to remember that I'm the one who needs to follow her? Flirting with my target isn't going to help this mission."

Shane popped the top off his beer after handing Remy one. "You're following her, not dating her. Not that I want to date anyone right now, but if I was going to date someone, I could hang out with her. Have you thought about the fact that she might be easier to handle if someone's friendly with her?"

The idea kind of threatened to fry his brainpan, and that didn't make a lick of sense. Not a bit. He wasn't interested in her. He'd meant that. So why was he acting like such a possessive jerk? She'd stood there with her designer clothes and a purse that likely was worth more than a week's worth of bar receipts and his dick hadn't cared that she was a poor rich girl whose family could afford to spend insane amounts of money so she didn't have to have a moment's discomfort.

And those shoes. Those fuck-me heels made her legs long and sleek and would look good wrapped around him while he thrust his cock inside her.

Friendly? There was nothing friendly about this.

"Did I mention I wasn't looking for anything serious?" Shane asked, backing up slightly. "Or at all. I've decided to give abstinence a chance. You know, I think she actually reminds me of my sister."

"You don't have a sister," Remy heard himself say.

"Yeah, well, if I did I would treat her with the careful sexual distance I'm now going to treat Lisa Daley with," Shane replied, leaning against the bar. "You look crazy right now. Like a little on the psychotic side. I'm serious. Drink that beer and chill out. No one's touching your shit, man."

Remy sighed and dropped down to the couch. He'd known going in that this wasn't a simple assignment. He could force himself not to think about her when she wasn't around. Mostly. How was he going to handle watching her constantly? "She's not mine. Not in any way. Well, except she's my client. But she's not. Her sister-in-law is my client. I can't even let her know I'm guarding her."

"That's rough, but you might want to rethink that whole 'she's not mine' thing because seriously, you almost lost your shit, and I was only talking about hypotheticals," Shane pointed out. "You're attracted to her."

Like he'd never been attracted to a woman before. Hell, he'd been married and he hadn't wanted his wife the way he wanted Lisa Daley. At first he'd told himself it was because he liked Laurel, and her family seemed warm despite their incredibly elite status. Now he wasn't sure where the hell his head was at. "I don't want to be."

"Why?"

For so many reasons. "She's not my type. Physically she's my type, but I'm not into high-maintenance women."

Shane chuckled. "All women are high maintenance. Relationships are high maintenance. If they aren't, then they're probably shallow."

He nodded. Finally someone understood. "Yes, that's what I want."

Shane stared at him, the inherent "dumbass" right there in his expression. "Well, then you're doing great, buddy. You've fucked just about every good-time girl in North Texas. You do know most of those good-time girls wanted a relationship with you, right? Women are funny that way."

"I am very clear about what I will and won't give to a woman." He didn't want to hurt anyone.

"Yeah, well, a lot of women get it in their heads that they can change a man," Shane replied. "They figure it out in the end, or they don't and keep right on running through guys like you until guys like you no longer look at them or want them."

"I'm not the bad guy here and I'm especially not the bad guy when it comes to Lisa Daley." But he was going to be. He was being paid to be. This morning it had seemed all right. Seeing her again… Well, the thought of hurting her made his stomach twist.

Of course he could potentially hurt those delicate snowflake feelings of hers or she could get shot, and that made his stomach twist even tighter.

"I heard you mention she's a Sanctum girl," Shane said. "Sub?"

Shane didn't play, but that didn't mean he was ignorant of his surroundings. "Yes, she's definitely submissive when it comes to sex. I don't know what that bullshit out in the hallway was. Wade said he hadn't seen a trainee so eager to try everything. And it wasn't like she came in a couple of times and then disappeared. She was a fixture every Thursday night, and Sundays she worked the nursery. And this was for over a year. Nah, I don't buy the whole 'I got bored' thing. This is about me."

"You?"

"She came on to me a few months ago and I didn't handle it well." That was putting it kindly.

"She came on to you?" Shane asked. "Like threw herself at you?"

"No. She was sweet about it. Polite." The way she almost always was, though now she avoided him like the plague. "She asked if she could have a moment of my time and if I would consider a scene with her."

He'd scened with almost every single sub in the place, and some of the married ones. Not that the married ones had led to sex. They'd been more about teaching the sub's husband about suspension play. Lisa had to know how many subs he'd played with. Everyone but her.

How had that made her feel?

"And you handled it how?" Shane asked as though he already knew the answer and it wasn't pretty.

"I told her I wasn't interested and walked back to the locker room." Stumbled in his haste to get away, but Shane didn't need to know that.

Shane winced. "Yeah, that would do it. You said *I'm not interested* and nothing else? Like you were refusing a mint?"

"I panicked."

"You don't panic."

"I do around her." He moved to his computer. "I don't know why but she unnerves me."

"Because you're attracted to her," Shane started. "Insanely attracted to her."

Suddenly there was movement in his doorway and Wade strode in, a box in his hand. "Are we talking about Lisa Daley? Because for some reason he doesn't want to be attracted to that sweet thing. And he doesn't want the rest of us to be attracted to her either. You should watch out. He kind of growls when one of us gets too close."

"I can't believe you got that monstrosity of a couch in," Declan said, setting down the box he was carrying. "I was so sure that wasn't going to happen."

"It's all about physics and geometry, my friend," Shane replied. "I've got both brains and beauty."

Riley groaned, entering the apartment with Remy's microwave in his hands. "Yep, you're a beauty queen, Landon. Remy, this place is way better than your ramshackle piece of crap. It deserves a microwave that was built in this century."

Ah, his crew was here and they would give him plenty of shit. "Hey, it works. Not everything has to be beautiful as long as it functions. Put it over there on the bar, and my ramshackle piece of crap is going to put me over the top financially."

Riley set the microwave, that really did seem like it had seen more of US history than a small appliance should, on the bar and held out a hand. "I'm happy to hear that, though I'm going to be sorry to see you go, brother."

There was that tug he hadn't expected, the one that let him know this was his home, too. He shook Riley's hand. "You're not done with me yet. I've got this one last job, and it could take a good long while. Hell, by the time I get home, my brother might have burned the place down."

Zep wouldn't mean to. He was just a dumbass who couldn't seem to stay out of trouble to save his life. He was a human Mouse Trap game, specifically the little ball that through no real fault of its own caused all those traps to fall into place. More than once he'd picked his younger brother up at the jailhouse with Zep scratching his head and wondering what the hell had happened.

He would have to deal with that all over again. Then there was Seraphina and her wretched taste in men, and his momma's penchant for shooting people.

Maybe he should stay here.

"I thought you were taking a vacation," he said to Riley. "That usually means crawling into some woman's bed, not helping a buddy move."

"Maybe I've grown over the years," Riley mused. "Sharla can wait. Or was it Charmaine? Champagne?" He waved it off. "I can have sex whenever I want. Apparently my time with you is running short. So I thought we could hang and do manly shit. Then I walk in and we're talking about your tender feelings. Landon, you totally should have been a relationship counselor."

Shane tossed him the bird. "Fuck you. It's an op. He's got to watch her but not look like he's watching her."

Riley nodded. "He should totally fuck her."

Declan shrugged. "It's the best way. Can't lose track of her if you're on top of her. Also, she can't take a bullet if you're on top of her. It really works all the way around. And she's pretty cute. I don't see the problem."

Wade frowned Declan's way. "Morals."

Dec looked around like he didn't understand. "Yes, the moral of the story is if you're sleeping with her, she'll probably do what you say in the field."

"I meant do you have any morals, asshole. What about her feelings?" Wade asked.

"I thought she would be feeling an orgasm," Declan replied. "I don't see what's wrong with that. Unless…"

Remy rolled his eyes and took a long drag off his beer. "I can give her an orgasm, dumbass. What Wade is saying is that it's not fair to sleep with her when I don't intend to hang around. I'm always upfront and honest. If I sleep with a woman, I tell her what I'm willing to give and what I can't. I'm leaving soon."

"Sometimes that's the perfect time," Shane pointed out. "Not that I don't agree with Wade wholeheartedly about the morals thing, but we've all been put in positions where we had to do sketchy shit to protect a client."

"Or two," Riley said with the smooth smile of a player who knew how good he was at the game. "Or three."

Dec snorted. "Misti, Janice, and Crystal weren't clients. They were the client's sisters."

"And they needed protecting, too," Riley replied, a wistful look on his face. "Such sweet, innocent ladies."

He was a lost cause. "Look, even if I wanted to be honest with her now, I doubt she would talk to me. She practically ran down that hallway when I said hello to her. I'll be lucky if she doesn't start looking to move." Speaking of moving. "Shane, could you pull up her GPS? Her sister said she planted the tracking device I gave her on Lisa's handbag. I didn't see her car in the lot. I need to tag that, too."

Dec shook his head. "I didn't either. You said it was a late-model Audi. I saw a couple of those, but not a gray Q5. I don't know. All those hipster cars look the same to me."

"I'm not sure you understand the meaning of the word *hipster*." Shane fired up the laptop. "But I didn't see it either. She must have parked outside the lot. Let's see where she's going."

"So you don't want to sleep with her?" Declan asked. He had

slumped onto the sofa as though tired. "Because again, she's pretty cute."

Why had he invited his friends over? "If I thought I could get in and out of her bed without causing a shit ton of problems, I would do it in a heartbeat. She's gorgeous and she's exactly my type physically, but she needs more than I can give her. That's why I told her I wasn't interested the first time she asked."

Riley stared at him. "You did what? Like you told her you had a girlfriend or something, right?"

Wade was shaking his head. "Shit. You didn't bald-face tell her that, right?"

Even Declan seemed surprised. "Dude, I'm terrible at expressing myself and even I would have found a way to let her down easy. You're screwed. Unless she's got no self-esteem. Did she ask you more than once?"

"Oh, she hasn't talked to me since," he admitted. And now he wondered if she'd actually left Sanctum to get away from him. He didn't like how that made him feel.

Could he be honest with her? Tell her that he was leaving soon, but he wouldn't mind spending some time with her. Explain what had been going through his head. He wouldn't be lying to her. He just wouldn't be telling her the whole truth.

According to her family, she wasn't dating anyone and hadn't in over a year. Apparently there had been a graduate school boyfriend who'd left her for someone he was now married to.

Maybe she was as lonely as he was and wouldn't mind passing some time with someone who knew what the score was.

"I think she's on the train," Shane said. "There's no road, but the light-rail goes through there."

Riley moved in behind him. "I think you're right. Otherwise she's the Flash and she doesn't mind running across fields. Yep. That's the red line. There's a stop within walking distance of this building. Where do you think she's going?"

"Why is she taking the train?" Remy asked.

"You know some people take it to save the environment," Dec replied with a yawn. "Yeah, I know that sounded stupid. Is her car in the shop? Do you want me to go break in to her place and see if I can find out?"

"I think we'll keep the break-ins in our back pocket," he replied, staring at the screen with the others. His brain was still on what they'd talked about before. Sleeping with her would be the best way to keep track of her. She didn't have a job right now. He would have to pretend to go to work and then follow her, but she couldn't know how much vacation time McKay-Taggart owed him.

They could have some fun and then when the case was done, he would say good-bye and she would be a nice memory. They couldn't work out long term, but maybe she wouldn't mind slumming for a few weeks.

"She's off the train. Two stops," Shane was saying. "Not the best part of town."

Like all cities, Dallas was a hodgepodge of the wealthy, the middle class, and what could only be called the not so nice parts of town. And they weren't all that far from each other. He could be in a super-wealthy neighborhood one block and within four have gotten to a section he needed a gun to feel safe in.

He doubted Lisa Daley carried a gun. "Where the hell is she going? That section of town is nothing but dive bars and…"

"Hey, I know that one," Wade said, pointing at the screen. "Cherry Pies Strip Club." He frowned suddenly, noticing that all eyes were on him. "What? It's got a good buffet."

Sure it did.

Holy shit. He stared at the screen, knowing exactly what building she was going into. Wade wasn't the only one who had been to that part of town. Lisa Daley had just walked into one of the skankiest strip clubs the city of Dallas had to offer, and he doubted she was asking for directions. "Gentlemen, I think it's time we took this party on the road."

"Thank god," Riley said with obvious relief. "A strip club is way better than moving the rest of Remy's sad shit."

"Will there be naked women I get to ogle, or is this some crazy 'rescue the grownass woman from herself because I'm a possessive caveman asshole' mission?" Declan asked. "Because if there's boobs and a buffet, I'm in."

"I don't think anyone should eat strip-club food," Shane said. "Is that even sanitary?"

Riley rolled his eyes. "The strippers don't touch the food. Hey, do you think Lisa's stripping? Because then I'm totally in."

And then Remy would punch any dude looking at her. But no. He wasn't a possessive caveman asshole. Even when he wanted to be. "I definitely think we should figure out what she's doing there, and that means taking a field trip. Let's take two cars in case I need to follow her somewhere else."

It could be a mistake. She could have gotten off at the wrong place, or maybe she was meeting a friend. At a strip club. Sure.

Was she stripping for cash? She didn't need cash. Her family was loaded and they didn't hesitate to hand it over. If she was stripping, then she liked to have eyes on her, enjoyed the thrill of being the gorgeous woman every male eye watched. If she was stripping, she was doing it for thrills.

He could be thrilling. Maybe she was looking for a walk on the wild side and he'd misinterpreted their situation entirely. He'd seen a polite rich girl he couldn't keep, but maybe she was the curious rich girl he could have for a brief time. For a mutually pleasurable time.

He locked up as he followed the others out, each laughing and joking, their camaraderie easy. So why did he feel like it was all changing on him again, like they would all be different soon? Why did he feel like Lisa was going to be the catalyst for his own change?

Any way he looked at it, he knew she would be trouble. But maybe he was ready for a little trouble in his life.

Chapter Three

Lisa looked at the clock. Seven hours. She'd only been here for seven hours? It seemed like much longer. It seemed like forever.

Cherry Pies smelled like a combination of beer, poor life choices, and shrimp cocktail sauce. And desperation, though she was fairly certain the desperation was mostly coming straight from her.

"I like the getup," one of the cocktail waitresses said, putting her tray on the bar. "It's classy. Makes you stand out. Tell me something. Is it Velcro?"

What? She could barely hear over the pounding music. "No. It's Chanel."

The cocktail waitress shook her head. "Nah, Chanel don't wear that uppity shit. She's old school. Nothing but nipple clamps and a thong. I keep telling her she should wear more clothes if she wants her act to last longer, but no one listens to me. I need four beers and a daiquiri."

The music died down a bit as this particular show ended, and thank god, the clapping wasn't nearly as loud. These "gentlemen" showed their appreciation with dollar bills, not enthusiasm.

"What kind of daiquiri?" Who the hell ordered a daiquiri in a strip club? In the hours since she'd been thrown to the lions, she'd poured about a hundred beers, made up dozens of tequila and whiskey shots, and a couple of sidecars and boilermakers.

The fruity drinks hadn't come up, though she had plenty of citrus. She'd been surprised at how well stocked the bar was. Normally a dive like this would be nothing but beer, whiskey, vodka, and tequila. Cherry Pies sported all the liquors of a good bar and three types of vino—red, white, and a pink of indeterminate origin.

The cocktail waitress, who was in fact topless, shrugged. "No idea. I asked and he said if you didn't know what a classic daiquiri was you weren't a real bartender. I told him this is a strip club, ain't nothing real here, but he insisted. He's hot, too. Damn, we don't get many men in here who look like that, and there's a table of five of them tonight. I thought JoJo was going to bust an implant shaking those things their way, if you know what I mean."

She didn't. She understood very little. Since the moment she'd walked in, the world had been a loud, weird place where nothing seemed to stop and glitter rained down from time to time. Certainly the drink orders hadn't stopped, nor had the head bartender's orders or Jai's leering. Or the constant comments about her boobs. Which were covered, and yet the men of Cherry Pies believed in equality. They harassed a woman no matter her age, size, color, or amount of clothing she wore. These men were serious about their sexual harassment, and no amount of clothing would stop them.

Her "interview" had consisted of Jai looking her over, nodding, and then tossing her to the wolves. She'd been there five minutes when she was thrown into the pit, as she now affectionately called the large bar at the back of the establishment. She'd poured her first beer, gotten her first one-dollar tip, and told herself life was going to be okay.

Seven hours later, she was fairly certain she was in purgatory. It wasn't quite hell because she could still find stuff to laugh at, but her feet hurt so much she wanted to die. It defo wasn't a good place.

"A classic daiquiri?" It was such an odd request for a place like this. She sighed, realizing who'd ordered. "Is this for Jai?"

It would explain a lot. This whole evening was her interview and she would be told at the end of the night whether or not she'd gotten the job. Then there would be normal things like corporate videos on safety—don't cut yourself, don't spit into the drinks no matter how much you want to—and procedures. There would be tons of paperwork. There was an odd comfort in paperwork.

The cocktail waitress Lisa had named Whiskey because of her throaty voice shook her head. "Nah. Jai likes Jäger. This is a superhot guy. I'm planning on going home with this dude. He's with the cowboy. Don't know his name because he always pays cash, but he comes in once a week or so. Usually during the day. Weird guy. I think he actually comes in for the buffet."

With a wince she turned and poured the beers. Bartending had gotten her through college. By the time she'd gotten into grad school, Will had started making enough from his practice that he'd asked to pay for her school. He hadn't liked her spending long nights at bars, but the truth was she kind of missed it. There was something deeply human about a good bar. A good bar could be a community, form a makeshift family for those who desperately needed one. Working in bars had taught her that kindness lurked in the oddest of places, and that sometimes those who were the most broken could also be the most human of all.

"What's up with the daiquiri, New Girl? You don't know how to make one?" Whiskey asked. She was a tall bleach blonde with beautiful golden-brown skin and a slender body. She had on a tiny mini skirt, sky-high stripper heels, and nothing else. "I could go and get Jazz, but she doesn't like her breaks getting broke, if you know what I mean. I'm surprised because honestly so far you've been real solid back there. I lost a bet to Rosie. Said you wouldn't make it an hour."

She opened the fridge and thanked god that at least Jai had a proper bar. There were lots of chilled pub glasses for beers and exactly five classic cocktail glasses. She pulled one out and reached for the shaker. "I'm stronger than I look."

One part Bacardi. One part simple syrup, but not the crap Jai had bought. Lisa hated over-the-counter simple syrup. Something about the processing gave it an aftertaste she couldn't stand. Her first boss had taught her to make her own each and every night. Simple syrup was easy enough to make. During her break, she'd gone into the kitchen and met the cook, retired Staff Sergeant William Batten. He'd been more than happy to let her use a sauce pan and his stove top. She'd noticed that a few of the girls had come through looking for snacks and he'd treated even the mostly naked ones with the kindness of a father to his wayward daughters. He would shake his head, avert his eyes, and pass them the sandwiches he'd made.

"Rosie said any woman who can walk in those shoes belongs here," Whiskey replied.

Her sad, hand-me-down Louboutins reduced to stripper shoes. Although now that she looked at what the other ladies were wearing, she suspected that perhaps Mr. Christian himself was a strip-club fan. She cut a lime in half, shoving it into the juicer and squeezing with a practiced hand. "Good to know I have proper footwear. And the thing about the daiquiri is it's a little like a test. You know how chefs test each other?"

Whiskey shook her head. "No. Wait. Do they go at each other with knives? Because that's how my uncle Antony did it and he owned an Italian place back in the day."

She couldn't help but smile even as her feet ached. It made her realize how much she'd isolated herself over the past six months. Since the debacle with Vallon, she'd been holed up in her apartment feeling sorry for herself. She was an extrovert. She needed the energy of being around people to thrive. And she was kind of a weirdo, so the odder the people she was around, the better. "No, not like chef fight club. When chefs test cooks coming in, they tend to ask them to cook an omelet. It's seemingly simple, but easy to screw up. The theory is if you can't cook an egg, you can't cook at all."

Whiskey placed the beers on her tray with a nod. "Ah, you're saying the daiquiri is a test. It's like the omelet."

She shook her simple three-ingredient drink and poured it into the cocktail glass. "Yep. And it's an old enough style drink that I'm surprised anyone would ask. Most people these days want some kind of daiquiri, not the base drink."

"Oh, you know my momma loves her strawberry daiquiris," Whiskey replied.

The music started up again and finally there was no one at her bar. It looked like the main billing of the night was up. Whiskey had explained to her that the really hot girls didn't perform until after ten. All the tables around the stage were full now.

Jazz strode up, the head bartender looking no more relaxed than she had when she'd walked away for her break. The woman was a good foot taller than Lisa and she was way better dressed for her job. Jazz wore a sexy sleeveless jumper with a plunging neckline that showed off her toned body. Her long hair was back in braids and even white teeth shone against her perfect skin. It probably wasn't Jazz's fault that the smile still looked a bit predatory. Jazz stared down at the cocktail in Lisa's hand.

"We got some weird bridal party in tonight?"

She shook her head. "I think it's a test."

Jazz wrapped an apron around her lean waist. "It ain't Jai. Jai doesn't know what a daiquiri is. Well, then, go on. I can see that you're curious, but if you aren't back here soon, I'll assume you don't care about that tip jar."

Mystikal's "Shake It Fast" started rocking the building and Lisa knew she couldn't pass up this chance. She wanted to know who was testing her. She still wasn't sure it wasn't Jai, or perhaps the actual owner was here. Jai called it his club, but he was merely the manager.

"I'll follow you," she told Whiskey. "This is too full. I don't want you to spill it."

Whiskey gave her a one-armed shrug and started back out into the fray. Lisa followed along, her feet aching. Maybe she should have given up the daiquiri. She wasn't as sure on her stripper heels as Whiskey was. She'd made it halfway across the floor when she suddenly found herself blocked by a large man in a softball uniform that proclaimed he was one of the mighty Rebels of Caruth LTD. She wasn't sure what he was rebelling against, but he was in her way.

"Excuse me," she said politely as the strobes began to flash.

"Excuse you," he slurred. "Teacher lady, I need a new drink. I wanna round of Fruit Loops shots for my buddies. Why are you dressed like a teacher lady? Reminds me of Mrs. Hoover. Third grade. She was a bitch."

Okay. "I will get those to you in a few minutes."

She started to go around him.

"Wait, teacher lady. I need a drink," he said. "Do you know who I am?"

He was an asshole. "Nope, but I'm busy and I'll get to you in a moment."

She started moving again, walking around him and catching a glimpse of the table ahead. Was that…?

"Hey, lady, I said I want drinks for my friends," the dude who looked way too old to be in a softball uniform insisted. "My dad owns this place and he won't be happy you ignored me."

He reached for her, but that was the moment the strobe light went off and everything seemed to go in slow motion. One minute he seemed to be going for the drink in her hand and then in a flash, he was stumbling, his hand finding her breast.

She heard a shout over the din of music, and glitter started to pour down from the stage. It probably should have hit Miss Mischief, as she'd been announced, who was shaking her thing for all she was worth, but one of two fans picked up a stream and blasted it straight into Lisa's face. The drink in her hand dropped and she watched in abject horror as Softball Uniform tripped and slipped, and before she knew it he was taking her down to the floor with him.

The floor that was covered in glitter and potentially heretofore undiscovered hemorrhagic fevers. One minute she was standing up, tall and proud and confident in her ability to mix a proper daiquiri, and the next she was a glitter-covered patient zero with a large man on top of her.

"Hey, now this is more like it." He reeked of beer and sweat.

"Get off me." She'd just said the words when the man was lifted off her and tossed to the side.

"Are you all right?" a familiar voice asked as Remy dropped to one knee in front of her.

She was fine. Probably.

She started to get to her knees, but softball dude had gotten up before her.

"Hey, Teacher Lady," he began, getting back into her space.

"I am not a teacher," she growled and pushed him back.

He stumbled a bit and then somehow managed to smash right into the cold buffet, sending shrimp and salad and oysters flying. Some of those suckers seemed to have caught air and soared out into the crowd.

She slipped in shrimp cocktail and went down again, her heels wobbling underneath her. She hit the floor hard, looking up at the ceiling and wondering if anyone ever dusted. At least she'd stopped moving.

But a loud howl signaled all was not right in her world. The lights suddenly came up and Lisa realized everyone was staring at her. Well, the people who weren't trying to help the dude in the softball uniform. He was lying to her right and his arm seemed to be at the wrong angle. He screamed louder than Mystikal could rap.

"Lisa, are you all right?" Remy was down on one knee.

"I dropped your drink." She didn't move to get up. Nope. There was no reason to. She was covered in perfectly made daiquiri, man sweat, and glitter that might have gotten into her lungs, and there was zero reason to get up. She could die right here. And she knew it had been Remy who'd ordered the drink because it only made sense. Bad things happened to her when he was around. "Jazz can make you another one."

"Don't worry about that right now, *chère*." His blue eyes looked her over with what seemed like genuine concern.

A whole bunch of guys she thought were probably McKay-Taggart employees stared down at her.

And then Jai was staring at her. "Jesus, Lisa, that's Billy Caruth. His dad owns this place."

She didn't move. She might have gone a little numb, actually. "I'm fired, aren't I?"

She suddenly felt strong arms lifting her up and she was cradled against Remy's big body.

"Yeah, I don't think you're right for this job," Jai replied with a frown.

Story of her life.

Jazz strode up, shaking her head. She counted out a bunch of ones. "Don't spend it all in one place, princess."

Forty bucks. She'd made forty bucks in seven hours, would probably get sued by a douchebag, and now had to deal with the hottest man she'd ever met.

All in all, not the worst day of her life, and that was pretty shitty when she thought about it.

* * * *

Remy looked down at her as they made it to the parking lot. She didn't seem to weigh a thing in his arms. It took all he had not to crack a smile. She looked completely shocked, her eyes fixated on someplace in the distance, her hands clutching a bunch of sad, crumpled ones. Her sweet face was covered in glitter of all colors. Somehow she'd gotten a napkin stuck to her hair. He was not going to mention that it made her look a bit like a unicorn.

She was so cute he could almost eat her up. He wanted to cuddle her and promise her that everything was going to be all right. He wanted to tell her he'd been an ass and she needed help and he was very, very interested in being helpful to her. Shit, it was right on the tip of his tongue to whisper to her that she could count on him.

Then she blinked and he caught sight of the hollow look in her eyes. "I forgot my purse. I have to have my purse."

Shane jogged up, carrying what looked like an expensive handbag. "Got it. Wow, that dude will be lucky to use his arm after what you did to him. That'll teach him to touch you again, hot shot."

Her bottom lip quivered, but she took the purse. "Yeah. I can stand now. I'm good."

He wasn't sure she should. Despite the fact that she glittered like a disco ball, he could see that her skin was on the pale side. She felt fragile in his arms. Still, she seemed determined, so he eased her down. It was time to get her home and cleaned up and figure out what the hell was going on because it obviously wasn't what he'd thought. He'd watched her for hours, and no woman worked that hard without a reason. Hell, no human being worked that hard if they didn't have to.

He turned to his group. "Can y'all fit in Shane's truck? I think I should take her back to her place right away."

"Definitely," Riley agreed. "She's in shock."

"I asked the cocktail waitress about her. Said this was her first night and she'd never seen her around before," Wade said. "According to her, Lisa walked in late this afternoon and was working the bar fifteen minutes later. Said the manager likes to throw newbies into the fray to see what they can handle before he hires them."

"She did a good job." Remy wanted her to hear it. "It was that asshole's fault. He wouldn't leave her alone. I should have gotten there faster."

The minute he'd realized that big guy was harassing her, he'd nearly jumped out of his own skin to get to her. He should have been watching, but he'd been waiting, wanting to hide out so she didn't catch on to the game.

Meanwhile, she hadn't been playing a damn game at all.

"I got the info on that asshole who wouldn't let her through," Dec said. "I wrote it all in a text that I sent to you. He is the youngest son of the owner of the LLC that runs fifteen strip clubs in the area, including this one. Also, I might have explained to him that I would come see him if he decided to sue. After hours and off the clock, of course. I think he realizes the error of his ways. But I would still like to get hold of the security footage. I don't want them dumping it."

Wade nodded. "I can get it. My old CO is actually the cook here. It's why I come in. We'll go back in and see what we can find to protect her."

It likely meant she wouldn't get sued, but they wouldn't be able to get her job back. Job. She'd come for a job and she'd clutched those wadded up bills like she'd needed them. Desperately. She'd worked that bar like she knew what she was doing. Where the hell had that poor rich girl learned how to work a bar?

"Do you think she's trying to make it to the train?" Riley asked.

Remy turned and Lisa wasn't where he'd left her. She was slowly making her way across the parking lot. Every now and then she would roll an ankle because those heels hadn't been meant for city street walking, but she would straighten up like a trooper and keep her long march going.

"Damn it. Why is she walking?"

Shane nodded Lisa's way. "You know exactly why she's walking away. That girl's got pride. I believe you told her you weren't interested and she took you seriously. Time to turn that around, man."

"Women don't like to hear they aren't interesting," Riley said with a sigh.

"All of you suck." Remy jogged to catch up with her, hearing his friends chuckling as they turned to head back into the club. "Lisa? Lisa, honey, where are you going?"

"Home." She didn't look back.

It didn't take him long to catch her since she kept stumbling in those shoes. He would have too if he'd spent hours and hours in uncomfortably high heels. She'd likely thought she was coming in for an interview, not for a full shift. "*Chère*, you can barely walk."

Now she turned to him, planting those heels on the concrete with one finger pointing his way. In the moonlight she looked a little crazy. "Don't you call me that. Don't you use that Cajun accent on me."

He held his hands up, surprised at how intimidating a petite woman could be. "In my defense, I use it on everyone. It's my accent."

"Pick another one. Everyone at McKay-Taggart knows different accents. I've heard Taggart use a Russian one during scenes, and the Irishman can sound awfully American when he wants to."

Oh, he needed to soothe her savage beast. She'd obviously had a hell of a night and needed somewhere to put all that anger. She could take it out on him or he could show her he wasn't the bad guy here and she could count on him to make things easier. He made his tone as soothing as possible and gently plucked the napkin from her hair. It seemed to have been held there by some kind of sauce. "That's because they used to be spies. Apparently different accents and languages are a plus for spies. I was nothing but a dumb grunt. Having a different accent wouldn't stop me from taking a bullet, and that's what I was there for. This is the only accent I have. Well, I used to do a good Elmer Fudd."

She nodded, but her eyes were on his face, almost as if she couldn't look away. "Good, use that accent. But don't you dare call me *chère* or honey or baby or anything but Lisa or Ms. Daley or Girl I'm Not Interested In. You know what, don't call me anything at all. Go away."

He sighed as she started to walk away again. "Chèr…Lisa, come on. Let me give you a ride. We're going to the same place."

She turned on him so fast he almost fell back on his ass. "No. No, we're not because you're going to move. I was there first. I call dibs."

What the hell? "You can't call dibs on an entire building. I signed a lease. I can't break it now."

At least Charlotte Taggart had. He jogged and managed to get in front of her. He'd dug himself a deep hole and now he realized he'd lied. Not interested? Bullshit. She scared him. She reminded him of Josette. Josette, who'd always been too smart for him. Josette, who'd convinced him she could be happy staying in Papillon Bayou.

Josette hadn't even liked walking into Guidry's, much less would she have been caught behind a bar. He was being an asshole who was putting punishment on a woman who hadn't earned it.

"What can I call you? Because Lisa is pretty, but I'm a Cajun and we live to call women pet names. It's in our natures. And I'm sorry about what I said to you those months back. The truth of the matter is you scare the hell out of me and I reacted poorly. Please forgive me."

She stared at him. "I scare you?"

Yep. She did then and she did now, too. Even with her face glowing like a damn disco ball and half a strip club buffet still somehow hanging on her, she was the most tempting thing he'd seen in years. "You scare the shit out of me, chè…woman I lied about not being interested in. The trouble is I've always known I was going home. That's why I've kept all my relationships light. When you walked up to me that day, well, I knew you weren't the type to have a one-night stand, and that's about all I do."

"Because you don't want to hurt someone?"

It was good she understood. "That's right."

She rolled her eyes. "Or because you want to sleep with as many women as you possibly can. Do you think we don't hear that excuse from the time we're old enough to come in contact with a player? *Hey, baby, you're gorgeous and beautiful, but I'm all wounded and shit so I can't touch something as lovely as you. What? You want to heal me through some sex. It probably won't work. I can't even think about a relationship that lasts past tomorrow because of all my wounded bullshit, but if you're sure, then hey, let's do this thing.* Yeah, heard it all before."

He sighed. "I'm not trying to play anyone. I'm not. I never used any of those lines on you. I acted like an idiot because I had no idea how to handle you."

She stiffened in the moonlight, her shoulders squared and rigid. "You handled it fine. You were honest."

"That's what I'm trying to tell you. I wasn't honest, and even if I had been being honest, I wasn't kind."

"I haven't known many men who cared much about kindness."

"Well, then you haven't known me."

She was silent for a moment, as though trying to decide what to do. She sniffled. "Did you order the daiquiri?"

He felt himself frowning. "Yes."

A humorless chuckle came from her throat. "Of course you did. You're the whole reason I left the bar. If it hadn't been for you, I would have a job right now. I would have a place to be. I would have a home that hadn't been invaded by an asshole. Why? Why did you order that fucking daiquiri? And think long and hard before you lie to me."

Shit. His first instinct was to tell her, damn girl, NOLA boy loves himself a daiquiri, but there was something wicked in that girl's eyes, something desperate that told him she needed to be handled with care this evening and that while he'd thought he was being honest with her before and that hadn't worked, honesty was definitely required now. "I was curious. My family owned a bar, you see. I grew up in one an hour and a half south of New Orleans. We owned the bar and the wharf attached to it. I consider myself an expert. I was working before I could drink. The sheriff would look the other way. He didn't care that I would help my pop-pop out as long as I wasn't sampling the merchandise. I'd watched you all night and you looked like a woman who could handle herself, but there are tests."

She touched her chest with her free hand. He didn't mention that it caused something to fall out of her hair. "My daiquiri was perfect. Fucking perfect, asshole. I even made my own syrup. I was great for that job and you came in here and fucked it up for me."

There was something about hearing those filthy words coming

from her pretty mouth that settled him. She'd always been polite around him, so ladylike, but there was a genuine woman in there and he'd hurt her. He'd been less than kind and he hadn't meant to be that. "Lisa, I'm sorry, but that is not the place for you. You don't belong there, chèr…damn it. You don't belong there, *ma crevette.*" My little shrimp. He couldn't help it. It was what he did when he was being affectionate, and she did have a shrimp hanging on her shoulder, though it wasn't petite. Cherry Pies believed in jumbo sizes for their crustaceans. "Let me take you home. Please. I'll call around and I swear I'll help you find another job tomorrow if that's what you need. I know some people. That's what you need, right? You need a job?"

He'd been an ass and he meant to have the story, but it was obvious he'd been wrong.

"Yeah, I need a job. I have an MBA and I can't find a job." She looked down at her shoes. "I've been out of work for six months and it's getting bad. I had some savings, but I've gone through it. I turned in my car a few weeks ago rather than have it be repossessed. I'm at the point where I'm not sure if I can buy groceries next week. I only have an apartment because my brother insists on either paying for it or moving me in with my sister Lila and her creepy boyfriend."

Creepy boyfriend hadn't popped up at the meeting. Remy would have to look into that. "Why don't you ask Will for more money? From what I understand Bridget has plenty."

It wasn't surprising that he would know her brother and sister-in-law. They were regulars at Sanctum and Will often joked that his knowledge of the human brain and how to fix it paid nothing compared to his wife's knowledge of how five men could penetrate a woman simultaneously.

Her eyes came up and he recognized something fierce there. Pure pride. "Do you go to your siblings for money? Do you ask for handouts, Remy?"

Hell no, he did not. "No. So let me help you. Help isn't charity. Help is…well, it's simply what we should do for each other. If I was walking down the road at night, would you stop and pick me up?"

One shoulder shrugged. "I don't know. If I found you interesting, I might."

He groaned. "I wish I'd never heard that word before. Please, Lisa Daley. Please let me take you home. I'm worried stray dogs and cats are going to think you're a movable feast and some random club kids will decide you're a walking rave and party around you."

She grimaced. "That bad, huh?"

"I think you're cute as a button, *ma crevette*," he admitted.

"Okay. But only because my feet are swollen." She stuffed the dollar bills into her bag and then the shrimp that had been on her shoulder fell and she shrieked but managed to catch it.

"It's not alive," he said quietly, looking around to see if anyone was calling the cops on the massive dude and the tiny woman who had screamed. She stared at it for a long moment and then he heard her stomach rumble. Damn. The woman was hangry. He could understand that. It was one part of her savage beast he could soothe easily. "Are you thinking about eating that?"

"Yes," she admitted. "But that would be gross. Right?"

In the distance he heard the sound of a siren wailing. It appeared the ambulance was coming for her erstwhile former customer. Remy pulled the shrimp out of her hand and tossed it away for some lucky roaming cat to find. This particular kitten had just gotten herself a keeper. "Pizza is on me."

He lifted her back up because he couldn't stand the way she stumbled in those shoes and walked to his massive truck, tucking her inside and doing her seatbelt himself.

"I would like that," she said, her lips curling up.

It was the first real smile he'd seen on her all night and he didn't want to think about what that smile did to his insides. He drove out as the ambulance was pulling in.

She was right where he needed her to be—at his side. Now he simply had to find a way to keep her there.

Chapter Four

What the hell was she doing? Lisa finished drying her hair. He was still out there, still walking around her apartment. Why had she agreed to eat pizza with him? She needed to be...what? Resting for her big day tomorrow of absolutely no interviews and no job to go to? Crying because this evening had been awful and horrible and she was sick of feeling humiliated by life? That was a plan.

"You doing all right in there?" Remy's voice came through the bathroom door. "The pizza's here and I found a bottle of Pinot Noir amidst the boxes over at my place. Unless you prefer a white. I could try to find a convenience store."

Just the sound of that wicked accent made her head rush and reminded her why he was here. Because she couldn't seem to help herself around the man. It was why she'd stayed away from him. She couldn't resist him even when she knew it was for her own good. Even when she knew it would end in heartache. "Red is fine, but you don't have to stay. I thank you for the ride, but I'm okay now. I know it's late and you have to work in the morning. I only need one piece of pizza and then I'll probably fall into bed."

Alone. Like she had for almost two years now. She'd thought once she'd hit the floor at Sanctum that she'd plow her way through hot Doms, enjoying the sex and making no apologies for it. After she and that weasel Gary had broken up, she'd decided to not make a single apology for what she wanted sexually or otherwise. There had been exactly one Dom she'd plowed through and then she'd hit a wall. A wall of muscle and tan skin and a smile that fritzed out her brain.

And then the only Dom she wanted was freaking Remy Guidry,

and he hadn't wanted her.

"I would rather stay with you," he said quietly. "If you don't want company, I understand, but I hate eating alone and that's all I seem to do these days."

She wasn't going to let him know how much those soft, sincerely spoken words meant or how much his puppy eyes did to tear down those carefully constructed walls she'd put up. Well, she'd thought they were carefully constructed. Now it appeared they'd been made of pretty tissue paper he easily tore through at his will. She wasn't even looking at him and she could see those eyes.

She opened the door, her robe tucked firmly around her now crustacean-free body. She wished she could say the same for the glitter, but damn it was hard to get off. "You don't take your dates out for a meal before getting down to dessert, huh?"

She knew she sounded like a brat of the first order, but she couldn't help it. If her walls were coming down, sarcasm was her last line of defense.

He stood there in the hallway, his massive body taking up all the space. He looked a little like a lion who felt regret for his prey. "Like I said, there was nothing at all intimate about those relationships. No relationship at all. I found a woman and hooked up for sex and sent her on her way in the morning. Sometimes she would come back for seconds, but only if I truly believed she didn't want anything from me but sex. It has been pointed out to me recently that the way I behave makes me some kind of a douchebag."

Did it? If she didn't want to be slut shamed for what she wanted, she couldn't exactly do the same to him. Stupid logic. Maybe if she hadn't had all those dumb ethics and philosophy classes she could have been self-centered and intolerant. "You said you were honest with them?"

"Always."

"Then you weren't a douchebag. You were a healthy male looking for sex and trying to be upfront about it. Believe me. I know a douchebag when I see one. I dated several." She looked up at him, tilting her head so he could take in her face and neck. "How bad is the glitter?"

He reached behind her, picking up the washcloth she'd used. "Not bad. Just some right here."

He drew the cloth along her jawline and on her neck, right down to her clavicle. She was deeply aware she was naked under that robe and all he would have to do to make her drop it was tug that knot loose. "There. That's some of it, but I think it's going to take multiple scrubbings to be free of it. You know it does make you glow."

She was way too aware of how close he was, how easy it would be to brush her body up against his. She wasn't sure it was the glitter making her glow. Being close to him seemed to make her whole body light up. "You said there was pizza."

If she stayed too close to him, she didn't trust her dumbass self not to go up on her tiptoes and brush her mouth against his. She dreamed about sucking that plump bottom lip into her mouth.

He smiled, an almost self-deprecating expression. "Yeah. There's pizza. I'll even suffer through a few veggies, though they don't really have a place on a pie."

Good. That was good. If they were talking about his eating habits, then he wasn't staring down at her lips like he wanted to devour her, glitter and all. "I hardly think mushrooms and olives count as vegetables."

She followed him down the hallway to her small bistro kitchen where the heavenly smell of pepperoni and sausage with the aforementioned "vegetables" permeated the air and reminded her that she hadn't eaten for most of the day. She'd downed the last of the oatmeal she had and had a piece of buttered toast before going to the interview.

She'd been planning on stopping at Laurel's in the morning because her sister always made breakfast for Mitch and their toddler and usually had extra. Except she'd forgotten she didn't have a car.

"Hey, don't get sad on me again," he said, holding out a chair for her. There were only two, and Remy looked like he'd made the most of the small space. The table was set beautifully with her nice plates and the good silverware. Two wine glasses sat at their spots, and the bottle had been opened and allowed to aerate.

The man might not eat vegetables like a good boy, but he knew how to present a meal.

She sat down, Remy handing her a paper towel like he was passing her fine linen. He poured the wine with one hand, by the bottom of the bottle, with perfect grace and control.

"You pour that like a sommelier, not a bar owner," she mentioned, trying not to let him know how attractive she found him and his impeccable manners. There was something about the controlled grace he displayed that fascinated her. She wondered what his bayou bar was like.

"A dive bar owner," he corrected with a wink. "But wine is important where I come from. Food is important. We take both of those things seriously in Papillon Bayou. My grandfather loved wine and he taught me all about it. And here you thought I was a beer-swilling mongrel."

She picked up the wine glass. "Well, you apparently were surprised I knew how to pour a drink."

"Touché," he replied, sitting down across from her. "I was, actually. When did you start tending bar?"

He allowed her to get a slice first before pulling his own.

"I put myself through college tending bar. Mostly scholarships, but I worked about twenty hours a week at this dive bar up in Denton. It was right off the TWU campus. It took me a while to realize that almost the entire clientele was female."

He grinned. "Lesbian bar?"

"Yep, and they were awesome. I was this dumbass thing who'd barely been out of her trailer park. The town I grew up in wasn't small, but it was oddly isolated. Everyone was very homogenous. I got to Denton and it was like this huge city and I was overwhelmed. That bar became my family," she said. "They taught me…well, everything about living in the larger world."

He sat back, his brow furrowed. "I'm sorry. Laurel once mentioned a trailer park, but are you telling me you actually grew up in one?"

She nodded. She didn't like to think about the year she hadn't lived in that rundown trailer park. Not ever. "Yes. We couldn't afford anything else."

A hand ran over his head as though he couldn't quite process the information. "You. You and Laurel and Lila and Will came out of a trailer park?"

That made her smile. It wasn't the first time someone questioned her background. "Hard to believe?"

"Damn near impossible. Those shoes you had on tonight are worth more than a lot of people make in a month."

She waved that off. "I didn't buy those. Bridget gets bored with shoes and I get hand-me-downs. Bridget did grow up wealthy, but my side of the family? Hell no. We worked our asses off. My mom was in and out of prison and Will raised us. He was the one who taught us that our grades had to be damn near perfect if we wanted out. He made sure there was food on the table and all our school forms were properly completed. He would do odd jobs after school and that was how he'd buy us stuff. My brother is the single best man I've ever met. He's the reason we're all alive and successful. Even my mom. She got married to a man she met in AA and they're doing well. Will made that happen. He paid for her to stay at a house that helps recovering addicts from prison ease back into the real world."

He stared at her as though seeing her for the first time.

She found herself sitting up straighter. "Does the fact that my mom is an ex-con shock you?"

"In ways you can't understand, *ma crevette*."

She should figure out what that was, but it sounded sweet coming from his mouth. "Well, she is and I'm not ashamed of her. I'm not ashamed of how I grew up."

"Why would you be? You bloomed without water. You became something more than you should have, according to our society. I thought you were some kind of rich girl who'd breezed through life."

Holy shit. Was that why he hadn't been "interested"? Oddly enough, she could forgive that. She wasn't interested in over-privileged men who couldn't understand the world she'd grown up in. She might run from that, too. "Because my brother's a neurosurgeon? Not all surgeons come from wealthy families."

"Your brother is a neurosurgeon. Your sister-in-law is a best-selling author. Your sisters work in legal and medical professions that require college degrees, and your brother-in-law is Harvard educated. His brother and sister-in-law own a massive corporation. All in all, those family ties don't scream I grew up in a double wide."

She shook her head. "No, no, my friend, that beauty was only a single wide. With one bathroom and wood paneling straight out of the seventies." The wine was starting to work on her, relaxing her and reminding her that she hadn't had the money to waste on wine in months. Waste? Wine was necessary. Maybe she should take a play from her brother's handbook and ask if she could do odd jobs in exchange for wine. It would make poverty a ton more fun. "The Daleys are perfect examples of what a family can do when they band together, work hard, and help lift each other up. I'm the only failure."

He sat back as though considering how to handle her. "You have an MBA. That's not a failure. The job market isn't great right now. That's not your fault."

Of course, he didn't know the whole story. "I got a job easily enough. Two weeks out of school and I was making seventy K. Then I blew the whistle on my employer. Apparently that gets around."

He frowned, the expression doing nothing to make him less gorgeous. "Blew the whistle?"

"I work in accounting. My old boss runs the biggest valet service in DFW. Lots of cash," she began.

His eyes widened. "Cash? He was laundering money?"

Well, no one could accuse him of not understanding how the world worked. She hadn't even considered it. She'd walked into that job like fucking Snow White, with birds singing on her shoulders. Everything was happy and shiny in her eyes. "See, that's what Bridget said the minute I mentioned he offered valet services. She told me I had to be careful because cash intensive businesses are magnets for the mafia and drug dealers and…how did she put it…douche canoes with dirty money. Have you ever met a crazed, paranoid person who turns out to always be right? It's annoying. Something happens or we meet someone new, Bridget comes up with some crazed theory and we all laugh and bam, a month later the guy who sent Lila flowers for saving his life in the ER is taken away on a seventy-two-hour psych hold after trying to break into her house."

Remy shook his head. "Your sister had a stalker?"

Lisa sighed. "Yeah. And he seemed super nice."

"Maybe you should listen to Bridget more often."

Bridget thought she should be in a safe house. The idea sent a shiver through her. "Anyway, I found the doctored books, went to the cops, and now my old boss got off on a technicality and I'm left without a job or any way to get a job because I have zero references and oddly enough, no one wants to hire the whistle-blower."

Remy had sat back up, his spine going straight and that hawkish look he got when he was hyper aware coming into his eyes. "Whoa, are you telling me the man you tried to send to jail is out and you were walking around this afternoon without any protection?"

Did everyone think she was an idiot? "Of course not. I have pepper spray."

"Pepper spray isn't going to stop the damn mafia."

"Well, neither did the truth, so I don't see why they would come after me now." This wasn't the conversation she wanted to have with him. Of course she wasn't sure what she wanted from him.

Except sex. Except comfort. Except one night where she didn't sit up and worry about what was going to happen to her.

He was leaving soon. Not merely leaving the apartment building. He was leaving town and he wouldn't be back. That actually made it way easier. Was she brave enough to ask him again? He'd said he was scared of her, but if she promised she wasn't looking for anything but a couple of hot nights from him, would that change his mind?

Or had it all been bullshit? Had he been attempting to be kinder to her than he'd been before?

"Lisa? Are you listening to me?"

Nope. "Yes, of course."

He stared at her like he knew she wasn't listening. "I was saying you need to take this seriously. You're in a dangerous position."

"Jimmy isn't violent. He's a jerk but he's not violent." Suddenly she wasn't hungry. The whole day had been one long mistake. Did she need to cap it off by making one more? "You know what? I'm really tired. I think I'm going to go to bed."

His stare pinned her. "So I hit on a touchy subject and you punish me by sending me away?"

"No, I'm tired and I had a shitty day and I want to go to bed."

"I want to go to bed, too," he said, his voice low.

The moment seemed to stop, his words right out there in the open, his eyes intent on her. There was heat in those eyes.

"Ask me again, Lisa. Give me another chance."

All the reasons she shouldn't fell away because damn it, she was an optimist and at some point in time her luck had to change. She didn't want to miss that because she was too scared to try. "Would you like to go to bed with me, Sir?"

"Tell me why you left the club."

Damn it. That wasn't an answer. "Because I gave up my car and I didn't want to admit it to my family because they're nosy as hell. Because I've been too depressed to play. Because I couldn't play with the man I wanted to play with."

His hand came out and he tugged her up, maneuvering her until she was sitting on his lap.

And what a comfy lap it was. She fit easily, her butt on his big thigh, his muscular arm around her waist making her feel dainty and feminine.

"I'm going home soon and I probably won't be back," he explained.

She nodded. "It's okay. I wasn't looking to get married. I'll be honest. When I asked you six months ago, I was looking for a Dom, but not now. Now I just want someone to help me get through the night."

"I don't want to hurt you, *ma crevette*," he whispered. His cheek rubbed lightly against hers, letting her feel that masculine scruff he always seemed to have. "But I have to go home and it's not a place where you would be happy."

"I have a home, Remy." God, how had she gone from bone tired to every cell in her body awake and alive with anticipation? "I don't need some man to come in and save me. Well, except from how long the nights are lately. I could use a rescue from that. I'm not asking you to be my knight in shining armor. I'm asking if you want to spend tonight with me."

"No."

She stiffened and started to get off his lap, but his arms were a cage around her.

"Hush," he admonished. "We're talking and we're negotiating. I'm not about to lie to you again. I'll want more than one night with you. I won't be able to hop into your bed and hop back out again and pretend like it didn't mean anything. I've wanted you for far too long for that to happen. Can we make a deal? A contract?"

A contract with her dream Dom? It was one more bad idea in a long line of them, but she found herself nodding. Why would she say no? Her pride? Her pride hadn't gotten her anything good lately. Because she was worried about being hurt? She'd been numb for so long that being hurt seemed like a halfway decent trade-off for feeling anything at all. He was being upfront with her. "Yes."

His hands moved on her waist, brushing up toward her breasts. "God, *chère*, this is where I'm supposed to set you across from me and we talk about what we want and need out of this contract."

"I want an orgasm, Remy," she stated plainly. "Can we forgo the negotiations tonight and agree that we're going to get into bed and not leave again until you've made me come a couple of times?"

"Oh, I like how you negotiate," he whispered. "But one thing needs to be made clear. I'm the top. You're the sweet bottom when it comes to sex. For now, you tell me to stop and I will, but you're not a novice. I'm going to want some fairly kinky things from you."

The word *kink* sent a thrill up her spine. It made her wriggle and squirm. It had her nipples hard, and she was very aware of her pussy. Soft and getting wet, her pussy suddenly seemed like the core of her being. "I'm good with that."

"Take off the robe for me."

Her hands went to her waist, undoing the tie that held the robe together. She let it fall open. This was what she needed. She needed to forget about all her worries for a while and merely listen to the sound of his voice. She needed to let go and give over to a man she could trust to take care of her.

"Oh, fuck, you're even more beautiful than I expected. All these months I've avoided watching your scenes because I knew when you got naked you would be even better than what I could imagine."

"There weren't all that many scenes," she admitted.

He moved his arm, allowing the robe to drop away and giving him access to her naked flesh. "How many? I need to know how much experience you have. I don't want to move too fast."

Talky Dom. "I'm not a virgin. I'm good. Let's go."

He shifted her, picking her up with strength that took her breath away. One minute she was sitting on his left thigh and the next she was on both his taut quadriceps, her knees hooked over his. He spread his legs out, causing hers to follow and leaving her completely vulnerable to him, her pussy open and wanting. She couldn't sit up. She needed to lie back against him to find some balance. This was what he wanted, her dependent on him, helpless against what he was going to do to her.

It was how he liked to play.

"Here's the first lesson," he growled against her ear. "Don't push me. I'm going to take my time. I agreed to your demands. I promise I won't get out of your bed until you've passed out from how many times I'm going to make you come, but how we get there will be all my way. Do I make myself clear?"

His way. All the way. All the way to screaming orgasms. "Yes."

She felt the fine edge of his teeth on her ear. "Yes?"

She was out of practice. "Yes, Sir. Yes, Master Remy."

The threat of his bite was replaced with the shivering pleasure of his tongue stroking along her outer ear. "That's right. Now like I said before, you'll tell me if you want me to stop."

"I don't."

His hands moved up from her waist, both big palms cupping her breasts and sending crazy pleasure sizzling through her. "Such a naïve thing. I promise to keep you as naïve as possible."

She didn't want him thinking she was some innocent thing. "I'm not naïve, Sir. I might look like some princess, but I assure you I've got scars that you can't see."

"Well, I don't intend to give you any more. I'm going to treat you like a princess. A submissive princess who likes to obey her servant when it comes to pleasure, but a princess all the same. Have you had D/s sex?"

She nodded. "I'm afraid I was one of the trainees who experimented a bit with her partner."

He chuckled. "That's only to be expected. I take it the relationship didn't last outside the training class? And by the way, my training partner and I fucked like bunnies the whole six weeks we were in our class together, so it's perfectly normal."

She still thought fondly of those days. "We were too different. Good partners when it came to training, but we wouldn't have made it in the real world. We were too much alike. If I've figured one thing out it's that opposites attract. Maybe not direct opposites, but truly good partners in life need to support each other's strengths and fill in on the flaws. Will needs Bridget because she's oddly romantic, and she needs Will to ground her."

"Mitch would be alone without Laurel's patience," he said. "I know because I was there. But I don't want to talk about your family. What did you like about D/s sex that you didn't get from vanilla?"

"This, Remy. The fact that you're touching me and talking to me and thinking about me. You're not fumbling around and guessing and hoping you get off and out of my apartment as soon as possible. I can't think about anything else but what you're doing to me because you're keeping me here in the moment with you." Vanilla sex hadn't been bad, but sometimes it had frustrated her. D/s required she talk about what she needed. It stripped away the embarrassment and left her truly communicating with her partner.

"I don't want you anywhere else, and you're right. I'm not thinking about anything but you. You and how to please you, how to torment you in the sweetest way, how to make you happy and eager to obey my every order when it comes to the bedroom. You have the softest skin. It's so perfect." He kissed her neck. "It makes me want to mark you."

Her whole body shook as he bit the back of her neck ever so gently, the faintest hint of danger making the whole thing all the more erotic.

"Oh, god, do it. Bite me." She wasn't sure how far she wanted to go. She'd never tried it but something about the way he'd said he wanted to mark her had her dying to feel his teeth on her sensitive flesh.

"I always said you were way too tempting." He nipped at her skin, a hard but quick bite.

Her whole body shook with pleasure. It was the kind of thing that she knew would hurt if she hadn't been incredibly ready for it. But when she was aroused, pain sent her to new heights. Not like she was a pain slut or anything.

But damn she liked his bite.

His tongue replaced his teeth, sending another thrill through her as he eased the spot he'd marked. "It was just a little bite. Nothing that will be there in the morning."

"Then you'll have to do it again tomorrow." She liked the idea that there was a mark from him on her body, that she could hide it or show it off if she liked.

His hips rolled under her and she could feel the hard length of his erection against her ass. "You are not at all what I expected."

She rubbed herself against his cock, needing to move in some way. "What did you expect?"

"Not that you would be this gorgeous, sexy bitch in heat." His voice had gone deep, his accent thicker than before. "You're not going to run away because this junkyard dog is coming after you, are you, *chèrie*? You're going to get on your knees and take everything I have to give you. You're going to demand I give it to you, aren't you?"

Oh, he needed to understand a few things. "Yes. I swear if this is some kind of joke, I'll hunt your ass down and deal with you myself. I won't send my brother. He would be far too nice. I'll be the one to take your balls if you walk away from me tonight."

"That's what I want to hear." His tongue traced the shell of her ear before nipping at her lobe.

Her whole body was tight with arousal, on edge and waiting for his next touch, next bite. "Really? It's not very submissive."

"Oh, but it means you want me. You think the Dom doesn't want to hear that? Your submission is something I'll earn, but I need to know that you want me inside you so badly you're willing to fight for it because I damn straight feel the same about you. Never wanted a woman as badly as I do you right now. But I'm going to kiss you first. I'm going to do this right. Turn around because I want to kiss that sweet as sin mouth of yours the way I've always wanted to. Straddle me like I'm a beast you want to ride."

He was a beast and she definitely wanted to ride him. On shaky legs she turned and repositioned herself, praying her cheap dining room chair could handle them both, but she wasn't stopping. She wanted that kiss like she'd never wanted anything in her life.

She stopped before straddling him, looking down at that gorgeous man who'd haunted her dreams for over a year. Remy Guidry always held himself apart. Even with his friends there seemed some careful distance he placed between himself and everyone else, as though he needed to not need. Not this Remy. This Remy had his hands out, begging her to come closer. This Remy did need.

He needed her.

Normally she never thought of herself as sexy. She was klutzy. Nerdy. Way too attached to her Kindle to be considered a sensual creature, but something about the look in his eyes gave her confidence. He was fully dressed and she was naked, and somehow that seemed all right with her. It was good to be naked for him. There wasn't anything dirty about it.

She eased one leg over his lap. "I'm going to have to do some laundry for you, Sir. Because I'm about to mess up these jeans."

His eyes went straight to her pussy as she lowered herself down. "You're already wet."

She rolled her hips. Yes, now she could truly feel that big cock of his where she needed it. The rough denim contrasted with the silk of her feminine flesh, rasping gently as she stroked herself over his cock. "I'm incredibly wet, Sir."

His hands moved, finding places on her back so he could pull her up, bring her in to the point that their mouths almost met. "You're wet for me. Say it. Tell me all that sweet arousal is for me and me alone."

That was easy. "It's all for you, Sir. I haven't been with anyone in a long time. There was my training partner for six weeks and then before that, I had a long-term boyfriend from grad school who never once got me this wet this fast. But all I need to do to get my motor running is close my eyes and think about how hot you are."

His lips were right there, so close she could feel the heat of his breath. "Then I better make this good because I never like to disappoint a lady."

One palm found the back of her head, fingers tangling in her hair, and he forced her down. Their mouths met and Lisa worried her whole body was about to go up in flames. He kissed her over and over, moving her with ease as though this was something they'd done a million times. There was nothing awkward about it. She followed his lead and soon enough his tongue ran along her lower lip and she let him in. Warmth filled her as their tongues played and she could feel his dick rubbing, working her right where she needed it. His free hand played, exploring her back and all the way down to the cheeks of her ass. He gave her a squeeze and then began to direct her, rolling his hips up while his tongue plunged in.

"Rub yourself against me, *chèrie*. Make yourself come. I want to watch you because I'm not sure how long I'm going to last once I get inside you. Make it good. Show me how much you want my cock."

That wasn't a hardship at all. She held on, bracing her hands on his broad shoulders as she rubbed against his erection. The denim of his jeans rasped against her clit, but it felt good. So good. Her whole body was on the edge and then she saw him watching her, his eyes trained on her face even as she could feel his cock pulsing beneath the grind of her hips. He wasn't lost in sensation. He was lost in her. Something about his focus sent her right over the edge, pure pleasure pounding through her.

She didn't want it to end, but she had to breathe, had to pause as she threatened to go boneless in his arms.

"That's what I wanted. That's all I needed from you." He kissed her and with effortless ease, stood, lifting her into his arms. "Well, not all. I think I'm definitely going to need to get inside you and soon, but look at me."

She glanced up and he was staring down at her. "Yes, Sir?"

"I misjudged you," he said. "I won't do it again. I meant what I said about going home, but don't think this isn't a special time for me. I want to be with you until I leave, and I'll think about you for the rest of my life. Can that be enough for you?"

She brought her hand up, needing to touch him, to feel that scruff under her skin. "Yes."

A fond memory, something she could take with her. That didn't sound bad. They were two adults who knew they would go their separate ways, but that didn't mean they couldn't enjoy each other while they were together.

"I'm glad because I don't think I could walk away now." He started for her bedroom.

Lisa hoped the night never ended.

* * * *

He'd been honest with her and she'd said yes. He wasn't thinking about anything else tonight. He wasn't thinking about the fact that he was her hired bodyguard and she didn't know it. That was a separate thing altogether and had nothing to do with his relationship with her beyond the fact that it gave him access and another level to protect her.

He eased her down on the bed and then reached back to pull his shirt over his head. What a complete moron he'd been, but then it wasn't surprising. He was the kind of man who saw something that looked like it was too good to be true and decided it was. He hadn't even given her a chance and he was going to make up for that now. He was going to take care of her in every way he could until he had to leave her.

He shoved that thought aside as quickly as he did his jeans. He was desperate. Fucking desperate. He hadn't felt this hot for a woman since he'd been a horny teen.

Lisa moved back on the bed, settling herself against the headboard.

"Knees up, feet flat on the mattress, and get them nice and wide for me." The order came out on a low growl that might have scared some women.

Not her. She bit her bottom lip and slowly complied, letting him watch as she spread herself open for him. That was what he wanted. She was a princess. It didn't matter that she'd grown up poor. There was something about Lisa Daley that would always remind him of a spritely fairy princess. Perhaps it was the light in her eyes or the air of mischief that followed her around, but he could see her with a delicate crown on her head, waving to her adoring subjects.

And then submitting sweetly to her lover when the doors were closed.

He stalked to the end of the bed, watching her. Even in the low light from the lamp on her bedside table, he could see how wet she was, how that pretty pussy glistened. He breathed in her arousal, so much sweeter than any other smell.

That was all for him. Perhaps he'd made a mistake by not taking a submissive. Only now did he feel how hollow his other relationships had been. There had been a power exchange, but it hadn't lasted more than a night. He would sign a contract with this woman. She would be his. His to fuck and play with. His to take care of. His responsibility.

He was surprised those last two words didn't scare him in the least. The real revelation was how much he craved that responsibility when it came to her. Now that he understood who she was, where she'd come from, he intended to make these weeks with her special so she would know what she deserved from a man, to ensure she wouldn't accept less ever again.

She was staring at him, her eyes boldly on his cock. He stroked himself, taking a moment so he didn't simply fall on her and fuck her senseless. He wanted this to last, to make this first night something she wouldn't forget.

Or maybe he wanted to make it so good she wouldn't kick him out in the morning when she realized he had no intentions of keeping this relationship to the bedroom. How would she handle it when she found out exactly how in control he meant to be with her?

"*Tu es la plus belle des femmes*," he said slowly as he moved on to the bed with her.

"The French stuff gets to me, Sir."

Yes, he could tell. He'd always used the fact that his mom-mom considered English a barbaric language in his favor when it came to the fairer sex.

"It means you're the most beautiful woman," he translated as he moved between her legs, his palms on her knees. "It sounds better in French."

She reached up to him, as though asking for his weight. "And the other? That thing you call me. *Ma crevitte?*"

"*Ma crevette*," he corrected with a grin. He could feel the heat of her core against his cock. So much hotter than before. There was nothing between them, though there would be. He'd fished a condom out before he'd tossed his jeans aside. He leaned over, trapping her. "It's a term of endearment. It means my little shrimp."

"What?" Her eyes widened and she tried to push him off.

But that was why he'd trapped her. He couldn't help but chuckle at her horror. He easily kept her where he wanted her and enjoyed how her struggles brought her pussy right where he needed it to be. "My pretty little shrimp. Well, you told me not to call you *ma chère*."

She couldn't quite keep the smile off her face. "That's a terrible nickname. Shrimp?"

"We take shrimp seriously where I come from." He kissed her forehead as he explained. "The whole of Papillon depends on shrimp, therefore calling you my beautiful little shrimp means you're precious to me."

"You are smooth, Guidry." She stopped her playful struggles and her arms went around his neck. "A girl could get in trouble with you."

"Or a woman could stay out of trouble by sticking close to me," he replied, laying kisses across her cheek.

"I need something to call you. Is there a male version of my little shrimp?"

He groaned and ground himself against her core. "There's nothing shrimpy about me down there. Now, *mon loup* would suffice. My wolf. I can be your wolf, *ma crevette*."

"How about you show me how a wolf kisses and I'll see what I can do."

She could get to him so easily. There was no artifice, no playing around in her eyes. She wanted him and didn't care that he knew it. Because she was honest in her desire, and that was the sexiest thing he'd ever seen.

"You know tomorrow we sign a contract and then you're in trouble," he promised before covering her mouth with his.

Kissing Lisa Daley was everything he'd worried it would be. The world melted away and he couldn't think of anything but the soft woman in his arms and how warm she was, how good she felt plastered against him, how right it was to kiss her. He tangled their tongues together, sliding against her over and over again. There was nothing awkward. They fit together like they'd been born to nestle their bodies and flow into a new form.

But he wanted to taste more than her mouth.

He kissed his way down her neck and over her collarbone. Such sweet, delicate skin. When he rubbed his whiskers against her, she turned a lovely shade of pink. He would have to be careful when he spanked her or caned her. He would love the marks he left, but he wouldn't do anything permanent to her.

He wouldn't ask her to pierce these sweet nipples. He wouldn't think about the fact that he could torture her by tugging on the rings. He sucked a nipple into his mouth hard, her body arching against his. He could feel the rush of her arousal coating his dick. Careful. He was close to heaven, but he wasn't ready yet. He wanted her hotter, wanted her begging for it.

Her hands ran through his hair, tingling along his scalp as he suckled her breasts, one and then the other. He licked and sucked, gently most of the time and then giving her a hard nip or tug that would have her body shaking under his.

When those pink nipples had turned a lovely ruby, he kissed his way down her body again, loving the heady scent of her arousal. He was surrounded by her softness, her scent, and all that crazy thick hair. When it was down, it hit her waist and seemed to go everywhere, drawing him in and catching him. As long as she was his, she would never wear it up when they were alone. He wanted to be able to tangle his fingers in that hair and drag her down for a long kiss.

He eased his body down despite the raging protest of his cock. It could wait. He needed more than a little taste of her. He needed her all over his tongue.

He pressed her thighs wide, settling himself in. "You see, I meant what I said. You're the most beautiful. Even here. Most beautiful pussy I've ever seen."

Then there was no more reason to talk. He set his mouth on her and let himself go. This was what he'd fucking dreamed of since the moment he'd met her. Even when he'd thought she was all wrong for him, he'd wanted her. He'd wanted her writhing under him, her legs wrapped around him and begging him for more.

"Please, Sir. Oh, please."

Yes, that was the desperate sound he wanted to hear coming from her lips. She was trying to buck up, to force him to give her more, but he had her right where he wanted.

He split her labia with his tongue in order to lap up all that sweet cream she was making for him. She tasted like sunshine and fresh fruit, things he couldn't get enough of. He speared her, penetrating her with his tongue and making her moan. His thumb found her clitoris and he pressed down and around, working to make a rhythm she couldn't deny.

It was only moments before he felt her come against his tongue, her body shaking.

He got up on his knees and was surprised at how unsteady his hands were. Sex was a bodily function, something he fed because he operated better with it. This was different. He was engaged emotionally with this woman, and he couldn't stand the idea of not pleasing her. Bringing his partner pleasure was always important, but this wasn't some random woman he'd picked up in a bar. This was Lisa.

"If you don't get inside me soon, I'm going to throw a hissy fit. Have you ever seen a hissy fit, Sir?" She was staring up at him in a way that made him wonder how long he'd hesitated.

"I have a younger sister. I have seen the power of the hissy." He opened the condom wrapper and rolled it on his cock, stroking himself. "I want you to be sure you want me. I don't want to hurt you."

And he wasn't talking about the physical. He didn't want to be the reason she cried. He didn't want to be one more man who disappointed her.

"Come here, Remy. I want you. For however long I can have you, I want you." She reached for him and he was through fighting it.

He let his cock find her pussy, pressing in and thrusting in small passes. He was careful but she was a stubborn minx. She tilted her pelvis up and he groaned as he slid inside her, those tight muscles squeezing him like a vise. The pleasure damn near made his eyes roll back and he had to take a deep, steadying breath.

"Damn you feel so good, *chèrie*." He held himself hard against her, locking their bodies together.

Her legs wound around his waist and he could feel her nails in the skin of his back. He welcomed the minor pain, wanted her mark on him, too.

"Come on then, *mon loup*. How does my wolf fuck?"

Yeah, the dirty girl did it for him. He leaned over and kissed that filthy mouth of hers. "Like he'll die if he doesn't get more of his girl."

He pulled out and thrust back in, setting a hard pace. Over and over he fucked her, giving her all of him and holding nothing back. For the most part he went easy on a woman, but this one was his. This one was made to take him and break him and put him back together again.

Lisa's nails dug deep as she matched him thrust for thrust. She tightened around him and his name gasped from her mouth as she came.

Remy lost it. He lost his rhythm, lost his control, lost something he wasn't sure he wanted back from her. Pure emotion drove him as though he could brand himself on this one woman and somehow make himself complete.

Instinct drove him. He pressed in and let go, let himself feel every bit of the pleasure she brought him.

He fell on top of her, giving her all of his weight. Peace surged through him. Always before, he was as anxious to be alone again as he'd been to have sex, but now he let his head rest next to hers.

"Okay, that didn't suck," she said with a low chuckle.

"Didn't suck?" He managed to bring his head up. "That was phenomenal and you know it."

Her arms wrapped around his neck and she sighed. "It was, but I think you can probably do even better."

Well, he'd wanted a woman who challenged him. "Oh, I'll show you better, *ma crevette*. I'll show you everything."

He kissed her again, ready to make good on his promise.

Chapter Five

Remy woke up to the sound of Lisa laughing and the smell of bacon. Damn. That was the perfect way to wake up. He sighed and turned on his side, looking at the place where she'd lain next to him all night. Well, when he hadn't been on top of her. Or under her.

His cell phone trilled. He glanced at the clock, a bit surprised he'd slept in. It was almost eight thirty. He didn't have to be in the office since he was already on duty, but he usually woke up before his alarm went off.

Something about sleeping wrapped around Lisa's petite body had been good for his beauty rest.

He picked up the phone and answered quickly because the number was familiar. "Momma?"

"No, it's Seraphina, big brother," a female voice said. "Momma is at church praying for your soul. Like she does every Wednesday morning. And Sunday. And Friday. And those are merely the Catholic services. I won't tell you about the hoodoo priestess she meets with every Thursday."

She didn't need to. His momma told him enough. "How is Miss Marcelle? She still running that hair salon of hers?"

"I'm telling you that woman doesn't age. She's got to be a hundred and ten and she's still scaring the shit out of tourists with those snakes of hers. Her daughter, Sylvie, and I have regular therapy sessions. Well, we drink a lot of vodka and wonder what it would be like to have normal mothers. You know, the kind who don't come up with plans to haunt the new nail salon and run it out of business. Momma dressed up and everything. I'm fairly certain there's a lawsuit brewing there."

So everything was the same in Papillon. "You know she's always had odd notions about how to protect her town."

"I don't trust Jean-Claude, Remy. He's up to no good and I think it has something to do with you buying him out."

He yawned. "I signed the papers of intent. I've got forty-five days to come up with the money. The bank here is going to approve the loan and everything's going to be smooth sailing from there. We'll have the wharf safely back where it belongs and a mountain of debt over our heads. It'll be just like the old days."

"Then why is he still meeting with that slick as snot developer?" Seraphina asked. "I was in New Orleans yesterday visiting a friend. He doesn't know I saw him having lunch with that same city ass who came through a couple of months ago telling everyone he would buy up their land."

"He can talk to the man all he likes. According to the way Pop-Pop's will was written, he's got to give me a chance to buy him out before he sells to a stranger. Don't worry, Sera. I've got this. I'm going to be home soon."

"That's what you've been saying for years," she said in a perfectly stubborn tone.

"Well, I mean it this time. And you can't count the Army against me."

"I can indeed. I can be as unreasonable as I like." She was silent for a moment. "We miss you."

"I'll be home soon," he promised. "I'll be back and I'm going to take charge. I'll make everything right."

She was quiet for a moment. "Right? What do you mean by right?"

How could she not understand this? "I mean I'm the reason we lost our half in the first place. I'm the reason Zep is twelve kinds of screwed up. I'm the reason you haven't gotten married. I'm coming home and I'm going to fix everything."

"Maybe Momma's right to pray for you. You sure are taking a lot on those shoulders of yours. Before you come home, think on this. Yes, you married poorly, and yes, Josette demanded that you give her the money from half of your half of the wharf. That was her choice, not yours, and when Momma or I tried to find a way around it, you plowed on through and sold to Jean-Claude. I know it was a lot of money, but I wish you had given us a chance to try to figure it out. Zep was an awkward kid. He is not a kid anymore. You'll be surprised at how baby brother has grown up, and I haven't gotten married because I don't want to. Think about that before you walk back in after seven years of barely being home, three of not seeing us at all. You think before you try to walk in as the patriarch of this family and start issuing orders. And remember that Momma taught me how to use a gun. I would remind you that I think Jean-Claude is going to try something, but you know better than I do. Good-bye."

She hung up with a decisive click.

Shit. His sister was pissed. Somehow he'd thought he would march back into Papillon as the returning hero. He might have to rethink that.

He set the phone down and heard a masculine laugh. Remy sat straight up in bed.

The first thing he was going to write into their contract was a clause where she didn't let strange men into her apartment. He reached for his jeans. It could be Will. Her brother might have stopped by, and wouldn't old Will be surprised to find the bodyguard he'd hired was taking his job seriously?

"You should have seen him," a deep voice that did not match Will Daley's said. "He's standing on that ramshackle porch of his with two babies and a dog and I swear he started to cry as we drove away. I'm pretty sure that blonde of his escaped at the earliest opportunity."

He practically ran out the door because Ian Taggart was here, and if he was fucking up Remy's job, they were going to have a problem.

Lisa laughed. "Are you insane? You left your precious baby girls with him?"

"No choice. It was that or take them with us to the hospital and watch them burn the place down before their baby brother could be born," Tag replied. "Honestly, he turned out to be the best of my iffy babysitting choices. The girls lived and no one got shot with an arrow."

"Poor Boomer," Lisa said with a shake of her head. It sounded like everyone had heard about that night. "I heard Theo did a good job stitching him up."

"Like Boomer noticed. Charlie made him a couple of hot dogs and he didn't even sue. I had a long talk with Kenzie about that. Told her she was legally on her own when she starts hunting down the most dangerous prey." Taggart looked up, one brow rising. "Hello, Remy, we were just talking about your secondary job."

"I am way smarter now. I see you or Charlotte outside my door and I hide. Obviously, Lisa hasn't learned that trick yet." God, he hoped the kids weren't here. Though at least he could bet Lisa wouldn't storm out of the place like what's her name had.

Lisa was smiling like nothing had gone wrong. She poured him a mug of coffee and handed it over. "Big Tag came by to check on me."

"She hasn't been in the club in a couple of months, and quite frankly my girls miss her," Tag said.

Sure, that's why he'd shown up out of nowhere. He wasn't at all checking up on how this high-paid assignment was working out.

"I explained about the car," Lisa said. "And he said no sob story was complete without bacon and walked over to the grocery store. Now we have bacon and eggs and pancakes for breakfast."

"Her refrigerator was completely empty with the exception of a half a pizza and some highly suspect milk." Taggart's eyes had narrowed.

She flushed. "I've been way too busy to shop."

A lie, but one to save her pride.

"Well, you should expect your man here to feed you," Taggart replied. "He's doing all kinds of other things on your behalf, including forcing his coworkers to look into some legal case involving valet services. I was surprised when he called last night, but now I get it. This is new, I take it. I'm confused because you've been coming to play nights, but Lisa hasn't."

Shit. Tag thought he needed to know something so he'd stopped by on his way to work and run into Lisa, who naturally would want to know why he was here. He'd given her a line about the girls being worried about her only to discover Remy was here and not in his own apartment, where he should be. Now he seemed intent on giving Remy hell about it.

"It's brand new," he explained. "I moved in across the hall yesterday while I'm getting my house ready to sell. Lisa and I started talking and decided to spend some time together while we're living in the same building."

"It's casual," Lisa said breezily.

"We're signing a contract this morning. It's not that casual." Had she changed her mind?

Lisa flushed again but this time he didn't think it was embarrassment. "All right. It's temporary, but not casual."

"I'm glad you two seem to have worked out the important stuff." Tag did not look impressed.

Lisa turned to Remy. She was wearing a pair of boxer shorts and a tank top that showed off her luscious breasts. A silky kimono thing was wrapped around her, giving her a bohemian vibe he liked. That crazy mermaid hair of hers was in a bun on top of her head. Without a stitch of makeup on, she was still the prettiest thing he'd ever seen. "You called Big Tag about my old job?"

This was going to be sticky. Unless he played along. It would be natural. "I texted him last night. You can't expect me to be in your bed and not look into this. That's not the man I am. It's not the Dom I am."

"But the Dom you are lets her starve?" Taggart asked.

"I've been her damn Dom for less than twenty-four hours. I supplied the pizza," he groused. "I haven't had time to take her grocery shopping."

"I don't need him to…" She stepped back slightly, pointing her spatula their way. "Do you know you both look very intimidating right now? Way to Dom a girl. And Remy's right. He hasn't had a chance to go all freaky protective, get-all-up-in-my-business Dom on me. He did buy me a pizza before blowing my mind in bed. Four times."

Remy actually felt himself flush. "He did not need to know that."

"Was it a good pizza?" Tag asked.

She shrugged. "I didn't eat much of it. I jumped him pretty fast."

"Maybe you're the one I should be talking to," Tag replied, obviously relishing the gossip he would share the minute he got into the office. Hell, he wouldn't wait that long. He'd call Charlotte the minute he walked out the door. "Sub, you have to feed your Dom. He gets cranky and starts speaking French and shit when he's hangry. When he starts speaking French, I get nauseous because it's way too French."

"Did you get me the info I asked about?" He hadn't asked at all, but Lisa needed to think his interest in this case had coincided with his interest in her.

"I sent you the file Hutch worked up late last night. You owe him a big bag of Red Vines." Tag looked over at Lisa, who flipped a pancake onto a plate. "That's the secret to a truly successful business.

You've got to find employees willing to work for food. Hutch is all about the candy and Boomer is happy as long as there's a plate of something in front of him. Julian Lodge taught me that. The whole first year when he was funding McKay-Taggart he refused to pay us in anything but Chilean sea bass. The rich are weird, Lisa. Stay away from them."

She grinned as though she truly loved Tag's antics. "I don't think that will be a problem. Honestly, I'm not that into rich guys. I know I'm supposed to be all about the billionaire, but give me a blue-collar boy any day."

"Or a redneck because that's what Remy's blue collar is hiding," Tag said.

He'd been so wrong about her because she simply grinned, her cheeks flushed, and it wasn't all because she was cooking. He winked her way and then tried to get Tag back on task. "You said Hutch found something?"

"There's nothing to find," Lisa said, holding out a plate. "The case is practically dead. Now, Sir, what's our protocol on which massive predator I throw meat at first? My Dom or our guest?"

"Unlike our guest, we're a perfectly civilized couple. Guests first, and you're wrong. He did find something. That's precisely why he's here," he replied even as she set the plate in front of Tag.

The big guy looked up and the sarcasm fled for a moment. "Thank you, Lisa. This looks delicious. Remy's right. Hutch and Michael are working on a comprehensive file on the actual court case, but we already have some underground intel that makes me nervous. I have information that a man named Francesco Biondo is in town. Does that name ring a bell?"

She shook her head as she made a second plate and passed it to Remy. "I've never heard of him."

"He's an Italian national, known as The Blond in certain circles," Big Tag said between bites.

Remy's appetite fled in an instant. McKay-Taggart kept files on anyone Interpol flagged. And some Interpol didn't even know about. "Are you talking about the assassin?"

"I am." Big Tag sat back. "He's known for his professionalism and his skill. His weapon of choice is a long-range rifle, but he's used close-up tactics as well. The good news is Lisa doesn't have a car for him to rig to explode. He's an expert at that, too. Now we don't know that he's here for Lisa, but I find it interesting timing."

She stopped and stared. "Why would someone assassinate me? The trial isn't even going on. I doubt it will. They lost their best evidence. The prosecutor told me he didn't think he would retry."

"I think you're their best evidence," Taggart said quietly. "You can still testify."

"But without the books to back me up, it's my word against his," she pointed out.

He saw exactly where Taggart was going and wished the boss would stay out of his damn business. He had this handled. "That's true. That must be why the prosecutor is taking his time figuring out if he's going to file the case again."

"The fact that he doesn't file the case now doesn't mean Vallon's off the hook. As long as you're out here and willing to testify, this will hang over his head for years," Taggart explained.

Lisa nodded. "I know, and I know what you think I should do. You want me to go into some kind of witness protection, but I'm not giving up my life, Ian."

"You've already given up Sanctum," Remy pointed out.

"That wasn't about Vallon potentially offing me to keep me quiet. That was about pride. I can't get myself there anymore. Next time, you should put the club next to a handy rail station," she replied.

Taggart shuddered. "That would be horrible. Those things are human cattle movers. Have you smelled one in the middle of August? My point is you should come back. The last thing you need right now is to be isolated. That does nothing but help out the people who might try to hurt you. Someone will pick you up and take you home. I assure you no one will mind."

"I'll take her." He didn't like Taggart trying to arrange things for his sub. Not that they'd signed a contract yet, but they would. And he already had plans to keep her safe. Two nights a week at Sanctum would be two nights where nothing bad could happen to her. He was going to fix the other nights, too.

"I thought you were leaving." Taggart winced. "Oh, was she not supposed to know that?"

"He told me," Lisa said quickly, a hand on her hip. "He's moving back home. That's why he's in the apartment. He has to get his place ready to sell. He's been upfront and honest with me, so stop baiting him, please, Master Ian."

"Well, since you asked nicely," Taggart replied.

"I'm going to take a shower. I have a busy day of staring at the computer and applying for jobs," she said, putting her spatula down.

"You're not going to eat?" He didn't like the look in her eyes. It didn't come close to matching the smile on her face.

"Poverty has killed my appetite. I'll get something after my shower," she replied. "You two try not to kill each other. And I'll be happy to come back. I missed the kids, too."

Taggart nodded. "See you soon, then. And thank you for breakfast."

Lisa smiled and walked back to the bedroom.

Remy turned on his boss. "You massive, meddling asshole. What exactly are you trying to do?"

Taggart was looking at him without a hint of sarcasm on his face. "I am trying to ensure that a woman who has been a sub in my club for years isn't getting played by one of my operatives. I thought you had better sense than this. Do you know why I picked you for this job?"

"Because everyone else was taken."

Tag pointed a finger his way. "Because you're the sane one. You're the stable one, and I know that says something about my hiring practices, but you're the one who knows his limits and can control his goddamn dick. You think I don't know what happened with her earlier this year? The whole club saw that."

He was never going to live it down. "I didn't mean to make a scene."

"No, but you did make the right choice," Tag shot back. "You should have softened that blow, but you were smart enough to not take what she had to give because you got nothing to give back to her. I would like to know what happened between then and now. Tell me this isn't some play to make the time pass. Tell me you're not fucking her because she'll be easier to keep up with if you're on top of her. Damn it, I told her brother we would take care of her. I owe him and I owe her brother-in-law, and I damn straight owe Bridget."

"I'm fucking her because I want her more than I've ever wanted a woman. I'm fucking her because I can't stand the thought of not fucking her. What's the difference? I was stupid before and didn't see past her family's money and accomplishments to consider who she was as a human being. I saw a pretty face and expensive shoes and didn't think she would have the depth to be able to care about a man like me for more than sex. I was wrong and I've corrected the mistake." And yeah, he'd thought about how sex could make his job easier, but that had flown out the window the minute he'd realized who she really was.

"Have you given a single thought to how she's going to feel when you leave?"

"Yeah, and she assures me that she would rather have these weeks than not have them, and I feel the same way." He was getting a bad feeling in his gut. "If you're going to fire me, do it, but I won't leave her alone. She's mine for as long as we're together, and I won't give up the right to protect her. I'll stay here until I'm sure this thing is done."

"She's part of our family." Taggart sat back. "She's been in the girls' lives since they were born. Her sister-in-law is Serena's best friend. She's more than a client. It's why I came here this morning. I thought I would talk to you. Lisa was taking out the trash and caught me walking in. Imagine my surprise at that. She was walking around outside like nothing was wrong. An infamous assassin is in town and she's taking out the trash and making sure the recycling went into the right bin."

It made his heart threaten to seize. "I was asleep. We agreed last night to not think about our contract until this morning. I'll put in protocols. I'll make her understand how serious this is. I think she'll let me protect her if she doesn't realize her brother's paying me. She's got a strong streak of pride, but she's reasonable."

"And if she catches you following her?"

This could work. "Then she catches her very real Dom making sure she's safe. I'm serious about that contract with her. There's nothing fake about this. I care about her."

"But you're leaving her behind."

Though he'd slept well the night before, the conversation was making him weary. "I have to go home. You heard her. She's not leaving her family. I have to do what I can to save mine. We're adults who've made our decision. Stop playing her dad and be my damn boss and help me protect her."

Tag took a deep breath, seeming to consider the problem. "I can try to find someone to back you up. I can bring Riley off vacation. He'll be pissed but he'll do his job."

"No, I can handle this, but I have some out-of-the-box thoughts on how to keep her safe. You just gave me two nights where I don't have to worry. She'll be safe at Sanctum."

"You can take her on other nights," Tag mused. "Sanctum is the safest place for her. You're her Dom. You sign that contract with her and you trump her brother. Will can deal with it."

"I was actually thinking she needs a job," Remy explained. "And I might know a place where the employees would watch out for her. Where the employees are mostly ex-military."

Taggart's eyes narrowed. "And what would she be doing at this place that I own a large piece of?"

"She's a hell of a bartender." Remy had thought it out last night in between sessions. It was the best way to protect her and give her something to do while they waited to see what would happen with the trial. "You know Linc could use some help."

"So let me get this straight. My company is paying for an apartment you are no longer really going to live in because you'll be in her bed every night, and now you want me to hire the client and pay her a wage so we can protect her. You are taking the bulk of the money the actual client is paying. Do you see the business problems with this?"

Sure he did, but he wasn't about to admit that to Taggart. "I'm nothing but an old country boy, boss. I don't know a lot about the financial stuff. I leave that to way smarter minds than me."

"Sure you do, asshole." But Taggart was already pulling out his phone. "Tell her to be ready to interview with Deena this afternoon, but of course she's got the job. We actually can use the help. Ally's pregnant and Macon's being seriously overprotective with her, so Lisa will have to bounce between the bar and service, but I suspect she can handle it. And I'll head over there and brief everyone on what's happening."

"I'll drive her to and from work, and when she's safe, I'll work with Hutch or whoever to try to figure a way out of this for her. You're right. Even if they don't prosecute now, she's still a threat." Their best bet might be finding something else to nail Vallon for, something that didn't involve Lisa.

Tag nodded. "We'll be on the lookout for Biondo. I'll have someone monitoring the CCTV cams around the restaurant and this building. Luckily you have security cams here. I'm talking to Adam about bringing in...god, what's it up to now? Miles-Dean, Weston, and Murdoch Investigation. Couldn't they find a better name? They sound like a bunch of lawyers. I suggested Wolverine Investigations. Or The Angry Badger. See, both of those say 'I'm going to find your missing person or someone will get torn apart by claws.' The other says 'we're a bunch of brogrammers in suits.'"

"Brogrammers?" Sometimes he didn't understand Tag's language.

"It's what Adam is. It's worse than a nerd because he talks about computers a lot and yet also reminds me of a fraternity asswipe. Still, he knows what he's doing and his facial recognition software is brilliant. If that man shows up on camera, we'll catch him," Tag promised.

An assassin was in town. Dallas was a big place, but still, his instincts told him something bad was coming. "I want work-ups on all the power players involved in this case. It's federal, but Maia Brighton probably knows something."

Maia Brighton was Dallas's duly elected district attorney. She was also a pain in Big Tag's ass. A devoted sex addict, she was one of the smartest, most ruthless women Remy had ever met. If anyone could get them information, it was her. The problem was her intelligence wasn't free.

Tag groaned. "I just got rid of her. You can't buy her info for money, man. She'll want something sexual, and all my brothers are whiny losers who can't give it up because they're married and said vows and shit. And this new generation? You would think they're a bunch of shrinking violet virgins. Ask them to fuck for information and you get a lecture on something about how their bodies make choices."

"Boss, aren't you the one who walked in here all self-righteous about the possibility of me hopping in Lisa's bed to protect her?"

Tag stood up. "Did I? You must be mistaken because that totally doesn't sound like me. I'll get back to you about those reports. Have her at Top this afternoon. I'm sure Lincoln will be more than thrilled to have some help. Especially from Lisa." He walked to the door. "And Remy, try to remember that plans can change. What you think you want and need, those things can change, and very quickly."

"I don't understand. Are you talking about the job?"

"I'm talking about life, brother. Take care of her. And get some damn food in her fridge. That's sad. Send me the contract when you're done and I'll file it. That way Will can't question your rights at Sanctum. Because he's going to. You need to think about how you're going to handle that whole family. Good luck. I wouldn't want to deal with Bridget." He closed the door.

He hadn't thought about her family the night before. He'd been too busy thinking about how damn good it felt to finally sink into Lisa. It didn't matter. They would have to accept the relationship or they could tell her the truth, and no one wanted Lisa freaking out and running headlong into danger. Will would simply have to see that his youngest sister was fully capable of making decisions for herself. And she'd decided on him.

He heard the shower running in the bathroom and suddenly food didn't seem all that appealing. There was something he wanted way more.

God, this desire in his gut was like nothing he'd ever felt before. He'd thought it would be banked this morning after how well they'd fed it the night before. Instead, it was as though now he knew how good it was between them and his dick couldn't wait. His dick had a taste and didn't want anything else.

It was going to be all right. He could handle this. He could take care of her and enjoy her, and when it was over they would both have a fond memory. That was all. They would go their separate ways and not regret having cared about each other for these weeks or months.

She hummed while she was in the shower.

He stood there listening to her for a moment, the sweet sound piercing him in a way very little did anymore.

Was he the one in over his head?

It didn't matter because there was no going back now. Warm heat hit him as he entered the bathroom. Through the opaque shower door he could see the graceful lines of her body. He dropped his jeans and joined his new sub in the shower. It was time to put their relationship on solid ground. It would be good for her. Despite the fact that this relationship was real, he would be foolish not to use it to help keep her safe.

She turned, her lips curling up. Her hair was wet, dropping down slightly past her waist. Yes, she was a siren calling him away from safety. Calling him right to her. "You got rid of Big Tag pretty fast."

"I can work miracles when I need to," he promised, reaching out for her. "Come here, *chèrie*."

When she moved into his arms, nothing had ever felt so right.

Chapter Six

"Hey, you!" Serena Dean-Miles waved her way as Lisa walked through the ladies' locker room. The locker room at Sanctum was a posh space with everything a submissive or Domme could need to pamper herself silly. Serena was sitting at one of the vanities, brushing out her brown and blonde hair.

Lisa waved back, moving out of the dressing area and into what she liked to call the "primp station." Here there were a bunch of beautifully lit vanities where a woman could perfect her makeup or dry and curl her hair.

"Good to see you're back," Avery said with a wink as she moved a flat iron over her dark hair.

"I'm happy to be back," Lisa replied.

And she was. It was incredibly good to return to Sanctum. And to have a job. And a Dom waiting for her in the lounge. That was a completely new situation. In all the months she'd played at Sanctum before, she'd never had a Dom who was hers.

Three days into their "relationship" and she still hoped he didn't catch her drooling. Life was looking up. She had a job she hadn't gotten fired from on the first day, one where the vents didn't spit glitter at her and there was no public food for her to fall into. She was required to wear comfortable shoes. There were all kinds of things to eat in her refrigerator because her Dom believed in regular meals and they'd made a deal. He bought the food stuffs and she turned it into something he wanted to eat. And yes, she did put those quote things around the word "relationship" even in her brain, but damn he was fine.

"Where have you been?" Serena gave her a quick hug before sitting back down. "The kids have missed you."

She hadn't even met the baby yet. Serena had a new baby girl, but it had happened after she'd left Sanctum. "I got way too busy with my old jerk-face boss's money laundering, and then it turns out when you're associated with money laundering, no one wants to hire you even though you were the good guy who turned the boss in."

"That's rough," Avery said. "I heard you're working at Top now."

Remy had gotten her the interview. Hell, Remy had gotten her the job. She'd interviewed with Deena Vail, who was running the business end of Top while Sean Taggart was on some mysterious mission in Fort Hood. She switched between bartending and waitressing. "Yes. I know Will is going to say I'm wasting my degree, but I actually love it there. I might have made a horrible mistake going with the accounting degree. Turns out it's kind of boring."

"I can't imagine," Serena replied. "But I would love to hear about the money laundering. Is the case over? Is that why you could come back? Are you playing tonight? Because I thought I saw Bridget walking around earlier."

"Yeah, my Dom says he doesn't care what deal I made with my brother's tender eyeballs." That was kind of how he'd put it. "He likes to play when he likes to play, and Will can get blinders."

She was a bit worried about how this would go. Will had never actually seen her with a Dom. He'd been careful about it. She'd offered to try to find another club, but that idea had damn near melted her brother's brainpan.

"Sanctum is big enough you can avoid each other," Avery said. "I'm just glad you're here."

"Me, too. And I'll be in the nursery on Sunday night." She was eager to get back to the babies. She'd missed those kids.

"You're working the nursery? Remy usually plays on Sunday. I heard you were with him now," Serena said.

"He's taking a dungeon monitor shift," she replied. "But we're kind of, sort of together. I mean we're totally together, but only until he's ready to move. He's going home to Louisiana, but we've got a contract until then."

A frown crossed Serena's pretty face. "Are you okay with that? Short-term contracts can be hard on a girl. They're kind of made of heartbreak. It's why an awful lot of romance novels start with one."

"We've been completely honest with each other. It's an affair," she said. "Not every relationship lasts forever. We're two adults who've consented to enjoy each other while we have the time."

Though it felt like more. It was awesome. Remy spent much of the days with her. Apparently he was taking some time off his job while he got his house ready to sell. He dropped her off at work in the afternoon and then showed up around an hour before closing and hung out at the bar and then ate with them before taking her home and making love to her until she couldn't hold her eyes open. Then they would wake up midmorning and start it all over again.

It was practically heaven.

Avery sighed. "An affair. I had one of those. I met this tall, dark, and handsome American in London. He was the most amazing man I'd ever met. And the sex was incredible."

Lisa felt her eyes widen. She couldn't imagine Avery with anyone but her Irish husband. "Wow, a London affair. That sounds hot. Does Liam know? Like later on, do you still miss the hot affair when you're happily married?"

"She can't miss him. The sexy American turned out to be a sexy Irish guy on a mission. Yeah, she ended up married to him," Serena replied with a sly smile. "Actually, now that I think about it, I started out thinking Jake and Adam were a pleasant way to spend a little time. An affair, nothing more. You should watch out, Lisa. Affairs around here tend to turn into weddings and babies and, in my case, way too much laundry. Everyone warned me about the laundry, but I didn't listen."

It wasn't going to end that way. Not for her. There was an ache in her heart, but she ignored it. She'd made her decision and she was a big girl. Remy was signing paperwork with the bank in a few days, and then he had to go down to Louisiana sometime after that to close on the property. When he talked about his home, his eyes lit up and he practically beamed.

He wasn't going to change his mind. He was going home and their affair would end.

But that didn't mean she couldn't enjoy it while it was here. He'd done so much for her already. How had she ever thought that man was cold? He was the warmest person she'd met, giving and thoughtful.

Some day he would make a magnificent husband.

But for now, he was her Dom. Her first real Dom. She said good-bye to her friends and stopped to give herself one more look-over. She was wearing exactly what Remy had bought for her. Ruby red corset that cinched in her waist, tiny, clingy boy shorts, and a pair of heels that made her legs look way longer than they were. She'd left her hair down as he'd requested. He seemed to have a real thing for her hair. She put it up when she worked, but every night, even before they got to his truck, he would pull it down and tangle his fingers in it and hold her head still for a long, luscious kiss.

She was going to play with him tonight. She would be the one he lavished all that masculine attention on. She would be the one he used his ropes on, to tie her up so she was helpless, and he could have his way with her.

For tonight she was his sub.

Lisa walked out of the locker room, head held high, and ran straight into Bridget.

"Tell me you're not sleeping with him." Bridget was in a long, see-through skirt and white bra, her round belly on display. No high heels for the pregnant chick. "I heard a rumor that you signed a contract with Remy Guidry. A D/s contract. Tell me that's not true."

There was a hint of desperation in Bridget's tone that worried Lisa. Bridget was cool. She was the one who shrugged off most things. Well, not things like someone cutting her off in traffic. Then she let the volcanic rage flow, but family shit kind of washed right off her.

"I don't know why that's a problem."

Bridget's eyes closed. "Oh, you will. I think Will is going to make it into a big old problem. Me, personally, I get it. The man is hot, and honestly, it solves a whole bunch of problems, but Will is not going to see it that way and he's on the protective side. He's going to explode when he hears about that contract. Maybe if you walk out now, I can convince him it's all a joke."

"Since when does Will get a say in who I date?" She got it. Big brother was protective, but she wasn't a teen. She didn't have to have her brother vet her dates. He'd been weirded out when she took the training class, but he hadn't tried to stop her. When she'd started playing, he'd gone a bit green, but worked out a schedule rather than telling her to go somewhere else. "Look, Bridge, it's not even a long-term thing. Remy's going home in a couple of weeks. I'm not going to hide the whole time."

Bridget took her hand. "Is Remy waiting for you in the lounge?"

"Yes." Before she could say another word, Bridget was hauling her up the stairs that led to the swanky lounge and the primary play space. To her left she could see someone already had a sub on the hamster wheel.

Hopefully Remy didn't decide she needed cardio. That hamster wheel was the only punishment she actually feared here at Sanctum. It took a lot of energy to get that sucker to turn green.

"Why is this upsetting?" Lisa struggled to keep up. "Why does Will care who I date? It's not like he's some ex-con without a job who sits on my couch and cheats on me all day. He's a good guy."

"I know he is. He's done a lot for our family. I'm surprised he would decide to start a relationship with you when he knows it's not going to work. I think Will is worried that you shouldn't be dating anyone right now," Bridget replied.

"Thank god." Laurel was suddenly rushing over from the bar. She was dressed for play, her corset a lovely purple with a matching thong. Ah, family life. They were having a family crisis in the middle of a BDSM club. It was perfect. "Mitch and Will are on their way up and they know. They know. Someone told them in the locker room."

The look on Laurel's face didn't make a lick of sense. "Stop. First of all, is Lila about to drop down from the ceiling to put her two cents in, too? And second, since when do we treat my dating life like it's highly classified and we'll all get in trouble if the guys know?"

Remy looked up from where he'd been sitting at the bar and she damn near melted at the look on his face. His eyes were like lasers focused in on her. He stood up, his big body encased in leathers and his cowboy boots. She could see the wide swath of his chest where the vest didn't cover. He was all muscle, all man, and it didn't matter that she'd already had him ten times. She wasn't ever going to get tired of the way it felt when he looked at her like he couldn't get enough.

"Whoa," Bridget said. "I know that look. That look is bad. That look is something you don't come back from."

She was going to ask her suddenly insane sister-in-law what she meant by that, but Remy had closed the space between them.

He reached out and took her hand in his, bringing it up to his lips. "*Tu es la plus belle femme du club, ma crevette. Et je suis l'homme plus chanceux.*"

She had no idea what he was saying, but it made her girl parts pulse.

Laurel and Bridget were watching him, too, their eyes wide like neither could think of what to say after that.

"If you're done speaking douchebag, perhaps we should talk about what the hell you're doing sleeping with my sister," a dark voice said. "Did you think I wouldn't notice that?"

She turned, putting her body in front of Remy's and saw Will wince. Probably because her boobs looked good in a corset. Her brother stood there with Mitch, both in leathers similar to Remy's, though neither man could fill them out the way hers could. And it was weird. He was right. It was creepy and weird to see her brother dressed for sex because she wasn't sure she was ready to accept that he had sex. Even though he was working on baby number two and Bridget freely talked about their sex life. It was easier to pretend like Bridge was talking about one of her crazy characters instead of her brother when he wasn't standing there in front of her.

"It was French and not douchebag," Remy said. "That's what Tag speaks when he starts talking about brogrammers and getting his manties in a wad. French is a perfectly civilized language."

"So is the law, buddy, and you're going to understand that when I sue your ass," Mitch said.

"Mitchell." Laurel managed to make her husband's name an admonition.

"Why would you sue Remy for sleeping with me? I'm going to tell you I'll be a very bad witness because I'll go into ridiculously explicit detail on how good he is at it," Lisa swore.

Everyone was watching them. Big Tag had Charlotte on his lap across the lounge. It looked like he'd been talking to Alex McKay and Liam O'Donnell, but now all eyes were on the Daley family as they hashed out their issues in public. They weren't alone. Simon Weston and his wife, Chelsea, had been sitting with Jesse and Phoebe Murdoch, and there was no way to miss how the two couples were now avidly watching the scene in front of them. Jesse even asked Simon to pass him the bowl of mixed nuts on their table.

Damn it. They couldn't have done this at home like normal people?

"Really? You think you know him?" Her brother had his best judgey face on. It had been the one he'd used on her when she'd come home late from a date or gotten a B on a test. "I don't think you know all the facts, Lisa."

Remy's hands came down on her shoulders. "I don't think *you* know the facts, Will. First of all, your sister is a beautiful, highly competent woman who is capable of taking care of herself, but she's been struggling and everyone needs help now and then."

"Yeah, not the kind you're offering her," Will shot back.

"Exactly how is your dick helping her?" Mitch asked, which promptly got him an elbowing from his wife.

Remy continued like Will and Mitch hadn't said a thing. "I'm going to admit that I didn't think I had anything to offer her until we met up again a few days ago. As many people in this club know, I've stayed away despite my attraction to her for that exact reason. But things changed recently. I moved into her building while my house is getting ready to go on the market. Some of my friends helped me move and we... Well, I took them out for drinks at Cherry Pies. Not the best establishment, but you know my boys will be boys. I was surprised to find Lisa working there."

She went completely still. Had he meant to mention that?

Will's eyes widened. "I'm sorry, what?"

"Cherry Pies?" Bridget asked with a look that let Lisa know she understood exactly what the business was about.

Yeah, she hadn't planned on mentioning her one-day job at a strip club to her overprotective family. She'd been planning on hiding it altogether. "It was an experiment. The guy who manages the place lives in my building and he offered me a shot at a job. It didn't work out. No biggie."

"What is Cherry Pies?" Laurel asked, looking from Lisa to Mitch to Will. "Is it a pie shop?"

Bridget sent Laurel a sympathetic look. "Oh, sweetie, you're lucky you're gorgeous. I do believe Cherry Pies refers to a woman's virginity. You know, I got me some of that sweet, sweet cherry pie."

Will looked down at her. "No one talks like that."

"Tell that to Warrant and much of the 80s hair metal movement, and then you can explain why a strip club calls itself Cherry Pies," Bridge shot back.

"You know it's really false advertising," Mitch pointed out. His eyes had gone a bit soft, a sure sign he was either thinking about his family or musing about a class action lawsuit. "I'm going to bet there's not a single virgin in that place. Well, not females."

Will seemed to know it was time to take control. "I don't care about virgins. I care about why my sister was dropping her freaking clothes." He went a little pale. "Holy shit. How did this happen? One job. I had one job."

"Oh, god, he's going to talk about the pole." Bridget had her hands on Will's arm, stroking him. "This baby is a girl and he fears the pole more than anything."

"I wasn't on the pole." She was absolutely certain she'd gone beet red. "Remy, please tell them I wasn't on the pole."

"She was behind the bar where the topless waitresses hang out," Remy explained helpfully. "Apparently they worked her eight hours without a break, and when I found her she was being accosted by a heinous drunk who ended up causing her to fall into the cold buffet. They proceeded to shoot glitter so hard out of the venting system that she's still got a little glow about her even after we scrubbed her forty times. Mitch, some of that had to have gotten into her lungs. There's your lawsuit. Anyway, when I got hold of her again, she was walking to the train station because she turned her car in months ago and didn't tell you. She preferred to turn it in rather than allow it to be repossessed. Your sister was walking down the dark street, clutching forty ones to her chest like they were her lifeboat, and she was covered in glitter that likely would have shone in the moonlight like a Bat signal for rapists or other criminals."

She turned on her lover, her hands in fists at her sides. "You are not helping the situation."

Remy managed to look as innocent as a two-hundred-plus-pound ex-soldier could look. "I am explaining the situation to your brother. I'm explaining how I'm not the bad guy here. I'm the guy who picked you up and put you in my truck. I'm the guy who fed you that night and got you a new job the next morning. I'm the guy who drops you off and picks you up and makes sure you're safe and happy because I'm the guy *you* chose."

"I'm still stuck on the fact that Cherry Pies has a cold buffet," Bridget said. "Was there shrimp?"

"I don't want to talk about shrimp," Lisa said with a shudder. She might never be able to look at a crustacean again.

"Sorry, I'm kind of hungry. Pregnancy cravings." Bridget looked up.

"We are not going to a strip club for shrimp. We are civilized. We'll find a Long John Silver's." Will turned to Lisa. "You turned in your car?"

She hated this. She hated everything about this. The pity in her brother's eyes was far worse than losing her car. Lila would never be in this position. Laurel would have figured a way out of it. Only Lisa was the loser in the family. She was the one who hadn't known what she wanted to do with her life, the last to make it through college. The first to fail. "I couldn't afford it."

"That is no excuse," Will replied and she knew she was in for a long lecture.

Remy moved to her side. "No excuse? Her pride is no excuse? If you had been in the same situation as Lisa, would you have turned to your sister-in-law and asked her to pay for your car? I don't think so."

Laurel shook her head. "He wouldn't. I wouldn't. Will, you raised us to be proud and not live beyond our means. We married really wealthy people. We don't have to worry about money. Lisa is not in the same boat as the two of us."

"I would have paid for the car," Bridget said.

"That's not the point." Laurel held her hand as though trying to give her strength. "Lisa wants to make it on her own. You taught her that, Will."

Will's jaw tightened and he eyed Remy. "She let him help her."

"I'm sleeping with him. He should help me. Not for the simple fact that I'm sleeping with him but because he cares about me. And he's not handing over cash. He helped me get a job. He bought food and I cooked it. It's a more even exchange." Lisa looked at her brother. He was way more like a father when she thought about it. He'd had a hard burden at a young age and handled himself and them with grace that most teenage boys wouldn't have had. He'd kept them all together, but he needed to understand that she made her own decisions now. "Look, Will, I love you, but I'm a grown woman who makes her own choices, and I'm choosing to be with Remy for now."

"You don't have all the facts," Will said, his voice tight.

"Will, please think about this for two seconds," Bridget warned. "Do you want to start a war over this? Because what happens when you force her to choose? Believe me, I know what a family looks like after that. She might choose her family, but your relationship with her will never be the same. And she'll be far more likely to rebel than you can imagine. Think about everything that's at stake."

There was some weird subtext conversation going on that she

didn't understand, but Bridget and Will could be like that at times. They had a whole shorthand no one else got.

"Will, I've been open and honest with her about how long I'm going to be in town and what I can offer her while I'm here," Remy said quietly. "I've been attracted to your sister, well, since the moment I saw her. I stayed away because I didn't think I was good for her, but we sat down and talked and I *can* give her something for these weeks. I can give her my full attention and my full promise to be present every second I have to spend with her. We've signed a contract with an end date, and we're both going into this knowing that it will end and agreeing to be friends afterward."

"That is the stupidest thing I've ever heard in my life," Will said. "A contract with an end date. Who does that?"

Bridget's eyes went wide, like supervillain, she-could-kill-you-with-lasers-from-her-irises wide, and everyone took a step back. Even Remy seemed to know Hurricane Bridget was about to get her storm on. Remy's arms went around Lisa as though he could protect her from the coming winds.

Will had the good sense to turn a bit pale. "Now, baby, I wasn't talking about us. That was a totally different thing. Totally."

Bridget pointed a finger his way. "Signing a contract with an end date is stupid? Is it, Will? Is it? Because you're calling the mother of your babies stupid, mister 'I don't know what the word love means so let's take it real slow.' Oh, hey wait, the sex is pretty good. We can go another month but stop using that *love* word."

"I love you, baby," Will said. "I love you so much. See how trainable I was? Am. You recognized that in me right away. Trainable. I don't think he's trainable."

"Trainable, my ass," Bridget shot back before she looked over at Remy. "If you hurt her, I will skin you alive and then I'll sew the skin back on and let it heal and skin you again for the fun of it. Do I make myself clear?"

"In a very intense way, Mrs. Daley," Remy said from behind her. "I have no intention of hurting Lisa. I genuinely care about her. I intend to protect her and take care of her until I have to go home to my family."

Bridget studied him for a moment and then looked over at Laurel, and the two seemed to come to some kind of decision.

"He's just a dumbass," they said at the same time.

Laurel gave him a grin. "It's all right. We both married dumbasses. Dumbassery can be cured."

Mitch put a hand on Remy's arm. "Usually with pregnancy. You want to keep your dumbassery, wear a condom, brother."

"I thought we were sticking together as the men of this family." Will sent his best friend a dirty look.

Mitch slung an arm around Laurel. "I think the ladies are right. He thinks this is going to go one way, but it's going to swerve, brother. It's going to swerve hard, and that's when you wake up and suddenly there's a kid in your arms and she's got this ring on her finger and you kind of scratch your head and wonder how you got there, but then you figure out *there* is really fucking nice. *There* is warm and happy and good. And suddenly all those reasons you limited the contract in the first place seem fuzzy and vague and you kind of give in. I give him three weeks."

Will's eyes had narrowed, seeming to fixate on that place where Remy's hands touched her. "I'll take that. He looks even more dumbassy than you did. Five weeks before they elope."

They'd changed tactics on her. Assholes. "We're not eloping, guys. It's not going to happen."

"I have to go home. I'm buying my family's business back," Remy said, as flustered as she'd ever heard him.

Yet he held on to her. "It's okay, babe. They're trying to scare you. They figured out they couldn't make me back down so now they're working on you."

Will seemed to have settled, his shoulders finally dropping from around his ears. "No. No, I think Mitch and the girls are right. I've played this whole thing out before. A long time ago, I signed a short-term contract with a woman I thought I could get out of my system. Turns out she was a necessary part of my system."

Mitch smiled. "And I didn't use a condom."

Laurel huffed and slapped her husband gently on his six-pack.

Mitch laughed and cuddled her close. "I wouldn't go back for anything. I would throw all my condoms away, baby."

"Hey, do we have an over/under yet?" Taggart yelled across the room. Charlotte was grinning in his arms.

Will nodded. "Yeah, let the betting begin." He moved over to Lisa. "If he hurts you, I'll let Bridget do all the horrible things she likes. In addition to the pregnancy cravings, she also gets a wee bit violent when she's gestating. I love you, sister." He kissed her forehead. "Now please put on some clothes. You, too, Laurel. I thought we had a deal."

"All bets are off now. If Lisa gets to play any night she wants, I do, too." Laurel winked her way. "We get dibs on the office space. I'm his horny secretary tonight."

"And any night you want to be, baby," Mitch said with a smirk.

"Well, I call privacy room where I don't have to see my sisters play," Will said. He smiled down at Bridget. "And I already had the room stocked with snacks and massage oil and hot cocoa, and my iPad is full of Grey's Anatomy, the season you missed while breastfeeding." Will sighed. "Sometimes kink comes in weird packages around here. I'll be watching you, Guidry."

Her brother strode off with his wife.

She turned and Remy was looking a little pale himself. "Are you okay? That was a heavy scene."

"Lisa, I…"

Shit, she was going to kill her brother. Everyone was betting on them. Everyone was looking at them. "Remy, it's okay. It's not a big deal. These guys fuck around with everyone."

He stared down at her. "I don't want to hurt you. Your brother… I'm not your brother. It's not going to go that way for us. If I took you with me, god, Lisa, I would be taking you into something you don't deserve. My family is difficult and the town is weird and you deserve your life."

He wasn't changing his mind. She wanted to tell him that she liked weird, but he'd been honest with her. He was worried she would get hurt if she started to believe that she could change him. Hell, she didn't want to change him. It was okay. "I'm not asking for more than you're willing to give."

Maybe if they'd had more time before he needed to leave. Maybe if he'd said yes to her the first time, but he hadn't and she couldn't ask a man she'd been with for three days to take her with him when he left town.

Even if she really wanted to.

"But your brother…"

"My brother likes to screw around with people," she said. "I don't take him seriously and neither should you. Consider that nothing more than a bit of hazing. And all the betting is going to be for nothing. Maybe we should get in on that. Would that be fair?"

He reached for her hand. "Maybe I should back off."

Now tears threatened. "If my family makes me less desirable to you, then yes, we should reevaluate."

"Nothing in the world could make you less desirable to me," he said. "Not now that I know you." He brought her hand to his mouth, kissing her. "But I'm not Prince Charming."

"I don't need you to be." She wished he was, but she was going with the flow, taking what life had to offer her. "I need you to be Prince Right Now. And if you want to tie me up and do nasty things to me, all the better."

He took her hand. "Now that I can do."

He started to lead her toward the playroom, and she swore that she would live in the moment. It wouldn't be that hard. After all, the future wasn't all that bright.

* * * *

Remy led her to one of the small rooms off the main play area. It was a room specifically done up for suspension play. It was the room he spent most of his time here in. All of his life he'd been around rope, learning to sail from an early age. It wasn't surprising that a lot of his kink centered around ties and knots. He'd grown up being told to make sure his precious boats were secure or they might drift away and all would be lost.

He felt the same way about the woman trailing after him. He had the sudden desire to make sure she didn't drift away, the waves of life taking her far from him.

"You know what I like to do, right?" The sex had been fairly vanilla up to this point. Oh, he'd used her panties to bind her hands together and spanked her pretty ass. She had a couple of bite marks because it turned out she enjoyed the sensation, but he hadn't gotten around to his central kink.

"Suspension," she replied with a sigh to her voice that let him know she wasn't going to be scared.

He was starting to think nothing at all scared Lisa Daley. "It doesn't look like anyone's in here yet, but that doesn't mean we'll be alone the whole time. How far are you willing to go?"

"How fast can you get these clothes off?" Lisa replied.

Damn she was going to kill him. "Pretty fast."

She followed him into the room. "Does it bother you? I wouldn't do it anywhere I didn't feel safe, but that's kind of the point of Sanctum. And I think I might have some exhibitionist in me. When we were training partners, Linc and I would do it in his truck in the parking lot and the thought that someone could catch us kind of did something for me."

"Excuse me?"

She flushed slightly, as though realizing her mistake. "The class would get us all hot and bothered and we would... You know how it can be between training partners. Especially when you agree it's all about sex and nothing else."

A rush of indignation shot through him. What had she said? She hadn't... "Lincoln? Linc was your training partner? The same Linc I recently got you a job working under?"

Lincoln ran the bar at Top. Lincoln had smiled brilliantly when he'd been told Lisa would be working with him. Remy had been watching them across the dining room. At the time he'd thought how nice that the big guy would give Lisa such an enthusiastic greeting. He'd thought it was good because she needed some enthusiasm in her life.

That bastard had probably been thanking heaven she'd walked back into his life and he got a second shot at getting into her pretty panties.

"I didn't mention that?" She had a cute, quizzical expression on her face. "Huh. I guess because it was so long ago and it didn't mean anything. Now he's just a friend. It's cool to be working with him again. You know it's always nice to catch up with an old friend."

Oh, but Linc wasn't old at all. "He was the last sex you had."

She shook her head. "No. It was the last *good* sex I had. Before you." She stopped, her lips curling up. "But you're way better. You have nothing at all to be jealous about."

Except that Linc was younger than he was. Linc was staying around. Somehow he couldn't quite believe the whole "let's simply have sex for six weeks because the class makes us horny and you're convenient" thing had been Linc's idea. He would have been a moron for not using that time to convince a woman like Lisa to settle for a dude like him.

Of course, that was exactly what Remy was doing, but he knew he was a moron.

"I'm not jealous."

Her smile dimmed. "Of course you're not because there's nothing at all to be jealous about."

He pointed her way. "I'm righteously pissed, and if he touches you in any way that doesn't concern making sure you don't fall or pushing you out of the way of danger, I'm going to have his ass. I don't care that the bastard goes psycho from time to time. If he touches my damn sub, he's going to find out how psychotic a Cajun boy can be. Do you understand me?"

She held her hands up as though letting go of the argument. "I understand that I am somehow surrounded by crazy, freaky overly protective men."

He needed to make something plain to her. He wasn't her brother. Not even close. He took her by the shoulders and got into her space, so close that she had to tilt her head up to look at him. "Your brother is overly protective, and maybe I can be considered that, too, but this is me being stupid and overly possessive. It's not a pretty thing to be, but I can't deny it. I know we've got an end date, but I can't stand the thought of that pretty boy putting his hands on you."

She groaned. "He's the pretty boy? Let me get you a mirror, Sir, because it's obvious you have no idea what pretty is."

Her smart mouth did something for him. "Get in there and I would like to see a proper greeting for your Dom before we get to the night's fun."

She stepped back, her head bowing in perfect submission. It was all play because that *chèrie* bowed to no one and nothing she didn't choose to bow to, and it would only work as long as she believed she was being treated fairly.

Like the queen she was.

She walked into the room, her heels clacking along the floor. He watched as she disappeared into what they liked to call the blue room. It had been painted shades of midnight blue, even the ceiling, to give the illusion that the sub was suspended by ropes that stretched up into the night sky, as though the night itself could hold and cradle the submissive close. All theater, of course. It would be him and his ropes keeping Lisa secure and ready for pleasure.

He entered the room and Lisa was in slave pose, on her knees, head down.

That was when he realized he wasn't the only person in the room.

A woman was suspended a few feet off a red pad on the floor. She was elaborately tied, her torso held in place and one leg pulled up behind her. There was rope threaded between her toes and wrapped around her foot causing her foot to curve. She lay in place, breathing steadily, as if remaining still would save her. It was obvious the sub had found a fairly comfortable position. However, eventually she would have to try to stretch, and then she'd be trapped, the tension of the rope forcing that leg higher and torturing her foot.

Predicament bondage. He only knew one couple who played that way on a regular basis. Predicament bondage put the submissive between a rock and a hard place. No matter what happened, the submissive would end up in a tortured position, often having to choose between two bad outcomes. It took a sadist to come up with the scenario and a masochist to find it fun.

He kept quiet, holding a hand out to indicate Lisa should do the same. They might have to find another space.

Kai looked up and smiled. "Hey, you two. Come on in. There's plenty of room."

"Hi, Kai," he said, finding the Dom sitting in the shadows, watching his sub. "Kori, you're looking lovely tonight."

Kai stood up, his mouth curling in a slightly evil smile. "I think I've finally figured out what to do when I want her to stop talking. If she moves even an inch, the rope around her foot tightens. Doesn't she look pretty all perfectly silent?"

Without moving another muscle, Kori's right hand middle finger came out.

"Love you, too, babe," Kai replied with a chuckle. "Hey, Lisa. Good to see you back. Kori says, hey, too. You know, if you want in on this we could tie them up in such a way that they have to decide between giving themselves pain or forcing their partners to take it. It's a fun game, man."

He looked over and Lisa's eyes were wider than he'd ever seen. "I don't think my girl's quite ready for that level of kink. We're just going to tie her up real nice, suspend her so she knows she's helpless, and then make her scream. Is that going to disrupt your scene?"

"Not at all. We've got a bet going. If she makes it an hour like this, I have to adopt another dog, so dear god man, make your sub scream. Any help I can get. We've already got two and one's a chewer. Like he chews on everything, but she insists that number three is going to be a perfect angel."

"You go, Kori. Get that puppy," Lisa said, her voice positive but low.

He frowned her way. "I'm sorry. Did I give you permission to speak? This is my space, *ma crevette*. This is where I rule."

He'd given her his most intimidating voice, but she simply shrugged, her eyes focused on the floor. "You didn't say I couldn't talk."

"Master Kai, maybe I should rethink." He moved around her, breathing in her beauty. She was so damn gorgeous. She was always gorgeous, but like this, she was damn near perfect. "I should rethink what I said though. It wasn't perfectly true. This is our space. This is the space where we can drop our daily roles and find that other part of ourselves. When we walk into this room, I want you silent unless I ask a specific question. Would you like to take off your clothes or do you want to do this with the corset on? I assure you I can make it work."

"Naked works for me. I told you, Master Remy, that I have some exhibitionist in me."

"Have you ever watched me scene?" He thought he knew the answer to that, but he wanted to see if she would reply honestly. He moved to her back, reaching down to let the laces of the corset out.

"It was my hobby while I was here, Sir. I think I caught most of your scenes. I'm surprised you came back here. There are hard points on the stage you usually use."

"I wanted some intimacy this time," he replied. "I don't want a huge crowd because like Kai here, I'd like to let my freak flag fly, and there are things I like to do when I hold a sub dear that I don't on a simple scene partner."

Like fuck her silly. He didn't mind having sex in the club, but he wanted more intimacy with her. And then there was his other kink.

"Ow. Ow. Fuck you, Kai," Kori said.

"I believe my lovely wife is making those hand gestures because she wants to know if you would like us to find another spot," Kai said. "Yes, keep it up, love. The rope is doing its job nicely. Your poor foot. I could help you, you know."

"You were here first," Remy replied. "And what I'm going to do won't bother you. Now if Big Tag was here, I'd gag him." He didn't do this often, though the words flowed through his head every time he picked up a length of rope. He wanted to do it with her. He wanted to give her the words that flowed like an easy river. "You have a safe word. Will you promise me to use it if I scare you?"

"I promise, but I don't frighten easily and I've waited for this," she whispered. "For a long time."

He eased the corset off her. "I've waited forever to see your skin. To make it my canvas. I won't use paint. I'm not an artist whose strokes hang in a gallery. There is no immortality in my work. It takes this flesh and binds it."

He'd prepped the rope he would use and called the dungeon monitor, who seemed to have properly set up his scene.

He dropped the length of jute in front of her. "This is my only artistry. My one talent. To bind my *chèrie* in rope worthy of her, to hold her close so she knows each wrap of my rope is a manifestation of my affection, my need. Can you accept my gift?"

She looked up and tears were already in her eyes. She nodded slowly.

He reached down. "I don't mean to make you cry."

"Don't you dare stop. If I only get a few weeks, I want all of you. I want this part. You let me feel it all. You don't hold anything back on me. I want it all and I definitely want those words. I used to watch you and you would take your hair down. I waited for that moment because that was the moment you took control."

"I cut my hair because I had to have surgery," he explained as he began to wind the rope around her torso. "I'll grow it back out and it wasn't a huge deal. I've got a metal plate in my head from an injury."

"What?"

"Hush, this is my time. In my head, this is a lush dance. In my mind, this is art."

She went still, her obvious trust in him allowing him to find that place again.

"You think I'm hard in this place, this top space, but this is where I find peace." He worked the rope, the ties perfectly familiar, his fingers moving almost without his brain. The muscle memory took over, knowing where to go as he concentrated on her. On how the rope looked against her skin, how it would leave an indention he could touch and kiss for an hour after. "This is where I let go, allowing my body to serve yours, my mind flowing like that river, gently easing everything out to sea."

He started in on her breasts, working the rope around each sweet mound. "My rope binds you to me, reminds you that I am the one who touches you, brings you to the ultimate pleasure. My rope binds me to you, reminds me that this connection, the one that flows through each wrap and binding, comes only from this soul I wind myself around. For I am in this rope, in every tie, every inch that caresses you. This rope is the touch of my hand, the loving touch of my mouth and tongue, the offering of my body to yours."

He let the words flow as he worked his rope. He spoke of her beauty, his affection and need for her, all the while winding the rope around her body, showcasing her breasts and preparing her for more. She wanted the full experience? He could give it to her. He would let her feel it all.

Not every scene had to be hardcore. For Remy, D/s was about having a spot where he could open himself up, allow himself to be as vulnerable as the submissive he was about to suspend. He'd been looking for the right sub, the one who would relax him enough to allow him to be exactly who he was without self-consciousness or fear.

"You look perfect with my rope your only clothing, nothing between us. Do you want to fly, *ma chèrie?* Because I will take you there," he said as he tied off the last rope that would connect her to the rope he would suspend her with. He'd attached it carefully, her safety his highest concern. It was attached at two points on her "flight suit," forming a triangle that would hold her up and let her float.

"Yes. I want to fly," she said, her voice tremulous.

He pulled on the rope and she was in the air, her lovely body hanging and dependent on his craftsmanship. He pulled her up so she was roughly at the height of his chest. He could reach down and touch her, caressing her skin through the ropes. She was facing up, unable to see what he would do to her, only able to hear his voice. "My ropes leave marks, tiny indentions to prove I was here, but they will fade to memory. No, my mark will not stay on this perfect skin because I would leave no scars to mar you. But remember the feeling, remember the care when you are alone. When I am far from you, remember how I lavished you with affection, with worship."

He sighed, a blissful but bittersweet breath. He could smell her arousal and see the way she relaxed, giving over to the experience. He looked up at her, at the beautiful way her luscious cheeks pressed against the rope. She was safe and secure, and he'd done this for her. He reached up, letting his fingertips trace along her body, skimming from flesh to rope and back again, loving the shudder that went through her body.

"I have worked this rope a thousand times before, and yet this one is new. This one is fresh, and I want to hold it, too. I want the marks on *my* skin, to make them indelible so I do not ever forget this first night. This first night, one of a handful I will spend with you. One of a handful of nights, of scenes that will feed my soul for the rest of my life. Looking at my angel, flying. Not free for now, but safe and warmed and cared for in my ropes."

He finished the poem that ran through his head by going on his toes and managing to capture her lips with his. He knew some of his counterparts would tease him for the poetry that he sometimes wrote down but mostly left in his head, but those words were as much a part of him as the way he fought or how he did his job. He accepted them, used them when he needed to.

How many times over the next forty years would he form words in his brain that spoke of her? He forced the thought out of his mind. He had to live in the now when it came to her. This whole damn night before he'd taken her in here had been walking a tightrope. He'd planned on talking to Will in the locker room, but he'd missed the man and then he'd been sure Will was going to out him. Not that he was doing anything wrong. The relationship was real and the job was real, and the fact that he was involved in both didn't make either less important.

"How do you feel?" He meant the question to come out in a patient tone, but he kind of ended up growling the words her way. There was something about the words playing through his head that made him anxious.

"I feel good, Master Remy. I like suspension, but I wish your hands were on me," she whispered. "I like this, but I like being close to you more."

The words in his head started to shift from pretty poetry about emotions to something more primal, dirtier, and yet still very much how he felt. "For some subs, this is what they want. They want to sit here in suspension and float for a while. Others, well, they want things a little different."

"I want whatever gets your hands on me. Please. But nothing, I mean nothing, ever made me feel as close to you as your words. It was beautiful. I never heard you talk like that during a scene. Were you quiet about it with the others?"

Oh, she needed to understand. "I've never done that in a scene. The words run through my head, but I never shared them with a sub. And honestly, what would have come out of my mouth with other subs had nothing to do with the things you make me feel. All my life these words have run through my head, but I never felt like I had to say them until tonight."

"If you don't fuck me hard, I'm going to die because I've never wanted a man in my life the way I want you. I want the poet and the Dom and the, god, I want the dirty, filthy lover I can't get enough of. You say you've never done that before. Don't you stop now. Give me all your dirty words, too. I want them."

He let his hands find her breasts. He'd bound them tight to make sure she would feel them, be deeply aware of them. "This is the sweetest fruit there is, your feminine beauty. Never have I seen anything I wanted more. I worship here." He tweaked her breasts before moving under her. He had to shift her slightly to get those pretty nipples in his mouth, but he moved back and forth, licking and sucking them. "These buds are the softest flowers…" He stopped because his head was suddenly filled with words he couldn't speak.

I see children here.

I see life here.

I see future here.

He stepped back, desire churning inside him, but there was more. He knew what lust felt like, what pure molten sex felt like when it rolled through his body in a volcanic state. This was something more. He wanted her but more than her body. He wanted her soul, her future, every ounce of love she had to give. It wouldn't last. The love inside her would grow and multiply as she grew their children. As her body bore their future, she would love more. Her love would be endless, growing forth from their children and grandchildren and sparking beyond.

This woman had been made for him.

He couldn't tell her that. Those words were caught, strangled by his past because he couldn't give her what she deserved. All he could offer her was hard work for years, an entire community that depended on him, responsibility after responsibility.

He could love her, but he didn't deserve her.

He moved to the rope that held her up. She was too high. He'd wanted her to feel suspended, but in order to join her, he had to lower her down.

God, wasn't that a metaphor for their relationship? To have her, he had to drag her down. He had to bring her low. She deserved the world and he could only give her a dive bar in flyover country.

But he could give her this now.

He eased the rope down, lowering her to the perfect height. He could see the look on her face, trusting and relaxed, as though she knew he would give her everything she needed. He would give her what she needed tonight. She needed a Dom who was crazy for her. He would show her.

"This body is mine. Its beauty infuses me with light, makes me strong. This gift is more than I deserve, but I will give you, *mon ange*, a gift of my own." His hands went to the ties of his leathers, opening them with ease and releasing his cock. He stepped between her legs. He'd tied her thighs apart for just this moment.

His cock strained as desire pounded through his system. Somewhere in the back of his head, he knew they'd drawn a crowd, but he couldn't care about that. They'd been perfectly silent so he ignored them. He stroked his cock, getting ready to roll the condom on. "Pleasure is my gift, but more I want comfort for you. Physical comfort in the form of my cock, my ropes, the warmth of my hands on your skin. Soul comfort that comes from knowing my whole being is here in this moment with you and I would be nowhere else." He rubbed his now sheathed cock against the heat of her pussy. She was wet and ready, and he could see how her fingers curled around the rope, seeking balance. "I worry I will come back to this place, this night, this moment when we are together again and again, that I will stay caught here. It's all I can hope for—to be young and yours forever."

He stroked inside her, words failing him. All that mattered now was giving her what she needed. He thrust in and pulled back out, going slow at first so he could feel every inch of the slide of his cock against the delicate but strong muscles milking him inside her. He wanted to stay here, right in this moment. The world could end right this moment and he would be perfectly happy.

But the world didn't work that way. The moment lengthened, time moving forward, and he couldn't hold out forever. He stroked into her, moving faster and faster, finding the rhythm that sent them both over the edge. He felt the moment she came, her body tensing around his, clamping down hard and causing him to fall with her.

Pleasure hit his brain like a runaway train, making his eyes roll back as his body took over, pulsing out and thrusting in until he'd given up everything he had.

And still he had things to say to her. He put a hand on her belly, keeping them connected. "And still, after the moment is done, I would stay with you because the after with you is as sweet as the during, more meaningful than the before because we are one."

She looked down, staring at that place where his hand rested possessively on her belly. "Because we are one."

Tears rolled from her eyes, but it was all about feeling. She felt. He felt, and it was good.

"You can have the puppy," a low voice said. "You can have all the puppies."

Kai had his wife out of her suspension and wrapped around his body. He lifted her up and started out of the room, kissing her even as he headed for the privacy rooms. His hands moved over her, holding her close and making obvious his passion for her.

"Hey, what's up with the poetry stuff? Is that like spoken word Cajun version?" Adam Miles asked.

Big Tag's hand came out, smacking the back of his head. "Hush, Charlie liked it."

Charlotte was draped over her husband's lap, her head in the crook of his neck, and Big Tag was whispering something to her. Something that made her glow and cuddle close. Whatever he said made her kiss his jawline and say something back.

Serena frowned at Adam and shifted closer to Jake. "It was beautiful."

Adam turned a nice shade of red. "Sorry. I didn't get all the talky parts."

Jake grinned and settled their wife firmly on his lap. "I love it when I'm the smart one. Remy, you know every dude in the company is coming to you now to write our Valentine's cards."

Damn. It was a good thing he was leaving soon.

"Get your own poet, ladies," Lisa said. "This one is mine."

He moved back reluctantly. He was hers. For now. He had to find a way to make that time count.

Chapter Seven

"What can I get for you?" She grinned at Remy as he settled onto the barstool three nights later.

Damn that man was fine. She wondered if she would ever get used to how hot he was. Maybe if they stayed together for many, many years she would, but that wasn't going to happen. She feared she would go to her grave with him perfect in her brain.

Remy smiled, his lips curling into that half grin that made her a little breathless. "Get me a beer, *ma crevette*. How's your evening going? Is Top treating you well?"

"I love it." The people were all great. Javier Leones was the acting head chef and he ran a tight, but happy ship. She loved the family atmosphere. Every night after service they sat and ate together before cleaning up the place. No one did that in corporate America. No one cared. "I think I'm going to gain ten pounds this week though. Macon has been stress baking and I'm his go-to girl. Have you ever had bread pudding made with Krispy Kreme donuts? Because I did. I'm a little hopped up on sugar, babe."

"I can tell," he replied with a wink.

She grabbed a chilled stein and started the pour. "Did I mention how happy I am to have a job?"

"You might have a couple of times," he replied with a wink that reminded her she'd paid him back in orgasms. "I'm happy to see you happy."

She slid the stein in front of him. "Are you closing on the wharf tomorrow?"

His expression dimmed. "Yes. Uhm, it's at three tomorrow. I'll sign everything and it'll be overnighted to the firm in Louisiana that's handling the sale. It won't take too long. I'll be able to bring you to work. Don't worry about that."

Bittersweet. That was what this time would be. There were only so many days between them and it lent something primal to the time they did have. She wasn't going to hide from it. She wasn't going to pretend it wouldn't happen. She would be grateful that she'd had this time where this amazing man had wanted her, had taken such sweet care of her. "I wasn't worried. I want to make sure you don't miss your meeting though. I understand how much making everything legal means to you. I don't want you to be late. Linc can come and get me."

A single brow rose over Remy's eyes. "Linc? Why would he pick you up?"

Linc walked up, winking her way. He moved behind the bar. He was six foot four inches of pure ex-Special Forces, heavily accented with the PTSD crazy. Linc had light brown hair and broad shoulders and could probably be considered gorgeous, but now she compared everyone to Remy and no one could match. "I'll be happy to pick Lisa up. I will absolutely make sure she gets to work on time."

Remy was suddenly sitting up straighter than he had before.

But she had to think about him. Linc could get her to work one day this week. "He's got a very important meeting tomorrow and I've got the dinner shift, but I can come in early if I need to. Do you mind?"

Linc put a hand on her shoulder. "Not a problem. I'm thrilled to have you here. I've missed you."

"From training class," Remy said, proving he hadn't forgotten a thing she'd said. After their scene, he hadn't mentioned it again.

That scene. God, she couldn't get her head off it. Never in her life had she felt as connected to another human being than she had when Remy had wrapped her up and spoken those sweet words to her. She'd been his art, his words a natural result of what their bodies felt. They'd been so peaceful afterward, she'd kind of forgotten he'd been jealous.

Linc pulled out the cocktail shaker as Tiffany, one of the waitresses, dropped off an order. "Training class. Sweet days, my man. I will tell you that there was never a better day than when I got paired up with Lisa. You know what it's like. You're standing there feeling awkward in those leathers, praying you don't get the chick with the crazy eyes. And then whoop, there crazy eyes is and she turns out to be pretty awesome."

She slapped at his arm. "I do not have crazy eyes."

Linc had been the best time. They'd made an agreement that first day that they were going to have fun during their training time and go their separate ways. Not once had she regretted that. Certainly not now. He was funny and sweet and not for her. They'd had fun in bed, figuring out what they liked and what they didn't as a top and a bottom, but that had been the extent of their chemistry.

When she thought about it, it was a bit like what she'd done with Remy. She'd known she and Linc would end, but she'd been okay with it. Not once had she cried over him. She didn't dream at night that he somehow changed his mind and took her with him when their time was up. They'd shaken hands at the end of training class. Oh, they'd also joked that if they were still without permanent partners in five years, they would take each other back, but that was all a joke. Her backup Dom.

"Yeah, Lisa and I got paired up that first night and we kind of clicked. You know how it is when you meet someone you fit with. Nice and easy. No drama," Linc replied. "It's so weird because I hadn't realized how much I missed her until she walked in that door. It's really great to have her here, you know."

"I know how much I like having her in my life," Remy said, his voice careful. "And that's why I'll make sure she gets to work on time. I can manage it, but thanks for offering to watch out for her."

Linc nodded. "No problem. I'll have plenty of chances to help out when you're gone. I hear you're heading back to Louisiana soon. The good news is, you won't have to worry about Lisa because she'll have a family here who will be happy to look after her."

She watched as Remy's hand closed around his beer and she prayed he didn't break the glass, but what exactly was she supposed to say? He *was* leaving. It made her heart ache, but he hadn't mentioned some miraculous change of plans. He was leaving her behind and she would need a ride. The train stop was a couple of blocks away and she worked late some nights. She wasn't going to start up with Linc again, but she would take a ride from him if he didn't mind.

Remy's jaw went tight and she was almost sure he was going to start an argument when something caught his eye. He turned slightly and looked over at the lobby. "There she is."

Lisa looked up and her day took a deep dive. She wasn't sure who the woman was, though she looked vaguely familiar. Blonde hair and perfect makeup, the woman was tall and model skinny, a designer briefcase in her hand and sky-high heels on her feet.

But the man she was with, oh, Lisa knew who he was. Matthew Scarsdale, federal prosecutor. He was in his late forties and was every bit as labeled up as his female counterpart. Lisa recognized a designer suit when she saw one. Bridget forced Will into Brooks Brothers and Armani whenever she could. Mitch had his Tom Ford suits fitted to his big body.

Remy Guidry would probably never wear a suit and she was perfectly fine with that. He looked better in a T-shirt and jeans, and the brilliant part was if he didn't like to dress up, she didn't have to. It was exhausting and she liked shorts and tank tops way more. That was what she needed. A job that required shorts and sneakers and let her sleep in late.

She forced herself to stay at the bar when what she really wanted to do was walk away. Why the hell was her worst nightmare here? Okay, maybe her worst nightmare was that assassin dude, but anything that reminded her of the ax hanging over her head was bad.

"You, little brunette girl who needs mascara, I want a martini and I want it properly prepared. Do you understand what that means?" the super-aggressive woman asked as she set her briefcase on the bar.

Oh, like she'd never dealt with overly aggressive power women before. "Yep. It means you pretty much want me to put some ice in a cocktail shaker, wave a closed bottle of vermouth over the cocktail shaker, pour out the ice, and fill a martini glass with vodka and we'll call it a martini. I'm betting no olives, but you do know a twist of lemon is pretty and contains no calories."

The other woman practically purred as she looked Lisa over. "I take back the mascara part. The natural look is good on you, honey. And yes to everything. And I do mean everything."

"Mine, Maia," Remy growled.

Oh, shit. The infamous Maia Brighton. That had to be who she was dealing with. She'd heard the tales of the groping DA. Maia Brighton was on a high-powered career path, had turned sexual harassment into a fine art, and she didn't discriminate.

A lot of people talked about her time at Sanctum.

"I think that chick is hitting on you," Linc whispered as she started the martini.

"I think she hits on everyone." Lisa looked at Matthew. "Is there something I can get for you, Mr. Scarsdale? I take it this isn't a date."

Maia laughed. "Oh, honey, Matty here has a major stick up his ass, and not in a kinky way. In a weird Mommy-didn't-love-me way. He's married but I'm fairly certain she's a cover for his illicit love for a blowup doll who might or might not be male."

"Excuse me?" Scarsdale said, his face going a florid red. The man might have been attractive if he hadn't had that perpetually pinched look on his face.

Maia waved him off. "Don't worry, hon. The psych eval is free." She winked at Lincoln. "And your friend is right. I hit on everyone. Well, everyone I find attractive. This is my favorite restaurant because I swear Sean Taggart doesn't hire unattractive men."

"I thought Taggart made it a habit of hiring ex-soldiers," Scarsdale said, looking around the place with something like distaste. "The crippled kind. Though I suppose that one doesn't look too bad."

He was talking about Linc, who smiled a feral expression that held absolutely no humor. "Oh, don't let the fact that I'm not scarred fool you. I lose my shit from time to time, and when I'm in the bad place in my head, I like to take it out on whoever happens to be nearby. I won't mean to kill you. I promise I'll feel bad about it later."

Maia reached out and put a hand on Linc's. "Don't mind him. He's an asshole and you know you and your team are the absolute sexiest group of men I've ever seen. Those scars are manly as fuck. Too bad you're all getting married. I heard we lost the sommelier to the pretty blonde."

Okay, Maia wasn't all bad. She'd managed to put a smile back on Linc's face.

"It was a lovely wedding," Linc said.

"Can I steal your pretty partner for a moment?" Maia asked. "I promised Big Tag I would help move things along for this case the feds fucked up. You know how the feds fuck up, don't you, honey?"

"I do indeed," Linc replied. "We're dead tonight anyway. I'll be in the back doing inventory. Lisa, call me if anyone shows up."

He strode off and Maia turned on Scarsdale. "The next time you're rude to one of these men, I'll let them have you."

"You're one to talk about rude," Scarsdale shot back.

"I know when to be rude and when to show some damn respect," she replied. "The men and women who work here gave more than you can imagine so you and I can live our posh lives. Even that one right there who is ready to take me apart because I hit on his precious." She turned to Remy. "Open your mind a little, Guidry. Three-ways can be fun."

"My mind is perfectly happy with the kink I already got. One woman is all this poor country boy can handle." But he was smiling, too. "And I thank you for setting this up. He won't return my calls."

Maia took the drink from Lisa. "Someone like this, you have to walk in, grab 'em by the balls, and lead the way." She took a sip and sighed. "Yes, that's a martini. Do you have any idea how hard it is to get a martini this good?"

It wasn't. It was just vodka with a twist, but hey, whatever got her through a day.

Remy had planned this? Remy had been calling about her case and he hadn't once mentioned it?

"I want to know where you are on the Vallon case." Remy got straight to the point.

Scarsdale huffed, scowling Maia's way. "I guess you don't want to talk about that job. This was some kind of setup?"

Maia shrugged. "I'm perfectly happy where I am. My office actually tries to prosecute criminals. Now answer the question or you'll be the one looking for a job. Don't think I don't have some power with your office. I assure you I have shit on some of your bosses that would make you blush, Matty. Now spill. Are you going to re-file the case or not?"

Scarsdale sank onto his barstool. "I don't know. If it's up to me, absolutely not. It's a losing case because the local cops fucked up."

"I'm surprised because DPD is usually quite careful," Maia said, suspicion plain in her eyes.

"Not this time," Scarsdale replied. "Apparently the officer got a call from her babysitter about a break-in at her home. She panicked and raced there. There was a burglary of her house that night and her young daughter was injured, though it was minor. The books were left on the front seat of her squad car, and there's proof that she didn't lock the vehicle."

"She was terrified for her child," Lisa pointed out. If it had been one of her nephews, she would have flipped out, too. "You can't expect her to ignore that."

Scarsdale shrugged, still holding his briefcase like he expected to need it as a shield any moment. "This is why I don't particularly think women should be cops. A man would have done his duty. Anyway, the defense argued that leaving the books in the open at another crime scene broke the chain of custody. And something was definitely done to those books. Several pages were missing."

"That's interesting," Remy said, his fingers drumming along the bar.

She supposed she couldn't expect him to not look into the case. He was a bodyguard by trade, but he'd done some PI work as well. He worked for a security and investigation firm. If he hadn't shown some concern about what was going on with her case, she would know he was truly only interested in sex. The fact that he was looking into it, spending time on her when she couldn't pay him a dime had to mean something, right?

Because she was a stupid girl and she was already wondering why they had to have an expiration date. Louisiana wasn't that far away, after all. It was about eight hours in a car, and by plane? Well, by plane there was only an hour between New Orleans and Dallas.

She'd started to think a lot about where Remy's family lived.

"So you can see why I don't think it's a good idea to retry the case," Scarsdale said.

"I'm interested in who broke into the officer's house," Remy said quietly.

"You would have to ask DPD," Scarsdale replied. "That's not in my purview."

"Oh, I think I will ask some questions." Remy sat back. "So Vallon's back in business?"

"We still have his accounts frozen." The prosecutor adjusted his glasses. "But we can only keep them for another few days. We have to make a decision."

"It sounds like you've already made your decision." Maia downed the last of her martini and gestured for another.

"There's some argument in the office. My second believes that the girl here would make a good witness. Apparently she remembers numbers quite well," Scarsdale said. "One of the pages that ended up missing had a series of numbers that might or might not have been accounts."

"Oh, they were accounts." Lisa was happy to have something to do with her hands. "I'm pretty sure they were Cayman accounts. I could write them down for you."

Scarsdale looked slightly ill. He stepped back from the bar. "No. It wouldn't help anything at all. No one is going to believe some waitress can remember numbers like that."

"She's an accountant," Remy shot back. "With a master's degree. I think she can handle a few numbers."

Scarsdale stood up, his shoulders straightening. "Well, I think it's a bust and law enforcement moved too quickly, and all on the word of a twenty-nine-year-old working on her first big job. If we lose this case, it makes my whole office look soft. I'm not willing to risk that. Now, if you have any other questions, I hope you'll refer them to my admin."

Remy stood up, too, getting in Scarsdale's way. "And what about her? What about Lisa? She's the only one who can corroborate those books. Why wouldn't Vallon come after her?"

"Vallon isn't violent," Scarsdale replied.

"What about the men he launders money for?" Remy wasn't letting this go. He sounded a lot like her brother in that moment.

Scarsdale sighed like the whole thing bored him. "I don't know who they are. If I did, I would be able to indict them."

"But you suspect," Remy shot back.

The lawyer shook his head. "Suspicions don't form a case. I can't put my reputation on the line when all I've got is one woman's memory as my witness."

"She's the only witness," Remy pointed out. "Give me one good reason they don't come after her."

A long sigh went through Scarsdale. "Why would they come after her if we're not going to prosecute?"

"Because they know damn well someone with more balls could get your job the minute politics change, and then they're fucked. I would take her out if I had skin in the game." Maia shook her head Lisa's way. "Which would be a shame because you're the only one who knows how to make a real martini. But I would totally have you offed."

"I understand." She passed Maia the second martini.

"The police aren't going to give her protection on a case that isn't being prosecuted," Scarsdale said.

"So what you're basically saying is you don't care." There was a dangerous tone to Remy's words.

"I'm fine, Mr. Scarsdale." She needed to bring down the threat level. She'd known for weeks now that the federal prosecutors didn't care about what happened to her. And no one had come after her. "Remy, why don't you finish your beer? We can talk about this later, maybe after work."

Scarsdale moved around him, giving Remy a wide berth. "Besides, it's not forever. If we don't prosecute, and we won't, the federal statute of limitations runs out in five years. Why would they risk adding murder to their list of crimes until we decide to prosecute? In five years, it won't matter what she remembers. Look, if you think someone is watching you, get me some proof and I'll go to the cops with you, but until then, there's nothing I can do. I have other cases, more important cases to deal with."

He strode away from the bar.

"Asshole," Maia said. "But he's right about providing her with a safe house. They don't have the resources for the people they actually owe protection to, much less for a witness on a trial they aren't pursuing. Look, I would have little Miss Math write down those numbers and hand them over to me, but they're meaningless without her testimony. I didn't see the numbers. You didn't see the numbers. She's the only one who can tie those numbers in her head to that accounting book."

Remy watched Scarsdale as he disappeared through the front door, every line of his body tense. "Yeah, I get that. I find it an interesting coincidence that the cop's house got hit at the precise time she should have been taking the books into evidence."

"You should look into that." Maia downed her second martini and stood up. "Tell Taggart I'll investigate a little on my end. I like to meddle. Especially with feds. It's a fun hobby, but he knows anything I dig up comes with a price," she said sweetly. "I'm going to need access to Sanctum again and he needs some Doms who aren't all married and ethical and shit. There's nothing worse than being in a candy store and finding out all the sweets belong to someone else. Tell him to import some from The Club if he can't find them himself. You know the only person I'm actually afraid of in this world is Julian Lodge, so I'm left with Sanctum. Taggart is a teddy bear comparatively." She pulled out a fifty and slid it Lisa's way. "I hear this one is leaving soon. Sacrificing himself to the wilds of the bayou or something. If you decide to walk on the alternative side, give me a call, sweetie."

"How about *you* call *me* when you know something?" Remy said, his voice dark. "She's my responsibility. Taggart's already offered you another year-long membership if you bring us something we can use. I'm your contact. I'm the one who'll decide if you've earned it."

Jeez, he sounded super serious. When the dude wanted to intimidate, he could do one hell of a job of it.

Maia winked up at him. "Oh, I'll earn it. And watch out for Scarsdale. I don't trust him. Those uptight ones are always hiding something. Have fun, kiddos."

She floated away on a cloud of vodka and self-confidence.

Lisa had to wonder what it would be like to have been born with absolutely no fucks to give. That was what it was like to be Maia Brighton.

"Well, that was fun." She glanced at the clock. Almost time to close, but it looked like there was still someone in the dining room.

"There was nothing fun about that," Remy shot back, his eyes still on the door as though trying to see where the two lawyers had gone.

"Yeah, that was sarcasm, babe."

His eyes came back to her. "Can the sarcasm when it comes to this. You need to start taking this seriously. It's apparent to me that you're not thinking straight when it comes to the situation you're in."

She was surprised at how grave he sounded. He was normally very laid back. "Why are you bringing this up? I understand that you are invested in the top thing, but I have to wonder about this. You leave soon. There's no reason for you to get involved in this part of my life when you're about to walk out of it."

"No reason? I care about you. And I won't leave until I'm sure you're safe," he replied.

Somehow she doubted that. "So you're going to put your plans on hold for the next five years or so? That's how long they have until the statute runs out. You planning on hanging out until then?"

She halfway wanted him to say yes. More than halfway.

"I intend to solve the problem before then," Remy replied, his irritation obvious. "But I can't do that if you don't work with me."

Was he irritated with her or with the situation he found himself in? He needed to go home and his conscience wouldn't let him. She hated the thought of him leaving, but she wasn't going to let him resent her. "There's no problem. You heard Scarsdale. He's not re-trying the case and I don't think he's leaving the federal prosecutor's office any time soon, so everyone is cool. No one wants to take on a case they don't think they can win. Vallon can go back to scamming everyone around him. I can ease into underemployment and you can go home."

"It's that simple, huh?" Remy asked.

"Yes, it's that simple," she replied, her heart aching. "You get your wharf tomorrow and we say good-bye. That's what we agreed on. I'm not your responsibility. We were having fun, that's all."

It was a lot more than fun. She was in love with him, but then she'd always known that would happen if she spent more than five minutes with the man. It had been foolish to think because she told herself she could handle a short-term relationship with him that she could actually do it without heartache. He was everything to her. There wasn't a part of him she didn't adore. Even his stubborn insistence on fixing this problem for her. It was all a part of the lovely, caring, passionate man he was inside.

Tiffany Lowe walked up, her gaze cautious as she approached the side of the bar. "Hey, I need another whiskey sour. I told my only table that it was last call. We close in ten minutes. He's almost done with dinner and he's the last table left. I think we'll be able to lock up on time."

That sounded good because this might not be a conversation she wanted to have with Remy in her place of business. She remembered table nine had wanted Jack Daniels in his whiskey sour and poured it out, all the while sensing Remy watching her with his impatient eyes. His fingers tapped along the bar as she handed Tiffany the glass and registered the drink in the system.

Tiffany gave her an encouraging smile as she walked away.

"So you're having a good time?" Remy simply picked the argument up again as if they hadn't been interrupted at all. "You call losing your job and potentially being the target of a mob hit fun?"

"No, I didn't say that," she replied, wondering what had him so testy tonight. "I said being with you has been fun, but I certainly don't expect you to change your plans in order for you to solve a mystery. I'm a big girl and I can handle myself."

He shook his head as if he couldn't quite believe what she'd said. "You can handle the mob? Will you take two minutes to listen to yourself? Do you have any idea how stupid you sound right now?"

"I'm stupid because I don't agree with you?" She was rapidly coming to the point where she wouldn't care that they were hashing things out in public. Why was he talking to her like this? She'd done nothing to deserve it. She'd held up every single end of her bargain.

"I didn't say that."

"Then maybe you need to say something, Remy, because I don't understand what's going on here. I don't understand why my temporary lover is messing around with something that's far better left alone. It's been weeks. I'm fine. I have a job now. No one's going after Vallon except you. You're the one who's going to get me in trouble."

He stared at her for a moment. "I can't figure out if you're honestly this naïve or if you simply don't care."

She resented the implications on both sides. "I do care, but what am I supposed to do if the federal prosecutor won't do it? What do you want, Remy? You want me to play the vigilante and go to the press with the account numbers I remember? Maia told you they don't mean much if no one believes I can remember them. They're to Cayman accounts. They're only meaningful to the people who own the accounts or if I can corroborate them with the book. Good luck with that. And I'm not naïve. I know what's going on and I also know there's not much I can do. I think you're paranoid. It is far smarter for whoever Vallon was working with to sit still and be patient. If someone shoots me, the cops will notice."

"And if the cops are in on it?" Remy asked.

Now he sounded like Bridget. She set her towel down and lowered her voice because it looked like their last customer of the night was heading to the bathroom. He passed behind Remy, whose back was to him. It was likely a good thing because Remy had a hard look in his eyes that might scare off anyone who didn't know him.

"The cops aren't in on it," she said, her voice low as the man in the suit turned toward the bathrooms. "If anything I feel bad for the cop who broke chain of custody. I would have, too, if it had been my kid. I don't blame anyone. It happened and sometimes the bad guys get away with it. That's it. You're the one who's trying to kick a hornet's nest but I'm the one who'll get stung, Remy. Have you thought about that at all?"

"Have you thought at all about the fact that I'm doing this because I don't want you to get stung? Someone has to. The feds are being useless." He ran a frustrated hand over his head. "Just trust me. And I meant what I said. I'm not leaving until I know you're safe."

She let the words sit between them because they'd been so flavored with anger. Bitterness, like he resented being here a moment more than he absolutely had to.

Maybe the last few days hadn't meant the same to him. Still, she could come up with one plan. "All right. I'll go to Louisiana with you."

His head came up. "What?"

It made sense. "You don't feel like you can leave here until I'm safe. I might not be safe for a long time. I don't know what will make you feel like I'm safe. I can only imagine it would be putting Vallon and his cronies behind bars. That could take a long time. You can't take over your family business from here, and it sounds like someone needs to. Hell, I can even help you with it if you need someone to make sure the books are in order. And who would come looking for me in Louisiana? Therefore the logical solution to our problem is that I go with you to Louisiana."

She said it all reasonable like, but inside her heart was pounding because damn but it solved the problem she had with him leaving her behind. It solved the problem of her broken heart.

The look on his face told her that wasn't a solution at all and that her heart was definitely getting broken, and sooner than she'd expected. A look of horror came over his face and he pushed off the bar. "Absolutely not."

She stared at him for a moment because there were no words. Only a few days before he'd tied her up and let her fly, his careful hands on her, telling her all the while how he wanted to stay with her. That night had made her think maybe he was too scared to ask her to come with him. She was dispossessed of that notion now. It had been stupid to think Remy would be scared. He was a man who knew what he wanted.

"I'm not taking you with me," he said carefully.

Well, she had that answer at least. Wow, that hurt. She'd even known what he was likely to say and it still felt like someone had kicked her in the gut. She wasn't going to cry in front of him. "Okay. Look, I've got to close up. It could still be an hour or two. Someone can give me a ride home. You don't have to sit here wasting time."

"Linc? You going to ask him to give you a ride home? Is he the reason you suddenly want me to go home so badly? You want to see if it can be good with your old training partner?"

"That's not fair."

"None of this is fair, *chèrie*. That's what I'm trying to explain to you."

"I asked you to take me with you," she shot back. "So I don't get the jealousy thing. Look, I'm not having this argument with you here. I made my play. It didn't work. I think this is more serious for me than it is for you."

He stood in the middle of the bar, his hands on his hips. "I didn't lie to you. I didn't tell you I would take you with me."

God, she needed to get out of here. She didn't want to be the chick who cried her eyes out her first week in. It looked like she would need this job quite badly. "No, you didn't, and that's good. It's my fault. I got in too deep, but it's time to stop. You said you didn't want to hurt me. We're getting to the point that it's going to hurt me and quite badly. So let's try to end this as friends. That's what we promised, right?"

A long huff came from his sensual mouth. "We don't have to end anything at all right now. I think that's what I've told you all damn night. I'm not going anywhere."

Why was he being obtuse? "I'm in love with you. Can you say the same?"

He was perfectly silent, but she watched his skin flush, saw how tight his body had gone.

There was her answer. She took off her apron. "Go home, Remy, and I'll do the same. I wrecked it. We had a good thing going for a week. I know that. Blame me. But we end here because I can't keep you. You'll end up hating me if you stay, so go and be happy."

He would find someone. Hell, maybe there was already a woman in Louisiana. Maybe that was one of the reasons he was desperate to go home. An old flame he'd never gotten over? It didn't matter. All that mattered was he didn't love her. She wasn't his one.

"Lisa, we're not done talking about this and I'm not going anywhere," he swore.

She shook her head. "I have to start closing."

She hurried through the small hallway that led to the back of the building. To her left there was another hall and the men's and women's rooms. Past that was the kitchen where the cooks would be cleaning their stations and getting ready to close down for another night. She walked straight ahead to where the offices were. Sean Taggart had the largest of the three, but Linc and Sebastian shared one. It was where they typed in inventory reports and ordered product and met with vendors.

It was a nice office. Maybe she needed to change her dreams. She'd thought of conquering the business world, but she felt happier in a place like this.

It might be the one blessing to come out of this whole debacle.

Lisa took a deep breath and hoped she didn't look like a woman who'd just had her heart plucked from her body and casually tossed away.

She couldn't get into Remy's truck. She couldn't slide in beside him and pretend like they were normal, like she didn't know what she knew. She wasn't sure why he was holding the line about not leaving until she was safe, but he could be stubborn. It would be ridiculous for him to put his life on hold for a woman he didn't love.

"Linc, I..." She started to ask him for a ride home as she opened the door and then stopped because Linc was on the floor, his big body at an odd angle and...oh god...that was blood. He was bleeding. He was on the floor and bleeding.

What the hell? She started to get to the floor to help him up.

"Hush, Ms. Daley," an accented voice said from behind her as a gloved hand covered her mouth. A strong arm wound around her waist, keeping her upright. "We're going on a little trip, you and I. Your friend is alive, but he doesn't have to stay that way. Nod if you understand me."

She went still. If she didn't, this man would kill Linc.

She nodded.

"We're going out this back door. I already have a car waiting for us and when we get where we're going, we'll have a nice chat, you and I. I don't want to hurt a lovely young lady like yourself, but you have something I need. Now nod again if you understand me and you're going to be a good girl. If not, I can knock you out, but then our talk will likely have to wait hours, and honestly I don't love it here. I want to go home. You understand, yes?"

She nodded again.

"Good girl. This will all be over soon and we can both go back to our lives." His voice was deep and it was clear from the thick accent he wasn't from Texas. He was calm. She didn't feel any panic from him, as though this was a normal part of his day. Kidnap the bartender. Check. Brush teeth. Check.

He started to walk her out of the office.

There was only a second or two that she was visible from the hallway, and then it was smooth sailing to the back. They were going out one of two entrances to the back of the building. Sean had recently put in this way for management to get into the offices without having to open the kitchen or the front. There was a small private lot he'd bought for parking.

It sucked that most of them took the bus or train because they lived close. As it was late, only Linc's Jeep was sitting out in the small lot. And a nondescript sedan.

Damn, but they needed to tow people around here.

"I'm going to take my hand from your mouth now. If you scream, I'll have to put you under." He kept one hand around her waist. She stayed quiet for the moment. Closing time in the kitchen was always noisy. They would turn the music up and the sounds of pots and pans clanging would fill the air.

She wouldn't shout if she thought no one would hear her. Not until she absolutely had to.

There was a beep and then the trunk to the sedan opened.

Her feet hit the cement and she realized what he was about to do. She dug her heels in. "No. No. Not the trunk."

Not a dark cramped space she couldn't get out of. No. Panic welled inside her and she could feel a scream threatening.

She heard someone shout. Maybe it was her. The sound curdled her blood and she was twelve years old again, being forced into the darkness. She couldn't feel the concrete anymore. She was barefoot and the peeling linoleum of her "father's" house poked at her skin. She'd tried so hard, fought so long, and she'd still gotten swallowed up. She couldn't go in that room.

"*Merda!*" The man shoved her hard and she hit her head on the way in.

Lisa kicked out, not thinking about anything but staying in the light. She had to stay in the light. There were things in the dark, things that hissed and struck. Things that she had nightmares about, but they were real. The screaming wouldn't stop and her knuckles hit metal as the trunk slammed shut.

She was alone in the dark again and she felt the moment her mind cracked and the nightmare began again.

Chapter Eight

Remy watched her walk away and felt something inside him break.

What the fuck had happened? One minute everything had been fine and the next she'd been telling him… Fuck, she'd said she loved him and wanted to go home with him.

He'd frozen. The idea of Lisa, sweet, beautiful, highly educated Lisa, in his backwater hometown had poleaxed him. She needed a man who could give her a big house and a reliable car. He would put everything he made into his business for years, potentially for the rest of his life. His mom-mom hadn't had a cushy life with fancy clothes. She'd worked every day of her life. He could still remember how her hands had been rough from labor, how some of his New Orleans relatives had looked at her with distaste and offered to get her a manicure.

Had she been unhappy? He couldn't remember a time when she wasn't smiling except the day his pop-pop had died. Then she'd wailed her mourning to the world. She'd been unashamed. She'd told him later that she hadn't hidden her love for her husband. She wouldn't hide her grief, and yet six months later she would talk to him like he was standing there with her.

A sudden memory hit him as clean and clear as the day it had happened. He'd stood in the room where his mom-mom had been lying in her bed, dying of cancer. He'd held her hand as the hospice nurse had given her pain medications and the light overhead had flickered and flared.

And he'd known. She passed an hour later, his hand in hers, but Remy had felt something infinitely warm cross through him and he'd known what it was. His pop-pop had come to take her home one last time.

What if he could offer Lisa that? What if all this shit about giving her a cushy life meant nothing if what he could give her was a life where he loved her with everything he had? Until the end and beyond. A life where he promised to come for her. To take her home. Forever.

Was he capable of that?

He didn't know and he hated feeling this...stupid. He didn't know what he wanted. He wanted to be different. He wanted the fucking world to be different. She'd worked hard to drag herself out of poverty. How could he drag her back into it?

How could he take her home with him where he was responsible for everyone? Seraphina would need someone to watch over her. Zep...god, he didn't like to think about Zep. Zep needed round-the-clock watching. Hell, it wasn't like his momma was a saint. She could get into some kooky situations. Lisa was used to her siblings being high-powered and helpful. Being the head of his family wasn't an easy task, and then there was the fact that he knew damn well the minute he walked back into town, they would want him to take charge.

What could he do with a woman like Lisa by his side?

He shoved the thought away because he wasn't taking her home with him. She would take one look at the wharf and run the other way.

He sucked down the last of his beer. What a fucking day. He'd spent the whole of it signing paperwork for his closing tomorrow. So much debt. So much hanging over his head and she wouldn't even acknowledge she was in trouble. She sat there like it was no big deal.

What the hell was he going to do? The minute he signed the papers, Jean-Claude would hand over the keys and there would be no boss at the wharf. But he couldn't leave Dallas until he was certain Lisa was safe.

He pulled his phone out and made a few quick notes. The only way out of this problem was to solve the case himself. Something was wrong with Vallon and the way the prosecutor's office had handled his trial. He needed to talk to the cop who'd broken chain of custody and try to find out what happened that night. He could get the internal report from one of his buddies on DPD. That was where he needed to start.

And Vallon himself. He'd spent the last couple of days going over the thorough dossier Hutch had put together on Jimmy Vallon, including a lot of the reporting around the trial. One of the things that he'd been surprised by had been Vallon's complete and utter calm. Even the arresting cops had talked about how cool the man had been. It ran counter to how he was in his normal life. He was known for being a bit paranoid, accusing close associates of coming after him.

And yet he'd been perfectly quiet those months he'd been held without bail. His only words when the case had been thrown out had been to thank the judge for his wisdom.

Not the normal words of a mobster, but he couldn't exactly take Vallon's attitude to the cops.

His cell trilled and he immediately picked it up because it was Simon Weston. "This is Guidry."

"Hello, Remy. I've been monitoring the city-wide search for our Italian friend. He's excellent at keeping his head down, but I believe CCTV caught him at a red light two blocks away from Top exactly forty-five minutes ago. I'm going to pull everything I have around the restaurant, but the city is upgrading the streetlights around downtown and we've had some problems with connectivity as they bring the new system online."

Remy looked around. The dining room was perfectly quiet. "Tiffany? Did the last customer leave?"

She'd mentioned she had one customer left. He hadn't paid much attention because his whole focus had been on the fight with Lisa.

Tiffany glanced down and reached toward the table. "He left me a hundred-dollar bill. Damn, he's a good tipper. I thought he'd gone to the bathroom, but I guess he was done. I knew it was my lucky night when I heard that accent. Now I can spend way too much on a bottle of Riesling Sebastian wants for his birthday."

Remy stopped. "Accent?"

Tiffany nodded. "Oh, yeah. Italian. I could listen to him all night. Don't tell Sebastian though. He gets jelly."

Remy wasn't sure why the sommelier would want to do that, but he didn't care. "Tiffany, get into the kitchen."

Her eyes widened and he could see she was about to question him. He didn't have time for that.

"Now!" he shouted. "Tell the chefs to put the place in lockdown, and I'm going to need them to clear every single room."

Tiffany nodded and took off for the kitchen.

"Si, he's here and I have to expect that he's after Lisa. I need backup and I need you to get those cameras online in case he's taken her." That wasn't the likeliest scenario. The likeliest scenario was that the assassin would find Lisa and quietly put her down. Remy was probably looking for a body.

Her body. The one that had given him pleasure and comfort, her arms holding him close. The one that housed her soul and kept her here on earth with him.

"I'm on it," the Englishman assured him. "And Jesse and Michael and I are on the way. Chelsea is taking over the tech side. Hang on. I'm getting in the car now. Our ETA is seven minutes."

"Understood." He shoved the phone in his pocket. Seven minutes would be far too long if Biondo was as good as he was supposed to be. Remy exchanged the phone for his gun, pulling the Colt out and starting for the back of the building.

"Where do you want us?" Javier Leones showed up with Macon and Sebastian and Javi's new wife, Juliana. All four of the ex-soldiers had guns in hand and looked ready to deal with the situation. "Tiffany and Ally are in cold storage with Calvin watching over them. He's solid. He'll secure the kitchen and take care of the women."

The women who weren't ex-soldiers.

"Jules, secure the front of house," Remy ordered. "I need Sebastian to clear the bathrooms. I'm going out back. I haven't seen Linc and I believe our friend was after Lisa Daley. Consider this man armed and highly dangerous. He's a known assassin."

"This is the best job ever." Jules winked her husband's way. "Stay safe, babe."

Javi took Remy's six. "If he wants to get her out quietly and he's cased the place, he'll take her out the office side. There's a small parking lot. If it's not full, we don't complain about who parks there."

There was a terrible knot in Remy's gut, but he had to ignore it. God, if his last words to her had been to reject her love…he had no idea how he would live with himself. That couldn't be the last thing he said to her. He needed to see her, hold her.

Macon nodded quietly and moved down the hall to start clearing the offices. He stopped at the first door. "We're going to need a bus. Shit. Linc's down. He's breathing but he's not conscious."

That was when he heard the scream.

It was a sound that went straight to his soul. Lisa. Lisa was screaming.

He heard Javier say something, but the words didn't register. He was running down the hallway, the only thought in his head to get to her, to save her. She was screaming for him to save her and he couldn't let her down.

His heart pounded in his chest as he slammed through the door.

Where was she?

The world seemed to slow as he stopped and took in the area around him.

She screamed again and then there was the sound of something slamming shut.

Remy pivoted and ran to his left. That was when he found himself standing right in front of a tall man with icy blond hair. He wore a suit and trench coat and pointed a slender pistol Remy's way.

"Well, that didn't go the way I thought it would," the man said in a heavy Italian accent.

Lisa was in the trunk. The nondescript sedan shook with the force of how hard she was fighting. She was still screaming.

And then she went suddenly silent.

"The police are on their way," Javier said, standing beside him.

"Then it's time for me to take my leave," Biondo said. "You should get her out of the trunk as soon as possible. I released a gas that will smother her lungs in four minutes. You can follow me or save your girl."

Biondo took off running.

Remy didn't even think twice. They were in the middle of the city and despite the late hour, there were still people milling around downtown. And besides, all that mattered was Lisa. She was suffocating in the trunk. She'd gone quiet. Was it already too late?

He felt Javier starting to chase Biondo, but all Remy cared about was that car.

Pure panic flooded his system. He didn't have the keys. She was dying right fucking now and he didn't have the keys.

He wouldn't get the trunk open. He had to see if he could get in the car.

Miraculously, the doors were open. With shaking hands he found the trunk release and it popped up.

He raced around to the back and there she was, blood all over her face. Without thought to the gas, he leaned over and pulled her out.

He held her close as the sirens could be heard and prayed they would make it in time.

* * * *

"Biondo lied," Will said three hours later, closing the folder in his hand. "I got the tox reports back. There was nothing in her system. There was no trace of gas at all. She's got a minor concussion that I'll monitor overnight, but otherwise she's fine."

He was still shaking. All this time later and he couldn't stop his hands from shaking. Even after the ER nurse had come out and promised him she was awake and fine and being given all the best care, he could see her lying there still and pale, the blood on her skin a pure shock to his system.

"Remy, she's okay," Will said, putting a hand on his shoulder. "She'll spend the night here and I'll stay with her. She can go home sometime tomorrow. All in all, I'm calling this a win considering the fact that she tangled with a known assassin. Big Tag sent me the file they have on him. He's the real deal."

Will hadn't been working, but he'd been at the hospital roughly ten minutes after the ambulance had brought Lisa in. Apparently when a man is the head of neurosurgery and his sister gets taken into the ER with a head injury, someone calls and fast. He'd shown up with Bridget and their son in tow because Bridget wasn't about to be left behind. Lila, Laurel, and Mitch had been hot on their heels.

The waiting room was filled with Lisa's family and friends, and the whole staff from Top there for both her and Linc. All those people who loved her and he was going to disappoint them all because that girl was his and she was coming home with him.

"Did he hit her with something? Like he took out Linc?" The night had been such a crazy one. He'd had to talk to cops and give Big Tag a rundown on what had happened. The problem was he wasn't sure what had happened.

Why had Biondo tried to take her? Why hadn't he killed her then and there? It would have been easy to put a bullet in her brain, but he'd tried to kidnap her. Hell, the infamous assassin hadn't even taken out Linc. He'd hit the man over the head, but Linc had only a minor concussion. He was already sitting up in his hospital bed, eating popsicles and flirting outrageously with all the nurses.

"I don't think Biondo hurt her physically at all. I believe she hit her head while she was inside the trunk," Will explained. "I talked to her after we did her CT. She said Biondo told her he wanted to talk to her. She said he didn't say a thing about gas or killing her. She said he wanted to talk and then they could go on with their lives."

"Assassins lie," Remy said. It didn't make any sense. What could he want to talk about?

"Don't assassins tend to assassinate?" Will asked, altogether too reasonably.

Remy sighed and leaned against the wall. "Yes. I don't know what happened tonight, but I'm going to find out. Big Tag is already looking into it. Will, I'm sorry. I thought we were safe at Top."

"It sounds a lot like you were," Will replied. "It sounds like if you hadn't been there and you hadn't moved as quickly as you did, he would have gotten away with her."

"Damn it, Will. Why the fuck are you being reasonable? I nearly lost her. You should be punching me, fucking firing me." He would feel better if the man did. There was a restless anger in his gut that wouldn't go away.

"Remy, you did exactly what I asked you to do. Hell, you did more. You got her a job to distract her from her trouble. A job in a safe place, and then you watched over her. You saved her when the time came. It was always going to come. It's why we were willing to pay you so damn much. And beyond that, you care deeply about my sister. I can tell. This isn't merely a job for you. The EMTs talked to me."

Likely about how they'd found him crying over her body, how he'd begged them to save her. How he'd behaved like a lost child when they'd lifted her from his arms and how he wouldn't leave her until they'd taken her back for tests.

And then she'd woken up and asked that he not be allowed into her room to see her.

He'd been shut out until Will had come to find him.

"Remy, I'm sorry. I didn't realize that this is truly serious for you. I thought you decided it was the easiest way to deal with her. I didn't know you're in love with her. That changes a lot. And I'm calm because she's healthy and I do believe she's now taking this seriously. I'm trying to find a silver lining. She can't pretend nothing is wrong. Now we can sit down with her and try to deal with this. I'm not mad. I'm incredibly relieved that you were there. Now tell me why she won't see you."

He groaned. "We had a fight. She told me she wanted to come to Louisiana with me. I told her I wouldn't allow that to happen."

Will winced. "Well, that would do it."

He put both hands up. "It was stupid. I reacted in the moment."

"Why?" Will asked. "It's easy to see you care about her. Why are you insistent on ending the affair?"

"I'm not anymore," Remy assured him. "I was scared. I'm going home to save my family business. It's a piece of crap bar for the most part, but we own the wharf most of the town's shrimping and tourist industry depends on. It's hard work. It's get up at the crack of dawn and pass out at midnight because you can't keep your eyes open a second longer. She worked hard to get through school. She should be in an office, not working from dawn to midnight serving drinks and selling bait and making sure the rental boats work."

"I think Lisa was bored in the office and that a business like that could do amazingly well with a smart woman running the financial side. She's not afraid of hard work."

"And then there's my family. We're fucked up. My sister recently had a baby out of wedlock. I don't even know who the father is. My brother. My brother started drinking young, and he's well acquainted with the inside of a jail cell. My momma. I don't even know how to explain my momma."

"My mother was a hardcore drug user," Will replied quietly. "She left us alone for long periods of time because her favorite vacation spot was the state penitentiary. There are four of us and I'm fairly certain we all have different fathers. You look at us and see something that's not there. Every family struggles. No matter how shiny the image is, there is tarnish beneath. How we deal with those trials and tribulations—that's what makes us rise or fall as a family. If you love her, share your burdens with her. That's what I've learned, what my Bridget taught me. I wanted to keep her but I was too scared she wouldn't want me if she saw the real me. Silly, really. She'd always seen past my walls and then I realized I didn't need them with her. Do you honestly believe you can drive away from Lisa?"

"No." He wasn't lying to himself or anyone else anymore. "Absolutely not. I can't leave without her by my side. Seeing her like that, well, I can't leave her again. But she heard me rejecting her and now she won't talk to me. God. I can still hear her screaming. She was so afraid. Do you think she blames me for letting it happen?"

Will's jaw went tight and he was silent for a moment. "I'm going to tell you a story that I wouldn't normally share with anyone outside my family, but you need to understand. I meant what I said. I do not believe Biondo physically hurt Lisa at all tonight. He scared her, but he didn't harm her bodily. Lisa's injuries tonight were self-inflicted."

"What?"

"Lisa has problems with claustrophobia, specifically when dealing with being locked in with no way out and darkness. She can handle a tight elevator. She can be in a small room as long as she knows she can get out."

"What the hell happened to her?" That scream. It had been beyond calling out for someone to save her. That scream had been from her soul, a desperate, hollow cry.

"I explained about our mom. There was a distant relation who lived in the same trailer park we did. A cousin of our mom's. She would sign the paperwork, agree to be our guardian on paper for the powers that be. She had no intention of actually taking care of us, but the girls and I would help out around her place and she would give us a little money and let us be during those times when Mom was in prison."

Remy couldn't imagine Lisa growing up in those weeds. She was such a gorgeous, well cared for flower. "None of your dads cared enough to take you all in?"

"Lisa's dad was the only one Mom ever acknowledged," Will replied. "He was a pastor. Not the regular kind. Not the kind who took care of his flock and fostered a family there. It's funny because I avoided church for years because of that man. Another thing Bridget helped me with. But Father Frank, as he called himself, was the guy who went to college campuses and told coeds they're going to hell."

He knew the type. They were nothing like the kindly pastors and priests from his home. "He came for Lisa?"

"I was an adult at the time, but I didn't have legal custody of my sisters. That would have required far more cash than we had. I still don't know how he found out where we lived, but he showed up with a social worker who decided Lisa needed her father. Naturally Mom had just started a six-month stint for possession. I remember how powerless I felt. I couldn't admit that I was the one taking care of them and Cousin Marie simply signed the papers and let her go. Lisa had never even spent the night away from home."

"What happened to her and is her father still alive?" Because Remy got the feeling he was going to want to kill the man.

"From what I understand it wasn't bad at first. Frank had married and the woman seemed fine, but they refused to allow Lisa to contact us. We were poor influences, according to her father." Every word out of Will's mouth was measured, as though he was forcing them out, forcing the tone he used to be calm. "Luckily we were in the same school district. She and Laurel were in the same school, so we at least had that. But then one day, Lisa stopped coming to school."

"He kept her at home because he was abusing her?"

"Not in the way you think," Will replied. "According to Lisa, he never hit her or touched her inappropriately, but his punishments could only be considered cruel. When she wasn't respectful enough, he took away things. Not things like her cell phone. He took away the light bulbs in her bedroom and her toothbrush, and shut off the water to her bathroom. He refused to wash her clothes. He locked away the soap and shampoo in the house and she was told that if she wanted them back, wanted him to provide for her as a father should, then she would be a good daughter to him."

She'd been young and vulnerable, and her father had taken all her comforts. She would have been embarrassed to have no way to stay clean. "And this asshole thought she would bow down to him?"

"He didn't know her very well," Will allowed. "The problem got worse because Lisa got good at finding ways around him. She showered at the school. She wasn't on a team, but the coaches came to believe her family was poor and had the water cut off. Lisa did not disabuse them of the notion and soon those coaches had used their own money to supply the girls' locker room with everything she and any other girls without means would need. Shampoo, deodorant, toothpaste, pads, and tampons. When her father wouldn't feed her, the actual real live pastor in town and his wife would find her on their doorstep on her way back home and give her a bowl of soup or a sandwich. Pastor Edwards called the county a dozen times, but every time child services left her there and it got worse. Until one night, Frank got angry enough that he locked her in a shed in the back of the house. It was pitch dark and she couldn't move because the place was filthy and there were tools everywhere."

"She must have been terrified."

"Oh, yes. There was also a nest of snakes in the shed. By the time he came to let her out, she'd been bitten many times. Luckily they weren't venomous, but she'd panicked and stepped on a garden hoe that cut her up pretty bad. They refused to take her to a hospital. I think his wife tried to clean her up, but the cuts got infected. We think she was there for at least three days, lying on a bed, dying of sepsis. My mom got out of jail and I have never seen her... She wasn't the best mom, but she did love us. She didn't wait for the caseworkers. She borrowed a shotgun and her cousin's beat-up Ford and she brought Lisa to the hospital and then home. I don't know what she said or did that day, but he never came around again. He died a few years later of cancer. Mom was all right for a couple of months after that. While Lisa was recovering, we were almost like a normal family. It didn't last, but I remember those months fondly."

"So when Biondo shut her in that trunk, it was like she was going into the shed all over again." His heart ached at the thought and he wished he could go back in time, step in front of that man, and save his girl all that pain.

"I can only imagine. This is why we couldn't put her in custody like that," Will said. "Even a locked door can trigger her. She can lock herself in, but she has to know she can get out. And she can't sleep in the dark."

"Yes, she can. That night-light thing of hers bugged me. I'm a total-dark sleeper. She told me she would turn it off if I would hold her. She can sleep in the dark if I'm there to hold her. Will, I'm in love with your sister. We need to talk about the payment. I can't..."

Will held up a hand. "One thing at a time and I know what you're going to say, but I think Moneybags will insist. You need it. I would rather you got it from family than a bank. We can work out terms down the line, but I want Lisa to have a steady home. She deserves it."

His pride made him want to turn it all down, but Will was right. Pride would leave them both without jobs and his town in shambles. Their town. "All right, but she won't talk to me."

"Yeah, she can be stubborn. You're going to have to insist, I'm afraid. The good news is she's being moved to a private room. Lila's with her, but I think she needs a guard on her door," Will mused. "You up for the task?"

He was. He was going to talk to her, to make her understand. "Yes, I believe I am."

* * * *

Lila looked down at her, examining the bandage around her brainpan. "You did this to yourself, you know."

"Lila!" Laurel sat in the chair to Lisa's right, sending their big sister a what-the-hell look.

Sometimes her know-it-all nurse of a sister was kind of a bitch. "Well, I was bored and there was nothing to do but bang my head against a heavy metal trunk lid. What can I say? It's a hobby."

Laurel leaned over, putting a hand on Lisa's. "You're okay now."

"I'm as okay as a traumatized chick with a mafia assassin after her can be," she qualified. Yep, an assassin. She would be in the hands of an assassin had Remy not saved her. At least that was what everyone said. She hadn't talked to him. "And I probably am out of another job. I hope I dented that asshole's trunk and they charge him for it. I'm pretty sure that was a rental. Good luck getting back that deposit, asshole."

She wanted Remy here with her, holding her hand. When she'd woken up, her head aching along with every muscle in her body, she'd been wheeling down the hallway, her brother looking down at her. All she'd wanted was Remy, but she remembered well that he didn't want her.

Absolutely not. I'm not taking you with me.

She could still see the look of distaste on his face, feel how her heart seemed to stop.

Lila frowned, letting her know she didn't appreciate the sarcasm. "I would have thought you would have gotten over that particular trauma. You would have if you'd attend therapy like I told you to."

Laurel sighed. "No one gets over that kind of trauma."

She groaned. "Can I get another nurse?"

Preferably one who didn't know all her childhood damage.

"Nope," Lila replied, picking up her chart and looking through it. "Though I'm not technically your nurse. And yes, you can get over trauma, Laurel. You simply have to work hard and be open and honest with yourself. Now, do you want to tell me why there's a sad-looking Cajun stalking the halls instead of sitting in here with you?"

"I don't want to see him."

Laurel stood, looking down at her with soft eyes. "What happened? You seemed happy the last time I saw you. And I heard about that scene at Sanctum. Oh, Charlotte hasn't stopped talking about how romantic he was. Does he really recite poetry while he ties you up?"

Lila's nose wrinkled in distaste. "There's nothing romantic about that."

Oh, it had been incredibly romantic. "He doesn't recite it. He makes it up as he goes along." She wanted to complain bitterly, to throw his hot ass under the bus that was her sister's disapproval, but she couldn't. He hadn't really done anything wrong. He simply hadn't loved her the way she loved him. "And we broke up. That's all. We knew it would happen. He has to go home."

"So go with him," Laurel said.

Lila huffed. "She's not going to some backwater Louisiana town. Don't be ridiculous. She's got an MBA. What would she do there? Besides, all of her family is here."

"But her heart is going to be there," Laurel insisted.

"Lisa is smart enough to know that her heart doesn't make the decisions," Lila shot back.

Oh, how little her eldest sister knew her. Lila was being optimistic about her intelligence. "Nope. I totally went with my heart on this one. I asked him to take me with him."

Laurel smiled. "I knew you would make the right decision."

And Laurel was obviously optimistic about everything. "He turned me down flat. Said he wouldn't take me with him."

"Smart man," Lila said under her breath. "At least one of you is thinking with your head."

Laurel ignored their sister. "He'll change his mind. He likely already has. You know the EMTs talked about how he reacted to finding you in the trunk. He cried. Men like that don't cry over women they don't love. They found him crying while he was holding you, begging you to come back. He didn't realize you weren't dying. That Italian guy told him he'd gassed you."

"Remy's a good guy." She tried to imagine that big, tough guy crying over her, but she couldn't see it. "We're friends. I know he cares about me, but he doesn't love me."

"I don't know about that." Laurel patted her hand. "Men can be strange. Sometimes they get this notion in their head that they aren't good enough for us and they should walk away."

"Oh, sweetie, they don't honestly believe that." Lila shook her head in sympathy. "That's an excuse they give to take what they want and leave. It's the same thing as the 'it's not you, it's me' excuse."

"Tell that to my husband." Laurel's eyes narrowed. "And Will. He said roughly the same crap to Bridget."

"Neither one of them…" Lila began and then sighed, one shoulder shrugging. "I just think it's different."

No, she didn't. Well, she thought it was different, but there was no "just" about it. Lila had intended to say something, but she'd stopped herself. "What's different about Remy?"

"Besides the fact that he doesn't exactly belong with the rest of us?" Lila asked.

"What does that mean?" She didn't like the implications.

Lila crossed her arms over her chest. "Come on, Lisa. You have to see it. He doesn't fit in. Can you honestly see bringing him to family dinners and taking him to church with you? Look, this family has come a long way. He's not the man I see you with. You need someone educated. Someone who fits in with your family. The man is basically a mercenary. He takes whatever jobs come his way."

She'd never realized what a snob her sister was. "He's been doing that to save money. And he protects people."

Lila nodded like Lisa had made her point clear. "People who can pay him outrageous sums of money."

"No, you don't get it both ways. He can't be bad because he doesn't have a ton of money and bad because he gets paid a lot of money. Pick one."

Lila's head shook. "I didn't say the man was poor. God knows he's not. I'm saying he's uneducated and doesn't fit into a successful family. Laurel married a Harvard-educated lawyer. I don't particularly care for what Bridget does but there's no way to deny she's successful at it. I'm dating the CEO of a company."

She exchanged a look with Laurel. They both hated Brock. When had Lila gotten snobby and rigid? What had happened to make her that way when the rest of them were laid back? Yes, they were successful, but Will didn't judge. Laurel didn't. Mitch and Bridget were super chill. Mitch constantly complained about how he hated to deal with other lawyers, much less hang out with them because they were successful.

"Remy is excellent at what he does and he's responsible." She felt the need to defend him.

Lila's eyes rolled. "Somehow I don't think sleeping with a client makes him professional."

The whole room went quiet and Lila flushed. Laurel looked over at their sister, her jaw dropping.

"What?" Lisa asked and then shook her head. "I don't care what he's done in the past. We've all done things we're not particularly proud of."

But there was something about the way Lila had flushed... How would Lila know gossip about Remy's past? And if she didn't know about his past then she must be talking about the here and now. Why would Laurel have gasped and looked shocked unless Lila had been spilling something she shouldn't have?

Of course now she could look back and see that she was really the idiot in the room. Why had her brother suddenly gotten comfortable with her staying alone the same day Remy Guidry had moved into her building? He'd stopped showing up every single day. He'd stopped pushing her to move in with one of them.

Because he'd solved his problem.

That was why Remy had been at Cherry Pies that night. He'd followed her. He'd gotten her a job where he could watch over her.

Why had he pushed it? Why had he slept with her when it was obvious he hadn't meant anything except to pass some time on his final job? Why had he taken it that far?

"I heard a rumor," Lila started.

Lisa shook her head. Now that she knew, she wanted to know all of it. "No, I get it. How much?"

Laurel frowned. "How much?"

"How much did Bridge fork over so Remy would follow me around twenty-four seven for...gosh, it's been a week already. It would likely last longer if I hadn't caught on. Like how much?"

"We only want to protect you, Lisa," Laurel said. "It wasn't a bad thing."

"It was a hundred grand," Lila replied matter of factly.

"Lila!" Laurel admonished.

Lila shrugged, her expression going perfectly stubborn. "She should know. They broke up anyway. Now she can move on to find someone more suitable. Someone who doesn't think it's fine to take money for being professional and then turn around and sleep with his client."

Put like that, it did sound bad. Achingly, heart-breakingly bad.

She'd been sure he'd wanted her. When she'd been in his arms, she'd felt like a different human being. God, she hadn't even been afraid of the dark when he was there. It was like the rest of the world melted away and he was all she needed.

Had he sat up bored while being forced to hold her at night? Had he wondered when it could all be over, and as time had gone by, he'd gotten more and more irritable? That made sense because how long did he expect he could pretend to want someone he didn't care about?

He was good. She would give him that. It had taken a whole three hours to get into her panties, and then she'd done absolutely everything he'd wanted her to do. She'd taken the job he found for her, stayed in when he wanted her to, become his perfect submissive, and all he'd had to do was tell her she was pretty and make up some bullshit poetry.

A hundred grand? They must be terrified. Although Bridget was used to throwing Scrooge McDuck sized wads of cash at all her problems these days.

There was a brief knock and then there he was. Remy stepped in, his big body filling the space, and despite the fact that she knew about his lies now, she couldn't help but sigh. He was the single most beautiful man she'd ever seen.

If only he could have loved her…

"Remy, this might not be the best time," Laurel said, a hitch in her voice.

"I need to talk to Lisa," he said, not looking at Laurel. His eyes were steady on her. "Could we have a moment alone?"

Lila stepped in front of him. "No, you may not. My sister has asked that you not be allowed into her room. We take our patients' needs seriously at this hospital. Now you can leave or I'll call security."

Lila sounded so damn sure of herself. It was funny. She was angry with Remy, but she really wanted to kill that tone in her sister's voice, too. "He can come in. Shut the door on your way out, Lila, and you don't have to come back tonight."

Her eldest sister turned, frowning her way. "Of course I do. We need to talk about what we're going to do now. You're going to have to stop being such a brat and move in to my guestroom."

"Where your boyfriend can hit on me on a daily basis? I think not." She sat back at the sound of Lila's gasp. "Well, I thought we were being all kinds of honest today. Your boyfriend is a skank and I'm not putting myself in a position where he can harass me. Now leave because I need to talk to my ex."

"Lisa," Lila began. Her skin had paled.

Laurel stepped forward. "No, you've done enough damage. We're leaving."

As she turned, Lisa saw tears in Lila's eyes. "I wasn't trying to cause damage. I was trying to save my sister from making a bad choice."

"You're being a bitch and we're going to talk about that right now," Laurel promised.

The door brushed closed and she was left alone with Remy.

"I take it I'm the bad choice she's trying to save you from?" Remy asked, his eyes on the door.

"She doesn't have to save me from you." How was it that a mere few hours before she'd been looking forward to nothing more than going home with him? She'd even started calling it their home because Remy didn't spend any time in his own apartment. He'd kind of moved in after that first night. All the better to do his job. "We broke up."

"We had a misunderstanding," he corrected.

Oh, she'd misunderstood plenty. She wondered how far he would go with the deception. "What did I misunderstand?"

"I misunderstood myself," he said. He strode over to her. "Damn it, Lisa. I was wrong. You were right. Look, we started this on the wrong foot. I said I was being open and honest with you and it was all bullshit because I wasn't honest with myself. I pushed you away all those months ago because I had this vision of who I thought you were."

"I know that. You thought I was some kind of rich, entitled person who never struggled once in her life. You kind of do that with a lot of people. You're like the opposite of my sister Lila, who assumes everyone without a college degree is a vagrant."

"I'll work on it. Maybe there is something there. I can be close minded. I was called trash my whole life by anyone who didn't understand where I came from. I expect it from women. All my life I was the guy you screwed, not the one you married. Hell, the one I did marry divorced me because she said she could do better."

She knew he was divorced, but this was the first time he'd talked about it. "So you thought it would be fun to get into the rich chick's panties and turn it all around on her?"

"What? No. That's why I was afraid of you," he said. "I now know that there's something I'm way more afraid of and that's losing you. Come home with me, *ma crevette*. I don't think it will be home if you're not there. I know it's soon, but I swear I'll do everything I can to make you happy and comfortable down there. I'll have to work…"

"Is my brother paying you more to take me with you?" Will must be desperate after tonight.

Remy stopped for a moment, his whole body going still. "Lisa, that is an entirely different discussion."

"Yeah, one we probably should have had. It could have started with you knocking on my door and introducing yourself as my bodyguard, bought and paid for."

"Your brother didn't want you to know," he replied carefully, as though thinking through his every word. "He thought you would be upset."

"He was right. I'm upset. I'm upset that you lied to me."

He leaned in, his voice going soft. "I did not lie to you and the relationship between the two of us had nothing to do with the job. Absolutely nothing."

"That's ridiculous. First of all, why would my brother not tell me?" She frowned because she knew exactly why. She'd told him to stay out of her business. She'd kind of yelled it at him.

"Because he knows how reckless you can be," Remy replied. "Because he knows how scared you can be when someone else is in control of you. Someone you don't trust."

Now it was her turn to go still. Why would he say that? "What do you mean?"

He couldn't know about that. She hadn't told him. She never told anyone about what happened that night. No one except her siblings. She hadn't meant to tell them, but one night she'd woken up screaming and she hadn't been able to hold back. No one should know how weak she'd been.

Remy reached out, covering her hand with his, and for a moment she wanted so badly to turn her hand over and tangle their fingers together. She wanted to ask him to climb into this stupid hospital bed with her and hold her for the rest of the night. Maybe it was all a bad dream and she would wake up and none of today would have happened. She would hold on to him and tell him about her dream and he would laugh and tell her she was silly because he wouldn't lie to her and he would never, ever really leave without her because the truth was she was his home now.

Instead she stared at him because she knew she was awake and this was real.

His hand was warm on hers. "*Chèrie*, you don't have to worry. I fucked up tonight. I let you out of my sights. I'm not going to do it again. And you are in charge. I have to work when we get home, but I promise I'll do everything I can to accommodate you. You're not locked away. No one will ever do that to you again. Ever."

She pulled her hand away. "He had no right to tell you. That was private."

"I needed to know. I can't truly protect you if I don't know what you're afraid of, what you've been through. Lisa, you could have really hurt yourself. You need to understand that I'll come for you. I'll find you. No matter where you are. I will find you. I promise. I won't stop until I find you."

"Yeah, I guess losing that hundred K would put a damper on your day." She didn't want to listen to his earnestness. He was an excellent actor when he wanted to be. He could make a woman melt when he started talking. "I'm afraid your game is up. They're going to have to pro rate your fee because I'm done playing the fool."

He sat up, his lips firming before he spoke. "You aren't a fool of any kind. I told you. The fact that I was your bodyguard has nothing to do with being your lover. They're two different things. I assure you I reacted like your lover earlier this evening and not some cold-ass professional bodyguard. If your brother should fire me for something, it's that. I panicked when I thought I lost you. I couldn't think. I didn't even try to follow him. It wasn't even a choice I made. Javier had to. He still lost him, but at least he tried. All I could do was cry and hold you."

She couldn't buy into it. Oh, she wanted to because the man could sell it. But she couldn't trust him again. And she definitely couldn't trust herself. She made bad, bad decisions.

"I think you should leave now." The last thing she wanted him to see was how she was going to cry over him. The tears were right there, weighing on her, desperate to get out.

"I'm not going anywhere." He sat back. "Lisa, this is not a problem. I told your brother earlier tonight that he could keep the money. I would do all of this for free. I'll find another way to buy the wharf. My house might bring in more than I think it will."

She'd driven by his house all those months ago. Stalker. Pathetic, sad stalker. "I doubt that. Take whatever they'll give you and go home, Remy. Be happy. I'll try to do the same here."

He shook his head. "I cannot be happy without you."

"Then you should have thought of that before you lied to me." She could handle a lot but trust was everything to her. He'd broken it and broken them. She wouldn't be able to trust him again. Every word that came out of his mouth would remind her that he'd started their relationship with a lie.

Had he ever wanted her? Maybe he was like most guys and he could get an erection from a stiff breeze.

Her whole body responded to him, to the mere fact that he was in the room with her. The minute she sensed him close, her skin became electric, her body magnetic and flowing to him. Briefly she'd felt whole.

He stood up, pacing the floor. "I want you, Lisa."

"Not enough to tell me the truth."

Remy turned to her, his whole face flushed, his eyes pleading. "Please don't give up on me."

The moment seemed to stop, her looking at him and those words burrowing in, blasting past her defenses. But she was stronger now. She knew who he was. He was trying to save his job. Trying to save his family and his town.

She wished he'd simply asked her.

"Remy, could I have a moment with my sister?"

Will was standing there. Will was in the room. The one damn person in the world she couldn't ever turn away.

Remy looked like he didn't want to leave, but he finally turned to Will. "I'll be outside. I'm going to stand guard. I won't allow her to be alone."

"I know." Will put a hand on his shoulder, stopping him before he could leave. He looked at Remy, as serious as she'd ever seen him. "I know where you are, brother. Let me talk to her."

Remy nodded and looked back once, his eyes empty.

She was relieved when the door closed behind him. But then she was alone with another man who'd betrayed her. "How could you tell him?"

"He deserved to know how you got a concussion, Lisa. He has to know how to take care of you and what he cannot do even if it seems like the right thing in the moment. I don't want him locking you in for your own good. He won't do that now. He'll find another way to protect you. That man loves you. He deserves to know."

She shook her head. "You don't get to decide that. And honestly, that's probably your conscience talking. Do you feel bad about pimping me out, brother? How did you ethically process this one? Sell my body to save my soul?"

"Oh, don't underestimate how damn worried I am about your body, sister." Will was a little pale. He approached her bed. "You were almost kidnapped tonight. If Remy hadn't been so fast, that man would have taken off and god only knows what could have happened to you. Don't even try to make me fucking feel bad that I hired a bodyguard for you."

"I'm not upset about that, though a heads-up would have been cool." She'd been so stupid. Had they all been laughing at her? How many people knew?

His brows came together in that way that let her know he remembered that conversation differently. "I told you I thought you needed one. We argued about a bodyguard for hours. You yelled at me to stay out of your business."

She sat back, her whole soul weary. "Will, I'm sorry about that. I was frustrated at the time."

"You think I'm not frustrated? Up until two weeks ago I hadn't slept in months. I sat up every damn night waiting to find out someone had killed you. I know you think this is another funny episode you'll one day tell your kids about, but it's serious, Lisa. Someone wants you dead."

She wasn't positive that person was Biondo, but she did understand that this was more serious than she'd considered before. Someone wasn't thinking logically, but then a potential life in prison might make a lot of criminals go a little crazy. And her brother, oh her brother had taken on all the responsibility. He'd been more like her father. How could she stay angry with him when she was alive and whole because he'd kept them all together? Everything she knew about love she'd learned from this man. Love and responsibility and sacrifice.

"All right, Will. I'll take a bodyguard. I feel bad because I can't afford it. I feel like I'm using you."

"I'm your brother," he shot back, his exasperation obvious. "I love you. You staying alive isn't using me. This isn't like you're borrowing money so you can buy new shoes. This is your life."

And there was no way out of taking on a bodyguard now, not unless she wanted to go into some kind of protective custody. But this time they would do it right. This bodyguard wouldn't get close to her, wouldn't sleep in her bed and whisper to her at night, his arms wrapped around her. He would do his job and she would ignore him as much as possible.

God, she was going to miss Remy.

"Can I interview a couple of candidates?" Lisa asked. "Do you know if Big Tag has some female operatives?"

"Sweetie, all of Big Tag's bodyguards have jobs right now or they're on personal time."

Wow. There must be something in the water. "Okay, do we know other security firms? Doesn't that Julian Lodge guy have some bodyguards?"

"I believe Mr. Lodge has his own personal guards. I don't think he lends those out." Will took a deep breath as though steeling himself for the argument that was sure to come. "There's only one bodyguard available."

"Are you kidding me?" She looked toward the door where Remy would be standing stalwart and unmoving.

"I am not kidding you," her brother replied. "He's our only option. I don't trust the other firms."

This couldn't be happening. She couldn't handle being close to him again. "I don't trust him."

"I do trust him. I get it. You're pissed, but I'm the one who asked him not to tell you he was watching over you. You can be reckless."

"I'm not stupid."

"And getting a job at a strip club where you would have to walk to and from a lonely train station after midnight was a great decision." He held up a hand when she would have argued with him, shutting her down. "No, you don't think properly when your pride is on the line. So I'm giving you one of two choices."

"I'm an adult. You can't force me to do anything." But she could hear the stubbornness in her voice.

"I'm calling it all in, Lis. I'm calling in everything I ever did for you. Every report I helped you write. Every burn I got from trying to figure out how to feed us. Every late night I worked to have the money so you didn't go to sleep hungry."

Oh, he was afraid, and in the face of her brother's love, her pride seemed a petty thing. She reached out, tears falling now. "Will, stop. You don't have to call anything in. I'm sorry. I'm angry and hurt. What are my choices?"

She would do it for him, so he could find some peace.

"You can go with Remy to Louisiana until McKay-Taggart figures out what's going on and comes up with a better way to protect you."

She wasn't doing that. "Hard pass."

He nodded. "All right, then I'm moving you into my place. I'll have someone from the company come out and make sure our security is as tight as it can be. But Lis, I can't drive you to and from work. You know what my hours are like. Mitch might be able to do some of it."

She couldn't go back to work. She'd almost gotten Linc killed. And if she moved in with Will, she put them all in danger, including her nephew and Bridget and the baby in her belly. What the hell was she supposed to do?

She was supposed to do what her brother had taught her. She was supposed to do what was best for her family, even if it meant sacrificing her own happiness for a brief amount of time. It wouldn't be forever. The other bodyguards would come back from their assignments eventually. She would be first on the list to get a new one. The investigators would figure out what was really happening and they would find a way to deal with it.

"I'll go with Remy." She had no idea how she would sit beside him, work next to him and not go crazy. Maybe she would catch up on her reading. Or her napping. She would nap a lot. "But I get my own room."

Her brother's whole body seemed to relax. "I'm sure we can arrange that. Lisa, you won't regret it. I promise as soon as we can, we'll bring you home. But you should think about forgiving him."

"Or I could think about all the ways to twist a man's balls off." Forgiveness wasn't a word she wanted to hear.

Will sighed and sat down on the bed. "Do you know what I put Bridget through?"

She'd heard the story. Most of it. "It's not the same. You didn't lie to her."

"Oh, I did. She was looking for a date to her sister's wedding.

Amy's first wedding, the fake one, was held in Hawaii, and Bridget needed a fake fiancé. Of course there was one man she refused to ask."

She hadn't heard this part. Bridget talked. Bridget talked a lot, but the really personal stuff, she kept close. "You? Was it because of me? I remember she thought you had three women coming in and out of your apartment at all times. She didn't realize we were your sisters until much later. So she changed her mind when you told her the truth?"

"Well, I might have already put a plan in motion by that time. I didn't realize what the problem was. I might have made deals with every Dom in Sanctum that not a one of them would say yes to her."

Poor Bridget. "You asshole. She had to ask them. Do you have any idea how hard that is? Jerk."

He chuckled. "It was not my proudest moment, and when she found out, she was pissed. Incredibly pissed, but she finally came around and gave me a chance."

"It's not the same."

"Isn't it? He took the first chance he had to be with you."

"No, I gave him a chance. He turned me down."

"We're a rather intimidating family and he knew he wasn't staying around. When he got close to you, he couldn't resist. When he got to know the real you, he fell in love," Will insisted.

"No, he saw how easy his hundred K could be. I can't get in trouble if he's on top of me."

Will grimaced. "I thought that in the beginning, but then I heard what he said to you. I heard what he said and I recognized the look on his face because I had it on mine the night I begged Bridget not to give up on me."

The hitch in her brother's voice made her heart ache. "Oh, Will."

He put a hand on hers. "We're not smart. Men, I mean. We get a couple of scars on us and decide it makes more sense to shut down the softer part of our natures. We go into a relationship because we want sex and companionship and we're happy when we have it. We don't think to ask for more. You have to show him how to love you. That's what he means when he asks you not to give up on him. He doesn't know how to say he loves you, but he wants to."

"He's not you, Will." For a moment she'd thought she'd found someone as awesome as her brother, but that was gone now.

"Oh, but sweetie, at heart we're all the same. I promise to bring you back as soon as I can, but I think you should take this time with him to figure out if he's what you want. He offered to pay the money back."

But she knew how much he needed it. "Oh, no. I won't go unless he's getting paid and every single penny you promised him."

"Going to use that as a shield, huh?" Will looked a bit disappointed, but she wasn't backing down. "Just know that if you decide to give him a shot, Bridget and I would rather make it a wedding gift."

"There's not going to be a wedding. I promise I'll be a good girl and behave, but I'm not touching that man again." Because if she touched him, she would melt and she knew it. If she let him in again, she would become one of those doormat women who accepted less than she should. No. She'd been burned by that man twice.

He wasn't getting a third chance.

Chapter Nine

Remy drove, his eyes on the road in front of him, but his brain was working overtime trying to figure out how to reach the woman next to him. Lisa was sitting not two feet away from him but she couldn't be further away.

They were nine hours and forty-five minutes into a ten-hour drive. He'd tried to convince her to stop at a motel somewhere, but she'd put a quick kibosh on that. She wanted to get to Papillon, and then he had the feeling she was planning on going into her room and locking the rest of them out.

He'd tried everything he could think of to get her to talk, to find anything of the always-curious, lively Lisa he'd grown to love. The problem was he couldn't figure out if it had been the kidnapping or he himself who'd sent her into the tailspin.

"We're only two hours from New Orleans," he said quietly.

She looked up from the e-reader she'd had in her hands the whole day. "Somehow I doubt I'll be partying in New Orleans anytime soon."

"We could drive in for the day," he offered. "I'll have to go into the city often to pick things up."

She turned away from him and seemed to realize there was a world outside the cab. She hadn't looked up as they'd moved from the flat prairie land of North Texas into the Piney Woods that connected the state to Louisiana. She'd ignored the world outside as they'd driven across the long stretch of highway that bridged the Atchafalaya Basin, and he was fairly certain she'd napped as they'd passed around New Orleans.

But she looked up now. They were crossing the long bridge that connected Papillon to the mainland. The one-lane highway was one of two ways to get into his hometown. The other involved an airboat and a certain tolerance for the swamp.

"That's the bayou the town's named after." He kept his words quiet, academic. He didn't want to scare her back into her book.

She turned and stared out the window. The sun was starting to set, the sky lit with pinks and oranges and yellows. Massive cypress trees leaned over as though dipping branches into the slow-flowing waters, Spanish moss dripping from the limbs like a gothic shawl. This time of year the place was green and lush, the water seemingly blanketed in bright green lily pads.

He'd grown up here, but even he knew the bayou was a different world, alien and beautiful. Like nothing on the planet.

God, he'd crossed the globe and nothing, nothing in the world had ever been as beautiful as this stretch of road taking him home.

Nothing except her.

She gasped and sat up a bit straighter, as though trying to see. "That's an alligator. It snapped at something. That was a real live alligator."

There she was. "Don't get too impressed. You'll get used to them. They're kind of part of life around here. We name them."

She turned to him, her jaw going stubborn again. "I won't be here long enough to name one." She pressed her lips together as though holding something in. "Except that one. He's Chompy."

Yeah, there was no way she'd be able to hole up in her room. That's what he had to count on. Her natural, vibrant curiosity.

God, he'd forgotten how beautiful it was here. He'd forgotten how it felt to be home. It was an actual ache in his chest. He was home.

"How long has it been?" The question came out of her mouth as though she didn't want to ask but couldn't stop herself.

"Three years since I came back, but I've been gone for almost seven. I went into the Navy, took the hardest assignments I could possibly find for as much pay as I could make. That's why I immediately told the recruiter I wanted to be a SEAL."

"You must have been in your mid-twenties when you enlisted. Why did you wait so late? Most kids I knew went in straight from high school."

At least she was talking. He wished they were talking about

something pleasant, but he would take anything he could get. And maybe it would help her understand. "I was eighteen when my grandfather died. Pop-Pop ran the business Papillon is built around, had for fifty years. In his will he left everything to my grandmother, of course, but with the provision that after she was gone, the wharf would be split between the grandkids who worked it while she was alive. There were four of us. Me, my sister, Seraphina, my brother, Zéphirin, and our cousin, Jean-Claude."

"So it was divided between the four of you?"

"Oh, no, *ma cre*...Lisa." He had to can the sweet names. She'd already told him she would smack him if he called her a shrimp again. He believed her. He was fairly certain she thought he was making fun of her. "Zep was far too busy drinking and getting into trouble to work. He dropped out of high school and ran off for a while with some girl he met at a concert. I didn't know where he was until I found him in prison for writing hot checks off the girl's mom's account. Sera was always wild. She tried college but dropped out and came home. She went to cosmetology school for a while. Finally ended up pregnant and never would tell me who the father was. So it was me and Jean-Claude. Two dumbass twenty-year-olds running a business before we were able to legally drink."

"How did you lose it?"

"The same way people lose most things. Someone took it away from me. I thought it was time to settle down. I was kind of the head of my family from the time my father passed. Like your brother, I had to hold things together. I thought I was ready to have a wife at the age of twenty-one. Josette was the prettiest girl in town and she said yes. I wasn't in love with her. I was just ready to start my life. I had steady work. It made sense I would have a family. She thought because I was going to own half of the biggest business in town her life was going to be easy."

Lisa chuckled but it wasn't a happy sound. "Businesses like that require an enormous amount of work. The upkeep alone is incredible, and you would have to constantly put money into it. You do work like that because you love it, not to get rich. Especially if you don't have a business degree. You would have no idea how to grow the place." She frowned. "I'm sorry. That was pretentious of me."

"Nope, you're one-hundred percent right," he admitted. "Pop-Pop was excellent at running the place. He could fix a boat, stock up on bait, run the bar. He had no idea how to invest money or how to negotiate the best deal."

"So did Miss Josette get tired of working?"

He turned as the bridge became highway again and he could see the Gulf in the distance. If he opened the window he would be able to smell the ocean. "Josie didn't work."

"You're kidding. That's a family business."

"Yeah, well, it wasn't much of one since neither my brother or sister worked either, and my momma…" How to explain his mother. "Well, when we let Momma work, she ends up causing trouble. She's kind of a con artist. Not a terrible-meaning one. She's always looking to make a quick buck. If she offers to read your palm, turn her down. She's got not an ounce of psychic ability, but she hangs out with the local hoodoo priestess a lot. They have a girls' night every Thursday."

"Hoodoo?"

"It's what we call voodoo around here," he explained. "Don't be afraid. It's not like the movies."

Her eyes had gone wide. "You have a voodoo priestess?"

"No, we have Miss Marcelle, who gives overblown ghost tours and sells blessings and candles to tourists. She's got a shop attached to her hair salon. You can get your hair did, as they say in these parts, and pick up a love potion before your date." They weren't far now, and he wished they had more time. She would likely run into the guest room and lock herself inside. He might not get to talk to her again for a while. "Miss Marcelle's daughter is named Sylvie, and she's the town's mayor. I still can't quite believe that. She used to throw mud pies at me."

"Smart girl," she said under her breath. "So Josette was too good to work?"

"She thought she was becoming a trophy wife. I think she watched too much reality TV. She hadn't been out of Papillon often. Her family lived out on the bayou. Her daddy wasn't the kindest of men. She was a couple years younger than me. I guess I felt like I was saving her. Anyway, she got bored because I couldn't take her all the places she thought we would go. I encouraged her to go back to school. I caught her fucking her history professor, who happened to know an excellent lawyer. By that point my mom-mom had passed and I owned half the business."

"She wanted her half in cash," Lisa said, her eyes wide. "She made you sell?"

"I couldn't sell my momma's house. I couldn't. It was the house or the business. I sold my half of the business to my cousin and then I left town. I enlisted and I sent back what I could. When I got my ass blown up so badly not even the Navy wanted me anymore, I got the job at McKay-Taggart. I saved up with the hopes that I could buy back in, but I knew there was a possibility Jean-Claude would tell me to go pound sand and I would stay in Dallas. There was a time when I worried I wouldn't go home at all."

"Ever?"

He shook his head. "Like I said, there was a chance. The first time I asked Jean-Claude, he didn't even give me a response. Then about a year ago, he told me he was open to the idea for the right price. Around the time you first approached me."

"We don't need to ever mention that idiocy again," she replied.

"Did I ever tell you how pretty you looked that day? I remember you were wearing a purple corset and your hair was flowing all around your shoulders." He'd run as fast as he could and then every time he would close his damn eyes, he would see her standing there asking him politely.

"I told you I don't want to talk about our nonexistent relationship," she said primly.

"Just because we don't talk about it doesn't mean it's not real. I told your brother to keep the money. I got the loan for a good portion. I'm going to tell Jean-Claude he has to wait for the rest of it. I'm going to sell this truck and my house in Dallas and we'll see where we go from there."

"Will wired your cousin the money this morning," she said quietly. "Once you hand over the check the bank gave you, the wharf is all yours."

"He did what?"

She didn't turn his way. "He paid you. I made sure you got paid. I told Will the only way I would come down here with you was if you got your full pay. I know you don't watch over me for free."

How could she? He'd tried to get them out of this position and she'd put them right back in. "That's not fair."

"No, not telling the woman you're sleeping with that you're on the payroll isn't fair."

"What would you have done?" he asked. "If I'd told you that I was your bodyguard. How would you have reacted?"

"We'll never know now. I might have been perfectly reasonable."

He stared straight ahead because that was utterly ridiculous. Nothing about her situation was reasonable.

She sighed. "I don't know what I would have done. I probably would have wanted someone who wasn't you."

There was a problem with that scenario. "I wouldn't have allowed anyone else to guard you."

"According to Will, you were the only one available."

"I wouldn't have allowed anyone else to guard you." At least he wasn't going to lie to himself anymore. He couldn't have handed her over to one of the other bodyguards.

"I want to talk about something else or nothing at all," she said stubbornly. "So you didn't think you would come home. Did you miss this place?"

He let the question settle over him, trying to shove out his irritation. "Yes, I missed it. I didn't realize how much until now."

"You didn't come back for three whole years?" she asked. "You came home after the Navy though, right?"

"I did, but it wasn't a good time. Zep was back, but he was sitting on Momma's couch doing absolutely nothing with his life. Sera was pregnant. We had a fight one night and Momma told me if I hadn't left it wouldn't have fallen apart. She blamed me. Sera did, too. Zep barely looked up from his beer long enough to say good-bye when I left. I had an old friend in Dallas from the teams. I crashed at his place for my final surgery and then I got on at McKay-Taggart."

"But then your cousin decides to sell out. That's when you put your house on the market, found a highly lucrative job watching a moron, and now you're coming home the conquering hero."

He couldn't let that by without clarification. "I put my house on the market, found a highly lucrative job, got involved with my client, and I assure you no one thinks of me as a hero here. I'm the fuck-up who nearly lost everything. I'm the one who married the wrong woman, who let his siblings become every cliché you can hang on a bayou rat. I'm sure the town is happy the business isn't getting sold to that massive chain, but I don't expect them to be happy to see me."

He should have come back more often, should have done more than send checks.

"Why didn't you?"

Had he said that out loud? Damn, he hadn't meant to do that. "I was ashamed."

She should know. He didn't want to keep anything at all from her, but these particular stories didn't show him in a good light.

"Ashamed that you had married poorly?"

His marriage was only part of it. "That I brought us to the point that I had to sell our business. It was my responsibility."

"You were a kid. You did the best you could. We all make mistakes." She looked back out the window. "I suppose in some ways I can understand why you did what you did. If my family needed me, I would do just about anything. Except Lila. We're fighting. I mean I wouldn't let her drown or anything."

"I didn't mean to hurt you."

"And yet, here I am." She was back to staring out the window.

"What did Lila say to upset you? I thought it was something about me, but I'm pretty sure you hated me by then."

"I don't hate you."

"You do a good impression."

"I don't hate you," she said quietly. "I'm angry with you. I'm worried that if I stop being angry with you, I'll make a fool of myself again. And Lila said a lot of things. She was being very snobby. She has this way of letting me know I'm not living up to her standards. Well, her standards include a disgusting pig of a boyfriend who hits on her sisters."

"Excuse me."

"Don't. That's not who you're supposed to protect me from. Trust me. Laurel and I can handle Brock." She sat back. "I feel bad that I said what I said to her though."

"She should know who she's dating, and I am going to protect you from everyone who means to hurt you. Or hit on you."

"I've tried to tell her before. She tells me I'm making a big deal out of nothing."

"She should believe you. She's your sister." His hands tightened on the steering wheel. "I could murder him for you if that would make you feel better."

"Hmmm, assassination. I hadn't included that in my decision pyramid. I'll slip that one in and let you know what I think."

"You won't look like a fool if you let me back in. And I'm going to pay your brother back. Every single dime." Shame rushed through him again.

She turned to him. "I'm already tired of being mad at you, but I can't go back to where we were. Take the money. You earned it. It's all right to take it. If I were in your position, I would take it, too. I'm not capable of being this angry for long, but I can't let you break my heart again."

"I won't." God, if she could forgive him, this would be an entirely different world. He might be able to survive this if she could forgive him. "I promise I won't ever break your heart or your trust again. *Chèrie*, I'm sorry. Do you have any idea how much I've missed you the last few days? I know I was with you, but damn, not holding your hand or seeing you smile at me has been hell. I've learned my lesson."

She shook her head. "You misunderstand me. I don't want to hate you. That doesn't mean I want to be back together with you. I can't. Not like that. Not again."

The hope he'd felt started to flicker out. "Then what are you saying? We should go back to being friends? I don't know that we were friends in the first place. I love you."

"I think that's guilt and a little bit of trauma. I've thought a lot about this. You feel bad that you let the Italian dude get close to me. We had that big fight and you sat there thinking how crappy it was that the last words you said to me were kind of mean."

That was almost exactly how he'd felt but she was putting the wrong spin on it. "I realized how empty I would be without you."

"You say potato," she began.

"Don't patronize me."

She looked down at her hands. "I'm sorry. I get sarcastic when I'm...well, everything. I'm sure a shrink would tell you it's a coping mechanism. Anyway, I think we should be civil. My first instinct was to find a room and hide in it, but that's going to last a whole day maybe and then I'll want to do something. Can I work at your bar?"

"Yes. I would like that." He'd known he would take her with him, but he wasn't going to force her to work. The fact that she wanted to was a huge plus. "I would love it if you would give me advice on the strength of the business. I would pay you. Well, when I can."

"I'm a captive audience," she said, her lips curling slightly. "Looking through your books and making a study of the business could take my mind off things."

Things like the fact that an assassin was after her. Things like him.

It killed him that she was lumping him in with all the bad things in her life.

She looked up in the distance. "What's that?"

He squinted to see what she was talking about. Up ahead there seemed to be a bunch of cars parked on the sides of the main street running into town. "I don't know. It looks like something's going on in the square. It's not carnival season or shrimp fest. We party a lot down here. Once we get past the square we're only a few miles from the house."

"Uh, I don't think you're exactly the most hated man in town, Remy," she said, pointing at a huge banner that someone had draped across Main Street.

Welcome Home, Our Hero
Papillon's Favorite Son, Remy Guidry

He stopped the truck in the middle of the road.

Now that was something he hadn't expected.

* * * *

It had been the single hardest day of her life.

Okay, that was total hyperbole and insanely untrue, but sitting in Remy's big old truck as they drove all day with weird shit right outside the window and about a million places she would have loved to stop and explore along the way but hadn't been able to because she had been proving she could brood had been pure hell.

She hadn't even gotten to run around the massive Buc-ee's when they stopped for gas and to use the restroom. She had to pretend she wasn't interested in its thousands of weird candy choices and hadn't wanted to ask how they sold both barbecue ribs and garden gnomes, and a surprisingly large selection of socks.

No. She'd frowned and gone to the bathroom and hadn't bought that CD that promised all the country classics sung in chipmunk voices.

She hadn't gotten a waffle at the Waffle House they'd stopped at for breakfast. She'd gotten adult food, food that didn't require maple syrup, and it had sucked.

As they'd crossed the border from Texas to Louisiana, she'd had to conclude that she wasn't the girl who could hold a grudge. Not when there were places to buy daiquiris from. She'd actually managed to pass by a bunch of drive-in daiquiri places and not buy one. Or four. New Orleans had gone by and she'd still held her tongue.

And then she'd looked up from the book she'd been staring at and seen a magical place. It was like something out of a fairy tale, the trees rising from the water as though they floated there. Once she'd seen Chompy, it was over.

She couldn't help it that she thought the world was pretty cool. Maybe that made her a nerd, and it definitely made her a bad brooder, but she couldn't help it.

Besides, the whole time she was brooding, all she could think about was the look on Remy's handsome face when he'd said those words to her in the hospital.

Please don't give up on me.

She stared out the window of the truck. He'd stopped in the middle of the road. Not at a stop sign or a red light. Just stopped and looked up at that sign. For at least a solid minute.

Someone honked behind them.

"I think we're blocking the lane," she pointed out.

He sat there, staring at the sign.

She heard the peeling of wheels and an SUV drove around them, a fist shaking their way.

And there appeared to be a Ferris wheel. It lit up and started moving in the distance. Ferris wheel. Did that mean carnival food? Because again, she'd eaten like an actual adult all day and that meant she was super hungry.

There was a knock on the window and she nearly jumped out of her seat. There was a man in khakis and a greenish hat that proclaimed him Sheriff of Papillon Parish. He was a big guy who looked like he should be on a football field. Broad shoulders, piercing blue eyes, and a jaw cut from granite.

"You all right in there?" The sheriff stood up a little taller. "Remy Guidry. Remy, my friend, you get your butt out of that truck and go and see what your family and friends have done to welcome you home. What are you doing sitting there when we've got beer to drink and women to dance with?"

Lisa leaned forward. "Is there cotton candy? Wait, funnel cakes. I would rather have funnel cakes." She winced. She had to at least pretend to be something of an adult. "Okay, corn dog first because I skipped dinner and it has some protein."

Remy frowned her way. "You said you weren't hungry."

"I lied. I was all broody. Now I'm hangry and you should find a place where I can shove fried food into my mouth." And she was suddenly curious about his family.

There was a long honk and the sheriff turned, putting his hands on his lean hips. The man knew how to wear a set of khakis. "Gene Boudreaux? Is that you? You go around. Remy's trying to decide if he's joining the party or running back to Dallas. The man needs some space."

"Does he have to have it in the middle of the damn road?" a man screamed back.

"Oh, I will tase you," the sheriff promised. "You move around him. You think I won't?"

A white sedan raced around them.

The sheriff was back and smiling. "Don't worry about them. You take all the time you need." He reached up and tipped his hat her way. "You must be Miss Daley. I'm Armand LaVigne. You can call me Armie. Everyone does. Unless I'm arresting you and then I prefer Sheriff."

Oh, he was a charmer. She reached out her hand and shook his, her fingers brushing over Remy's as she pulled back. "How did you know my name?"

Armie grinned, looking younger than before. "Everyone knows your name, *chère*. There's a parking place on the square being saved for Remy. If you want to run, you should dump your cell phone. Seraphina tracks you on it."

"She does what?" Remy asked, his voice rising.

"Your sister tracks you. She flips out from time to time when it shows up in some weird foreign country and rushes into my office screaming that I have to go save you because you've been kidnapped. I told her there was nothing at all weird about a bodyguard going to Monaco. She didn't know where that was. We need to work on our education system. Someone needs to teach that girl geography."

Remy had flushed and it took a lot not to reach out to him. She reminded herself that they weren't together. They had never really been together. He didn't deserve her sympathy.

But oh she wanted to give it to him because he was floundering.

"We'll go and park, Sheriff." It was obvious someone had to make a decision. Also, hangry. Maybe not angry exactly, but there were definitely some feelings going on that she would like to medicate with fair food. If there was a beer somewhere out there, all the better.

"Why are they doing this?" The question came out on a tone that proved Remy was pretty emotional, too.

Armie leaned over, his eyes serious. "We screwed up the first time you came home, man. It wasn't a good time for the town, but we should have remembered what you sacrificed. We lost a boy about eighteen months ago."

"Yeah, I heard we lost Wesley Beaumont in Afghanistan," Remy replied grimly. "He was a good kid. I always hoped he and Sera would get together. They were friends, but she preferred the bad boys."

"We all felt his loss and we realized if we're going to mourn our dead soldiers, we should damn straight celebrate our living ones." Armie held out a hand. "Thank you for your service, brother."

Remy went still and she was worried he would stay that way. She reached out, putting a hand on his arm, and he seemed to remember to move again. He shook the sheriff's hand. "Of course. We'll go park and get my...get Lisa some food."

Armie stepped back. "You do that. And Remy, you're a hero around here for more than your service. We were sure we were going to lose the wharf. Everyone in town is breathing easier, and we know it's all because of you and your girl. Miss Daley, welcome home."

He gently tapped the hood of the truck and then turned to the back. "Is that Brent Cardet in his momma's minivan? What did I tell you? You do not have a driver's license, son. I don't care that your momma's too lazy to get her own beer. You're not allowed to buy beer, either."

The sheriff stalked off and Remy started the truck again.

"We could go back to the house instead if you like," Lisa began.

"Apparently my sister would know how to find me." Remy kept his eyes on the road, turning down Main, and she got a better look at the chaos going on in the square.

Zydeco music filled the air as the sun started to go down and the street lights came up.

"Sounds like they changed their minds about you," she said. It would be good. She wouldn't have to sympathize because the whole town loved him. "This is quite a party for a man you say they all can't stand. Oh, there's the spot."

She pointed at the parking spot. It was the only one open and the only one that had a massive, glittery star on the sidewalk in front of it. Was that Remy's face in the middle of all that gold glitter?

"They're just happy they won't lose everything," he replied. "If Jean-Claude sold out, their whole way of life would be gone. This isn't about me. It's about feeling bad over Wesley and being relieved they don't have to move or work for a large hotel that would send their property taxes sky high."

"Or they realize they didn't treat you well the first time." He was being way too pessimistic. "Why do you think he said that stuff about me?"

Remy shrugged as he parked the car and cut the engine. "I don't know. I told Momma I was bringing you with me. I didn't exactly tell her you're a client because I didn't want anyone to freak out. If this town thinks there's an assassin on the way, it could go poorly."

"Ah, they would want me gone." She was curious about the small shops that lined the square. It looked like something straight out of a movie about the 50s. Small town America at its finest. There was a drug store in front of her and it still boasted about serving the best milkshakes in town.

"Not exactly, but if it gets out that there could be serious trouble coming our way, then Miss Marcelle starts using magic to find out who's a criminal and who's a tourist, and she gets that wrong a lot of the time. Momma starts packing more heat than normal. They'll have town meetings. Someone always spikes the punch and then George Teague decides to fight a gator. It's a thing around here. It's best we keep quiet anyway. No one except your family and Ian knows where we've gone."

That was why they'd been on the road at the godawful hour they'd left at this morning. Remy had made a few rounds of the city before he'd been satisfied they weren't being followed. They'd left straight from the hospital. Laurel had packed for her. Lila hadn't even said good-bye.

"Don't you think we should tell your mom if we're staying at her place?" Lisa asked.

"We're staying out at the wharf. There's an apartment over the bar. Jean-Claude said he's cleared out so we can stay there."

"You don't want to stay at home?"

"I think it'll be easier to watch over you at the wharf," he said. "I should get to work. Jean-Claude wants to transition pretty quickly.

That means every minute counts. I'm going to find my family and thank them for the welcome and then we can go."

Oh, his panties were in a wad and she needed to get them all smoothed out if she was going to enjoy the night. "Or we could be more gracious and stay for a while."

He stared straight ahead. "You spent the whole day ignoring me. I don't think I can handle walking around a big old party with you not speaking to me. You can't go running off, you know. We have to stick together. I think we'll do that best if we don't have a bunch of people around."

Because he would have to explain her presence. He'd walked back into town with a woman on his arm. He'd left because of his divorce. How much would his pride be hurt if he had to explain over and over that she was nothing more than a client?

Well, he'd made that bed. He was going to have to lie in it.

It wasn't her problem. She didn't have to solve it for him.

"Okay, well, it's your town and if you don't want to go to the party, we won't." She opened the door to the truck and slid out.

And smelled the heavenly scent of food frying in greasy oil. Her stomach rumbled. And she couldn't help but smile because yes, that was Remy Guidry all done up and glitterfied. It was the kind of handicraft high school cheerleaders made for the star quarterback.

She might have to steal that.

"If I went to every party this town threw, I would never do anything else," Remy grumbled. "Come on. I'm sure my momma will be in the square. I'll thank her and then we can go."

He was going to be the grumpiest town hero ever.

They started walking down the sidewalk and she got a good look at the town that had produced Remy Guidry. It was weird. There was a barber shop complete with a blue and red and white pole. A café called Dixie's proclaimed it had the best chicory in town. There was a half-priced book store that shared space with a game shop and offered "the best souvenirs." A hardware store that also offered shipping services.

"A lot of these stores found they needed to diversify to survive," Remy said. "The local grocery rents out space to swamp guides. We do what we have to to survive."

What had he done to survive? Well, he'd taken a large contract for one.

She sighed. It would take a good long while to get over what he'd done. Even if she could understand it.

"Guidry, it's damn good to see you, son." A gray-haired man held out a hand.

Remy shook it and another couple. She listened quietly and figured out that these men belonged to the local Knights of Columbus and wanted to know if Remy would speak at their annual charity pancake breakfast.

Remy seemed to have lost the power of speech.

Was he actually shy? He'd never seemed that way around her, but now she had to wonder.

"Of course he will," she said with a smile. "I'm Lisa Daley. I'm hanging out here for a while and working with him at the wharf. Call me over there and I'll make sure it gets on his calendar."

"Thank you, young lady." He smiled suddenly. "I thought you must be Miss Daley. Not that you'll have that name for long." He held out a hand. "Oh, it's nice to meet you."

She shook his hand, wondering what he meant about her name, but she let it go. "And you as well."

She was introduced to the group and then Remy managed to shift them away. She waved good-bye while Remy led her by the elbow.

"You're handling my schedule now?" He stopped in front of a hot dog stand. "What was that?"

"It's called being polite and you said I had a job. I assume part of that is going to be answering telephones because if you're this growly on the phone, we'll lose customers." She hadn't meant to say that. "You'll lose customers. I'm kind of your temporary business consultant and the first thing I need to advise you on is your attitude."

"My attitude?"

She nodded. "It's bad today."

"You haven't smiled once all day. That's why I'm in a terrible mood. I'm never in a terrible mood. I'm an easy-going guy. Now I realize one petite woman can frown at me and the whole day goes to hell."

She wasn't going to let him make her go all gooey again. "Well, I'm smiling now because funnel cakes make me smile. But I'm an adult so I'll have a corn dog first. Aren't you hungry? You barely ate any lunch."

They'd stopped at a sandwich place, but she'd told him she wouldn't eat with him unless they stayed in the truck.

She'd been kind of a bitch. Did she really want to spend the next few weeks being a bitch? Did she want the end of her time with him to be filled with confrontation? Not that he'd been confrontational. He'd been...sad.

"I'm not hungry," he said. "But I'll try to smile more if it makes you happy."

"Don't." She looked away from him. "Don't try to make me happy, Remy."

"Okay."

Damn it. He was looking away from her, his eyes a little empty.

Why couldn't she be one of those cool chicks who once she was through with a man, she never thought about him again? Or the kind who could make it easy on herself and just off him? She bet Charlotte Taggart was a woman who could deal with an ex. But no. Lisa Daley was all soft in the middle. Lisa Daley lasted exactly two days before she started to worry about her enemy's tender feelings. She needed to harden up, get some of those shields everyone else had, build walls so tall...

"Cotton candy." Her mouth kind of watered.

Remy stared down at her and his eyes suddenly got steely. "You can't make me not try to make you happy."

What? Sometimes that Cajun accent could be hard to follow.

He turned on his heels and walked straight up to the cotton candy stand. The girl in the stand kind of giggled and jumped up and down and then passed him a big cone of frothy pink sugar.

He strode back over like a man on a mission. Gosh, he was big. Big and beautiful and so sexy it hurt her pussy to think she was never going to sleep with him again. It was an actual ache, like her girl parts were rebelling against her very reasonable plans to never let him touch her again. Not with those big hands. Those big, callused manly hands. Nope.

"Cotton candy." He offered it to her like he was offering something precious.

It was. It was cotton candy. She should go and get her own. Be strong and brave and he had sad puppy eyes. Gorgeous sad puppy eyes.

It was only cotton candy. When had a big old poof of sweet, sweet cotton candy ever hurt a girl? Well, there was diabetes, but she wasn't thinking about that tonight. She took the cotton candy. "Thank you,

Remy."

Those lips curled up in the most brilliant smile. Yep, her girl parts were singing again. And her heart rate had ticked up. It didn't matter. She wasn't staying. When everything was cool at home, she would go back and never think about Remy Guidry again.

Often. She wouldn't think about him very often. Probably.

"I was supposed to eat something adult first." Not that it stopped her from taking a big old bite. And then wondering what it would be like to share cotton candy with the asshole lying liar with the great abs and soulful eyes. She could take her bite and then share it with him by kissing him long and deep, their tongues mingling. Sweet kisses. They would walk around the fair hand in hand and share those kisses.

"Well, I have to do something about that. I can't have you on a sugar high. Let's see. Have you ever had a shrimp po' boy?" Remy asked. "Because if you have, I'm going to tell you that you haven't because you've never had one from here. The shrimp were caught today." He held out a hand. "Come on. I won't try to make you happy. I promise. I'll simply walk you around and introduce you to the weirdest people you've ever met and get you food at every single stand so you don't miss a thing. And then, I'll dance with you. Not to make you happy, but because it's expected at a party like this. There won't be any joy in it. It's merely something we're expected to do. It would be impolite to not dance."

She glanced over at the dance floor that had been set up in the middle of the square. Twinkle lights had just lit up making the whole place gauzy and romantic. She couldn't dance with him. That would be such a bad idea.

But then again, she was the new girl in town and she should probably be polite.

"Remy, my man!" Some dude strode up and passed him a bottle. "*De la cave de mon grand-père pour toi, mon frère. S'il te plaît profites-en.*" The young man winked her way. "*Et ta nouvelle femme est magnifique.*"

Remy took the bottle. "*Merci, Rene. Mais elle est à moi. Ne pense pas à faire plus que la regarder.* Lisa, this is Rene Darois."

Rene was a stunning man roughly the same age as Remy. He had reddish gold hair and a matinee idol smile. Unlike most of the men around him who favored jeans and T-shirts, Rene was in a full suit. His green eyes seemed to twinkle as he winked at her. "*Bonjour,* Lisa. I look forward to learning more about you. I'm interested in any woman who can take on our Remy. He's been a bear since the divorce."

Remy frowned Rene's way. "*Ne commence pas là-dessus. Moins elle sait, et plus mes chances sont bonnes.*"

She had no idea what he was saying but the man nodded her way and walked off after shaking Remy's hand. She did know that he was ridiculously sexy when he was speaking French. Like swoon worthy. She stuffed sugar in her face because what she wanted to do was jump on the hot Acadian dude.

He'd lied to her. He'd used her. Hadn't he? He couldn't love her and still have taken all that money from her family. Could he?

"Rene's family has been here since long before this was US land." He snagged a couple of glasses from one of the vendors and poured two cups. "You want one of these? Wine will make this evening much easier to get through."

She never turned down wine.

"Sure." Lisa took Red Solo Cup #1.

Remy took one, too. "Thanks for walking around with me. It would be awkward to be here alone."

Yes, it would, and they were stuck here for weeks probably. Maybe even months. "I think we should try for friendship. I understand why you did what you did."

"And I'm glad for that, but Lisa, I don't want to be your friend. I want to be your man. I want to walk you through this fair and have everyone know that you're mine."

She couldn't go that far. Not ever again. Not with him. "I'm trying."

He stopped for a moment, seeming to think. "And I'm pushing when I should be patient. You need to understand that I won't lie to you again. I'm in love with you and I'll do anything to make sure you don't ever leave this town again."

"That sounds really stalkery."

A brilliant smile crossed his face. "There's my girl. Let me be more romantic. I want this to be your home, here with me. But I understand you need time, so here's to friendship. You can always, always count on mine, Lisa Daley."

He held up his cup.

Could she ask for more? She wanted some peace between them, but this was a slippery slope. He was too beautiful, and she knew exactly what that man could do to her body. She would be smarter to retreat. And yet her hand came up, touching her cup to his. "You have mine, Guidry."

"Then let's have some fun, *chèrie*."

Red Solo Cup # 2

"Hi, I'm Seraphina and this is my mom, Delphine. It's nice to meet you. I'm surprised, though, since big brother never even mentioned you until he said you were coming home with him. I guess that's a lot like Remy, when I think about it. He plays everything close to the vest. Probably because we teased him mercilessly as we grew up. I was a horrible little sister." Seraphina was a lovely blonde in her mid-twenties.

Remy had walked Lisa around the town square. She'd learned she loved po' boys and gumbo. She'd foregone the corn dog in favor of a meat pie that had been the single greatest thing she'd ever put in her mouth. And yes, she'd said that and Remy'd had a witty double entendre that made her blush. She'd moved on to crab pistolettes and boudin balls and finished up with beignets before they'd found Remy's family sitting around a table on the far side of the square.

She was ridiculously full of everything except wine. She could use more of that.

An adorable toddler sat on Seraphina's lap. The boy, who couldn't be more than two and a half or three, sat up straight when he saw Remy. He had a mop of dark hair and seemed fascinated with the big man in front of him.

Not that Remy had a chance to greet his nephew. The minute they'd walked up, his mother had been all over him. Delphine was far too busy doting on her firstborn child. Delphine Guidry looked an awful lot like her son. She was tall, with dark hair and a feminine, older version of Remy's face. She put her well-manicured hands on either cheek. "I prayed for this day. Three long years, I prayed that my baby would come home. I told you all this day would come. I told you we hadn't lost him forever to that hellhole called Dallas." She pointed at some of the people watching the reunion of mother and son. "You doubted me but the saints spoke to me. They told me the time and the place and here he is. My son, the heroic soldier."

"But I called you and let you know I was coming home," Remy

said under his breath.

"This is the day the lord made," his momma continued, her voice rising.

Sera looked up at Lisa. "She didn't need Remy to tell her when you were coming through town. I have this app that watches where his phone is. Why the hell did you need to go to Malaysia? What is a Malaysia? I told the sheriff I thought it was one of those made up countries."

Remy shook his head, patiently allowing his momma to hug him. "I was guarding a businessman who had meetings there. It's a real country, Sera."

She turned back to Lisa. "It sure sounds fake to me. I totally watch Zep's phone, too, but it never gets farther than New Orleans. I was worried in the beginning that Zep's phone would give mine an STD, but Rene told me it doesn't work like that. And don't mind Momma. She's about to launch her new business. She reads tarot cards and palms and specializes in magical fixes. So when you get the whammy put on you by Miss Marcelle, Momma can give you some herbs and say some words and make you feel better."

"She is not planning another con," Remy said, shaking his head. "Damn it, Momma, you promised."

"It's not a if it works," Delphine insisted. "Those people seriously feel better. I'm helping them."

This was completely different than her family. Her family got scandalized when someone made a *C* on a test. The most scandalous thing that happened was when Lila mistakenly read Bridget's manuscripts and asked what figging was.

That had been a fun family night.

Remy wasn't having it. "It *is* a con if Marcelle is pretending to whammy people so you can charge to fix them. That is the exact definition of a con. Where is Zep?"

Delphine waved a hand. "Zep is a young man. He's out exploring the world of possibilities waiting for him. He's like the wind he's named after, Remy."

"What's the stripper's name?" Remy asked.

Sera shrugged. "He goes through them too fast for me to catch their names. He didn't come because he thought you would be more comfortable here without him. I tried to tell him things change."

"Oh, but Zep doesn't change." He seemed to catch sight of the toddler. He stopped, his whole face softening. "But there's something that did. Luc? Buddy, how did you get so big?"

She stood there as she finished off her drink, listening to the family reunion and going twelve kinds of gooey because no one could resist a superhot alpha male with a baby in his arms.

Red Solo Cup #3

"I'm the king of the world!"

Yeah, that was just what she said when she rode Ferris wheels. Five times in a row.

Red Solo Cup #4

Lisa twirled around the dance floor, the music lifting her higher and higher. Or maybe it was the wine. She was already on the tipsy side. She'd met the mayor, who had a big hug for Remy and the offer to sit down over breakfast one day this week and talk about how to deal with their mommas and their new short con plans...er, business plans. She wasn't sure how she felt about Remy having some intimate brunch with the lovely mayor, but it wasn't like she had a choice.

Although he had been a gentleman all night. He'd brought her wine and cotton candy and made sure she ate some shrimp. Shrimp here meant life. Shrimping was a way of life.

And more than once she'd heard someone called *ma crevette*. It wasn't some insult. It was a term of affection and endearment.

The wine was really strong. She promised this was her last glass. She'd danced with the mayor's brother and the man who owned the hardware store. She'd been twirled around by the local priest, who was an excellent dancer and apparently also was good with moonshine. But dancing with Remy was the best. The song turned slow and suddenly he was there. He let her current partner know she would be unavailable for all slow dances and then took her in his arms and started to sway.

"Magical," she said with a smile, looking up at him. "The whole place is magical."

He held her closer. "You might feel different in the morning when the sugar high has worn off and the alcohol turns into a hangover. Did I mention he makes that himself and it probably has a higher volume alcohol than you're used to when it comes to wine? You don't drink a lot and that particular wine can really sneak up on you. I should know. Most of my youthful indiscretions were because of that wine."

She shook her head. He was not taking her red Solo cup. Her red Solo cup was her friend. Her red Solo cup let her relax and not be worried or upset. Everyone made mistakes. Not everyone had piercing blue eyes and made love like a superhero. Those were very important things. "You will pry this cup out of my cold, dead fingers."

And he could dance.

"You also might feel differently when we get out to the wharf," he admitted. "It's not what you're used to. The apartment is a bit on the utilitarian side. We have a kitchen and a bedroom and living area. The bathroom isn't bad, but it's only a shower. I used to live out at my momma's, but I thought that might be weird, to say the least."

"Weird?"

"I don't want to share a room with my brother. He's a slob."

She had to laugh at the thought. "Well, I'll make sure I stay tidy."

He swayed and she followed. It felt so right to be in his arms.

"Thank you for tonight," he whispered.

"I didn't do anything except eat a ton of food." Such good food. If they did this kind of thing often, she was going to gain a bunch of weight.

"You made tonight special for me." He sighed and she could feel his body relax against hers. "I didn't think I would come home. I sure didn't think I would come home like this. If you hadn't been with me, I would have gone on to the wharf. I don't know how to deal with this."

"With people who care about you?" It was the easiest thing in the world to lay her head on his chest and just be. Between the music and the starry night and the man who held her, life seemed pretty perfect.

"It's a lot." His hand smoothed down her back. "I guess I've gotten more used to keeping my mouth shut and throwing myself in front of bullets. I used to be fairly good at dealing with people. I used to be able to negotiate and debate my way around things. Now the whole thought makes me tired. I guess I thought I would be happier."

She could understand that. "I get it. I worked super hard for my MBA and I was miserable at my first job. All I did was look at numbers. I'm good with numbers, but I need something more. I think you'll feel better when you get to the actual work. You enjoyed it when you were a kid, right?"

"I loved that place more than anything," he admitted. "I would run from the school bus straight to the wharf. My momma would yell at me, but I wanted to be there so bad. I didn't want to miss anything."

"Give it some time. Let yourself get back into a groove and I think you'll be all right. Some things do change, and it seems like these people know they didn't treat you right the first time around."

"They were angry," he admitted. "From what I can tell, Jean-Claude did things differently after I joined up. He was angry with me for leaving him there alone. Hell, the whole town was. They expect more out of my family. If we fail, the town fails. I do get that. I hope you can teach me some business sense before you leave."

She didn't like that word. Leave. She'd just gotten here. She didn't want to think about leaving. "I think we've got some time. And you probably know more than you think you do. Did I mention I really liked the wine?"

He chuckled and pulled her close. She loved it when he wrapped those big arms around her and squeezed like he couldn't help himself. She loved how big he was, how her head settled on his chest when he swayed and moved them across the dance floor.

He stiffened suddenly, all that grace stopping on a dime.

Lisa turned and realized they weren't alone. They'd made it to the edge of the dance floor and a lovely woman wearing what had to be a designer dress stood looking at Remy like she was something out of a gothic painting—the tragic heroine, the one who'd lost her lover to the evil villain's plans. She was only a few inches shorter than Remy and had the kind of blonde hair that Swedish supermodels wished for. Coupled with the ridiculously banging bod and classically beautiful face, she was one of the most stunning women Lisa had ever seen.

"Hello, Remy," she said.

Even her fucking voice was lyrical.

"Hello, Josette."

The world was a little on the hazy side. Remy was right about the wine. It was strong. So were her feelings about Remy's ex-wife, the tragic beauty.

"I was hoping we could find somewhere quiet. I think we need to talk," she said, completely ignoring Lisa. "You've been ignoring my calls. You can't ignore me forever."

"He can try," Lisa said. His ex-wife had been calling him? Seraphina tracked his phone. It was time for Remy to get a new damn number.

"Maybe some other time," he replied politely. He glanced around, seeming to understand that they were drawing a lot of curious eyes. "I probably need to get this one back to the wharf. Rene gave us some of his grandpere's strawberry wine. You know how hard that can hit you if you're not used to it."

She smiled, a wistful expression that belied the watery look to her eyes. Shimmering. Tears shimmered in her eyes. When Lisa cried nothing shimmered. She went red as a tomato and her nose turned Rudolph shiny, but Josette managed to shimmer.

"Yes, I remember many nights sitting with you on that big front porch and drinking strawberry wine until you carried me to bed," she replied. She put a hand on his arm. "Remy, I was wrong. I know that now. Please let me talk to you. Away from your friend."

Oh, that was not happening. "Hey, hands off."

"Lisa, maybe I should handle this," Remy said, getting in between them.

"Do we still have a contract?" Lisa asked. In the moment it seemed like a really smart thing to say. They had signed a contract.

He leaned over, whispering in her ear. "What happened to you never trusting me again?"

"Do we have a contract?"

"I did not tear it up and have been keeping up my responsibilities," he replied. "I want that contract and you know it."

Miss Too-Pretty-For-Words put a hand on her slim hip. "Who is that, Remy? I've never seen her before. She is not from around here."

"Her name is Lisa," he began, his voice wavering a bit. "She's…"

"I'm his fiancée so you better back off or you'll find out how Texas women deal with poachers," Lisa promised. Yeah, that felt right in the moment, too. No one here would understand the Dom/sub thing, and Remy needed to look respectable. Engaged was respectable. Right? The wine was totally with her. The wine thought it was a brilliant idea.

"Fiancée? You aren't wearing a ring, fiancée." Josette seemed to drop the fragile act, her voice losing the ethereal tones.

Oh, she knew she was in trouble, but the words kept coming out of her mouth. "Well, that's what happens when wife number one is a skanky bitch who steals her husband's hard-earned business and runs out on him, and now he can't afford an engagement ring."

"I can totally get you an engagement ring. I want it to be special. That's all." Remy's hand was suddenly in hers. "Baby, you should calm down and maybe think about this."

"You won't last a week in this town. And you don't look right with him. You're too short for him. He likes tall women," Josette replied.

"She makes up for her lack of height with her vivacious and constantly surprising behavior." Remy started to tug her away, but a crowd had formed. It looked like every single eye in the place was on the new girl vs the ex-wife.

It was time to make a ladylike retreat. She wasn't tipsy. She was drunk and the last few days had been hard on her. This was not the way to take out her stress. She needed sleep and then she could face the fact that the whole town now thought she was about to become a Guidry.

Except wasn't that what they'd been saying all night long? God, they'd already thought she and Remy were together. Why else would her brother have written that check? That had to be it. And suddenly she didn't want these nice people with their yummy food and twinkle lights and complex French names to think she was nothing more than a client.

He looked down at her and his smile was gone. "It'll be okay. I'll deal with it in the morning."

"Everyone in this town knows you're marrying that uptight city bitch for her money. What does that make you, Remy? Huh? How do you feel having to whore your body out for that damn wharf?"

And that was when the Solo cup got pitched to the ground and the world went a nice shade of red.

As red as the cup.

As red as her ass was going to be.

Lisa didn't care as she proceeded to show the entire town of Papillon how a Texas woman defended her man.

Chapter Ten

Remy took the mug of coffee from his cousin's hand, the smell of that dark chicory waking him up in a way no plain roast ever would. "Thank you. I need this. That was a long night."

Jean-Claude had his own. "So I heard. Did your new girl really pull out Josette's hair extensions in the middle of the square?"

Remy groaned. He should have known there had been no way that story didn't make the rounds. He wasn't surprised Jean-Claude had already heard it even though he hadn't been at the party the night before. Of course, neither had his other guest this morning.

"I heard she told the sheriff she was keeping the longest piece as a war trophy." His brother, Zep, had been sitting in the bar when he'd walked out. He and Jean-Claude already had the coffeemaker working, a big old box of donuts on the bar.

Remy yawned, covering his mouth with his hand as he settled into one of the chairs. It was barely six in the morning. They didn't open for an hour. Oh, the regulars knew how to get around that if they needed something, but the tourists wouldn't show up for a bit. "Why are you two here? I thought Jean-Claude was ditching this town first thing he could and, Zep, don't you sleep until afternoon?"

"I had to come once I found out I had a brand spanking new sister-in-law." Zep was sitting across from him, one long leg crossed over the other. Despite his late night, Zep looked fresh as a daisy. Which turned out to be the name of the stripper he'd spent the night with. Daisy No Last Name. His younger brother was still raising hell. "I would also like to protest the horrible unfair treatment I get. Lisa and Josette go at it in the middle of the square and Armie lets them off with a warning that young ladies shouldn't fight over men. I get into one tiny barroom brawl and I spend the night in his incredibly unclean jail cell. It's discrimination, I tell you."

Discrimination, his ass. Remy downed a good shot of the chicory. "Lisa had a bit too much to drink and was merely attempting to ensure that Josette understood our relationship."

Remy didn't understand their relationship. One minute she could never trust him again, the next she was clinging to that platinum blonde extension like it was gold she'd won in a tournament. She'd wanted to know if they had a contract. She'd been the one to introduce herself as his fiancée. Oh, he'd known that was what everyone suspected—even Josette, who'd pretended to have never heard the name Lisa before. He'd known he would have to dismiss that rumor, but now maybe he didn't. There was a good chance that she would be so embarrassed by the night before that she would actually go through with a wedding. At least he thought there was a chance. He was willing to take it. He would take her any way he could. Of course, he was also well aware that she would be back up and ready for a fight this morning.

"Damn, now I wish I'd been there," Zep said.

"And why weren't you?" Remy eyed his younger brother. "Sera gave me some song and dance about how you weren't sure of your welcome."

"Well, I wasn't sure of my welcome at all, but you weren't the one I was worried about. That was mostly because Mr. Gentry found out that I haven't exactly been mowing his yard all these years." Zep had the good sense to flush. "I mean it started out that way, but after a while Mrs. Gentry paid the Smith kid to mow and she and I would spend the afternoon fucking. It's not my fault. It started when I was seventeen. I was too young to know what I was doing."

"Are you telling me you've had a Thursday afternoon booty call with Emma Gentry for the last five years?"

Zep shrugged. "Well, Momma told me I needed to get a job. I did. It led me to sin. And you know when you think about it, it's all old man Gentry's fault. He's damn near ninety. What's he doing marrying a thirty-year-old?"

"Well, I think it's called buying himself a gold digger," Jean-Claude explained.

Zep held a hand out. "Sorry I missed the party, big brother. It's good to have you home."

His younger brother was obnoxious and damn, but he'd missed him. "Good to be home, Zep. But you have to stay away from other men's wives."

"Oh, you have to be more precise these days, *mon frère*," Jean-Claude said. "It's not merely other men's wives. When it comes to adultery, Zep doesn't care if you're a woman married to a man or another woman."

"I was almost certain she wasn't a real lesbian," Zep explained. "Camilla, not Dawn. Dawn wore a wallet on a chain. I was pretty sure about her, but Camilla was on the fence."

"She wasn't on the fence. They had a lovely wedding." Jean-Claude shook his head.

"And then I had a lovely portion of their honeymoon. It's not my fault Dawn's a long-haul trucker and she needed to get some TVs to a Walmart in Reno." Nothing was ever his brother's fault. Zep just fell into bed with women. "And I'm glad you're home because maybe you can talk to Armie about his deputy."

"Old Paul?" He'd been around for twenty years.

"Nah, he retired. Armie hired someone from a SWAT team in the city," Jean-Claude explained. "Pretty thing. You would never guess she was a sniper in the military. Or that she would have terrible taste in one-night stands."

Zep's eyes went wide and innocent. "Or that she could hold such a mean grudge."

Remy held a hand up. "Nope. Your dick is on its own."

Zep leaned in. "Damn it, Remy. She's mean. She follows me around and punishes me for every tiny infraction."

"Translation, he speeds a lot. And parks wherever he wants to. And is often drunk in public. Armie gets lazy, but Deputy Roxie takes a hard line on all things." Jean-Claude shook his head. "You've got your hands full with that one. She's very interested in building codes and making sure everyone follows the rules at all times. I have no idea what Armie was thinking."

Armie had probably been thinking that bringing in a woman who didn't have ties to every single person in the community would make life easier on him. More than once he'd caught Armie trying to arrest his momma for her con games only to find her yelling that he couldn't arrest her because she'd changed his smelly pants when he was a baby.

"You're on your own with the deputy." He sat back, already falling into the old rhythms. The bar didn't open until noon. The bait shop opened at seven, but no one ever actually went down there until the bell rang letting them know someone was waiting. It made for some nice lazy mornings. "Either of you know what's up with Josette? We've been happily divorced for years and suddenly she's interested in talking again? What happened to the horny professor?"

"The horny professor also turned out to be the married professor," Zep replied between bites of his chocolate donut.

"And wasn't Josie surprised when he wouldn't leave his wealthy wife for her," Jean-Claude finished. "She tried for about a year after your divorce came through. Apparently a quarter of a wharf wasn't enough to entice him away from his wife."

"And that has what to do with me?" He'd been shocked when she'd called, but let it go. The fact that she seemed to be trying to get him alone didn't make a lick of sense. They'd said everything they needed to. And then, of course, Lisa had a few rough words for his former bride. Most of them four-letter words, but she'd been creative, too. "I haven't seen Josie since I left town."

Zep shrugged. "I heard she had a rough time the last few years."

Remy didn't understand. "How could it have been all that hard? She walked away from me with two hundred thousand dollars in her pocket. I had to spend most of my cash paying off her bills. By the time I was done, I had next to nothing."

"I don't know what happened from when she left town to coming back last year, but she's living out at her daddy's." Jean-Claude leaned back, looking thoughtful. "She wouldn't do that if she still had enough money for a motel. That girl fell on hard times. I guess when you're hurting, it's easy to go back to what you know. She wasn't counting on you finding a new love. Or that she would be so very forceful about your monogamy."

Zep laughed. "I hope someone got that on tape. I'm going to hit the head. Be right back. And I'm a little short of cash, brother. I thought I'd take a couple of shifts this week."

He disappeared into the back of the bar.

Remy groaned. "He spends all his time flirting with whoever's in front of him. Trying to get any work out of him is completely impossible."

"He's better than he was." Jean-Claude shifted in his chair as though trying to fortify himself for what was to come. "I'm sorry I pushed you the way I did. I'm sorry I blackmailed you."

"Why did you?" It had been plaguing him since Jean-Claude had reached out months ago with his demands. They'd been friends as well as family once.

"I have to get out of here." Jean-Claude stared out the big bay windows. "You know I never wanted this place. I did it because I didn't know anything else. The truth of the matter is I've been a terrible cousin to you. I could have bought out exactly what you needed to pay off Josette, but I forced you to sell me the whole thing or nothing. It was out of spite, and I hate myself for making you make that decision. I was jealous and mean spirited and I need to be more. I'm thirty-four years old and I've been waiting all my life for one woman to wake up and realize I was always the man for her. I can't be here with her back in town. I can't spend one more minute of my life pining over what I can't have."

Remy sat back, shocked. But it explained so much. "Josette?"

Jean-Claude stood up and walked over to the windows. The sun was up, turning the whole bay pink and orange. In the distance, the shrimpers were already moving out, ready for the day's catch. "I've loved her since we were kids, but she never once looked my way. I know she's a conniving bitch, but the heart is a stupid thing, Remy. I stood by you on your wedding day and that might have been the worst day of my life. I stood there smiling and saying all the right things, but there was hate in my heart. I was practically gleeful when you two divorced. I wanted you to leave so I might have a shot. Of course that didn't work out either. When she came back, I knew I had to leave and I put it all on you."

Holy shit. He wasn't sure how he felt, but he knew getting mad wouldn't change a thing. How many years had his cousin been hurting? "Jean, I didn't know. I'll be honest, if I had known, I would have walked away from her. I never loved her. I liked her. I was attracted to her, but I married her because it seemed like it was time."

"Yeah, that was the worst part," his cousin replied.

"I'm sorry. I didn't know. Maybe if you talked to her." The thought that he'd taken something from Jean-Claude made him sick inside. Especially something that had turned out so poorly.

A low, humorless chuckle came from Jean-Claude's chest. "You think I didn't? I went to her the night before you married. I went to her when you divorced. I won't go to her again, and that's precisely why I'm leaving this morning. My bags are packed. I'm offering you and Lisa the house if you want it. Consider it a gift to placate my conscience. The keys are upstairs. If you don't want it, I'll sell it off."

"That house has been in your family for a hundred years."

"And I'm the last of my line. I don't think I'm going to come back. View the house as a way to make up for all the blackmail. I know it's been damn hard on you and I made it harder." He glanced toward the back, as though he could see up the stairs and into the apartments. "You've got a woman now. You can't stay upstairs forever, and dear god if you want to keep that woman, don't let her live with your momma."

"I don't know how long she's going to be here." He had the sudden urge to tell his cousin the truth. After all, keeping things to themselves hadn't worked out. "She said what she said last night because she was drunk, and this is not a woman who gets that way often. She'd had too much wine and a bunch of hard days and I don't know, maybe she got a little territorial. Josette was bitchy to her and Lisa doesn't take a bunch of crap, if you know what I mean."

"I don't. Why wouldn't she stay? She's the reason you got the money on time."

"Her brother is the reason I had the money. Lisa is my client."

Jean-Claude's brow rose. "Your client? Like as in she requires your bodyguard services?"

Remy nodded. "She's got a mafia hitman after her. Don't worry. I was careful. I don't think he'll trace her back here. My company had an operative stay in her hospital bed, and this afternoon they'll try to draw Francesco Biondo out. Not that catching him will solve our problems. She's stuck here for a while. I didn't want to get the whole town up in arms, so I let them think she's my girl."

"Well, from what I heard, she's good at playing the part," his cousin pointed out.

"Yeah, well, we had some practice, and then she found out I was being paid to watch over her. She didn't know. Her brother asked me to keep my professional duties to myself. I thought I could have my cake and eat it too. The real problem is I figured out I love her too late. She knew she'd been lied to and she says she can't forgive me."

And yet she'd felt perfect in his arms the night before. He'd had to carry her upstairs and help her get out of her jeans. When she'd sunk onto the double bed, she'd pulled him with her, wrapping her arms around him and falling asleep. He'd known exactly what would happen if he stayed there. He would have woken up kissing her, cuddling her. It had taken everything he had, but he'd slid away and slept on the extremely uncomfortable couch.

He hoped she didn't hate him this morning.

Jean-Claude was shaking his head. "It sounds like she's already forgiven you. Oh, she'll tell you differently, but declaring herself your fiancée last night, that was what she wanted when she couldn't think straight, when the pain meant nothing and it was all about what she wanted with her heart. So don't fuck it up. Use this time to wrap her up and let her know you won't let go."

In vino veritas, as his pop-pop would say. Had she told the truth last night? Was that what she wanted?

"I lied to her," Remy admitted.

"Were you trying to hurt her?"

"Hell, no."

Jean-Claude pointed a finger his way. "You're one of the single best men I've ever met in my life. Unless something's happened in the past couple of years to change things, you're honorable and good to the people around you. You tried to make things work with Josette. You tried to give her what she told you she wanted. What she really wanted was an entirely different life where you didn't work your ass off and could spend all your time worshipping her and being the golden couple of Papillon. If this Lisa is anything like that, do your job and let her walk away."

"She's not," he replied quickly. "I thought she might be at first, but now I honestly think she might be looking for something to build. She didn't like her office job, but she might like this. She's good with people and she's smart. This job might keep her on her toes. And I know damn straight she needs someone who'll keep her out of trouble. It follows her around."

Could he use this very place he'd thought she would run from to catch her in his web? She'd loved the fair the night before. It was the kind of thing that couldn't be replicated in a big city. Oh, the big-city fair had more rides and attractions, but it didn't have the same sense of being a family party. They would be talking about the Lisa/Josette takedown for the next twenty years.

"Are you sure you want to leave?" Somehow the thought of losing his cousin just as they were starting to be honest with each other hurt. He hadn't understood the tension between them all those years ago. He'd thought it was about the wharf and their management styles. He hadn't realized it had all been about a woman.

"I have to," Jean-Claude said quietly. "If I don't, I'm going to end up bitter and I don't want that. You move her in. Keep the old place up for me if you can't accept it as a gift. I'm going to work for that conglomerate. Yeah, the horrible one that almost took our town down."

"Is that why you were in New Orleans? Sera mentioned it, but she thought you were making a deal behind my back."

His cousin frowned. "No, I was interviewing, and your sister is a menace. She's the worst gossip in town, and that's saying something. But yes, I took a job with them. It's going to take me around the world for the next several years. At the end, when I've seen something outside this town, maybe I'll want to come back, but I doubt it. You got to see the world. Now it's my turn."

What the hell was he talking about? "I got to see Afghanistan and Iraq. I got to see some shitty places in the jungle, and even then it wasn't a vacation. I got dropped in, someone shot at me, we collected the target or blew some shit up, and we went home."

A smile crossed Jean-Claude's face. "Well, then, I'm way smarter than you because I'll be in Paris tomorrow. Good-bye, cos. I wish you well, and call me if you can't find something, although Meredith knows where everything is." He held out a hand. "She's been my girl Friday for a couple of years. If only I could have loved her. I've got a plane to catch, cousin. You watch out for that girl of yours."

"I will." He shook Jean-Claude's hand.

"You know Zep is even right now sneaking into your room to get a look at her, right?" Jean-Claude started for the door. "Good luck with that."

A feminine scream split the air and Jean-Claude laughed as he walked away. Zep suddenly showed up on the stairs, trying to ward off a pillow attack from Remy's surprisingly feral-looking girl. Lisa was wearing a tank top and a pair of Remy's boxers. She looked sexy and slightly vicious.

"I'm sorry," Zep said, rushing down the stairs. "I just wanted to say hi. Your girl is mean. So mean."

He was going to kill his brother. Well, if Lisa didn't first.

* * * *

Lisa came awake with a groan.

Her brain seemed to have been replaced with a heavy bowling ball that kind of rolled against her skull. In a loud as hell way. She stared up at the ceiling. It wasn't her hospital room or her bedroom. There was a ceiling fan making a slow rotation around and around.

Oh, what had happened to her?

"I think it was Rene's strawberry wine," a masculine voice said. "From what I heard, you had quite a bit of it."

Shit. She sat straight up, hugging the blanket to her breasts. At least it looked like she was properly covered. She seemed to be wearing one of her tanks and Remy's boxers. How had she gotten into those? One minute she'd been swearing she wouldn't talk to the man again and a few tiny cups of wine later and she was wearing his shorts. Okay, they'd been rather large glasses. Still, she hadn't realized she was such a lightweight.

And now she had a strange man in her room.

"Many a bad decision has been made while downing that wine. I myself prefer a nice beer, but there are days when nothing else will do," the man was saying. He was a tall, slightly lankier version of Remy. A bit younger, but those years and maturity made all the difference for Lisa. Though she did like the longer hair.

Not that she would talk to Remy about growing out his hair because that wasn't any of her business. It wasn't her right to run her hands through that hair and feel it tickle her body as he kissed his way down.

Except…something played at the back of her head. Something she'd done. How had she broken that nail? And there was a rocking bruise on the knuckles of her right hand. She didn't remember any of that. She chose to deal with the problem at hand. "Why are you here? You're Zep, right? Remy's brother. You look a little like him."

"Although I'm considered the handsome one in my family. Zéphirin Guidry, at your service." He gave her a jaunty bow and a smile that didn't quite meet his eyes. "Tell me something, Lisa almost Guidry. If you're engaged to my brother, why is he sleeping on the couch?"

Oh god. The night flooded back in. The Ferris wheel. She'd

almost kissed him. When they'd reached the top, the wind had been chilly and she'd snuggled against him. She'd giggled as he won her a tiny teddy bear that only cost him an hour of his life and forty bucks.

The dance floor. They'd swayed and held each other, and in that moment the world had seemed perfect. The whole night had been perfect and she'd decided to forget about their previous problems. Who needed to think about the past when the present had cotton candy? That's what she'd told herself. Or maybe the strawberry wine had told her. She seemed to have listened to it a lot the previous night.

What happened next, that had been a product of her imagination, right? It was nothing more than a bad dream. She glanced over and there was a stupidly long hair extension on the pillow beside her, the one where Remy would normally sleep if he hadn't turned out to be a liar.

A liar who'd done what her brother had asked him to do. A liar who had his cash and no longer needed to be nice to her, but still had treated her like a princess the night before.

She needed to think and couldn't do it with unwanted guests around. "Do you normally intrude on your brother's bedroom?"

Again his eyes strayed back to those blankets on the couch and the pillow that had obviously been slept on. "Is it my brother's bedroom? Because you appear to be the only one sleeping in the bed."

"I don't think that's any of your business." But it would be Remy's when she found him. Had he sicced his brother on her? No. He wouldn't do that. He was somewhere in the building and had no idea his brother was being obnoxious.

"And to answer your question about how often I stick my nose in my brother's business, I do when I think something's wrong. You told the entire town last night that you're my brother's fiancée. Yet from what I heard, you didn't kiss him once last night. That's not like my brother. My brother is very affectionate. He also is the kind of man who would sleep with his fiancée. So if he's in trouble, if he's found some cold bitch who wants his property and nothing else out of him, then I think it's time I protect big brother for once. He can be foolish when it comes to women."

Wow. She hadn't expected that. According to Remy, his brother didn't care about anything but letting the good times roll. "I can understand that. I have two sisters and a brother, too, and we're always up in each other's business. As for Remy, we're working a few things out."

She needed to sit down with Remy and decide how they would deal with the mess she'd gotten them into last night. Well, him. She would leave one day and owe no one an explanation. He was the one who would be left behind, and he knew it. That was precisely why there was a thin blanket on a couch that couldn't have been comfortable to sleep on. It was far too small.

"Did you find out Jean-Claude was planning on giving him Chartier House?" Zep asked.

She put a hand to her head. It was too early for a grilling. And she had to deal with the ramifications of that hair extension. What would Miss Manners say about how to return someone's hair? *Dear Josette Hussy, I'm very sorry I pulled out your hair extensions when I tried to kill you in our catfight last night. I am returning them with best wishes. And stay the fuck away from my man. Love, Lisa.* Yeah, she didn't think that would probably be the way to go. "I don't know about any house. Where's Remy?"

And coffee. She needed coffee.

Zep stood at the end of the bed, his hands on his hips. "He's downstairs getting ready for the first customers to come. I think he's saying good-bye to Jean-Claude, too. Do you have any idea how much work goes into this place?"

"A lot. How would you know?"

"Oh, I know because I spent whole decades of my life avoiding it. My point is Remy needs a fiancée who not only gives him physical affection but who can work beside him. Unless you intend to spend your days at Chartier House hosting teas and trying to break into high society."

"Do you have that here? Because I was born in a trailer park and our high society was Miss MaryBeth's book club that was really more about drinking the hooch her husband made in the yard. Also, there was a nice couple who had a brand-new car, and that kind of made them the king and queen, but it turned out they were also making meth, so that didn't last long."

His eyes had gotten as wide as saucers. "What?"

She put a hand up, holding him off. "Your brother and I have already been down this road. I am not some princess who needs a man to take care of me."

"Fine. You're not exactly what I thought, but I wanted to have a few moments where we could be honest and put everything out there. You might have Seraphina and Momma under your spell, but I'm watching you, Lisa Daley. I've already seen one cold-hearted bitch tear my family apart. I won't allow another in. Do I make myself clear?"

"And what did you do about it the first time?" It occurred to her that she was being treated unfairly once again and she didn't have to take it. You know what? Zep absolutely had the right idea. They should get everything out there and take their proper places. He was going to be surprised where her place was. It seemed like the family could use an indulgent alpha female.

That seemed to stump him.

She pointed her scraggly nail at him. She was pretty sure she lost that nail while attempting to claw out Josette's crocodile-tear-shedding eyeballs and she would need to get that fixed. "Exactly. Nothing. You were way too busy drinking to help your brother with the business, much less to deal with the fact that he was obviously not meant for that soulless Barbie doll. Bayou Barbie, that's her new name. You didn't save him from Bayou Barbie and it cost him years of his life." She reached over and held up the hair extension. "You want to know how to handle her? You take her down. I already got one trophy, Zep. Don't make me take yours."

He stared for a moment. "I heard you got in a little tussle with Josie last night. I guess I thought they were exaggerating. Jesus, is that her hair? You took her hair?"

"She came after my...Remy and he did not want to talk to her. He was polite. She did not take his 'no' for an answer. That is the textbook definition of sexual harassment. I took care of the problem and it wasn't a tussle. It was a knock-down, drag-out fight and by drag-out, I mean Remy had to drag me out or I would have way more of her nasty hair for my collection." She rolled out of bed, grasping the pillow. "So you and everyone else in town needs to get something straight. I'm not some sad-sack city slicker you can intimidate. I'm here as long as Remy wants me here, and by the way, I'm the reason he has the wharf in the first place. It was my money that bought it." Well, her sister-in-law's, but he didn't need to know that. "So the next time you want to threaten me or want to make me look like some gold digger, you make a proper appointment."

She struck him with the pillow, his muscular arms coming out to ward her off.

"Hey, honey, I was only trying to look out for my brother." He backed out of her room though.

"I am not your honey, you infant." She was unwilling to allow that to be the end. "And while we're at it, my relationship with your brother is none of your business. You haven't shown him a moment's kindness in three years." Another vicious swat of the pillow had him almost to the stairs.

"I thought about sending him a card, but I got ADD." Zep started to back down the stairs with a strangely high scream.

"I don't care. You will treat your brother right or you're going to deal with me," she swore.

"I'm sorry," Zep said, turning and rushing down the stairs as though Remy could save him. "I just wanted to say hi. Your girl is mean. So mean."

She stopped, taking in the sight in front of her. It had been dark the night before and she was fairly certain Remy had carried in her passed-out body. She certainly hadn't seen this.

"You go up to our bedroom again when she's sleeping and you'll find out how mean I can be, brother," Remy was saying but she was too busy studying her new surroundings.

The bar was neat and clean, looking a lot like an Irish pub, but the lovely dark-wood bar and tables and chairs weren't what caught her attention.

She walked down the stairs, unable to take her eyes off the massive windows that showed her the bay. There was a big patio area where patrons could sit and watch the boats in the distance. Morning made the world gauzy and soft. Beyond the patio there were several piers with boat slips. Most of the large ones were empty, likely the big shrimpers, but the smaller personal boats were still docked in their places. Beyond the pier was endless ocean and gentle waves.

Her breath caught when she saw several fins break the surface. Dolphins. They had dolphins. And gulls flew in the sky.

There was nothing like it in the city, nothing that made her feel both awesomely small and entirely connected to the larger world. That view literally took her breath away.

"Yeah, it's something, isn't it?" Remy joined her, standing beside her. "I'm sorry about my brother. I've made it plain our room is off limits."

"It's okay. I think I made myself plain to him, too. Do you wake up to this every day?"

"I tend to see the sunrise and the sunset right here," he admitted. "I've missed this view but I know another one I'll miss even more."

She turned and he was staring down at her. She couldn't help but ask the question. Zep seemed to have disappeared and they were alone. "You don't have to keep this up. You have the money and Will doesn't expect it back. I promise I'm not going to be rebellious or sullen. I'll follow the protocols. I want to live through this. I won't make it hard on you."

His face turned solemn. "I love you and that's not about money. If you leave me, I'll be lonely for the rest of my life because I know I'll never meet another woman like you."

He knew exactly what to say to get to her. There was only one problem. "I don't know how to believe you anymore."

"Well then, you probably shouldn't have told everyone we're engaged. You know people take that seriously around here. I might be a ruined man if you leave me at the altar." When she didn't laugh, he turned serious. "It's all right, *chérie*. I'll tell everyone it was only a joke on your part. I'll have Sera spread the word that we're nothing more than friends."

"Can I have some time before you do that?" She was confused and the last thing she wanted was more curiosity about them. "I'm not going to lie to you. I think I was way more invested in our relationship than you were."

"Until I thought I lost you. Sometimes men are dumb and we get happy and don't want things to change, but we can grow up mighty fast when we need to. I'm not going to lie to you either. I want to marry you. If I wasn't such a gentleman, you might have found yourself with a ring on your finger this morning."

Ah, but the question was why the sudden change of heart? Did he feel guilty about the cash and marrying her would wash some of that blame away? Or had he realized he needed a partner in this business and she might be a good one? The situation was complex and she needed to think. "Can I have some time?"

"Time away from me? Not physically, of course, but do you want me to back off? Not touch you, not try to be close?"

Did she want him on the couch? She'd been willing to sleep with him when they had an expiration date. That hadn't changed except she had a decision to make. It would be smarter to stay away from him—

as far as she could and certainly emotionally.

"No. I'm a dumb girl. I miss you. I miss you holding me and kissing me. I want that for as long as I can, but I'm not promising anything else. I'll probably go home when this case is over."

"I'll do everything I can to make sure that doesn't happen." He turned to her, his hands cupping her face as he leaned over and kissed her. "Everything I can. I thought you would be miserable in a town like this, but you belong here. You need this weird place, and god knows we need you. Every town needs a queen."

She didn't know about that, but she melted in his arms. It was foolish, but she couldn't stop herself.

"Uhm, you want sugar with your coffee?" Zep was behind them, holding a tray. "The cook's already working if you want breakfast." He set the tray down at a table in front of the bay windows. "I'll bring out some beignets while you decide."

"Who are you?" Remy asked, looking his brother up and down. "You look like my brother, but he's usually dragging his ass home at this time of morning, not getting to work and looking like he actually had some sleep and a shower."

Zep sighed. "I'm too old to not have a steady source of income and way too young to want a real job. So I'm hoping you'll let me help out. I need cash to pay off my tickets. I think Armie's serious about letting Roxie arrest me this time. Apparently you're not allowed to park in front of other cars. Who knew that?"

"Everyone who took driver's ed." Remy pulled out her chair. "And yes, we can find something for you to do."

"Awesome. I need five hundred," Zep said.

Oh, that boy was beautiful, but it was time he learned how Lisa Daley ran a business. "Then you should get to work. Make sure you file all the proper tax papers. We don't pay upfront."

Remy grinned as he sat down across from her. "I'll cut you a check on Friday for everything you do now through Thursday. Welcome to the real world, brother."

His brother grumbled as he walked off.

"Tips are daily," Lisa shouted. "And you get to keep what you make."

Zep stopped and nodded. "Tips. I can make tips. All right then."

Remy groaned. "Now he'll expect me to leave him a twenty."

"Well, he can be disappointed." Her eyes kept straying to the bay.

"If I only have a little time, I'm not wasting any of it." He tugged her hand until she was sitting on his lap. He looked down at her hand. "Please tell me you're not going to carry that around like some trophy from battle."

She'd forgotten she still had that piece of Josette in her hand. "What else would I do with it? I'm certainly not going to tickle you with it. I risked life and limb so she couldn't touch you."

He grinned, a decadent expression. "We can superglue it onto a nice-sized plug and I can introduce you to pony play."

She threw it across the room. "Eww, you are deeply perverted."

"That I am," he replied, holding her close. "But I'm *your* pervert. Now, we've got some time before the rush is on. Let's sit here and watch the bay."

She cuddled up with her coffee and her man—for now.

Chapter Eleven

"Now, Josette says she's going to sue, but I think that's complete bunk because she doesn't have the money to afford a lawyer and we all know her family's reputation," Seraphina was saying two days later as they sat together in the dining room of Guidry's Pub House, established 1957.

Of course it was an odd bar, or maybe Lisa simply hadn't been around many family-friendly bars. Sera had marched in, gone to one of the storage closets, and hauled out a playpen. She'd set it up in the middle of the bar and before long little Luc was playing with a friend, a girl who looked to be roughly his age and whose momma was enjoying a burger and fries with a friend nearby.

"She's suing me? But I just got here. I can't already have a lawsuit." Was Mitch licensed in Louisiana? He was the only lawyer she knew. "And I sent her hair back along with a very nice note."

Seraphina and Delphine had shown up around one in the afternoon, clearly needing to talk to someone, and that someone was Lisa. They'd pounced the minute she'd walked out of the kitchen. She was spending the day getting in touch with some of the main processes. Not that anyone who worked at Guidry's understood what they did was a process. She'd spent the past few days meeting the five employees on the payroll. And dealing with the one who wasn't. Zep was awfully good at flirting with the women. Not as great at actually fulfilling orders.

She woke up at the crack of dawn and Remy was already out of bed. She fell into bed after midnight and Remy was still hard at work. After that first night, she'd convinced him he didn't have to stay on the couch. She would wake up and there would be a mug of coffee sitting on her nightstand and a warm pillow to her other side, but no Remy rocking her world.

He'd told her he would give her time. Oh, when she saw him, he would hug her and kiss the top of her head, but she was kind of going crazy because being close to the man made her hormones explode.

Sera grinned. "She's claiming you've given her PTSD. Now, I've seen actual PTSD and it doesn't involve sitting around and crying over that piss-poor wig of hers."

Delphine waved a hand through the air with dramatic flair. "I can cure her of it if she would only let me. There's a demon attached to that girl. Only I can convince that demon to flee. But she says twenty-five dollars is too expensive. Do you think I'm pricing myself out of the market, Lisa? Remy tells me you're a business guru."

Oh, she was not going to be the business advisor to a psychic. "I think that sounds perfectly reasonable. I know if I had a demon attached to me, I would fork that twenty-five over pretty quickly."

"She doesn't have a demon attached. She's got FOMO," Sera said.

"FOMO?" Delphine got that look in her eyes that Lisa already knew meant she was scheming. "I think I can cure that, too."

Sera's eyes rolled, but she reached out and patted her momma's hand. "It stands for fear of missing out. It means she didn't want Remy back then, but she doesn't want anyone else to get him."

"I told Remy it would never work out. He's seen his promised bride and it certainly wasn't Josette." Delphine lifted her iced tea glass. "He's got a touch of the sight, you see. Comes from my side of the family. The Dellacourts have always had a way with the sight. Now, everyone will tell you it comes from the Guidry line, but the Dellacourts are much more in touch with the other side, if you know what I mean. I've got a nephew who made something of himself. Now I am almost one-hundred percent certain he did it by making a deal with a demon. I've offered my services to him as well."

"Yeah, there's a reason we're the black sheep of that particular family," Sera explained.

"But to get back to my original point. Josette was never the bride the universe selected for my Remy. Not that anyone would listen."

"They had to listen. You talked about it at their wedding," Sera complained. "She actually stood up in the middle. You know when the preacher asks if anyone has just cause? Yeah, that was when Momma struck."

Wow, she never thought she'd feel for Josette. She knew she shouldn't ask the next question, but she couldn't help herself. "The sight?"

Delphine leaned in, her voice going low. "The sight, child. He gets visions of the future. He's seen his promised bride since he was a teenaged boy, but he never saw her face."

His sight needed an adjustment. And for a psychic he kind of sucked at figuring out cause and effect. A psychic should have seen that not telling his lady love he was being paid a shit ton of money to sleep with her would have a chilling effect on their relationship. Okay, anyone should have seen that coming from a mile away.

Which was why maybe he was exactly what Laurel had said he was—a dumbass.

"So he thought it was Josette? The vision he had?" She had been wondering why that hard-working man would fall for someone like Josette. Besides the perfect face and long legs and big boobs. Besides that stuff.

"Since we were kids he always says he sees his future wife here." Sera smiled over at her boy. Luc seemed fascinated with a toy truck, running it over the bottom of the playpen. "But the sun is too much and he can only see her outline. Of course he also said he could feel how warm she was, so that disqualifies Josette right there."

"Hello, lovely ladies," a masculine voice crooned. "Can I get you anything this fine afternoon?"

Sera frowned. "Yes, a damn waiter who doesn't take thirty minutes to take my order. I saw you over there with the Savoie sisters. Elva has a husband and Minnie is barely eighteen."

Zep shook his head. "I'm not trying to sleep with them, sister. I'm trying to get tips. I'm using my masculine wiles to try to pay off those damn parking tickets before Roxie throws me in jail."

Sera faced off with her younger brother. "I've got a tip for you. Stop using your masculine wiles. You've got none. You've got a pretty face and nice abs. No wiles whatsoever. Develop some serving skills, like table management and customer service, and the tips might follow."

Delphine stood up, putting a hand on her youngest child's back. "Don't you worry about her, Zep. You're doing a fine job. Your sister is merely hangry. I heard that word used and it fits Seraphina to a *T*.

Come on. I'll make her a *croque-monsieur* and she'll perk right up. I'll make one for my new baby, too." She reached out and patted Lisa's head. "You like ham and cheese, right, child?"

"Sure." She was just happy Delphine wasn't offering her a cleansing. Food she could handle.

Delphine led Zep away, but not before he stopped by the playpen and picked up his nephew. He smiled in a way that had every woman who wasn't related to him panting. He said some words that made the boy smile and then he kissed Luc and put him back down before following his mother into the kitchen.

Sure enough, the Savoie sisters both sighed as he walked past them.

Sera shook her head. "Now, see, those are masculine wiles. My brother isn't the most self-aware of men and he can be righteously obnoxious, but one of these days, he's going to be a good husband. One day a long time from now." She looked back at Lisa. "Though I think my older brother would make a good one right now. Don't listen to Momma about the sight stuff. And her Dellacourt relatives certainly didn't sell their souls. My second cousin Dante is simply very good with computers. And Remy is just plain good."

"Sera, I don't know that we should talk about this," she began.

"I think we should because I bet Remy isn't doing a lot of talking right now." Sera turned and it was easy to see the conviction in her eyes. "I don't know what happened between the two of you, but Zep says you're not sleeping together. There isn't a woman in the world who Remy can't charm into bed, so I have to think you're either lying to the town for some reason and my brother isn't your type, or he did something wrong. If you and Remy are nothing more than friends, you should know no one here is going to care. I know small towns have bad reputations for being intolerant, but that's honestly not who we are. If you like women, you don't have to hide it. Now, Momma will try to set you up with a woman named Christine. This would be a mistake. She's been trying to set up that crazed harpy for years. She made a bet with my cousin, Susan."

Wow, Seraphina could talk. "I'm not a lesbian."

Sera nodded slowly, as though thinking the problem through. "So Remy did something stupid."

"We're kind of taking a break. From the physical." Not that she wanted to. It seemed like Remy had become a bit prudish. Or he knew how much she craved his hot bod and he was manipulating her with it.

"Then he did something *really* stupid."

It didn't look like she was getting out of this one, but then this family seemed very nosy. Perhaps it was foolish to think they could sell this story to them. "He lied to me about something important."

"That doesn't sound like my brother. He tends to be incredibly honest."

She shrugged. And then told the damn truth anyway. "I think he thought he was doing what was best for me. But what he did hurt me a lot. I need some time to think about it and honestly, I have a family in Texas I should probably get back to. I came down here with him because I promised I would help him get Guidry's running smoothly."

Not exactly a lie, but Remy had instructed her she wasn't to tell anyone about the trouble back in Dallas.

"So you were with him but now you're not, and you nearly murdered Josette over a man you're not involved with," Seraphina summed up.

"Pretty much. I was drunk the other night. I lost control."

"Or your inhibitions were lowered and you showed us all what you want deep down." The pretty blonde leaned in, looking thoughtful. "The last time my brother was in town I didn't treat him properly. It was a bad time for me. I blamed him for walking away because once Remy's steady hand wasn't guiding me, I got very lost. I was an adult and he's only five years older than me. He's not my father. Our daddy died when we were in our teens. But I still blamed him for leaving me and Zep behind."

"My brother raised me." And he'd been the one who asked Remy to keep the secret. Will was the most important man in her life. Had been the most important man in her life before she'd fallen for that Cajun. What would she have done in his place? Had it started one way and turned out another? She hadn't gone into the relationship thinking she would fall madly for him. Why should he have done that?

Should he have held his hand out and stated that he couldn't sleep with her because he had more than one reason to do so? Or had he looked at her and all that mattered was that they both wanted it?

Still, there was that voice in the back of her head telling her she couldn't be that girl who simply forgave. That girl was a doormat. That girl was the one everyone rolled their eyes over and talked about how she was setting back every woman in the world.

"Then you understand how I feel about Remy," Seraphina said. "I want him to be happy. I think you make him happy. Oh, not lately. Lately you make him miserable, but the only reason he would be sad is that he loves you and he screwed up. Because if you were the one who'd screwed up and you'd done it honestly, he would have forgiven you. It's who he is."

She didn't like the idea that Remy was some kind of saint. "Like I said, he hurt me. Quite a lot."

"Yeah, well, I've been on the other side."

"What do you mean?"

"I've been the person who hurt someone." Her gaze went to where Luc was smiling at his playtime friend. He was heartbreakingly cute. His hair was darker, but those eyes were pure Guidry. What would Remy's son look like? His baby girl? Her heart clenched at the thought of Remy having kids with someone else. Seraphina continued talking, her voice wistful. "I hurt the hell out of Luc's daddy and I would do anything to make that up to him. I lie awake at night thinking about how good it would be to stand in front of him and drop to my knees and beg him to forgive me. Isn't that funny? Getting to my knees and begging, oh that's my sweet dream. Even when he doesn't forgive me. Even when he turns me away, I wake up smiling."

Tears blurred her eyes because there was only one reason Seraphina would smile at the thought of her lover rejecting her. "How did he die?"

Her nose had gone red, emotion taking over. "He joined the military after I broke his heart. He came from the richest family in town, so I know he definitely didn't do it for money. It was to get away from me. I didn't know I was pregnant when he left town. I didn't try to call him when I figured out I was pregnant. I got angry with everyone. I told myself I was going to give myself time to figure out what I wanted to do, and that meant staying angry with him because he left me. Yes, I was at fault, but he walked away. He didn't stay around, didn't call to see how I was. He left and didn't look back, and I thought love meant more than that. And then the soldiers came to his momma's house. Not mine. I wasn't his next of kin. I gave birth to his son and I still wasn't Wesley's kin."

The young man who'd died in combat. He was Luc's father. "Does his family know about Luc?"

Seraphina shook her head. "They don't care. They didn't even let me go to Wesley's funeral. I'm not from the right people. Because I'm his momma, neither is Luc. They've never asked about him, never come to see him. It's okay. I want it that way. I can't imagine life without my baby, and they would definitely not want me around him if they accepted him as a legitimate Beaumont. Wesley's got a brother so I'm sure they'll pass everything on to his kids. I don't need them."

"I'm sorry for your loss." She couldn't imagine it. She'd never had to lose someone like that. She'd gone through a lot, but she hadn't lost someone she couldn't talk to again, didn't have hopes of making things better with. Lila. God, her sister made her insane, and she had the sudden and deep desire to talk to her.

Forgiveness is the gift we give ourselves.

She'd heard the homily a million times. Sometimes forgiveness was easy. It was almost an afterthought. After she'd gotten away from her father and he'd died a few years down the road, she hadn't given him another thought. Oh, some of the things he'd done still lived deep in her subconscious, but she didn't think about the man himself. She'd moved on in her head.

Could she move on from Remy, her love for him only surfacing in those deep moments when everything else fell away and she was left with nothing but primal emotion? When she shed the society version of Lisa, would she mourn her choices? That she didn't give him another chance? So much was made of perfection. Men couldn't make mistakes because women couldn't be doormats. Any flaw was to be culled until the perfect mate was found.

There was no such thing as perfection. None.

Seraphina looked back at her, tears in her eyes. "I wish I had another chance. I wish he'd known he had a son. I kept that from him because I was angry. Isn't it funny how little that anger means now when I'm confronted with my son's grace? Luc doesn't care. He doesn't care that I screwed up. He loves me and it's pure and unconditional, and we can't have that from each other as lovers. I know that. There's always conditions on love between lovers, but shouldn't we try for something better? Shouldn't we hope we can love each other the way we were born to love?"

"It's not the same." She wasn't naïve. Seraphina wasn't telling her this story out of a need to share. This was about Remy. This was a sister's plea for her brother.

"I know, but I have to ask you—for me, for my brother—if you hold on to the wrong that was done to you, how do you have hands ready to reach out for what's right? I think I have to let go of Wesley and all my anger so when I get another chance, I can grab it with both hands, and this time I won't let go. If I get one more shot at really loving someone, at being a wife and a lover and a best friend, I'll let go of everything that went wrong before and I'll hold on for dear life. That's what I'll hold close to my heart. Love and not pain. I wish the same for my brother, but that choice has to be yours."

A red basket of French fries dropped between her and Seraphina. Zep stared down at them. "There. Those are hand-cut fries to go with the sandwiches. And I remember what both of you like to drink. Sweet tea and if it's a shitty afternoon, vodka tonic for Sera, and a super-buttery Chardonnay for you, Lisa. Because I do listen." He turned and then swiveled again on his heels. "And don't you dare give me tips. I don't take tips from family. I live to serve my family."

He walked away so primly she couldn't help but laugh.

Sera smiled, too, though tears slipped from her eyes. "A long time. Like years from now he's going to be a great husband to someone. Maybe it's someone who isn't born yet."

Lisa laughed and then sobered as Remy walked in. His eyes moved over the dining room until he found her. There was no denying how he smiled her way, how his whole body seemed to relax now that he saw she was here and okay. He winked her way and then headed for the bar.

And she wished he'd walked down and taken her into his arms and kissed her until she couldn't breathe.

"Think about what I said." Seraphina lifted her glass. "Until then, welcome to Papillon, Lisa. I hope you enjoy your time here, and don't sweat the lawsuit thing. The only lawyer who'll take her is terrible. Of course he's the only lawyer in town, and he mostly spends his time bailing Zep out of jail. We'll have Momma put the *gris-gris* on him."

"And then she can heal him." It was a pretty good business now that she thought about it. She clinked glasses with Seraphina and then turned at the sound of the door to the kitchen being thrown open.

Remy walked toward the patio, his hand on his brother's neck. "You wanted a job, brother. This is part of the job."

"I wanted to serve pretty ladies drinks and get tipped, Remy," Zep argued, his handsome face a bit pale. "I did not sign on to deal with stinky reptiles who don't know where their damn place in the world is."

Seraphina stood up and nodded. "Oh, Otis is visiting."

Lisa felt her eyes go wide as she followed Sera's gaze. A massive gator was strolling down the pier, out for a leisurely walk. He didn't seem to mind that one of the tourists damn near jumped out of his skin running the other way. "Holy shit."

Sera's hand waved. "It's okay. Otis is a sweetheart. He's only eaten a couple of tourists. As long as he's well fed, he's harmless."

Lisa watched in perfect horror as Remy obviously gave up on his brother and took that gator by the tail, hauling him back.

Damn that man was fine.

And she had a big decision to make.

* * * *

After he handled their reptilian interloper, Remy strode back toward the bar. Otis was an old visitor. He dealt with that gator the same way his pop-pop had.

"You are going to wash your hands, right?" Zep asked, falling in line beside him. "Because all the signs say you have to wash your hands before you go back to work after using the bathroom, and I think that should also apply to after you've handled dangerous reptiles. You don't know where that damn thing has been, Remy."

His brother had been no help at all. Zep had mostly looked like he was going to be sick. "I know where he was going. He was headed up to the parking lot. Having a massive gator in the parking lot tends to scare off customers, and then where would you get your tips? He likes to sun himself out there. The rocks are reflective."

"I'm only saying you should be more careful." Zep opened the door for him. "I know Pop-Pop used to do that all the time, but I think gators are meaner now."

"It was Otis." Otis was damn near a pet in some ways, and he was seriously getting on up there in years, but every now and again he got it in his lizard brain to make friends with the tourists. Tossing him back in the bayou usually worked because Otis was also pretty damn lazy, and the walk in was almost always a one-way trip. "I'm not a poodle, therefore I'm fairly safe around Otis."

But he would definitely wash his hands. He pressed through the kitchen, forcing himself not to look into the dining room where Lisa was sitting with his sister. He hoped she was passing a good time in there, but the image was too sweet for him. If he stared too long, he would find himself trying to sit down with them, to run his hand over hers, and he didn't have the right. But that in there—it was everything he wanted—Lisa taking her place with his family.

No, it was better he got back to work. It was hard to sleep next to her and not roll her over and take her. He thought she would welcome him, but he knew it wasn't forever, and suddenly sex wasn't enough for him. He needed to make love to her, needed to know she wanted him for more than an orgasm. Every night he worked later than he needed to, trying to ensure she was asleep before he came to bed and got in beside her.

He wasn't sure how long he was going to be able to hold out. And he knew every time he slept with her would make it exponentially harder to leave her.

He stopped at the sight of his momma holding a cigarette and stirring a pot of gumbo. God, he needed Lisa to take control of his damn family. He had forgotten exactly how crazy they were. Beyond crazy.

He washed his hands in the sink while trying to get a leash on his temper. "Momma, you can't smoke in here."

She simply smiled his way. "I'm just holding it for Michel. Apparently he heard that Otis was out there and that someone had called the sheriff. Michel's papers aren't exactly up to date. Now I tried to tell him ICE wouldn't come out for an Otis sighting, but he ran anyway. He'll be back soon. I suspect he's hiding in the bushes by the mechanic shop."

And now he needed a lawyer for his chef. And maybe a shrink, definitely someone who could help him stop smoking. He'd inherited a big old mess. Inherited? No. It was way worse. He'd paid for this sucker. Paid handsomely, and with maybe more than mere money since Lisa didn't seem to be coming around.

He might have come home only to lose the one woman who could have made it all worthwhile, because he was rapidly coming to the conclusion that she was the only woman in the world for him. How had he ever thought Josette could make him happy? He hadn't been thinking at all. He'd been certain it was time to settle down and she'd been pretty and willing.

Now he knew that wasn't nearly enough.

He looked at the kitchen. Someone was serious about salad. There were roughly twenty bowls of perfectly done salads ready to be delivered. Who the hell thought they would need that many salads?

His cell phone trilled. He pulled it out and sighed. It wasn't someone he could put off or drag by the tail back to the swamp. "I have to take this. Momma, put that cigarette out and go find Chef. Zep, stir the gumbo. You know how pissy he'll be if the bottom scorches."

Zep grumbled, but he was stirring when Remy stepped into his office.

Here he could see Lisa's handiwork. She'd already left an indelible impression on Guidry's. Everything in the office was neat and in its place. Jean-Claude hadn't been very organized, so making file folders and cleaning up in here had been Lisa's first task. She'd brought in nice curtains to frame the window and found him a much more comfortable chair. She'd even found some old framed pictures of his mom-mom and pop-pop, and photos of what Guidry's looked like decade by decade, and had made something she called a memorial wall.

His heart did a little flip-flop every time he looked at those pictures of his family over the years. He wanted a new picture up there on that wall. One of him and Lisa. Later, some of their kiddos.

He slid his finger across the screen. "Hello, Maia. Thanks for getting back to me."

"Hello, hot stuff," she replied, her voice low. "Heard from Big Tag you're back in the bayou."

"I am back home. Did you find anything out for me?"

He could practically hear her pouting over the line. "What, no flirting? You know you should buy me a drink before we get down and dirty, Guidry."

"I have a whole bar waiting for you if you ever decide to come down this way, but if this is good enough, you could be drinking at Sanctum tonight and making Big Tag crazy. So why don't you spill?"

"Fine," she said, satisfaction clear in her voice. "I'm sending you a couple of files that I'll forward to McKay-Taggart, too. I have some contacts on DPD who did some digging. Did you know the officer wasn't reprimanded for breaking the chain of custody?"

That was surprising. He knew it wasn't exactly her fault, but there should still be some kind of remark on her record. "She wasn't punished at all?"

"The incident wasn't even noted on her file. More, no one can now find record of the break-in. They're calling it a computer glitch. I'm calling bullshit," Maia said. "This is starting to feel like a setup to me, and I'm turning it over to Ian. I think you should hide your girl while he sorts this out, but I don't think it's going to take too long. If she's there with you, I think you're well set."

"What kind of setup are you thinking?" He was willing to listen to her.

"Did you know a young woman was shot outside Vallon's office building the day Lisa Daley called in her tip to the police?"

"No. I did not know that." A chill crept across his skin. "Was she a brunette?"

"She was, and roughly the same age and general description as Lisa," Maia replied. "I had one of our more intelligent investigators look into it. He said it was raining that day. The young woman actually worked two floors above Lisa, but she left that day at roughly the same time Lisa usually left. She was shot in the parking lot behind the building. She lived but it was a close thing. The police theory was a mugging gone wrong, but I have another one."

"They thought they were shutting Lisa up."

"I believe so. I think someone realized what she'd done. The feds arrested Vallon the next day, but obviously that was botched, and I'm not entirely sure that was an honest mistake. Someone is trying to tank this case."

"Why haven't they come after her again?"

"I don't know. I do know that the next day she was brought into the prosecutor's office, and she didn't go alone. She went with a little entourage, as it was described to me."

He could imagine who she took with her. "Her brother-in-law is a lawyer."

"Her brother-in-law is Mitch Bradford. He's not merely a lawyer. He's a pit bull. Her brother was with her, and Ian Taggart was, too. I think Mitch requested his presence, or likely someone from McKay-Taggart, to go in with them as background muscle. It's a smart play. It lets the feds know you've got money and power to protect the witness. Likely they'd already talked about protection for her. Taggart would have been there to assure them he could handle it."

"And them, if someone came after her." What a lucky play Mitch had made. The rumors would have gotten back to Vallon that she was protected by Taggart. "If Vallon has half a brain, he knows who Taggart is connected to."

"Yes, I suspect someone in his organization does, and they do not want to cross the Denisovitch Syndicate," Maia practically purred. "I think that's why they chose to go after the evidence and not your girl."

"Until the Italian showed up." But Lisa swore that Biondo had said he wasn't going to kill her. Wouldn't it have been easier to kill her there at the restaurant? Why take her somewhere else? He'd certainly been close enough. Why had he told her he wanted to talk? What did they have to talk about?

"Big Tag has way better contacts in that world than I do," she admitted. "I'm better with the crooks in suits who pretend they're not criminals. Anyway, I actually think you find yourself in a standoff. It's obvious they don't want to rock the boat with Taggart. They've managed to get the case shut down for now. I would let Taggart figure out what's happening with Biondo, but I think once they figure him out, your girl is probably okay to come home. She's in a cushy place because no one on Vallon's side wants to piss off Taggart's Russian in-laws."

She could go home soon? Would she rush off the first moment she could? Would she hop on a plane and never look back?

He felt his hand tighten around the phone as though he could crush the fucker and not have to listen to another moment. "Yes, we'll reevaluate after Taggart finds Biondo. Thanks, Maia. I'll let Big Tag know he owes you."

She was quiet for a moment. "And I'll be better behaved this time. Remy, if you want that girl, tie her up and don't let her go. She'll get used to it. If you let her come back, she'll get used to that, too, and you'll lose her. Sometimes you have to take the bold path to get what you want. That's my two cents. And I'll keep my eyes open here. If I can prove someone's messing with cases at the feds, I'm a shoo-in for a federal judgeship. Once I get there, I'll start using all those secrets I have because I'm going to be the hottest Supreme Court justice in history. I will rock that robe. They think RBG was notorious. Wait until they meet me."

He feared for a world where Maia had all the power, but for now he had other things to worry about. "Thanks, and give me a heads-up if you hear anything else."

She hung up and Remy wondered how long he had with Lisa. It

wouldn't be enough. She'd just started fitting in. No one in Dallas knew where she was, but if Maia was right, she might be willing to risk it if Will could be convinced they were at a standoff. She would want to go home to her family.

He felt heavier as he walked back out into the kitchen. At least Michel was back, though he was sporting leaves all over his clothes. His mother was trying to tell if he'd gotten into poison ivy.

"I can cure it, of course. I've got a lotion that will fix you up," his mother was saying.

Zep was stirring the hell out of that gumbo. "You should get to the dining room, Remy. We had a bus pull up ten minutes ago. They're on a swamp tour. Seraphina said it was thirty hungry, ancient people. Like really old. I bet it looks like the walking dead out there."

Somehow he didn't think that was what Seraphina had said. "Jean-Claude told me he'd started taking tour buses. Damn it. I shouldn't have given the other server the day off."

He hustled, ready to find the place in complete chaos, but it was quiet in the dining room. There were still ten tables occupied, and Mindy St. Clair was covering them. The college student was far better at table management than Zep.

"I heard we had a busload," he said.

Mindy smiled. "Yeah, Sera and Lisa handled it. They're on the patio explaining the food choices."

"She's passing out the menus?"

Mindy shook her head. "No. She talked to Michel yesterday and they're doing a prix fixe luncheon. They get one of two choices for three courses. Everything's ready. Michel only has to plate it. She's got the whole group on the patio and she's giving everyone who wants one a complimentary hurricane. I'm going to serve the appetizer in ten minutes, and I set the bus driver up with a private table. Lisa organized it all when she realized we had a bus coming in. It's okay, right?"

Of course she did. She'd been prepared and now this lunch was going to make money and run smoothly. "It sounds perfect."

"And tell Zep that he's got to actually spend time on the floor if he wants tips." She turned, her ponytail swinging.

"Unca. Unca."

He looked down and he was standing in front of the big playpen. Guidry's had always had one. He'd played in one when he was a kid, the work of the wharf going on all around him. Patrons would come in and drop their own toddlers in. When he was big enough, he would hang out on the playground off the parking lot, the same one that had been fenced in after Otis had started making his appearances.

Of course the best times were when his pop-pop would lift him up and walk him around. He reached down and hauled Luc up. "Hey, buddy. You getting bored in there? We'll put you to work. We can go see what Lisa is doing. Look real cute now. You're one of my best weapons in this war. You have to balance out Otis and your other uncle."

He started toward the patio but stopped. The sun was coming in at just the right angle and he held his breath. This was it. This was what he saw when he had the vision of his woman, of the life he could have. He'd never seen her face before, but it was her. He knew it deep down in his soul.

She came through the door, her sweet, sexy form backlit by the sun. His heart nearly stopped as she cleared the shadows and he watched her smile up at him.

"You looked awfully manly handling that gator." She ruffled Luc's hair. "Gotta go and get the drinks ready. I think that's going to be a rowdy crowd."

He watched her walk away.

And wondered how he could ever let her go.

Chapter Twelve

Remy locked the door and turned off the overhead lights.

Another day done.

A big low-hanging moon illuminated the bay, the light slipping across the dining room floor. On a night like this, he could sit and watch the bay for hours, letting the peace of the gently rocking waves fill his soul. This was what he'd come back for.

A deep sense of satisfaction filled him. It had been a profitable day. Zep had even seemed pleased. He'd walked out with a hundred and twenty dollars in tips after working two shifts. Whether he would use that cash to actually pay off his tickets had yet to be seen. The last time Remy had caught a glimpse of his younger brother, he'd been heading out with a set of red-haired twins. He'd promised to come back to finish closing up the marina, but Remy was fairly certain his brother would conveniently forget now that he had some cash.

But things were working and he rather thought they were working because of the woman currently counting cash and documenting the day on the laptop they used for accounting.

She was standing at the bar, her face illuminated with the light from the laptop. So damn pretty and she worked hard. "Can I finish for you?"

She looked up, her face softening. "I'm almost done. I loaded some accounting software. The program Jean-Claude was using was old and not very adaptable. I like to write my own code for some of this. We'll be able to see the data in a couple of different ways when we come to the end of the week, month, and quarter."

She loved to talk about data. Her eyes lit up when she started talking about how she could use the data to predict what to purchase, how many people to staff on any particular night, what to invest in. She got so animated when she discussed the business.

"Are you saying you're done for the night? It's barely midnight," she pointed out.

He'd found things that would keep him busy long after she'd gone to bed. He wasn't going to do that tonight. They were on a deadline and she could be far from him a week from now. "I thought we could talk."

Her brows went up in surprise, but she seemed to go with it. "About what? About the fact that Zep flirted with my senior citizens? I went out with dessert and he was letting those sweet old ladies pat his abs. I swear I expect to find him stripping for cash one day. He's incorrigible."

Remy couldn't help but laugh. "I'll talk to him about that."

She shook her head. "Don't. We've already got three new reviews on Yelp about how amazing our service is. And a poor review about how that young whippersnapper of a waiter should keep his clothes on. I expect the reservations for girls' night out to start flowing right on in."

If only his pop-pop could see them now. "I'll count on it."

"Are we staying here? Or moving into the house? Seraphina was asking about it. She said Chartier House is nice and has several bedrooms."

Well, that was one reason he hadn't moved her in. "I thought it was easier staying here in the beginning, but obviously if you don't want to share a room with me, I'll make arrangements."

Her eyes shifted away. "That's not it. I don't mind. Honestly, I was wondering if you were the one who doesn't want to share a room with me."

"Why would you say that?"

"Remy, you avoid me every night around bedtime. I thought we'd kind of agreed to be friends."

Friends. He wanted more than that. "Yes, that's why I've avoided you."

Her lips curled up in a slight smile. "Is there a reason we can't be friends with benefits?"

Because I need more than that. "You want to have sex?"

She sighed. "I wouldn't hate it. The way I look at it, we're not in such a different place than we were before. We know this won't go on forever. We can be friendly and if we consent, sure, why not have sex?"

Because I want to make love to you. She didn't want to hear that from him so he moved on to something she needed to hear. "I talked to Maia Brighton earlier today."

He hated how tense her body got.

"What did she have to say?" Even her voice was tight.

He moved toward the bar, wishing he had the right to wrap her up in his arms. "There's definitely something wrong with the way they lost those pages of the book. And there's something else. A young woman was shot in the parking lot behind your office building the same day you blew the whistle on Vallon. She fit your description."

Lisa dropped the pen. "Is she alive?"

He was so glad he could tell her the truth to that question. "She made it. I read the police report. It's up in my backpack if you want to read it. She said the man who shot her wore a mask and apologized as he walked away. We think he realized he shot the wrong woman and that's why he didn't finish her off. I should have told you earlier."

She shook her head. "Nope. I'm happy to have had the afternoon without that knowledge."

"It's not all bad news."

She shook her head. "It is for that young woman. I didn't drive myself home that day. I was unsettled after I called into the tip line and then talked to the FBI. I called Laurel and she and Mitch picked me up. That was when I told them what I'd done and Mitch turned into super lawyer. We picked up my car the next day, but I didn't go back to work. That poor woman."

"It's not your fault. You can't feel guilty about that." He moved behind the bar and grabbed a bottle of bourbon, pouring out two fingers between a couple of glasses. He passed her one.

She downed it in a shot. "Oh, I can feel guilty about a lot of things."

"She's okay," he promised. "And there hasn't been another incident until we came up against the Italian, and I'm starting to wonder if he really wanted to talk to you. Those numbers you memorized, they were account numbers, right?"

"I memorized all of them."

He shook his head. "I don't understand."

She turned the laptop around his way. "Ask me."

Was she saying what he thought she was saying? Was it even possible? "Okay, what was our take today at the bar?"

"We brought in two thousand five hundred and ninety dollars and twenty-three cents in credit card receipts and another seven hundred and thirty dollars and eighty-three cents in cash. Would you like me to split it up by type of credit card?"

So his girl was a machine when it came to numbers. "And you've been able to do this all your life?"

"Since I was a kid. I was a whiz at numbers and calculations. I wasn't as good at things like abstract math," she admitted. "But if what you're asking is could I possibly remember an account number, then yes, I can. I've got those pages in my head. Oddly enough it actually makes it easier that they took those two pages. Otherwise, I would be awash in a sea of accounts. Those two pages only held the data for four accounts, so easy peasy. If the Italian guy wants a number, I can give it to him. But I don't know how that gets the mob off my back."

"Taggart himself does that," Remy explained. "Charlotte Taggart has close ties to the Denisovitch Syndicate. By Taggart standing next to you in court, he was letting everyone know that he backs you and therefore the syndicate does as well. Now whether or not Dusan Denisovitch would go to war on Big Tag's word, I have no idea, but I don't think anyone wants to find out."

She sat there quiet for a moment, as though letting it all sink in. "So you think they'll leave me alone as long as there's no trial."

"I do. I'm talking to Big Tag tomorrow and he's going to sit down with Will," Remy explained. "They'll decide when it's safe to bring you home. They'll put some protocols in place, ensure you have all the safety features money can buy, and you'll be relatively free to move on with your life. Big Tag is trying to get in touch with Biondo to find out what his real motives are."

"So I could be home by next week." Her tone was bland, emotionless.

Was she desperate to leave him behind? "I think it'll likely be the week after. He has to be sure."

"But that time is coming." She turned back to the bar and opened the refrigerator. "Well, I want to know before I go and now is as good a time as any."

"Know what?"

She grabbed the simple syrup. He'd watched her make it in the kitchen before the lunch crowd came. "I want to see if I pass. The daiquiri test. You didn't get to try it before. I was too busy drowning in oysters and shrimp and glitter. Would this make me qualified to work here?"

"I would never put you behind the bar. You're too valuable to the rest of the place. I can train a bartender. I can't train an all-around manager." He actually didn't know what he would do without her. In the few days she'd been around, he'd come to rely on her. She'd made some changes that had helped out enormously and her processes, as she called them, forced the whole team to be prepared.

She placed the daiquiri in front of him. "Try it. I'd love to know what you think."

"I think it's going to be perfect because almost everything about you is perfect to me, *chèrie*."

"Almost?"

Damn but his whole soul ached at how beautiful she was. "Well, I'm not crazy about the fact that you're going to leave me."

She went still and for a moment, he prayed she would argue with him. "I have a life to get back to. I have a family in Texas."

And you lied to me. I can't trust you. I can't love you because I would always be waiting for you to betray me again. She didn't have to say those words. He could hear them in his head.

He'd had everything he wanted in his hands and he'd lost it all. Maybe not all, but certainly the best part. He would go on, moving through his days working in a place he loved, but now he wondered how hollow it would be without her.

He took a sip of the daiquiri. Simple. Cool. Perfect. Like the woman herself. "Yes, I would hire you on the spot. You know what you're doing." He slid off the barstool. "I think I'll head up to the office and get some paperwork done. You finish up here and get some sleep. I'll see you in the morning and we'll talk about Chartier House then. I suppose at some point we do need someone there. I have no idea when or if Jean-Claude is coming back. We can't leave it empty."

"Remy?"

He turned and she was standing, facing him with her back toward the moon. This was how he would remember her. So beautiful and full of life. "Yes?"

"I don't want to sleep alone. Even if you don't want me sexually anymore, I don't want a separate room. And you don't have to avoid me. I won't bug you. I feel better…happier when you're in bed beside me."

His heart damn near broke and he couldn't stay away from her a minute longer. He couldn't let her believe for a second that he didn't want her. He crossed the space between them and caught her face in his hands. "There's nothing I want more in life than to be by your side, *ma crevette.*"

He kissed her, devouring her mouth like a starving man. Days and days had gone by and he realized what had been missing. This. The way she relaxed when he touched her, how she softened and gave herself up to his kisses and touches. Having her close was wonderful, but he needed this to feel whole.

He dominated her mouth, his tongue delving deep and dancing with hers. He lost himself in the experience, in the scent and feel of her. His body came alive and he realized he'd been numb for days, going through the motions of life but not truly living.

How could this be one sided?

"God, I need this," she whispered when he moved to kiss the line of her jaw. "I need you."

He might have been able to back away if she'd kept it to the impersonal, but the idea that she needed him satisfied something deep inside. He wasn't the only one who felt it, this live-wire connection between the two of them. She was still going to walk away and that would break him in a way he'd never been broken before, but if she needed him, he would be there. He would throw himself into work and family, always knowing that if she called, he would go to her.

But he wasn't thinking about that now. They had a handful of days and he was done wasting them. He'd given her space and now she'd let him back in. That wasn't something he would take for granted. He would take her as many times as she would let him, branding himself on her body, making sensual memories to call upon when he was alone again.

He tugged her shirt over her head. Maybe he should make it his mission to make love to her in every damn room of this place. Everywhere he went he would be able to see her there, naked and waiting for him. They would play. He could tie her up on the bar after hours while he worked on paperwork, wrapping his rope around her naked form so he would have something pretty to look at. He would install hard points all over the place because he would want to suspend her everywhere. She was insanely gorgeous trapped in midair and waiting for her pleasure.

He wanted so badly to be her Master.

"I know you asked about it the other night, but you were also under the influence of all that strawberry wine." He whispered the words against her ear.

"I was under the influence of everything about this town." Her hands moved over his arms, brushing under the fabric of his T-shirt like she couldn't wait to get it off.

"I have to know. Is our contract still in place?" He wanted to dominate her, to take control and know she trusted him in this one way. It might be the only way she trusted him.

Her eyes came up and he was floored by the need he saw there. "Yes, Remy. Please take control. For however long we have left, I want to play with you. I want to be your sweet sub in the bedroom."

That was what he needed to hear. His cock was thick and long and thumping against his jeans. He knew exactly what he needed from her now. Complete and total submission. "Take off your clothes for me. Show me how beautiful you are. Let me know that I'm the boss here and now."

He pulled a chair out, easing into it. He wanted her to forget all the stress of the day, all the worries they would face tomorrow. He wanted her in the here and now.

"Yes, Remy. I like working for you," she said as she pulled her bra off and tossed it aside. Her breasts bounced free. She pulled the clip from her hair and it dropped out of its bun, cascading around her shoulders and chest. There was his lovely mermaid.

If he did take her to Chartier House, he would spend their evenings off playing around the pool in the back, skinny dipping and making love to her under the stars.

"You work *with* me, *chèrie*. Hell, sometimes I think I'm working for you," he replied. Yes, they were playing, but he needed her to understand how smart and capable she was. She needed to value herself so when she went out into the world again, she could find something that made her happy. He was surprised at how important it was that she be happy. With him or without him. "It's precisely why I need to be in charge of this. I have to be in charge of something or my manly ego can't handle it."

"I like working here and you have way less of a manly ego than I would have thought." She toed out of her shoes and he loved that she was slightly clumsy in her haste.

"I like having you work here. It reminds me of..."

She stilled, her hands on her jeans. "Your grandparents. You know from the stories your mom tells, they probably did stuff like this. She said they were pretty crazy about each other. I like that."

He shook his head. "Nope. Let's not think about that."

"But they were happy here and it must have been nice for you to have a happy couple after your dad passed away."

"Yes, they were happy and they made us happy. They took Momma in and treated her like their own. They built this place. I think you should consider helping startups get off the ground." He'd thought about it for a long time. She would never be happy as an accountant. She needed challenges to shake her up. "I think you should consult. But after you follow my orders, of course. The jeans and undies. Take them off now."

He did not want to get into a career discussion with her. He wanted her mouth working on something else. And he didn't want to think about who she would be working for in a few weeks. Here and now. It was all they had.

She shimmied out of her jeans and her undies and looked around. "Am I giving the night fishers a show?"

"Maybe, but I don't care. I'm the king here and they can deal with how I treat my queen. My queen is the most beautiful. In the evening light her skin shines like a pearl." He motioned her forward so he could get his hands on her hips, studying her body with loving eyes. "She is deeper than any ocean and far more mysterious to me."

He pulled her forward, the ripe berries of her breasts calling to him. How had he gone for days and days without this? He brought her close, her back bowing, offering up her nipples. Pretty pink nipples, and he knew how to play with them. He licked one and then the other, teasing them to points. He sucked one nipple into his mouth, gently at first, lavishing it with affection. She squirmed in his arms because he was going easy on her, and his girl liked a little bite. "My queen is everything to me. She is sun and moon, night and day. She is food and water to this old wolf."

He nipped her, his teeth sinking a tiny bit into her sensitive flesh.

She gasped and her whole body went tight and then relaxed.

"Please, Remy. That makes me crazy." Her hands found his shoulders, balancing herself.

"The words or the bite?" He licked the tortured nipple.

"All of it," she rasped. "All of it, *mon loup*. The bite, the words. God, I missed the words."

"You are earth and air to me and even if you are gone, the memory of you will be the solid ground on which I stand, the thought of you the oxygen in my lungs. But for now I take succor from the beauty of your body, memorizing every inch, every hollow and curve. For now this is my home."

He played for another long moment at her nipple. If she was his, he would talk her into nipple rings. She loved having them sucked on and twisted, and the rings would stimulate her further. He could run a chain through them when they played and tweak her at will. When they weren't playing, they would be a reminder that her Master always wanted her, was always with her.

He gave the other nipple a quick bite and she shivered in his arms. He could smell her arousal, tangy and sharp in the air. He could take her now if he wanted to and his dick would slide right in, she was so wet.

But he had other plans.

"Get on your knees, *chèrie*. I want you on your knees in front of me."

She dropped down to the floor, in between his legs. "I love it when you do that. Of course I also loved it when you dealt with that gator, though it scared me."

She was kneeling between his legs, right where he wanted her to be. "Otis is a known quantity around here. I wouldn't have done that with another gator, and you'll stay away from them altogether. I want you to open the fly of my jeans and take my cock out."

His whole body tensed in anticipation as she undid his fly and eased the zipper down. His cock jumped as though it knew exactly what came next, and the damn thing couldn't wait. He clenched his teeth as she reached out to move his boxers down, her warm skin brushing against his dick. Already he could feel the blood racing from all the other parts of his body to the most important part. Hard. He was so damn hard.

"Touch me. Let me feel your warmth and know your affection. Let me be enveloped by you."

She let her fingertips run over the skin of his cock, tracing the thick vein that ran along the underside. One finger moved from base, up the stalk to the place where the vein dove deep and his cockhead formed a V. And then she began again, this time taking him fully in hand and squeezing gently until his breath hitched and a drop of arousal coated the head.

"Lick it." His voice had gone guttural. This was a place where words seemed to fail him and all he could do was feel.

Her tongue came out, wetting those glorious lips of hers before she leaned over and curled her tongue around the head, sending pure lightning flashing through him. Every cell came alive the minute he felt her sweet heat surrounding him. He caught her hair in his hand, tangling his fingers in the soft thickness. He pulled it taut and was rewarded with a little gasp.

"You like that?"

"Yes, I like it a lot. I love it when you pull my hair just right," she said, the words humming along his dick.

It was a balance, a game he enjoyed very much. He tugged again and she sighed, a shudder going through her body but her nipples peaked.

"Suck me and don't stop until I tell you to."

She leaned over and his dick disappeared between her lips.

He let his head fall back. His hands remained in her hair, but he let her play. Her tongue ran all over the head of his cock. He wouldn't pull her off this time. They had all night.

She licked her way from the base to the head and then sucked him inside again. He watched her with heavy lidded eyes, his blood humming in his body, preparing for that moment of pure pleasure. He stared, taking in the gorgeous sight of her mouth closing over his cock. Her tongue whipped out, skimming across the slit at the head of his dick, drawing his arousal out.

"I don't want to stop at all." The words hummed on the skin of his cock before she sucked him deep again.

He guided her head up and down, his cock swelling with every pass of her sweet lips. Her hand came up, cupping his balls, and he couldn't hold out.

"Take what I have to give you. Take it all." He pressed in, tugging on her hair and letting her know what he needed. "I want to give it all to you."

She settled in, sucking him in earnest now, her head moving up and down, swallowing him in the best of ways.

He felt his balls draw up and then he was coming. He filled her mouth as he continued to thrust. He could feel her swallowing around him, taking in everything he had to give. Nearly blinded by the heat, he relaxed back as she softened around him. She licked at his satisfied cock as though unwilling to give up her prize.

Remy took a deep breath and vowed to pay his sweet sub back.

* * * *

Lisa ran her tongue down her Master's cock. Despite the fact that he'd recently come fast and hard, he was already showing signs that the evening wasn't finished.

She didn't want it to ever be finished. She wanted to stay here in this place with him, to work and build the business, to hold his hand when they went to the fair and have Sunday dinners where Delphine would do something wacky.

She wanted to go to bed with him every night and have him blow her mind. She wanted to play with him and wake up beside him.

Why did Ian Taggart have to have such a fearsome reputation? If the mob was still after her, she would have no choice except to stay. She might have to stay forever, and then things would take their course. The ache in her heart would ease, replaced with everyday affection, and one day she would be able to look past what had happened.

But if she was in Dallas when that came to pass, would he still be waiting for her? Would her stubbornness cost them a lifetime of happiness?

"Come here." His voice was deep, that dark whiskey sound that made her whole body light up with anticipation.

She'd loved sucking his cock, loved the way he'd filled her mouth. Mostly she'd loved how close to him she'd felt when she did it, hearing every moan of pleasure coming from him and knowing she was the reason he felt it. But it was good to move on to her own pleasure, too. A deep ache had settled in her pussy and he was the only one who could ease it.

She gave him one last kiss and got to her feet, her body languid. Even her bones felt submissive as she looked at him. No one in the world could do this to her, could make her want him the way this man did.

He tugged her onto his lap and his lips found hers. Long, drugging kisses. He could kiss forever and she would get lost in the way his tongue danced with hers. Over and over again, he kissed her until she didn't want to breathe, only wanted more of his lips and tongue.

His hands moved over her body, stroking her in long motions. It was easy to relax in his arms. He had her. She wasn't going anywhere. Being with Remy was like being in suspension. She could float and he wouldn't let her fly away.

"Your mouth felt so good," he said against her lips.

"Your cock tasted like heaven," she replied. She could still taste him on her lips, loved the idea that he would be able to taste himself on her tongue.

He chuckled as one hand found her breast, cupping it. "You kill me when you talk dirty. Every word out of that sweet mouth of yours goes straight to my dick. How did I ever once think you were some uppity intellectual?"

"You underestimated me. Or overestimated me. And I can be smart *and* dirty." It was a good combination, though one that only really worked around him. She'd never thought dirty could also be loving before she'd met him. Nothing was off the table with this man. She could try anything she liked because he would be there to catch her.

His hand moved down again, inching its way toward her pussy. "You can. You can be anything you want to, *chèrie*. Don't you forget that, and if anyone ever tries to tell you different, they will have to deal with me."

Because she wouldn't be with him. Because she was stubborn.

"I don't know what to do," she admitted, her heart torn. "I have a family and a life back in Texas."

He stared down at her as though he wanted her to feel his will. "And you would have a family and a life here. Your life. Our life. One we'll build together. I'll marry you tomorrow if you'll have me. I'll share this whole place with you."

After everything he'd gone through? She tried to sit up, but his arms caught her, keeping her close to him. "If you ever get married again, you have to have a pre-nup, Remy."

"I won't marry anyone but you." His hands tightened. "Spread your legs for me. I want to touch you."

He was killing her. She let her knees move wide, allowing him access to her pussy. "You can't risk the bar again. You have to protect yourself."

"It wouldn't be a risk with you. You would stay with me. You would have a family with me. We would give this place to our children one day. God, I hope we don't have a Zep." His fingers found her clitoris and brushed over the button, making it hard for her to breathe.

"I can't. I don't know." She couldn't marry him. He'd lied. And yet the idea of someone else making babies with him was insufferable. She couldn't think of anyone else getting to hold him and make him happy.

His fingers moved over her, touching her and making her squirm.

"I'll take *I don't know* over *I can't*. I'll take it until I turn it into a yes." His lips were against her ears, his words hot. "You like to say yes to me. You like to say, *yes, Remy, please fuck me with your fingers. Yes, Remy, please put your mouth on me and make me scream.*"

Oh, she didn't hesitate to say yes to that. "Yes. Yes, I want all those things."

She wanted everything he had to give. She was simply too afraid to reach for it. Or too busy holding on to something that didn't matter. If she let go of her anger, she might be able to hold on to him.

He stood, lifting her up with effortless strength.

He turned, setting her on the top of the table. Luckily she'd already cleaned up the place, and it looked like she would be doing that again because Remy shoved aside the basket of condiments and menus and laid her out on the table like she was the feast. Cool air hardened her nipples and sent a delicious chill across her skin. She'd served this table three times today. Two groups of friends and one family, but now it would be hard to look at it and not think about what it felt like to lie on top and wait for her Master's touch.

He stared down at her, his cock erect again. "You are the most beautiful mermaid a man ever found."

Mermaid was probably more beautiful, but she had to admit she liked her other nickname. "I thought I was a little shrimp."

His lips curled up. "I changed my mind. You're a mermaid." His fingers brushed over her, starting at her chin and drawing a line down. "You sing your pretty song and I'm lost because I can't do anything but try to find you, try to bring you back to me."

He dropped to his knees and suddenly she wasn't thinking about anything but how good it felt to have his mouth on her, his tongue sliding over her pussy. He made a meal of her, sucking and licking before he settled in, his long fingers penetrating her. They curled up inside her seeking that perfect spot while his lips found her clitoris. He kissed her sweetly and sucked on the little bud and sent her right over the edge.

Before she could process the first orgasm, he was standing up, shoving his jeans down and rolling a condom on. Through hazy eyes, she watched as he stroked his big cock. She wanted him naked. He was so beautiful naked, but it looked like he wasn't waiting around. Her Master was hungry.

"I don't know how I got through the last week without this." He moved between her legs, his big hands spreading her wide. "I don't know how I'll get through life without this. I'm utterly addicted to you."

She was addicted to him, to his touch and how he made her feel. Why allow one mistake to take that all away from her? His cock slid over her clitoris as he rubbed himself all over her wet pussy, preparing himself.

His eyes were perfectly serious as he looked down at her. "I shouldn't say this. I shouldn't make this harder on you, but please don't leave me."

He thrust up, joining them in the most precious of ways. Connecting them body and soul. His cock filled her, stretching her and making her aware of him. She reached for him, wanting nothing more than to be in this moment with him. One hand touched her face, cupping her cheek. He stared down at her while his hips moved, finding a rhythm. He drove her higher and higher, his words echoing in her brain.

Don't leave me.

How could she leave him? How could she leave this? She wrapped her legs around him, working with him, not wanting to lose the feeling of him deep inside her.

He stared down at her as though trying to memorize something. As though he wasn't sure she would listen to his pleas and he wanted some memory of her.

She reached up, touching that gorgeous face. His eyes closed briefly and when they opened again, she saw the pure willpower there.

"I love you." He picked up the pace, his hands on her hips, cock driving home. "I love you. I'll say it until you believe it and if you decide to leave, well, I can still show up on your doorstep. I won't ever give up on us. I thought I was wrong for you, but I'm not. No one in the world is going to love you the way I do."

Somewhere in the background she heard a phone ring, but she didn't care. The rest of the world could go to hell. All that mattered was the warmth he poured into her as he thrust up and pleasure coursed through her. It invaded her veins and took over her every thought until there was nothing in the world that mattered more than him.

He shuddered over her, holding on tight as he gave in. She loved how open he was when he let go and gave her everything he had.

He fell back into the chair behind him, but not before grasping her hand and taking her with him. They landed in a heap, the chair groaning under their combined weight, but like everything at Guidry's, that sucker held solid. This place and family were weird and crazy and strong.

She could be a part of this. She could belong here. There was still a little time to think. They were normal again and she could use these last few days to make her decision.

"You didn't even get your clothes off." She wanted to touch him, trace his scars and kiss his warm skin.

"Too busy. Needed you too much. Lisa," he began.

What should she say to him? It was too soon. The ache was still there in her heart, but she also knew they couldn't be done.

The blare of the house phone broke through their intimate moment and Remy groaned.

"It's probably my brother. He won't stop if he needs something. My cell is on the charger in my office, but he'll call any number he thinks I'll answer." He kissed the top of her head. "I'll go unplug the fucker. If he's caught at some chick's house and needs a ride, he can Uber."

She didn't want to lose the moment, but she scrambled off Remy's lap, reaching for her undies. If she was going to seriously think about becoming a member of this family, she had to take care of even the most obnoxious Guidry. "Answer it. I can't stand the thought of him desperately trying to get in touch with you. You can't leave him. Do you even get Uber out here?"

He fastened his jeans. "You're too soft hearted, Daley. And I've heard old Jacques tried to sign up until the company told him his riding lawn mower didn't qualify. Don't laugh. It's a real nice one." The phone started up again and Remy groaned. "I'll be right back and we can take this upstairs. I've got some toys I want to play with."

And they had a serious discussion to have. They could do it naked and wrapped up in each other. She watched as he hustled back to the office.

How could she leave him?

She put on her jeans and dragged her T-shirt over her head in case that really was Zep in need of a ride. Although knowing she was likely safe, Remy might not insist she go with him. Of course, it wasn't like she didn't have a choice. She could simply slide into the front of the truck beside him and he wouldn't leave her behind.

She sighed and straightened up the table. If he was going to end every night by throwing her on some random table, she'd better get good at putting everything back together. First she wiped it all down, spraying anti-bac everywhere. She carefully reset the basket, making sure they hadn't broken any of the condiment jars. Settling the menu back in place, she stopped and really looked at the back of the menu for the first time.

Guidry's didn't have some fancy menu like Top that changed every day and got printed on heavy cardstock. These menus had been printed on regular paper and laminated. The front announced all the options for burgers, gumbo, jambalaya, and the plethora of meats Michel could throw in a fryer. But the back was all about history. She stared at the pictures. There was one of a couple in a black and white photo standing in front of a smaller Guidry's. The bar had been roughly half the space and incidental to the wharf. The couple had their arms around each other, smiling proudly in front of their business baby.

Remy's grandparents.

Guidry's Bar and Grill was founded in 1957 by LC and Glendola Guidry. LC fought in World War II and when he came home, he wanted nothing more than to build a place like the ones he'd seen in Europe, a true family pub. Glendola's parents had left her the bait shop and wharf, so they expanded and soon Guidry's was as much a focal point of Papillon society as the local church. Always holding fast to the idea that this was a family business as their personal family grew, they did it at the restaurant.

Children have always been welcome and a generation of Southern Louisiana bébés grew up at the wharf. Guidry's became a place to celebrate at and to gather when the community mourned. It is a true American business, dependent on family and giving back to the community it serves. Though LC and Glen have departed this earth, their love lives on in the spirit of the business they built and passed down to the grandchildren. Welcome to Guidry's where we hope you pass a good time.

There was another picture, this one in color. LC and Glen were much older and surrounded by family, including a heartbreakingly handsome teenaged Remy. They all stood together smiling in front of the Guidry's she was standing in now.

Tears blurred the words. Once there had been two people who took a chance on each other. Had neither of them hurt the other? Were they utterly blameless and mistake free? She doubted it. They were human and hurting each other happened. No, she was sure there had been very bad times for that smiling couple. What they hadn't done was let it break them. She was mistaking stubbornness for strength.

Two people had taken what they had and built something great. They'd built a family that hadn't existed before—first through the children and then through this bar. They'd built something that lived on after they were gone.

She was never leaving this place. She had found her home and she would fight for it. She would work her hardest to maintain and grow what Remy's grandparents had given into his hands. She would learn from them and grow a family, her love for Remy expressed in new human beings, boys and girls she would love unconditionally, and this would be their birthright. This place and town, the bay and bayou would be theirs.

She loved her family in Texas but she would always be the baby, the one who needed help and protecting. The family she created here in Papillon would look to her for strength.

And one day, it would be her and Remy on that menu. Older, wiser, even more in love.

A loud knock from the front of the house made her start. She wiped away the tears on her cheeks. They were good tears, happy and relieved because she'd made her decision.

The knocking started again. How late was it?

She crossed the space with absolutely no intention of opening that door. There was a security monitor that would show who was out there and then Remy could deal with them. It was after midnight and if this was someone come looking for a drink, he would have to go somewhere else. Maybe Remy would drag him away and toss him back into the bayou like Otis.

"Remy? Remy, it's Armie. I need to talk to you," a deep voice said.

She glanced at the security station. Sure enough, the sheriff was standing at the front door and it looked like he'd brought some friends.

She couldn't keep the sheriff out. God, what if something had happened to Zep or Seraphina? Or Remy's mom? Her heart started to race and she found the keys.

"Remy, the sheriff's here," she called out. She wasn't sure he could hear her from his office. Her hands shaking slightly, she managed to get the door open.

Armie stood there, a frown on his face. "Lisa, these men are here with a warrant to take you into custody."

She looked at the officers behind him and knew her time was up.

Chapter Thirteen

Remy jogged into the office, thinking of all the ways he could murder his brother. No one else would call this damn late. Once Zep was gone, there would be no one to interrupt his playtime. Well, no one except all the other members of his family.

He would have ignored them all for Lisa, but his girl wouldn't have it. Of all the things that might tempt a woman to marry him, his insane family hadn't even been on the list. How odd that it might be the exact thing to push him over the top. Someway, somehow, his Lisa had fit right in as though they'd been missing an important piece, the piece that made them functional, and now that it was slotted in, they were back in motion. Unstuck. Sera smiled more, had matured into a good mother. His momma adored Lisa and she'd softened up. Even Zep was more tolerable while Lisa was around.

He picked up the landline and looked over to his cell. He'd forgotten to charge it earlier and had plugged it in when they'd closed. The screen glowed in the dark of the office and fear crept up his spine.

Ten messages. Why would someone leave him ten messages?

"This is Guidry," he said as he tried to see who'd called his cell.

"Thank freaking god," Ian Taggart said over the line. "I swear you've been gone for a week and you forget all our fucking protocols, one of which is to carry your phone at all times. Finding this number was insanely hard."

That answered his question. His hand tightened around the receiver. "What's going on?"

"Maia called about thirty minutes ago. The feds filed to put Lisa under custody as a material witness. They got a judge to sign off on the warrant outside of the courtroom. Maia only found out because she's got a mole over at the federal office. The fact that they did this in the dead of night scares the shit out of me. They'll be down there tomorrow morning to pick Lisa up. It's best we avoid the whole thing. They can't take her in if they can't find her. Get her out of there now. I'm sending someone else down so you can take shifts."

His mind was whirling. What the hell had happened? "Wait? What? The prosecutor said there wasn't a case."

"Well, he changed his mind," Taggart replied. "I don't know and Maia hadn't heard anything had changed about the case. I have to figure out what the hell is happening, but the first thing I need you to do is get Lisa someplace safe."

"They don't know she's here. Her brother doesn't even know exactly where she is. We left from the hospital and I made sure we weren't followed."

"Oh, but they do," Taggart replied. "They know exactly where she is. Apparently someone named Josette Trahan recently filed papers with the local courthouse. She's suing Lisa and she listed Lisa's address as the bar. Normally that wouldn't catch anyone's eye, unless they were looking for her and looking hard. Someone's been hunting her down in cyberspace."

Hunting her. The words chilled him to the bone.

"I'll call you when I have her secured. I'll make arrangements for someone to take over here, but they won't know anything more than we left. We'll be ready to send those feds on their way in the morning." He hung up and immediately went for the gun case.

"You won't have the chance, my friend. They're already here," a voice said.

Remy turned and a shadow peeled away from the wall. The man coming at him was roughly six foot two and lanky. Dressed in all black, but his shock of light blond hair gave him away.

Taggart was going to kill him for getting caught without a gun. The week had made him soft and now he was with a known assassin in his own damn office.

"I'm sorry to scare you in this fashion. I had to sneak in or I feared you would react the way you did last time." Biondo didn't have the same problem as Remy. He was holding a semiautomatic in his left hand, pointed right at Remy's chest.

In the distance he heard someone pounding on the front door.

"They're here and if we allow them to take her, they'll get the information they need and disappear, and we'll be left with her body. They will ensure it looks like someone else kills her," he said, his Italian accent thick. "They are…how do you say? Pretending. The paperwork will be perfect, but tomorrow the real police will show up and the whole thing will be blamed on criminal elements such as myself. They will blame Vallon or me. They will say we wanted to shut the witness up forever."

He turned to the door as he heard Lisa yell something. Something about the sheriff. Remy's stomach turned. "I need to get out there. I can't leave her alone with them."

"I agree, but you have to be calm, Mr. Guidry. She is not alone. Your sheriff is there. He doesn't understand the situation though. Of course, you don't either. I am not the enemy," Biondo said. As though realizing his actions didn't match his words, he lowered the gun. "I'm sorry, but after last time, I have to protect myself. You were not interested in talking."

"You tossed my girlfriend into the trunk of your car," he growled back. "You were about to leave with her. No, I wasn't interested in talking."

"I did not handle things with as much finesse as I should have. What can I say? I'm used to shooting people, not kidnapping them. And by kidnapping, I was only borrowing her. I would have brought her back safe and sound after I got what I needed."

Well, of course. "The account number."

He put a hand on his chest. "My account number. I used Vallon for years, and trust me, he's going to have a visit from me to speak to him about his business practices. He will not enjoy how this meeting will go. But for now, we have to get her away from these men. As I stated before, they look like police, but they are not. This is an intricate game and your woman is always the pawn. They are going to sacrifice her tonight."

"Why should I trust you?" He shouldn't trust the other man. Not for a second, but Remy knew what the answer would be.

"Because you have no other choice, my friend," Biondo replied. "You might not believe me, but I have a code of my own. I turn down more assignments than I take. I only take assignments where I decide the target deserves to meet me."

"An assassin with a conscience?"

Biondo went still, as though waiting for the decision to be made. "Like I said, I have my code. Now you have to make the choice. Will you let me help you or shoot me and go into this alone?"

"Remy?" Lisa's voice was closer now.

He was out of time. He couldn't let her walk in and see Biondo standing there. It would ruin the only advantage they had—surprise. "If you betray me, I'll never stop hunting you down."

"Just be ready," Biondo said. "I'll make some chaos and you get her out. Run with her. All I ask is when this is done, I want my account number and then she will forget she ever saw it."

Remy nodded. The last thing he wanted was for her to be in this man's way. There was something almost arctic in the assassin's eyes. He damn sure wasn't going to mention that she wouldn't be able to forget those numbers. "It's a deal, but remember who I work for."

He retreated, blending into the shadows as though they were his natural home. "I do not forget, Mr. Guidry. I have no wish to be on Mr. Taggart's list. Do not get on mine. Be ready to run."

He wanted to run right this fucking second. Instead he opened the gun closet and tucked his Colt into the back of his jeans and covered it with a hoodie he did not need. But it seemed better than walking out and letting everyone know he was carrying.

He strode out, his heart thudding in his chest, but he was calm, cool. He had to stay in control for her sake. He nearly knocked into her. "What's wrong, *chèrie?*"

Her eyes were wide with fear. "Some men are here and they said I have to go with them."

"Remy, these men are here to take Lisa into custody and transport her back to Texas. This is Marshal Jones and Marshal Porter." Armie was in street clothes, a sure sign that they'd gotten him out of bed to deal with this problem. "They say she's a material witness in a federal case back in Dallas. Do you know anything about that?"

He tangled his fingers in hers, giving her a reassuring squeeze as he faced the men who'd come for her. "Of course we know about the case. Lisa has been cooperating on every level. The last we heard, the prosecutor wasn't re-trying."

"Things have changed," one of the men said. Marshal Porter was tall and broadly built. He wasn't hiding the fact that he had several firearms on him. His jacket was off in deference to the heat and Remy could see he had two guns in holsters. "The prosecutor's office has new evidence. It's important that we get her to safety. Hence the warrant to take her into custody. No judge fills that out unless he knows the situation is serious."

"How am I not safe here?" Lisa asked, her voice shaking a bit. "I'm perfectly fine testifying, but I'm not going into some sort of witness protection plan."

"I have a warrant that says you will," the second man said. Marshal Jones was thinner than his partner, his eyes narrowed with irritation. "You will surrender to my custody and be removed to a safe site. From there we'll discuss your situation."

"Armie, did you check their badges?" He wasn't sure how much time Biondo would need. Talking seemed like the best way to give it to him. The minute he had the chance, he would go for one of the boats. If he could get to the keys.

Armie frowned. "Of course."

"I'd like to see them, please," Remy said. "And I'd like to see the warrant as well. Lisa, call your brother-in-law. I'll send him a picture of the warrant and he can advise us. Her brother-in-law is an attorney."

If he knew Ian, Mitch was already on it, but he wanted to give Lisa something to do and Mitch might be able to explain what was going on so she wouldn't be shocked. And Big Tag would know this was going down far sooner than they'd thought.

"Ma'am, there's no need to bring lawyers into this," Porter said. "You can call him when we get you to safety."

She was already dialing.

Armie seemed to sense something was off. He glanced between Remy and the two supposed marshals. "I think we should take this back to the station." He gave them an amiable smile. "No place is safer than the sheriff's office."

"Mitch, I'm sorry to wake…yes. Okay. I understand. Yes, that's happening now." She went silent, turning away but staying close to Remy.

Yes, Mitch was going to do his job and everyone would have a heads-up that this was going to go south and fast. She would know to follow his orders and his lead.

"Yes, I think that sounds like the perfect thing to do," Remy said. Keep 'em talking. Give Biondo time to get into place. Of course part of the problem was they were standing in the middle of the main aisle. They could easily block either the front entrance or the one that led to the patio and the dock. Biondo had been smart enough to find them, to track their opponents. He might wait until they had a shot at getting out either of the doors. He needed to move them further in. "How about Lisa goes and packs an overnight bag for the two of us and I'll get everyone some coffee? I assure you it's way better here than it is at the Sheriff's. That man drinks motor oil."

Armie smiled, an expression that didn't come close to his eyes. "I need pure caffeine. You're the only one who likes all those flavored things. But definitely make a pot. It's going to be a long night."

Jones put his hands on his hips as he followed them. "There is no need. Ms. Daley, I am an officer executing a valid and lawful warrant. If you do not come with me, I will have you arrested. If your friends here attempt in any way to stop me from doing my job, I will not hesitate to arrest them. Sheriff, I expect that you will also do your job."

"This is a highly unusual situation, Marshal," Armie said. "I don't usually have law-abiding citizens dragged out of their homes in the middle of the night. I am the duly elected sheriff of this parish, and one of the reasons I was elected was to protect my people. So while I will absolutely follow the letter of the law, I will also ensure that every *i* has been dotted and *t* crossed before I allow you to waltz out with one of my people."

"Porter, it looks like we're going to have trouble with the locals," Jones said with a frown.

Lisa had hung up and moved to the bar with Remy. "You're not going to have trouble. I'll go with you. Let me grab my bag. It's upstairs."

It wasn't. Her purse was sitting right behind the bar, but likely Mitch and Big Tag had told her to get out of the line of fire.

"I'll have the coffee ready for you when you come down, *chèrie*." He winked at her.

"Wait, I thought you were fighting us." Porter stepped in closer.

Where the fuck was that Italian? Remy was honestly ready to kill both these fuckers and let Armie sort it out. "Nah. Look, you're right. I don't want any trouble."

There was a loud banging as the front door came open. "Remy? Hey, did you know the door is wide open? Is everyone okay? Who the hell are you?"

His brother walked in and he was carrying. Too late. For the first time in his life, Zep had kept his promise and was here to check the marina before he headed home. It was dark out there and lots of critters came out at night. Which was precisely why Zep was carrying a rifle.

And Remy watched in complete horror as Porter reached for his pistol and shot his brother in the back.

* * * *

Lisa froze as Zep walked in, a worried look on his face. He had a rifle in his hand, but then she'd been told she shouldn't walk much past the parking lot without one at this time of night.

She was about to tell him they were all fine, about to lie through her teeth, when one of the marshals tensed and his hand went to his holster. He'd pulled that revolver and fired before she could shout out a warning.

Zep's eyes flared as though he couldn't quite understand what was happening to him. The rifle fell from his hands, clattering uselessly to the floor. "Remy? What was that? I can't…"

He pitched forward, his body hitting the floor with an audible bang.

She didn't think. She ran toward him, hearing Remy curse behind her.

Armie's gun was out, too. "What the fuck was that? Remy, call a goddamn bus."

She looked up and Remy already had his cell phone out. He dialed with one hand and gave short, sharp instructions.

"He came at me with a rifle," Porter said, his voice shaking.

"It's Southern Louisiana. We've all got a rifle, you ass." Armie knelt down beside Zep. "And he was turned away from you. You shot him in the back."

"Lisa, get back here right fucking now," Remy yelled.

She stopped but she'd gotten too close. Porter reached out and grabbed her, shoving that same gun he'd used on Zep into her side.

"Put the fucking guns down," Porter said. "Put 'em down or she's dead."

Remy immediately set his gun down and held his hands up. "Please let her go. You need to get out of here. I know you're not a real marshal. There's an ambulance coming. This is your chance to leave and disappear. I assume you're being paid. You've already shot one civilian. Do you want to have to shoot me and the sheriff, too?"

"What do you mean they're not cops?" Armie asked.

"I don't know who sent them, but the real marshals are set to show up tomorrow," Remy explained. "These two are going to kidnap Lisa."

That was what Mitch had explained to her on the phone. He'd gone as quickly as he could, explaining something was wrong with those two and she needed to get to safety so Remy could do his job.

Mitch hadn't counted on Zep showing up. God, he was perfectly still. *Please let him be alive.* Remy couldn't come home after all this time only to lose his brother. He couldn't.

She was still, so still she could feel how her heart pounded. "I'll go with you. I'll go quietly. It's okay. Whatever you need, I'll do it."

She would do absolutely anything to make sure that ambulance got here and was allowed to work on Zep.

"We're going to back out of here real easy," Jones said. "I see either one of you move and my friend is going to kill her."

"Lisa, you listen to me," Remy said, his eyes focused on her. "You survive and I will come for you. Do you understand me? And if my friend is here, now would be an excellent time because I have a straight shot to the outside. That door isn't locked yet."

Because Zep hadn't done the final walk-through of the marina.

Something pinged through the air and then she felt the body behind her go completely stiff and then perfectly soft.

Chaos erupted as Porter fell back, his arms loosening and setting her free. Remy tackled her. All the breath left her body as she hit the hardwoods. She glanced to her left and saw what she hadn't before. Porter was on the floor, a neat hole through his forehead.

"Stay down," Remy said. "I don't know where the other guy went and I have to get you out of here."

"But Zep," she protested. They couldn't leave Zep behind. Was he even alive?

"Armie's got him." Remy's voice was solid but she could still hear the emotion. "I have to take care of you, love. I have to get you out of here. Can you run with me?"

She wasn't sure she could move at all. The space had gone deadly quiet, eerily quiet, and then she heard the sound of a low groan.

Zep was still with them, but she had no idea how long that would last. What would happen if they got taken hostage? And who had fired at the man who'd had her in his clutches? It hadn't been Remy. She'd been watching Remy, and Armie had been on the ground beside her, trying to help Zep.

"Lisa?" His voice was insistent.

"Yes, I can run." It was time to do anything he asked of her. He was the expert here. He'd been a SEAL and a bodyguard. She was an accountant and this was only her second time in the line of fire. She hadn't fared spectacularly well the first time. "Where are we going?"

"Hold on to me. Hold on tight." Remy wrapped his arms around her and started to twist and turn them toward the back of the house where they could get to the marina.

Boats. He wanted to go for the boats.

"Don't do this, Guidry." Jones's voice rang out. "I don't want to kill you, but I will if I have to. Your sheriff took some fire. Your brother is down. Give up the girl and it all stops."

"You go, Remy," Armie yelled.

Lisa looked back and the sheriff had somehow managed to push a table on its side, giving him and Zep's body some cover. He'd also pulled a secondary weapon and looked perfectly ready for a firefight. The only thing marring the sight was the dark stain on Armie's left arm. He'd been hit in the crossfire.

Jones stepped out from behind the hostess station where he'd been hiding and took another shot at Armie. It wasn't the only bullet that went flying. From somewhere above, a bullet slammed into the wall right behind Jones's head. He cursed and disappeared again.

And Remy was up on his feet, hauling her with him. "Run. You keep running. Even if I'm not behind you anymore. Get to the airboat in mooring five. The keys are always in there. Fire it up and get into that bayou. I'll join you if I can. Go."

She didn't hesitate. She ran toward the door. Her heart thundered, hands shaking as she opened the door. Remy was behind her, but the bullets were flying again. They resounded through the space, though she couldn't tell where they were coming from except behind her. In the distance she could hear the sounds of sirens coming up the road. Surely that would scare off the pretend cop.

She pressed through the door and her feet hit the boards of the pier. Number five. Was it on the right or the left? Oh god, how could she run when Zep was dying?

Five. She turned to the left. Please let Remy be behind her. She wouldn't, couldn't leave without Remy. She would find a weapon and go back after him.

The boat in five was an airboat, the kind they would use to take people into the bayou. It was a flat-bottomed boat with a massive fan on the back. That fan might be a bit of cover from someone who was firing on the boat.

The boat swayed as she scrambled in. The keys. She had to find the keys.

And then the whole world seemed to sway as the boat rocked hard back and forth. Something heavy tackled her from behind and every bit of breath she had in her body fled. Remy. He was on top of her and that was when she felt something warm hit her cheek. The bottom of the boat was cool against her skin, but this was hot, and the coppery smell couldn't be denied.

Blood.

"What happened?" She breathed the words, shocked.

"He's coming. I took one to the shoulder, but we'll never get the boat started before he catches up. You stay down," he said. "Stay under me. Ambulance will be here in minutes. Don't underestimate those boys. Biondo will come, too."

The assassin?

"Love you, Lisa." His mouth was against her ear. "Reach into my pocket. Don't use it until you see his face. Not until then. I'm your shield."

He was willing to lie there and take every bullet that came her way.

She reached into his pocket and felt cold metal. She flicked off the safety. "Please, let me up. I can shoot. I can save you. I don't want to lose you."

Not when she'd just found him. Not when everything they'd ever wanted was right there, ready for the taking.

She felt his body shudder above hers.

"Not on your life, *ma crevette*. I'm your cover. Now and always. Never going to let you down again. Love you. Not until you see his face." He went still.

So heavy. His dead weight held her down, but the boat still rocked gently. It was dark. The lights had been turned off and only the moon illuminated the deep gloom of night.

Please. Please. Please. Let him live or let me go with him.

She would fight, but she couldn't see a life without him. What the hell had she been thinking? She couldn't leave him, couldn't leave her home.

The sound of hard-soled shoes hitting the wooden planks thudded along, getting closer and closer.

"Time to go, bitch," a deep voice said. "Fucking job wasn't supposed to get bloody. Scarsdale is going to pay. Come on. We have to get out of here now or I'll have to kill the EMTs. You don't want that on your conscience, do you? Not after you got all these other assholes killed."

She waited. Waited until the footsteps stopped. Waited until his voice was close. Waited until he leaned over as though trying to figure out exactly what he was seeing.

His face came into view and she swung the gun up, pulling the trigger.

Jones's head snapped back as the boat swayed again and he was gone from her vision.

What was happening? Had she hit him? "Remy? Remy, babe, please talk to me."

"Can't. My ear's ringing. So damn loud," he complained.

Yeah, that shot had cracked the air around them.

"Come, *mio amico*," a deep voice said. "Please don't shoot me, *bella*. I have very little time and I need to use this boat to disappear. Your man is going to be fine."

The Italian pulled Remy off her with a groan. She could suddenly breathe again. She scrambled up, the gun still in her hand. An assassin had Remy. He had Remy and there was nothing she could do.

"*Bella*, please lower that. I have no wish to harm you. Who do you think took out the other man?" Biondo laid Remy out.

"He's good, *chérie*. Come here and hold my hand." The words were the sweetest she'd ever heard.

Biondo held out a hand and helped her onto the dock. "You did a good job with the other. He fell back into the water, but the shot was true. Tell the authorities he went over on that side and they should be able to pull him out. Also, tell the authorities that he was working for the federal prosecutor."

Blue and red lights lit up the north side of the building.

"Biondo? Take the boat. There's a place marked on the map. Meet me there dawn Friday and you'll have your account. I promise," Remy said. "And thank you."

Lisa clutched Remy's hand as Biondo nodded down at him.

"I will be there." He hopped into the boat and started it up. He slipped into the bayou as the door to the patio came open.

"Hold on," she said, hoping the Italian was right.

He squeezed her hand. "I'm okay. Won't be using my left arm for a bit, but I'll recover as long as I have the right nurse with me." His eyes went stark. "Is my brother alive, Lisa?"

She held his good hand to her heart as one of the EMTs raced out and prayed the answer to his question was yes.

Chapter Fourteen

"We do this far too often," Taggart complained. "I hate hospitals. Why do I get called to them all the damn time?"

Lisa looked up from her chair in Remy's room. She'd spent the early morning hours going back and forth between rooms in the small hospital. Remy's surgery had been simple. Zep's had not. Eight hours of complex surgery had been required to remove the bullet and its fragments from close proximity to his spine.

It had been a long night, but they'd all breathed a sigh of relief when Zep had come out of anesthesia and managed to wiggle his toes.

Delphine and Sera were sitting in his room, holding hands and thankful it hadn't been worse. She'd been dozing when Texas had invaded.

"Maybe you need to hire people who don't get shot," Mitch said as he strode through the door.

Will merely walked in and started looking at Remy's chart. "Has he had a CT? From what the police report said, he landed pretty hard a couple of times. For that matter, Lisa needs one, too."

Oh, no. "You are not in charge here, Will. You don't even have privileges in this hospital, so don't think you can order up a battery of tests. I'm fine. Remy's fine now. And he took that bullet for me. He made sure I was in front of him when we were running away from the hired killers."

"That wasn't merely my job." He brought her hand to his lips. "It was my privilege."

Will set the chart down and she watched the moment he gave up the fight. His face flushed and he strode over to her, holding his arms open. "Thank god you're alive."

She got up and let her brother envelop her in a hug. "Only because of him. And because my family hired him. By the way, you hired him to save me, but he's really awesome in bed. I think I'm going to keep him."

Will groaned but he was smiling when he pulled back. "I did not need to know that."

"I think it's the other way around," Remy said, reaching for her again. "She's not only the most beautiful woman in the world, she's also the best manager. I'm the one who's keeping her. And Will, that money was a loan. We're going to pay you back."

"No, it was an investment in my sister's future," Will corrected. "And I told you it could be a wedding gift. I am going to assume there will be a wedding."

"Don't expect a big thing." She didn't want to wait months and months. "We'll go to the justice of the peace."

Remy's head shook. "Not once my momma and Seraphina find out. But don't worry. They can plan something fast. I think you'll discover the whole town wants to be in on it. We don't let a reason for celebrating get by us down here."

She was going to marry that man. She was going to be a part of this town and this family.

"I believe this means everyone owes me," Taggart said. "I took the way under on that bet. Which is a good thing because I got bills, man. Charlie wants to send the girls to school and that involves all sorts of expenses. Do you have any idea what school supplies cost? I say put one pack in the center of the kindergarten room and let them fight it out *Hunger Games* style."

Lisa was glad he wasn't the head of the education department. "You scare me."

Taggart's whole face brightened. "Thank you. That is the nicest thing anyone has said to me in forever. You know, it's like people think because you're the king of the world you don't need a few compliments."

Remy groaned and let his head roll back. "Will someone give me the rundown of what's happened? Were you able to connect any of the dots I gave you?"

Even as they'd prepped him for surgery the night before he'd been on the phone with his boss, explaining everything that had happened, telling him everything he knew.

"Your sheriff is apparently a rock star," Taggart replied. "While you were getting all prettied up for surgery, Armie LaVigne wrapped his bullet wound up and oversaw that crime scene. He had pictures for me within hours, and Adam found our two dead guys a couple of minutes after. Hutch worked some magic and connected our federal prosecutor to the wiring of fifty K each into the dead guys' accounts. He's in custody and singing like a soon-to-be incarcerated bird."

Will shook his head. "Bridget is completely and utterly insufferable now. She was right about everything. She heard the news and she hasn't stopped fist pumping. I'm worried for the baby. Her mother's self-satisfaction could ruin her before she's even born."

"I think we should learn to always believe Bridget," Mitch said with a sigh. "I'm just saying, she needs to go into crime fighting."

"You think *she's* going to be difficult to deal with? Maia Brighton is currently polishing her collar because she's got me by the balls," Taggart replied. "I'm going to find her the nastiest Dom I can and pray he can keep her under some kind of control."

Lisa was starting to understand. "Vallon wasn't merely laundering for the mob, was he?"

"Nope," Taggart replied. "When you turned him in, you also turned in a judge and prosecutor who were taking bribes to ensure good verdicts. All of Bridget's crazy pregnant lady conspiracy theories were true. We think Scarsdale has been working this for years along with the judge and a few members of law enforcement who helped direct things."

"You caused some chaos because you called in to the police tip line. The police started investigating and Scarsdale couldn't stop it once it had begun. You started a snowball that caught all the bad guys in it as it started to roll downhill," Mitch explained. "The best Scarsdale could do was force the officer who wasn't on his payroll to break the chain of custody so he could try to get the case thrown out on lack of evidence. He sent someone to her home to cause some chaos and then made sure she got the call when she was supposed to be driving back to the station. An officer who *was* on the payroll then took the pages that had Scarsdale's accounting."

"Unfortunately for him, that page also included the account number for an assassin known as Il Biondo." Taggart leaned against the sink. The whole room was filled with large predators, but somehow

Lisa had never felt safer. "You do realize almost no one in the world has seen the man's face and lived. He's the real deal."

"He told me he has a code," Remy said. "As far as I can tell, he meant it. He could have taken her with him last night, but he didn't."

"I had Hutch and Chelsea look into him. And hack some highly classified sites," Taggart continued. "We believe Il Biondo is a former operative of AISE, Italy's version of the CIA. We believe his legal name is Giovanni Vorenus. He comes from a wealthy Venetian family whose history apparently stretches back almost forever, according to the lore. Anyway, Gio was the last of his name until he married and had a son. That's where things go poorly. He returns from an assignment only to discover that his wife and son have been killed. He disappears the next day and resurfaces a year later with a dye job and a new business."

"That's terrible," Lisa said, her heart softening toward the man who'd tried to kidnap her.

"But it explains a few things. He wasn't going to harm you. He wanted the account number, but he didn't intend to kill you." Remy laid back. "He could have taken me out or left me for dead. He could have taken Lisa with him last night. I wouldn't have been able to stop him."

Taggart nodded. "Does he have what he…" He put a hand out. "I don't want to know. Just tell me if he's going to come for her again."

Remy shook his head. "No. He'll honor his word. Don't worry about him. Our business is done."

It wasn't, but Big Tag didn't need to know it. If Big Tag knew they were meeting Il Biondo on Friday, he would likely send out a ton of people to protect them both and scare off the man. Remy wanted this over with and Lisa agreed. It was time to look to the future.

There was a knock on the door and her sisters were there. They'd both made the trip, hurrying to get to her, and she realized that miles couldn't change her family. Laurel rushed in, but Lila hung back. If there was one thing she'd learned, it was that family required work and tolerance, too.

She looked at her oldest sister and waved a hand to bring her in. "Lila, please come here and hug me. I've missed you and I'm so sorry about some of the things I said to you."

Tears in her eyes, she joined them, wrapping her arms around her sisters.

"I'm sorry, too," she whispered. "I was totally wrong about Remy. He's a good man. God, we owe him so much more than money. I don't know why I was hard on him that day except I was being arrogant and I thought I knew best."

"She does that a lot." Laurel smiled, her head dropping to Lila's shoulder.

"I broke up with Brock. Laurel told me he'd been making you both uncomfortable. I didn't listen before, but I am now. I was holding on to something that didn't work because I so desperately want what my siblings have," Lila admitted. "Please forgive me."

Lisa hugged her sisters tight. "There's nothing to forgive, but you have to be nice to my fiancé and you can't be all snobby around his family. Or the customers at my new establishment. Or the gator. I've heard Otis can be sensitive about stuff."

Lila's eyes had gone wide. "Please tell me you're joking. At least about the alligator."

Taggart was shaking his head as he stood next to Will. "You seriously raised all that estrogen?"

"How I survived I do not know," Will admitted, but he was looking at them with an indulgent smile. "But if you ever need parenting tips on the teen years, I could write a book. Your number one job?"

"I know this one," Tag said, holding up his hand. "Keep 'em off the pole."

"Gotta keep 'em off the pole," Mitch said with a frown. "Laurel, we're never having girls."

Laurel winked Lisa's way. They would see about that.

She settled in next to Remy as her family talked around her. They had one last job to do and then she would be free.

* * * *

The morning air was almost cool as they shifted from the bay to the river, then turned off into the bayou. Darkness was all around them and the big cypress trees rose from the waters, shadowy figures that looked altogether different at night. At night the trees seemed to reach out for her, arms grasping.

"Hey, there's nothing out here that's going to hurt you," Remy said as he turned the boat down some path she couldn't detect.

"You're free out here. No one's going to ever lock you away."

She took a deep breath, letting the air around her remind her that she was with Remy and this was part of their home, one she intended to explore. Nothing would hold her back from making this place her home. "Thanks for letting me come with you."

"I wouldn't if I thought you were going to be in danger, but you deserve to be with me. This is our life, not merely mine," Remy said. "Besides, this is one of my favorite places in the world. I want to show you. I think it's a fitting place to start."

"To start?"

He looked back and she could see him as the world around her began to brighten slightly. Civil twilight. Not quite dawn. "To start everything. I was wrong. I was scared before, scared of screwing things up, scared of not being enough for you. But all I have to do is love you and be a good partner to you."

She moved in behind him, resting her head against his back. "You are everything to me."

"And I've been waiting for you since I was a child, waiting to find the other half of my soul," he said. "This is another part of my soul, *chèrie*, and I want to share it with you."

The boat bumped slightly as they ran aground, and she could see they'd made it to what looked like an island in the middle of the bayou. Remy tied the boat to a tree stump and then helped her out with his good hand. She jumped the last of the way, landing in a small clearing.

"Zep and Sera and I would come out here this time of year. Always at dawn because there's nothing like it," he said.

"Nothing like what?"

In the low light, she watched him smile. "Wait for it. We've got a few minutes. We can conduct our business and let our friend be on his way."

"Asking me to leave so quickly?" Biondo's voice came from the other side of the small island.

Remy stepped in front of her like they were in the presence of a predator. "We just want to move on with our lives. I need to know this is over."

The man known as Il Biondo stepped from behind one of the massive trees, coming out into the clearing. "If I get what I need."

Men. They were making this super dramatic. She moved from behind Remy, holding her hands up to show she didn't have anything in them because…again with the overly dramatic men.

"Thank you for what you did at the wharf. We would be dead if you hadn't shown up." She walked right up to the beast.

"Lisa," Remy said under his breath.

She gave the assassin her most brilliant smile. "Can I give you a hug?"

Biondo stilled, the question seeming to completely stump him. He looked over at Remy. "Mr. Guidry?"

Remy sighed. "Go on. She's a hugger. You'll hurt her feelings if you don't."

The Italian seemed awkward as he patted her on the back. She squeezed the man, willing him to feel how grateful she was. How long had it been since he'd had a kind hand on him? Had it been since his wife and child died?

"Thank you so much for saving us," she said.

He cleared his throat and stepped back. "I was only saving myself. You have the account number where I can access my money. Money is necessary to my lifestyle, and I don't merely mean to buy clothes. Money protects a man like me."

She pulled the account numbers out of her pocket. They were written on a pink sticky note and she'd finished it off with a heart. "Here are the four I remembered. I don't know which is yours."

"I can figure it out from here and move the money quickly," he said with a long sigh. "Then you can be as honest as you need to be if the time comes for you to testify. It won't matter because I'll be gone and so will my money. The rest will be sitting there to help incriminate whoever needs to be. I'll lay low after I do what I need to do."

"So this might not be over." Remy reached out for her hand, tangling their fingers together.

"I promise you this is finished, Mr. Guidry," Biondo said solemnly. "I will handle everything from here. If the wheels of justice don't move quickly enough, it's up to men like me to hurry things along. No one will come after the lovely Ms. Daley. She was trying to do something right and good. That should not be punished."

"Thank you, Mr. Vorenus."

He stopped, going still again, but not in any kind of an awkward way. Nope. This was the predator Remy was worried about and she didn't have a death wish.

Remy moved in front of her again. "She has no intentions of

telling anyone."

His eyes came up and there was such a chill there for a moment, and then it seemed to pass. His shoulders relaxed and a reluctant smile crossed his face. "Mr. Taggart, I presume. As you haven't brought a law enforcement team with you, I assume it was for his curiosity alone."

"The boss is a curious man, but he also knows what it means to have a job to do," Remy replied. "Ian's got his own family connections."

"Yes, the Denisovitch Syndicate. He's an interesting man, your boss. As long as he understands the world is not so black and white, we will be fine. You know it's been a very long time since someone said my name. Funny thing, my name. Where I come from it's attached to many interesting stories. Perhaps you will vacation one day in Venice and hear about how my family was descended from a vampire. Take the ghost tour and if I am in town, I will show you my city." He looked around. "You know, I'm really more of an urban assassin. Next time we meet perhaps it will be more civilized. *Arrivederci, sii felice.*"

He walked off and disappeared in the trees. After a moment she heard a boat motor turn over and he was gone.

Remy took a deep breath. "I can believe that man is descended from vampires."

Lisa wrinkled her nose. "They don't have babies, and now you sound like your momma. I have to say I love that my future mother-in-law thinks she can vanquish demons with sage and some Latin that I'm pretty sure she doesn't even understand what the words mean."

Remy pulled her close. "Latin? I'm fairly certain she made that shit up. God, Lisa, I'm glad you're here. Don't ever leave me."

She let her head find his chest. "Never. It's you and me and possibly Otis forever." She laughed, but the truth was they had battles ahead. "I know Zep is doing okay, but we have to help him get back on his feet."

"And we will. I promise. I'm going to make sure baby brother is back to normal. It's time we were a family again."

She held him for a moment longer, but then she yawned. This place was...very bayou. And they could seriously be home in bed. One of Remy's second cousins was opening Guidry's for them for a week so Remy could recover. They could be in bed, cuddling, maybe having some very careful, don't-pull-the-dude-who-got-shot's-stitches fun.

"This place is nice. Let's head home. I want to spend some time showing my sisters around town."

He sighed, a long-suffering sound. "Will you be patient? There's a reason I brought you out here. It's the perfect time of year."

"The perfect time for what? Is Otis going to make an appearance? We're in the middle of a swamp, Remy. I'm a little worried about your wounds. There have to be like a million bacteria running around here."

He chuckled. "I'll try to avoid swimming. Now be quiet. I don't want to scare them. It's almost time."

"Time?"

He turned her around and held her close. "Dawn's here. Look at that light coming up. Be quiet and listen to me. Did I ever tell you that when I'm out here the words in my head... Well, they're never louder than they are right here."

Okay, he was right about that. The world was suddenly orange and pink and red, the sun coming up and lighting the world with energy and hope. All around her, day rose from the bayou, lifting the world with it.

"Do you know why we call it Papillon Bayou, my love?"

She was watching the colors as they revealed the beauty of the world around them. The forest. The water. The greens and browns all waking up, all saluting the new day. There would never be one just like this. This day was unique and special, as were the days before and the ones that would come after. Her future spread before her filled with light and love, struggle and triumph, and most of all this amazing family built from both blood and those she'd chosen. "Because it's so beautiful?"

"Nothing is more beautiful than you, *ma crevette*. And we're going to work on your French. Say good morning, Lisa. Or as we say it, *bonjour*."

She gasped as she realized what he was talking about. They weren't alone. Not even close. They came from out of the ground, from the branches of trees where they'd hidden for the night, from under logs and rocks. They rose with the dawn, their wings spreading as though joy had suffused each small creature.

Butterflies.

Her world filled with wonder as thousands of the things took flight, ready for the day. They took off, circling for a moment as though saying hello or dancing to greet the sun before they swept up and scattered, taking their beauty to the world.

"Papillon means butterfly," Remy said, wonder in his voice. "I wanted to share this with you. I've been here with my brother and sister, but never a woman. The next woman I bring out here will be our daughter. This is their migration time. Every year they come back here. They always know their way home."

His arms were around her and there was only one more thing that could make this perfect, that could bring them closer. "Tell me what's going through your head right now, Remy."

"Here," he said, whispering the words in her ear because they were meant for her alone. She'd figured that out. Those glorious poems that ran through his head were for the two of them. "It is here we rise. Here on this spongy earth, where water and land mingle. Here, where the trees rise from the bayou and not flat dirt. Here we are born. Oh, our story might begin somewhere else, the once upon a time happening in a kingdom of concrete and neon. But happily ever after starts here. This is where two decide to become one. Where that odd one will multiply to three and four. Where the whisper of soulmates starts a new generation. Here on this soil, this soul we share, here where the butterflies live—we begin."

Tears blurred her vision, but she didn't need sight. She rested her head against his chest and let those words of his fill her soul as the butterflies danced around her. She could feel their beauty as they welcomed her home.

Butterfly Bayou was a magical place.

Epilogue

Broken Bend, TX
18 months later

Remy looked around the full barn at the Rockin' R Ranch. The entire barn had been remade into a shabby chic space, a gorgeous wedding and reception venue. Twinkle lights brought intimacy to the dance floor and candles lit each table. A cool breeze swept through the place.

"I can't believe it. We're all married. I would have told you that would never happen." Shane was sitting across from him, his pregnant wife, Talia, standing a few feet away talking with Lisa, Suzanne Burke, and Natasha Blade.

The women were all looking stunning and he had to admit, his old team had done a damn fine job. Each had married far above himself.

Riley sat back, his lips curling up in a smirk. "I would have totally bet against Dec."

Declan gave Riley his happy middle finger, but he was smiling while he did it. "Fuck you, Blade. Do you have any idea the things I could show you if I wanted to? I know some crazy shit now."

Riley frowned. "Hey, what could you possibly know that I don't? I get that your girl is in the business. We all love her show. But I've got Hollywood connections, too."

Declan had married a TV chef. Suzanne had a popular show called *Angel in the Kitchen*. Lisa enjoyed it and had made many a delicious meal from Suzanne's repertoire.

"Uh, Suzanne's connections are way deeper than Hollywood," Dec replied. "And Shane, I met a doctor who thinks Talia is the bomb.

Name's Eidolon and he's such a fan. Says he rarely sees humans as brave as Talia."

"Humans?" Shane asked.

"I mean researchers. You know, doctors who could make a shit ton of money off their work, but they give it up to the betterment of mankind." Declan had gone a little pink. "You know, humans. You have another word for it?"

Riley shook his head. "Dude, you have gotten even weirder since you left."

Declan's mouth went wide with a smile of pure joy. "Brother, you have no idea."

"Hey, I've seen some weird stuff in my day," Remy said. "Did you know that Lisa and I met this crazy assassin guy who thinks he's the descendant of a vampire?"

Riley and Shane chuckled.

"Which one?" Declan asked, his eyes perfectly serious.

He really had gotten weirder and he'd actually developed a sense of humor. "He didn't say."

"Probably for the best," Declan replied. He pushed his chair back and stood up. Wade Rycroft had just walked up, looking good in his tux. But then they were all wearing them since they were Wade's groomsmen. "Hey, there's the man of the hour. I see your old friend is here. Not many people get to say Emily Young was their wedding singer."

Sure enough, up on the small stage at the head of the barn, a band was getting ready to play and the famous country singer was smiling and preparing for a set. Wade had once been her bodyguard and was close friends with her husband, Cooper Townsend.

Wade joined them, a wide smile on his face. "Ah, you know I'm sure she does that for all her friends. She told me she misses playing small venues now that she does her own stadium tours. I say, hey, Em, gotta barn for you right here." He chuckled. "I'm happy she and Coop could make it. Did you get to see Sadie and Chase?"

"Yeah, she looks great," Shane said. "I did not tell her that we've gone through three receptionists in the year and a half since she left. No one can handle the big guy's bad temper."

"He does not handle transition well," Declan said.

"He doesn't handle transition at all," Wade agreed. "Shane and I have been trying to get him to refill the spots. He always finds something wrong with the candidate. Sometimes the candidate walks out in the middle of the interview. One of them actually ran. It's crazy."

"The big guy will come around." At least Remy hoped he would.

"Do you think so?" Riley asked. "After what happened with Ezra and his group? I don't know. He hasn't been the same since."

Remy didn't like to think about what had happened to that group of men they called the Lost Boys, but it hadn't been Big Tag's fault. "He can't blame himself. No one saw that coming."

"I've told him that same thing a hundred times," Wade replied with a shake of his head. "He's taking the weight of the world on his shoulders."

"No one could have known. He played everyone. We all thought he was…" Shane pushed back from the table. "I don't want to think about him. I want to forget what happened to those men and focus on the fact that we're all good. Our team. We were lucky. We're all whole and here."

Remy agreed, but he had to go and make sure Tag was fine, too.

Dec slapped Shane on the shoulder. "You're right. Tonight we celebrate."

"The dancing is about to start so grab your girls," Wade offered with a smile.

All around, the people started moving to the dance floor as the music started up and Mr. and Mrs. Wade Rycroft were invited to share their first dance.

Lisa was standing and talking with Charlotte Taggart. She glanced up and gave him a smile and a brief nod. Like his little shrimp could read his mind and give him permission to do what he needed to do.

Remy winked her way. Their wedding had been nothing like this, but it had been his best day. He stepped outside the barn. There was a temporary playground where the crazed army of lunatic children roared and several harried adults watched after them.

Sitting to the side, a beer in his hand, was Ian Taggart, his eyes on the kids. His mind…well, that was likely somewhere else.

"Hey, boss. How are you doing?"

Taggart was silent for a moment. "I'm all right."

"Do I have to say it?"

"If you do, I'll likely figure out a way to shove this beer bottle straight up your ass," he growled and then sat back and sighed. "I'm fine, Remy. I just need some time. I don't handle change well and we've had a whole lot of change lately." He stood up suddenly. "Kala, baby girl, let that little boy out of those ropes right now. Now. I don't care if you're playing superheroes and villains."

He stalked over and came back with a small length of rope in his hand.

"I have no idea where she got that," Tag said with a shake of his head. "And I always knew Jesse's kid would end up being a sub. Never tell Charlie I said that."

At least the big guy was still sarcastic and a little afraid of his wife. It was good to know some things never changed. Remy eased onto the bench beside his former boss. "You know you have to replace us, right?"

Taggart's expression never changed. "I could shut everything down and live the hobo life. That's always a choice."

Remy chuckled at the thought of the Taggart clan riding the rails. "I don't know that Charlotte's shoes survive that experiment."

Tag's lips curled up. "Yeah, well, she loves her shoes. Listen, I might have found a way to solve both our problems."

"I have problems?" Remy asked. He had several but he wasn't aware of any Tag could fix unless he had some skills Remy didn't know about.

"A little birdie told me you need a new refrigeration unit and you lost two boats in the storm a couple of weeks ago. Someone didn't have insurance."

"Yeah, Jean-Claude let that lapse." It had been an oversight. Business was tough. His business was complex, with a thousand moving parts, but then Taggart should know that. "We didn't realize the boats weren't covered, and that fridge is a million years old. Was."

"Find me a new team, Remy. You put together this one and it was a great group." Taggart took a long swig from his beer. "Do it for me again. Train them. Shane and Wade are too busy working. Give me a month of your time a year for the next several years and I'll keep you from having to take out more loans. This was the deal Julian Lodge made with me a long time ago and it worked out pretty well. Besides, you know you miss it. Fill the douche again, Remy."

Taggart's smile this time was pure amusement, and Remy realized he would be cool with the ridiculous nicknames if it put that smile on Big Tag's face.

How had he gotten so damn lucky? He'd worried he would have to take out another loan, but this did solve his problems. And there was nothing he wanted to do more for his old friend than give him a new team he could rely on. He held out a hand. "You've got yourself a deal."

Taggart shook it and sighed with seeming relief. "Thank god. If I had to take one more interview I was going to murder someone. Kala, your sister's hair is not a rope to climb on. Seth, stop eating dirt." He stood and nodded toward one of the women watching the kids. "I swear those kids are going to be the death of me."

"They will if you keep having them. What's this? Number four? And Erin's pregnant again. Are you building your own army?" He started back toward the barn.

"Charlie promises me this is the last, but I get a feeling that's not how it's going to work out," Taggart said, still smiling. "And I'm damn happy for my brother. They've been trying for a while. This is definitely their last, but at least Theo will be here for this one. I pray it's a girl. I'm the only one who walks around in a tiara. I forgot I had it on the other day. My brothers never let me forget. Well, hello, Mrs. Guidry, you're looking lovely."

Lisa slipped a hand in his. "Thank you. I'm happy to see everyone again. It feels like a reunion."

Big Tag wrapped an arm around his wife. "We should have them more often. Family is too important to let it drift away. Time and distance, those are our real enemies. Come on, Charlie. Let's show them how a tall white dude with absolutely no rhythm does it."

Charlotte was laughing as her husband led her off.

Remy leaned over and kissed his wife. "How about we show them how the Cajuns do it, *chèrie?*"

"We definitely do it with style," she said as he started for the dance floor. "Did he ask you to come back on a limited basis?"

So Charlotte had known the plan. "He did indeed, and I accepted."

"Good," she said. "I know you've missed it. Don't get me wrong. I know you love the wharf, but staying connected to your old world is good, too."

He took her in his arms and danced, surrounded by old friends and new. But she was the whole world and he wouldn't have it any other way.

* * * *

Thank you so much for joining me in this crazy crossover idea. And thanks so much to my fellow crossover authors—Larissa Ione, J. Kenner, Corinne Michaels, Carly Phillips, and Susan Stoker for giving these characters life and the happily ever afters they deserve. I hope you've read them or plan to because getting to see these worlds collide has been amazing. Of course, there is one bodyguard left. Though you saw a sneak preview of his story in *Close Cover*, all will be revealed and the final bodyguard will find his happily ever after in July's *Protected*. Until then, I hope you have fun with the crossover!

Sign up for the 1001 Dark Nights Newsletter
and be entered to win a Tiffany Lock necklace.

There's a contest every quarter!

Go to www.1001DarkNights.com to subscribe.

Discover the Lexi Blake Crossover Collection
Available now!

Close Cover by Lexi Blake

Remy Guidry doesn't do relationships. He tried the marriage thing once, back in Louisiana, and learned the hard way that all he really needs in life is a cold beer, some good friends, and the occasional hookup. His job as a bodyguard with McKay-Taggart gives him purpose and lovely perks, like access to Sanctum. The last thing he needs in his life is a woman with stars in her eyes and babies in her future.

Lisa Daley's life is going in the right direction. She has graduated from college after years of putting herself through school. She's got a new job at an accounting firm and she's finished her Sanctum training. Finally on her own and having fun, her life seems pretty perfect. Except she's lonely and the one man she wants won't give her a second look.

There is one other little glitch. Apparently, her new firm is really a front for the mob and now they want her dead. Assassins can really ruin a fun girls' night out. Suddenly strapped to the very same six-foot-five-inch hunk of a bodyguard who makes her heart pound, Lisa can't decide if this situation is a blessing or a curse.

As the mob closes in, Remy takes his tempting new charge back to the safest place he knows—his home in the bayou. Surrounded by his past, he can't help wondering if Lisa is his future. To answer that question, he just has to keep her alive.

* * * *

Her Guardian Angel by Larissa Ione

After a difficult childhood and a turbulent stint in the military, Declan Burke finally got his act together. Now he's a battle-hardened professional bodyguard who takes his job at McKay-Taggart seriously and his playtime – and his play*mates* – just as seriously. One thing he never does, however, is mix business with pleasure. But when the mysterious, gorgeous Suzanne D'Angelo needs his protection from a stalker, his desire for her burns out of control, tempting him to break all the rules...even as he's drawn into a dark, dangerous world he didn't know existed.

Suzanne is an earthbound angel on her critical first mission: protecting Declan from an emerging supernatural threat at all costs. To keep him close, she hires him as her bodyguard. It doesn't take long for her to realize that she's in over her head, defenseless against this devastatingly sexy human who makes her crave his forbidden touch.

Together they'll have to draw on every ounce of their collective training to resist each other as the enemy closes in, but soon it becomes apparent that nothing could have prepared them for the menace to their lives...or their hearts.

* * * *

Justify Me by J. Kenner

McKay-Taggart operative Riley Blade has no intention of returning to Los Angeles after his brief stint as a consultant on mega-star Lyle Tarpin's latest action flick. Not even for Natasha Black, Tarpin's sexy personal assistant who'd gotten under his skin. Why would he, when Tasha made it absolutely clear that—attraction or not—she wasn't interested in a fling, much less a relationship.

But when Riley learns that someone is stalking her, he races to her side. Determined to not only protect her, but to convince her that—no matter what has hurt her in the past—he's not only going to fight for her, he's going to win her heart. Forever.

* * * *

Say You Won't Let Go by Corinne Michaels

I've had two goals my entire life:
1. Make it big in country music.
2. Get the hell out of Bell Buckle.

I was doing it. I was on my way, until Cooper Townsend landed backstage at my show in Dallas.

This gorgeous, rugged, man of few words was one cowboy I couldn't afford to let distract me. But with his slow smile and rough hands, I just couldn't keep away.

Now, there are outside forces conspiring against us. Maybe we should've known better? Maybe not. Even with the protection from Wade Rycroft, bodyguard for McKay-Taggart, I still don't feel safe. I won't let him get hurt because of me. All I know is that I want to hold on, but know the right thing to do is to let go...

* * * *

His to Protect by Carly Phillips

Talia Shaw has spent her adult life working as a scientist for a big pharmaceutical company. She's focused on saving lives, not living life. When her lab is broken into and it's clear someone is after the top secret formula she's working on, she turns to the one man she can trust. The same irresistible man she turned away years earlier because she was too young and naive to believe a sexy guy like Shane Landon could want *her*.

Shane Landon's bodyguard work for McKay-Taggart is the one thing that brings him satisfaction in his life. Relationships come in second to the job. Always. Then little brainiac Talia Shaw shows up in his backyard, frightened and on the run, and his world is turned upside down. And not just because she's found him naked in his outdoor shower, either.

With Talia's life in danger, Shane has to get her out of town and to her eccentric, hermit mentor who has the final piece of the formula she's been working on, while keeping her safe from the men who are after her. Guarding Talia's body certainly isn't any hardship, but he never expects to fall hard and fast for his best friend's little sister and the only woman who's ever really gotten under his skin.

* * * *

Rescuing Sadie by Susan Stoker

Sadie Jennings was used to being protected. As the niece of Sean Taggart, and the receptionist at McKay-Taggart Group, she was constantly surrounded by Alpha men more than capable, and willing, to lay down their life for her. But when she visits her friend in San Antonio, and acts on suspicious activity at Milena's workplace, Sadie puts both of them in the crosshairs of a madman. After several harrowing weeks, her friend is now safe, but for Sadie, the repercussions of her rash act linger on.

Chase Jackson, no stranger to dangerous situations as a captain in the US Army, has volunteered himself as Sadie's bodyguard. He fell head over heels for the beautiful woman the first time he laid eyes on her. With a Delta Force team at his back, he reassures the Taggart's that Sadie will be safe. But when the situation in San Antonio catches up with her, Chase has to use everything he's learned over his career to keep his promise...and to keep Sadie alive long enough to officially make her his.

About Lexi Blake

Lexi Blake is the author of contemporary and urban fantasy romance. She started publishing in 2011 and has gone on to sell over two million copies of her books. Her books have appeared twenty-six times on the *USA Today*, *New York Times*, and *Wall Street Journal* bestseller lists. She lives in North Texas with her husband, kids, and two rescue dogs.

Connect with Lexi online:

Facebook: Lexi Blake
Twitter: authorlexiblake
Website: www.LexiBlake.net

Protected

A Masters and Mercenaries Novella
By Lexi Blake
Coming July 31, 2017

A second chance at first love

Years before, Wade Rycroft fell in love with Geneva Harris, the smartest girl in his class. The rodeo star and the shy academic made for an odd pair but their chemistry was undeniable. They made plans to get married after high school but when Genny left him standing in the rain, he joined the Army and vowed to leave that life behind. Genny married the town's golden boy, and Wade knew that he couldn't go home again.

Could become the promise of a lifetime

Fifteen years later, Wade returns to his Texas hometown for his brother's wedding and walks into a storm of scandal. Genny's marriage has dissolved and the town has turned against her. But when someone tries to kill his old love, Wade can't refuse to help her. In his years after the Army, he's found his place in the world. His job at McKay-Taggart keeps him happy and busy but something is missing. When he takes the job watching over Genny, he realizes what it is.

As danger presses in, Wade must decide if he can forgive past sins or let the woman of his dreams walk into a nightmare....

Momento Mori

Masters and Mercenaries: The Forgotten, Book 1
By Lexi Blake
Coming August 28, 2018

Six men with no memories of the past
One leader with no hope for the future

A man without a past

Jax woke up in a lab, his memories erased, and his mind reprogrammed to serve a mad woman's will. After being liberated from his prison, he pledged himself to the only thing he truly knows—his team. Six men who lost everything they were. They must make certain no one else gets their hands on the drugs that stole their lives, all while hiding from every intelligence organization on the planet. The trail has led him to an unforgiving mountainside and a beautiful wilderness expert who may be his only hope of finding the truth.

A woman with a bright future

River Lee knows her way around the Colorado wilderness. She's finally found a home in a place called Bliss after years lost in darkness. The nature guide prefers to show her clients the beauty found in the land, but she also knows the secrets the mountains hold. When she meets Jax, something about the troubled man calls to her. She agrees to lead him to the site of an abandoned government facility hidden deep in the forest. She never dreamed she was stepping into the middle of a battlefield.

A love that could heal a broken soul

Spending time with River, Jax discovers a peace he's never known. Their passion unlocks a side of himself he didn't even know he was missing. When an old enemy makes his first move, Jax and River find themselves fighting for their lives. But when his past is revealed, will River be caught in the crosshairs of a global conspiracy?

On behalf of 1001 Dark Nights,

Liz Berry and M.J. Rose would like to thank ~

Steve Berry
Doug Scofield
Kim Guidroz
Jillian Stein
InkSlinger PR
Dan Slater
Asha Hossain
Chris Graham
Fedora Chen
Kasi Alexander
Jessica Johns
Dylan Stockton
Richard Blake
BookTrib After Dark
and Simon Lipskar

Made in the USA
San Bernardino, CA
06 April 2018